CLOUD *of* BONE

CLOUD *of* BONE

A Novel

Bernice Morgan

ALFRED A. KNOPF CANADA

PUBLISHED BY ALFRED A. KNOPF CANADA

Copyright © 2007 Bernice Morgan

All rights reserved under International and Pan-American Copyright
Conventions. No part of this book may be reproduced in any form or by any
electronic or mechanical means, including information storage and retrieval
systems, without permission in writing from the publisher, except by a reviewer,
who may quote brief passages in a review. Published in 2007 by Alfred A. Knopf
Canada, a division of Random House of Canada Limited. Distributed by
Random House of Canada Limited, Toronto.

Knopf Canada and colophon are trademarks.

www.randomhouse.ca

Library and Archives Canada Cataloguing in Publication

Morgan, Bernice
    Cloud of bone / Bernice Morgan.

ISBN 978-0-676-97938-1
    I. Title.

PS8576.0644C56 2007   c813'.54   C2007-902464-5

Text design: Terri Nimmo

First Edition

Printed and bound in the United States of America

10 9 8 7 6 5 4 3 2 1

This book is dedicated to my uncles Clarence, Jack and Clyde Vincent of Cape Island and to the countless Newfoundlanders and Labradorians who served at sea during the Battle of the North Atlantic—hundreds of whom died and none of whom deserted.

"The struggle of man against power
is the struggle of memory against forgetting."

MILAN KUNDERA

I

They have been climbing forever—sea, sky, earth—
even time itself has dissolved in fog. The road, little
more than a ledge hacked into rock, is now so narrow
that they are forced to walk single file, keeping to the left, reaching out to touch the wet cliff, reassuring themselves it is there,
praying they will not step into air, plummet downward into the
ocean they cannot see but can hear—a dull, repetitive heave of
wave on rock, cut now and then by the razor wail of a foghorn
far out beyond Fort Amherst.

They are sailors, a volunteer honour guard, though no one
volunteers. "You and you," some officer yelled, culling two ordinary seamen from each Royal Navy ship in port, marching them
off to a memorial service for shipmates lost at sea. Sometimes
there are bodies; thank Christ there are none tonight—there
seldom are nowadays.

There are forty-six men in tonight's guard—forty-eight if
you count the English officer up front and the man lagging
behind. The officer is a shag-bag, nervous away from his own

3

kind. He's only spoken once since the climb began, barking, "Dout it, Sailor!" at some poor sap stunned enough to light a smoke.

Only one man knows precisely where they are, the man at the rear, the one not conscripted, the one not reaching out to touch rock—the murderer. His name is Kyle Holloway. He has come this way a thousand times. Winter and summer, rain and shine, he and his friends roamed these hills, took shelter in the church they are climbing towards. Weak with fatigue, eyes shut, almost sleepwalking, his body still knows when to lean into the grade, turning as the path turns. In order to keep behind he must stop every few minutes, must stand still until he can no longer hear the laboured breathing of the man just ahead.

They come upon the church suddenly. The officer bangs into its stone wall, swears, then shuffles sideways, fumbling for the latch. One of the men snorts some vulgarity about officers never being able to find the hole, and nervous laughter trickles down the line, dying as one by one the sailors reach the church, sense it looming above them like the entrance to some dismal cave.

The officer pushes against the double doors. They give and the men crowd in. The vestibule, cold and dark as night, smells of dust, of wax and linseed oil—and now of tobacco and sweat and the woolly damp of melton coats. They stand quietly while the outside doors are closed and noisily bolted. Only then does the Englishman open the second set of doors, revealing the silent sanctuary, dark wood, a high shadowy ceiling, an uncarpeted aisle that leads to the pulpit over which someone has draped the Royal Navy ensign. On the altar below the flag, three tall candles burn, make a shimmering halo of the white silk.

The sailors walk towards the pale light, file into the front pews but remain standing. The murderer comes in last. He steps into the back pew, stays next to the aisle, shoving his duffle bag out of sight below the seat.

The very air is familiar, that chill mustiness of a place that is never properly heated, the faint acid smell he knows is a combination of coal smoke and bird shit. There have always been birds in St. Mary's: seagulls, turrs, sparrows, ice partridges and pigeons; sometimes even Mother Carey's chickens, strange half-birds that blow in on storms, cannot take off from land and have to be flung into the air to fly. Bad design on God's part, Mr. Norman used to say.

Thirty years as a church verger has drawn Art Norman into the twin, and sometimes overlapping, studies of God and birds. Year after year he devises ever more bizarre ways to rid his church of the pests: shouting, pounding the organ, switching the newly installed electric lights on and off.

For the first time in days Kyle Holloway's thoughts have veered from churning water, from loud noises and violent death. His body feels soft, rubbery, he longs to sit down but dare not; movement might attract the officer's attention. So he stands and waits, reflecting on birds, almost smiling as he remembers Art Norman scurrying about the church waving a bamboo pole above his head, as if fishing in the vast dimness. Neither Kyle nor his friends had laughed back then—certainly not Cyril, although he must have been embarrassed by his father's antics. Not even Gup laughed, not even when the birds, ignoring sunshine beyond the open door, simply flew out of the pole's reach to roost on the high rafters.

So far as Kyle knows, Mr. Norman is still the verger here at St. Mary's, but he's gotten into the taxi business now, carting Yanks and their girlfriends around town. For the duration birds will have to escape on their own, starve, smash into windows or bash their brains out against the fluted glass of light fixtures. Birds have no experience of glass—another of God's oversights, in Art Norman's opinion.

Organ music drones suddenly upward, although no organist can be seen in the dark narthex. A man Kyle doesn't recognize rises from behind the White Ensign. Some old bat brought out of retirement, so frail he has to use the pulpit to pull himself upright. His movement disturbs a pigeon; it flutters from behind the altar and glides up into the frost-glazed rafters. The church is bitterly cold; darkness presses against windows, which, in accordance with regulations, are draped in black cloth.

The dreary music ends. The man behind the pulpit murmurs a few words, a prayer perhaps. He stops speaking but remains standing—they all remain standing, uncertain of what to do. The old man gazes down on them as if he's never seen their like before. His eyes move from face to face. Except for the officer they look identical; four rows of men, boys really, with short clipped hair, clean-shaven faces above navy blue jackets.

At last the minister nods and the sailors sit. The English officer holds his back stiffly away from the seat; the others slump down, sailorlike, making themselves as comfortable as possible on the uncushioned pews. Thankful for the security of walls they close their eyes, some even sleep.

The old man speaks. At first Kyle cannot make out his words, but gradually the quivery voice rises. He is telling them about land and inheritance, about all the continents, all the seas of the world, all the countries on earth—how England has dominion over them, dominion under God. He says this and much more. There is poetry, or what Kyle takes to be poetry, words following words, rolling down, making no sense.

Kyle feels light-headed, dizzy, then heavy-headed—one

sensation following another before he can name it. He has not slept for three days—three days and two nights—not since that moment when the knife came down, moving as if it were something alive, something apart from his hand, his arm, himself. It is always there now. Like a coloured comic, Kyle thinks, each awful square caught inside his head, repeating over and over— the downward slice of the knife, its grey tip slipping into white flesh, a red line appearing just above the ink-blue collar of Gup's guernsey. Gup's eyes staring into his—the stunned incredulity, the closeness of that shared second, as if they were one person, him Gup and Gup him. Then Gup's body crumpling, sliding under the rail and into the sea, Gup becoming what he will now always be.

Despite the cold Kyle is sweating, bent forward in the pew, head on knees, gulping air, panting like a dog. Stop! he tells himself. Stop or they'll hear you, cart you away—hang you! He imagines being led to a high window, the thick rope around his neck, imagines dropping into that blackness beside the courthouse.

He clamps one hand over his mouth, grips the edge of the seat and forces his body upright until his shoulders again touch the back of the pew. He wills himself to be still, to breathe slowly. He has only to stay calm a little longer, to stay awake a little longer. He will listen, concentrate on the words, try to make sense out of what the old frigger is saying. But words are elusive, insubstantial things; they dissolve, blur, slide into silence. Kyle Holloway's chin drops to his chest, his eyes close, he is asleep.

The organ wakes him in time to stand for the hymn:

> Eternal Father, strong to save,
> Whose arm hath bound the restless wave,
> Who bidd'st the mighty ocean deep

Its own appointed limits keep;
O hear us when we cry to Thee
For those in peril on the sea.

The singing ends, the minister bows his head: "Almighty
Lord, in whom we live and breathe and have our being, who has
recorded the names Marcus Dwyer, Edward Gill and Valentine
Gullage . . ."

("Gup! Gup! Gup! Me name's Gup Gullage!" the child bel-
lows. The teacher draws a line in the register, never again calls
his name.)

" . . . we commit these brave young men to Your keeping.
Although their bodies have been lost to the sea, we rejoice in
the knowledge that their souls rest in Your arms. We ask Lord,
that You grant protection to their comrades gathered here. Place
Your everlasting arms around them, keep them safe from terror
by night, from the arrow that flyeth by day, the destruction that
wasteth at noonday. May they go forth in the certainty . . ."

The old man falters, then stops. He opens his eyes and in a
confusion of grief stares down at the young men—*in the certainty* of what? He can no longer remember. He is weeping, tears
streaming down his face.

Even the likes of him knows we're good as dead, Kyle thinks.
Suddenly alert, he threads his fingers through the rope of his
duffle bag and slides sideways towards the aisle. He stands and
slowly, soundlessly, moves backward—fifteen steps to the inside
door. He counted on the way in.

He does not hear the blessing, has already stepped into the
dark vestibule, is feeling his way along the far wall, running his
hand over a shelf of frayed hymn books, moving towards a dusty
curtain behind which there is a trap door, steps and safety.

He wakes once during the night, heart pounding, thinking he is still at sea, thinking night on the North Atlantic, feeling the fear, the damp cold that seeps through cloth, through flesh and muscle into bone, so you can't tell where cold ends and fear begins. He panics, thinking he is on watch, has stopped beside the ship's warm funnel, to reassure himself that heat still exists—he must have fallen asleep, slid down against the funnel.

Minutes pass before Kyle realizes that the iron he lies against is cold. He feels no movement, no sting of sea spray and ice, cannot hear waves slamming the hull or smell the stink of bilge water and diesel—he hears only silence, smells only coal dust.

He has no memory of lifting the hatch or coming down the narrow steps. Yet here he is, in the furnace room below the Church of St. Mary the Virgin—the patron saint of sailors, according to Mr. Norman. All around are rock walls, solid granite quarried from the hill, rock rooted to rock—walls that will last a thousand years. Kyle Holloway has lived in fear for so long that safety leaves a gaping emptiness inside him.

He lies awake for some time, savouring the quiet, the emptiness of the church, thinking back on the service, the three candles, Gup's long-forgotten name being spoken, the old minister crying, going on about death and terror. But that must have been hours ago. The sailors are long gone, all back aboard ship by now. Some may already be at sea, some may already be dead.

And he is not out there—not standing on an icy deck watching dawn gulch in over the North Atlantic, not searching the grey ocean for the black snout of a submarine, that frill of white when its periscope is raised.

I'm not out there, he thinks, and that is enough. Enough to make him forget for a time that Gup is dead, forget that he too will soon be dead. In the safe darkness he slumps back against the furnace and is instantly asleep.

When he wakes again the windowless cellar has brightened. Pale light coming from somewhere. It softens everything, causes coal dust to sparkle from the gritty floor, to glimmer gauzelike in the air. Even the giant coal-pounds looming in two corners of the room glow like polished marble, even tools lodged neatly against the blackened wall, the chisel and pick Mr. Norman uses for breaking up the coal, the long-handled scrapers and shovels, the worn broom—all are beautiful beyond anything Kyle has ever seen.

The furnace room is large and almost empty. Except for the tools along the wall, everything is arranged within reach of a three-legged stool that stands squarely in front of the furnace door. Beside the stool is a full coal scuttle, a shovel and two iron pokers. On the other side are two cardboard boxes, one containing splits, the other newspapers. An old-fashioned toasting fork lies atop the newspapers.

This is Art Norman's work station, exactly as Kyle remembers it. He studies the familiar objects as an archaeologist might study the household goods of some lost civilization. The permanence of these everyday things comforts the young man, for whom the last eighteen months has seemed a lifetime.

Slowly, because he is stiff, he pushes himself to his feet and begins to pace the room—a sailor's habit, to keep the blood from freezing, or so his grandfather maintained. Kyle remembers watching his grandfather pace, his father too, back and forth, back and forth, a path worn in the cream and green canvas.

Pace and mutter, pace and tally, licking a pencil stub, marking their lives down on the back of a calendar; how much wood hauled, cut and stacked, how many barrels of vegetables in the root cellar, how much fish landed, how many quintals dried, how much credit left at the store? Enough to cover this year's flour? Next season's gear? On and on. This lifelong litany of anxiety is what Kyle remembers from childhood, from the bleak place he lived in until he was ten, the place his mother has gone back to, the place she wanted him to go back to.

A letter saying what he has done will be sent to her. Not about the murder—they don't know that—about his desertion. Desertion in wartime. For all he knows it might be worse than murder; he's heard tell people get shot for it.

Because Floss Vincent is postmistress on the Cape, his mother will have to go to the Vincent house to collect the letter. The Royal Navy has envelopes with a little flag—Kyle saw the one Mr. Norman got about Cyril.

Even seeing the flag, knowing the letter is about her son, Maeve Holloway will not open it—not in front of Floss. It surprises Kyle that he knows this, that he can tell, just by thinking, what his mother will do. She will walk back to his grandfather's house, walk the sea-swept length of the Cape, up the long beach and along the back path between the vegetable gardens. All that time his mother will keep the unread letter in her pocket, her hand holding it flat against her body, and she will be thinking he is dead.

When his mother discovers he's not dead but a deserter, will she be glad or sorry? What will she tell his grandfather? What will she tell the others—all the curious people who know she got a letter from the Navy. What will she tell them—?

STOP!

Concentrate on now—on what you see this second. . . . Concentrate on now! That's what the officer said.

It shouldn't be difficult. He is cold now, thirsty now, also in urgent need of a piss. He unknots the rope of his duffle bag, finds his heavy sweater and pulls it on. In the church upstairs there is a toilet, a sink too, with a cold water tap. But he will not go back up, will never go back up.

Studying the two coal-pounds, large as horse stalls, Kyle remembers that Mr. Norman always used one load of coal while holding another in reserve. "Not like English coal this slack Canadian stuff we're gettin nowadays—got to be aged, dried out like wood," he'd grumble, breaking apart the inferior un-English coal with a pick.

Kyle climbs into the pound he judges to contain the reserve supply, clambers around the mountain of coal to the back and relieves himself. It takes only a minute, yet when he jumps down it is broad day, a square of sun on the earthen floor.

The sight of sunlight in this place where he has known only dimness is shocking. Looking upward he sees that the trap door is wide open, pushed back, catching sun from above, from the vestibule window. He must have forgotten to pull the door down behind him last night. Thank Christ no one noticed! He steps into the square of light, stops for a moment to feel sun on his face one last time, then puts his foot on the bottom step.

Even going that short distance back requires immense effort, long minutes to climb twelve steps. After lowering the hatch Kyle jumps down. He is sweating, his breath rasping again. He picks up his duffle bag and walks quickly to the far corner of the furnace room. Carefully working his way behind a load of stacked pit-props he finds the opening, the earth floor just three feet below, and he jumps into blackness.

II

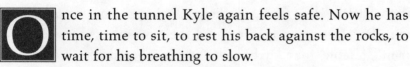nce in the tunnel Kyle again feels safe. Now he has time, time to sit, to rest his back against the rocks, to wait for his breathing to slow.

He must have been ten when they found this place, which means Cyril was nine and Gup eleven that year he made friends with them—his first year in St. John's.

Although he had never heard his father and grandfather argue, indeed had seldom heard them speak to each other, Kyle suspected some disagreement between the two men caused Steve Holloway to leave the Cape. He'd found work longshore, rented a narrow row house on Boggan Street, and sent word to his wife that she and the boy should come into town on the next steamer.

Kyle had never seen the Cape again. Neither had his father—dead now, smashed to bits under a crate of engine parts when a deck crane broke. Talk was the crane had been tampered with. Gup's uncles said longshoremen didn't want machines doing their work. Kyle never told his mother this. What use? Whatever the way of it, his father was still dead.

"When your time comes," one of the neighbours said.

His mother would have none of that. "Wasn't his time," she snapped. "He was only filling in for Mose Moyst down the road!"

"God knew that," the neighbour said.

Maeve Holloway pushed the townie out, slammed the door in her face and told Kyle they were leaving this unholy, unlucky place. "We're going back to the Cape," she announced, and with that began taking dishes down from the sideboard.

"Not me," Kyle said. For years he had been communicating with his parents in monosyllables. It was easier; the more he said, the more attention they gave him and the harder it was to do what he wanted.

His mother didn't give in. Right to the last minute down on the wharf in Job's Cove, she kept nagging at him to come back with her. Four men had lowered their meagre possessions—a trunk, a table, four kitchen chairs, a sideboard and two beds—into the ship's hold, then carried the pine casket up the gangplank and set it down on deck. And still his mother had persisted.

Finally she seemed resigned. "Ah well, Lydia Summers says you can board with them." She pushed several bills into his jacket pocket, her hand lingering on his chest. "Mrs. Summers said you can have young Kevin's room 'til he comes back. I told her you'd be no bother, be a good help around the shop."

The Summerses knew about the cigarettes and comic books he, Gup and Cyril regularly swiped from their shop. Why had they agreed to board him? To pacify his mother most likely— Mrs. Summers knew he'd never turn up, so she had agreed.

Kyle did the same. "Ya, Mom, that'll be great." He even patted her shoulder, pushing a little, easing her towards the gangplank.

He wanted her gone, wanted to be free of her, free of the obligation of standing beside her on this freezing wharf. As soon as she was aboard, he'd be off to find Gup and Cy, see what was on the go. The money in his pocket would buy bread, pickles, bologna, maybe a forty-ouncer.

Maeve Holloway didn't budge. "We always hoped you'd amount to something, like your Uncle Dan." She started again, telling him how easy it would be to finish his grade eleven on the Cape. "You'll be clear of that bunch of savages you run around with. You got a good brain, Kyle. If you attend to your books you could be a teacher in a few years . . ."

His mother was wearing her husband's old overcoat; it weighed her down, pulled her shoulders forward. For some reason he could not figure, she had her hat on, lipstick too. Red lipstick and her church hat—the only hat she owned, a black feathered thing that ruffled in the wind, as if a crow had crashlanded on her head and was not quite dead. She looked pitiful but Kyle refused to pity her. How could she go on about him becoming a teacher? Didn't she know that he hated every moment he spent in school?

The thing was his parents believed in stuff. Despite everything, they believed that hospitals made you well, churches made you good and schools made you smart—smart enough to become someone different from them, someone who worked in one of these holy buildings. God they were stunned!

Kyle moved away from her, turned towards the ship and noticed that his father's coffin had not been taken below deck, that a man was lashing the pine box down. Kyle watched, admiring how the deckhand handled rope. When finished the man straightened, nodded down at the coffin and made a quick, incomplete hand movement towards his forehead, as if lifting an invisible cap. The gesture made Kyle realize that this was a kind of funeral. The real funeral would be on the Cape, in that windswept graveyard out on the point, where headstones stand white and tilting against the blue-black sea. He would not be there and he was not sorry. This, he decided, was better, this returning home of his father's body—whatever was left of his father's body.

Kyle, who had not touched his father in years, suddenly recalled the solidness of that body. Remembered his father's arms holding him, swinging him up off the wharf, lowering him down into a boat, his grandfather catching him, setting him in the cuddy next to the breadbox.

It was a morning when he was six or seven, he had snuck out of bed at dawn and begged to go on the water with them. He'd enjoyed the ride out through the smooth bay, listening to the soft putter of the motor, watching sea and sky change colour as the sun rose, but as soon as they hove-to he started to feel sick.

His father and grandfather had paid no mind to the child, had begun hauling nets. Kyle squatted down against the box, eyes closed, imagining the contents of his stomach sloshing back and forth with the rocking boat. The screeching gulls, the heavy *thump* and *whoosh* of the trap coming in over the side saved him from vomiting. He'd opened his eyes then, squinting into the brightness, the dark bodies of a hundred birds diving between him and the sun, the outline of his father, dark as the birds, shoulders and arms straining against the net, thick-fingered hands hauling wet rope. Within the black outline his father glittered, hair and oilskins, even his old guernsey, all of him alight, fish scales and salt water sparkling in the sun.

The boy had been astonished by the glory of it, the movement and sound—the frenzy of wings above his head, the netloads of shining, flapping fish, gasping for life, squirming and flopping all around him. And his father. His father laughing out loud, calling over his shoulder to his grandfather, or perhaps to him, "Grand catch, old man! Jeezly grand catch!"

That must have been happiness. Gone now. All of it, everything his father had seen or felt, thought or wanted, everything he'd been, packed in a box, stowed and tied down. Kyle can still feel the horror of that thought, the cold weight of regret, the sense that he was teetering on the edge of something unknown, possibly dangerous.

Standing there in Job's Cove the shameful realization came that he was about to cry. He turned to his mother, thinking to touch her, to say something about that morning in the boat, his father shining, laughing.

But she was still at it. " . . . after you get your grade eleven you can come back in town if you want to." She too was holding back tears, her bottom lip bivvering.

"I'm through with school and I'm never going back to the Cape—you shouldn't either," he shouted at her, whatever he'd felt the moment before quite vanished. He took a gulp of air. "I'll be fine. Lots of jobs on the go—I'll get work someplace—down at Pepperrell or up in Buckmaster's Field."

He didn't speak another word. Fingering the money in his pocket he watched her climb the gangplank. Then he took off. He and his buddies would be down in under the church havin a feed before his mother was out through the narrows.

A letter from the Navy will take months to get to the Cape, Kyle thinks. It might never get there. Maeve Holloway could go the rest of her life not knowing what became of her son. That could happen. There's a good chance Cyril wrote *Boggan Street* on the form they had to fill out down at the recruiting station.

Gup often slept under the church, and after his mother left Kyle started sleeping down there as well. They were all the time on the pip—only Cyril was really still going to school, so he usually went home suppertime with his father.

If the furnace ashes were still hot the boys would toast bread, the two of them sitting with their backs to the warm iron, eating and drinking whatever they'd put their hands on: raisin squares and candy bars and Pepsi, bologna and pickles and whole loaves of bread hooked off the Mammy's Bakery truck. When there was no heat in the furnace they would go on into the tunnel and get a fire going in their usual place.

It was a good thing Mr. Norman never caught them lighting fires. Although he was more tolerant of boys than of birds, there was an understanding that St. Mary's could be their hangout only as long as there was no fire lit, no glass broken and nothing stolen.

Gup and Kyle were sleeping under the church just over a week when Gup said he was friggin fed up with the place and why didn't the three of them just go down to Duckworth Street and join up.

The girl at the recruiting office was a big surprise, young and pretty with red lips and a fluffy pink sweater. Kyle had expected a naval officer—a row of officers, like in the poster, with their hands out to welcome volunteers. But no, there was just this girl, not much older than them, all alone in a big office. She was typing when they shuffled in, hands in pockets.

"Just checking the place out," Gup muttered, studying the walls and ceiling as if he were a fire inspector or something. They had agreed not to sign up unless it looked like a good deal.

The girl came over right away, very brisk. She placed three sheets of paper on the counter. "A test for you gentlemen." She smiled, flirting a little. Her glance lingered on Gup, who was tallest, best looking. Then she went back to her desk.

It took a good while to fill out the forms. Neither Kyle nor Gup were that hot at writing, but Cyril could pass himself because Mr. Norman was all the time after him about homework. In the end Cyril filled out all three forms, writing their ages in as eighteen though they weren't even seventeen yet.

When Cyril finished, Miss Priss told them to wait in the hallway. "You will be called," she said.

So they went out to the hall and sat on a long bench. It was like in school, the brown floors, the gouged pressboard walls, the smell of Dustbane—like waiting outside the principal's office. There was even a picture of the King staring down from the opposite wall, looking sort of sad like he always does, as if being king were a big disappointment to him.

Some fellows farther along the bench were smoking. They didn't look any older than Kyle, Gup and Cyril, but their white shirts, grey flannels and St. Bon's blazers made them seem smarter somehow, superior to the other boys. One of them was even reading a book.

An hour passed and all the St. Bon's lot got called back into the office. Kyle figured him and his buddies must have failed. A dismal, empty feeling came over him—maybe it would be like this for the rest of their lives, three of them waiting. Always waiting. Never getting anywhere, never doing anything.

"Why would he want the likes of us in his Navy?" Kyle nodded towards the King's picture. "Why would he want us lot?" He was surprised at how bad he felt. After all, they'd only come down for a laugh, to find out what it was all about, see if they could pass for men.

Cyril was slouched over, chewing his hangnails, but Gup looked pretty relaxed. He was sprawled out on the bench, holding an inch-long butt to his lips. He didn't even open his eyes. "Who wouldn't want us?"

"The King. We're stunned. We can't read or spell. We don't know nuttin. Why would he want us in his Navy?"

"Don't be a dickhead—King don't give a shit if we can spell or not."

Like always the Gup was right. Not ten minutes later they were called back, sent to a separate office off to one side. A man with braid on his sleeve glanced at the forms, scrawled something across the bottom and directed them to a long, narrow room where you had to take off every stitch, be weighed and measured, poked and prodded.

The boys were embarrassed by their pale bodies and grimy underwear. When Gup said, "Jeez we're just like the horses down at Neal's," they all giggled.

The doctors may have been Newfoundlanders but they had a grand way of talkin and they didn't smile once, just tapped the boys' chests and squinted at their teeth.

Yes, Kyle thought, to them we are just like horses. A doubt flickered.

But the doctors all nodded, told them to get dressed and go to Room 6A. In Room 6A the poster officer was sitting behind a rolltop desk, beside him a Union Jack sticking out of what looked like an umbrella stand. In minutes the three of them were signed up; abruptly, no second chances, no one asking if they really wanted to be in the Navy. The officer simply ordered each of them to stand in front of the Union Jack, to put a hand on the Bible.

" . . . and do you swear to bear true allegiance to His Majesty King George and to his heirs and successors according to the law, so help you, God?" he asked.

They each said "Yes" a bit doubtfully, startled by the man's seriousness, by how quickly the thing had concluded.

Suddenly, thoughtlessly—the impulse of a second—swear on the Bible, sign a paper, slide a knife into white flesh. Unchangeable things should not be so easy.

STOP!

He stands and begins to move through darkness, following the rough rock wall, counting the support beams. Somewhere there is a beam with their names carved in it: GUP GULLAGE, KYLE HOLLOWAY and CY NORMAN, in order of age. It had taken a whole afternoon—one of those dead-boring afternoons in late summer, when the scattered thought that you are not really unhappy that school will soon start flutters at the back of your mind. Later, he will try to find the names. For now he must keep walking, must get to the place he's been thinking about for so long.

III

The girl at the recruiting office congratulated them on the way out. "I've got something for you." She smiled and passed black enlistment bands to Kyle and Gup. "Welcome to His Majesty's Royal Navy!" She made a kind of salute, then handed Cyril a little pin she said was for his lapel.

That was how they found out that Cyril had gotten into the Foresters instead of the Navy. God alone knows why. The girl said that was what he'd signed up for.

Cyril, who was deadly afraid of water, didn't seem concerned. He stood there trying to attach the pin to his baggy sweater. "Is all alike to me," he said, and gave up on the pin, sheepishly dropping it into his pocket.

Like always Cy's softness made Gup angry. "Ya stunned bugger! What's the matter with ya? Three of us come here to join the Navy and that's what we're doin!" Gup told the girl she'd made some mistake and it had to be straightened out. "This feller here's a better sailor than Mr. Churchill! He been in the races ten times for God sake!" He thumped Cy's shoulder. "Been on the sea all yer life, haven't ya, old man?"

Cyril kept his mouth shut and so did Kyle. Joining the Navy had been Gup's idea.

"Don't want ta be all the time penned up in barracks, marchin every Christly place ya have ta go," Gup said—and besides, he knew for a fact that girls went mad over sailors.

Kyle had no more love for the sea than Cy did. He wouldn't have minded if they all went into the Foresters; chopping down trees on dry land seemed a pretty good way to spend the war.

"I assure you there's been no mistake." The girl was talking to Gup, she'd stopped smiling. "Your friend's documentation is complete. The assessment officer must have found his talents especially suited to forestry." She swivelled her chair around and without another word began typing.

"Newfoundlanders makes great sailors—Mr. Churchill hisself says so." Gup was hanging on to Cy's arm, hauling him forward until they were both half over the counter. He was on a roll, talking to the girl's back, confident that he could charm her into doing what he wanted. "Come on, miss, just look at him—you can tell he's not all there, he's our retarded cousin. He'll be lost on his own. He'll chop his friggin hands off. Have a heart—just push his paper into the Navy pile—give him one of yer arm bands—go on, do it!"

The girl glanced over her shoulder at their hopeful, grinning faces. Even poor Cyril, now half convinced he wanted to be in the Navy, whined, "I wants ta be with me buddies, miss."

"No," she said, and went back to her typing, pretending not to hear. Even when Gup turned dirty, started tormenting her— asking for a date, asking if she'd been assessed, asking if she had falsies on, if she'd been with Navy men—she never raised her eyes from the document on her desk.

Kyle watched Gup size the place up—the lone typist, the row of empty desks, the distance between him and the doors behind which the officers worked—trying to decide if Cyril was worth kicking up a real stink over.

In the end he only shrugged, made a rude gesture in the girl's direction and turned away. "Well, Cy b'y, it's the woods for you. Musta made some half-arsed mistake on your form— told 'em ya used an axe once, sometin like that. Thank Christ is you not me—friggin well don't want ta spend the war cuttin down fuckin trees!"

He yelled, "Piss on the lot of ye!" over his shoulder, and the three of them pounded down the hall and through the doors, bursting onto Duckworth Street laughing.

Gup and Kyle stopped to pull the black Royal Navy bands up over their jacket sleeves before they took off for the Belmont. They had been kicked out of the tavern more than once, not just because they were underage but because the violence that simmered around these three made regular customers uneasy. Tonight would be different. Tonight their Navy arm bands would get them service and with any luck a few free rounds.

The barman at the Belmont told them it was the easiest thing in the world to get out of the Foresters. "Fellers doin it all the time. Just fill out the right papers." His own stepbrother had transferred into the Navy after two months in some godforsaken woods camp in Scotland. "Christ, why leave Newfoundland to chop down trees?"

Henry Sparks was the barman's name. He'd known the three of them ever since they started knocking around together, remembered how they used to drain the beer bottles he stacked in the alleyway out back. Henry had once dropped a baby mouse into an almost-full bottle of Black Horse, then watched from a window as they guzzled the beer down. He was watching now, remembering the mouse. Three big galoots—Henry wished they were already at sea, hoped they'd get their comeuppance.

"Stands to reason they'll take chummy here in the Navy—with the Krauts out there scuttling ships like they was rubber ducks, they needs good men like ye." Henry smiled. "I s'pose that'll all come to an end now you lot are takin 'em on."

Gup stared into Henry's eyes and sipped his beer, his fingers tapping a little tune on the bar. Kyle watched his friend's hands—narrow, almost delicate hands, wrists thin as a child's. The Gup had given in too easily back at the recruiting office—any minute now that beer bottle would come down on the bartender's foxy head, or smash against the mirror. Knowing Gup's fondness for glass, Kyle was betting on the mirror.

Just like in the westerns, people around them moved back, became quiet. But, "Cy's a good hand at fillin out forms," was all Gup said.

Cyril and Kyle laughed. Everyone relaxed, grinning, clicking bottles of India Pale Ale, toasting the brave lads who were off to fight for King and country. Men nearby began talking again, of war, of ships gone down, of friends and relatives lost. "Lost," they said, "Jim Kearney's boy was lost Tuesday."

"Young Ron Tobin's gone too, him and his cousin, Marge's youngster, the one used to deliver *Telegrams*—both of 'em lost aboard the *Northern Princess*."

"Ron's father's back in the corner," someone said in a low voice, nodding towards a man who sat staring at his untouched beer.

Men were lost, boats went down—the same conversations every night. The numbers were terrible. "Sixteen ships," Bill

Bowden said, "sixteen ships and over two hundred men gone to the bottom in the last two weeks." Others maintained casualties were much higher, that the War Office wouldn't let out the real numbers.

"Was a time seamen watched out for one another," one of the regulars remarked. "I minds back in '35 when the *Mabel Gosse* broke up off White Point. Three of us got hauled aboard a Russian vessel—gave us dry clothes and fed us, put us ashore in Halifax."

"Not this lot! Huns shoots drownin men in the water . . ."

"Blows up shiploads of innocent women and children—look at the *Caribou* . . ."

In the silence that followed, a man down at the end of the bar ventured that he'd heard tell of a crew that got saved by the Germans. "The *Sagona*," he told them, countering their disbelief with details. "One of them old scows in the salt-fish trade. She got boarded by Germans. Before scuttling her the German captain ordered the five crewmen, all Newfoundlanders they were, aboard a lifeboat, fitted them out with supplies and a compass. The wife's cousin was first mate—they made it to the Bahamas."

There was some angry muttering, no one wanting to hear anything good about Germans. Someone shouted, "Propaganda!" Everyone knew the Huns were savages. "Germans goes mad every twenty years—heard that since I was a boy," one man said.

"It's their beer, not enough nourishment in German beer," Henry declared, and that seemed to end the war talk.

Individual conversations broke out—tradesmen marvelling at how much construction was on the go, how free the Yanks were with money, with women too. Three taxi drivers were having a half-whispered exchange about how to lay their hands on car parts or extra gas, the possibility of getting a decent set of used tires tossed over the fence down at Pepperrell.

So this is what being grown-up is, Kyle thought. He felt well pleased with himself. Leaning against the Belmont bar, inhaling smoky air that smelled of rum and sweaty work clothes, listening to the boozy talk, his afternoon doubts seemed childish. Everything that had gone before, the vandalism and thievery, the violence and petty cruelty, did not count. Every man in the room had done the same things—they were part of boyhood.

We were just bein boys, no harm in us, he thought, and clicked his bottle against Gup's and Cyril's. Him and his friends were good as anybody.

An hour or so later Gup got into fisticuffs with some French Canadian who made fun of how Cyril was sayin Hedy Lamarr's name—Christ knows why Cyril was sayin her name. Anyway, Henry kicked them out before the fight came to anything.

It was just gone ten. They wandered aimlessly around until they found themselves up on the higher levels. People were coming out the Nickel, Newfoundland girls with smarmy Americans, every one of them dressed like officers though it stood to reason they couldn't all be. The odd girl'd be with a Canadian, her lookin sheepish because of the boyfriend's stunned outfit—uniforms made out of horse blankets and clodhoppers on their feet.

No one mentioned Bern Pittman and his big black overcoat lined with bottle-size pockets, but Kyle still had some of the money his mother gave him, so they dodged on in Freshwater Road towards Golden Arrow Coach garage where Bern hung out nighttime.

Long before they got to the garage they heard shouting. "A fight!" Gup yelled, and they took off towards the commotion coming from down Merrymeeting Road way.

Roller skating had just ended and the street outside the rink was aswirl with noise and movement; thirty or so Canadian Navy guys in hand-to-hand combat with an equal number of Americans. The Canadians were clearly winning, chanting, "Remember Pearl Harbor! Remember Pearl Harbor!" over and over as they slowly backed the enraged Yanks down Merrymeeting Road.

Coveys of girlfriends lined up on each side of the street, keeping abreast of the battle with sedate sidesteps. They were pretty, big-eyed girls in neat sweaters and pressed skirts, a few carrying white-booted roller skates on their shoulders. Some seemed frightened, one or two were quietly crying, but most of the girls looked happy enough, pink cheeked, calling out encouragement to their boyfriends, jumping up and down to see over the heads of a dozen or so locals. These young Rabbittown rowdies were not properly in the fight, just hovering, clapping their hands to the chant, occasionally bazzing a rock in the general direction of the Americans who, though retreating, still faced their tormentors.

Gup, Cyril and Kyle smashed through the line of watchers. Fists flying, they battered their way to the middle of the mob and commenced pounding the Yanks. Seeing three Newfoundlanders jump uninvited into the scuffle, other ruffians leapt forward in a mad burst of energy that so horrified the Americans that they turned and ran. Rocks pelted their backs but no one chased after them, the USO building and reinforcements being just two blocks away.

A general shout of triumph went up. No one had been badly hurt. Not a soul had come out of the darkened houses nearby. Things grew quiet, sailors searched around for caps, grinning sheepishly at their girls. The girls who had been with the Americans left quickly, keeping close to one another, not quite running. Other girls hovered, waiting for the backslapping to end and their dates to come walk them home.

"Who started it?" one of the Rabbittown boys asked. He'd arrived late but had managed to get a dilly of a black eye.

"Friggin Yanks!" a Canadian Navy man said. "Yanks think they own the world—all the women, all the movies, all the dance halls—every fuckin thing in this burg of a town. Well, the roller rink's *our* property!"

"Says who?" the boy with the black eye asked.

"Says us, Newfie boy!" The sailor spit on his white dicky, had almost finished wiping his bloody nose before the Rabbittowner's fist slammed into it.

The small peace ended. Newfoundlanders flung themselves at the Canadians. This was not for fun. The girls knew, and vanished down lanes and into backyards, taking shortcuts to another street. Pickets were ripped off fences, broken bottles appeared, Gup flicked open his pocket knife. Two Canadians began pounding the piss out of a fat boy everyone knew was retarded.

Someone could have been killed if the Shore Patrol hadn't pulled up in one of their transport trucks. Six MPs jumped down, barking orders, their boots hitting the ground like gunshot. They wore white gloves and leggings and brandished white billy knockers that glowed in the dark. They herded sailors into the great canvas-roofed cavern. Those who would not respond to prodding they lifted, two MPs tossing men like sacks in among their buddies.

As the truck rumbled away the driver shouted, "The Black Maria's comin to pick up you Newfie slackers!"

Half a dozen Rabbittowners raced after the truck, waving fists and pickets. "Stay away from this end'a town, ya friggin Canadian dogs! Piss off to yer kennels in Buckmasters."

Gup bazzed a beer bottle after the truck. It smashed into the iron frame holding up the tarp and sent a shower of glass down on the young toughs running behind. They whirled around and lunged at the three outsiders. "Shaggers from up the Brow—thinks yer smart, don't ya!"

The whole Rabbittown gang closed in, circling so close that Kyle could smell their sweat, see snot sliming out of one guy's nose.

Gup yelled "Run!" His hand shot out, knife plunging, and blood ran down the snotty bugger's cheek.

Then they took off, pounding down Merrymeeting Road with the other lot right behind.

It wasn't until they were well in Freshwater, cutting up through the dump, that Cyril called out, "Okay—we're okay!" and they stopped running, squatted down in the middle of the stinking garbage to catch their breath.

"Them fuckers was really gonna kill us," Cyril said, his voice full of wonder.

Gup made a dismissive sound, halfway between a curse and a snort. Nothing pissed him off more than having to run from a fight.

The dark mounds of ashes and tin cans, the rotting food and burning cloth, the smouldering carcasses of two horses—it all gave Kyle the creeps, but he wasn't about to say so, not with Gup in one of his dirty moods.

"Fuckin stunned havin the whole town in blackout and the dump burnin like Bonfire Night," he said, hoping Gup would laugh or make some crack. But he didn't; no one said a word and nothing moved except rats.

After a while they stood up and cut across the field, evading two guards on duty at the searchlight station. ("Got a mind to burn the place down," Gup said, but they were too tired.)

They came out on Pennywell Road, then drifted around the edge of town, working their way down towards narrower, more familiar streets. Every window in every house was curtained. Tin hoods shading turned-down headlights gave cars the sleepy, heavy-lidded look of large animals lumbering through darkened streets. It was cold and nothing was happening, yet they wanted to be here, to be together.

They were dying of thirst. With the last of Kyle's money they bought a bottle from the bootlegger on Young Street. After a few swigs they crossed over to Harvey Road and ordered three large from Stacy's fish-and-chip van. When the newspaper-wrapped bundle was handed out, they took off without paying, racing in and out of yards and back alleys. Even when they knew the chip man was not following they kept running—just for the fun of it—until they rounded a corner and found themselves at the foot of Boggan Street. There was not a light anywhere, the whole street black as a cow's guts.

Things just happened, aimlessly and without plan, the way things did. They ambled up to Kyle's old house, went around to the back, quietly jimmied the door and went in. Since Maeve Holloway disapproved of her son's friends, neither Gup nor Cyril had ever been inside the house. Feeling something was required, Kyle led them through the kitchen into the hall to the empty parlour, where wrinkled layers of dark wallpaper gave off a smell like fousty bread.

Cyril said it was creepy. Kyle agreed, worse even than the dump, though he didn't say so. They should have gone down under the church. There was no heat in the house, no light either since the electricity had been cut. Yet the place felt occupied, full of creaks and squeaks he'd never noticed, smells he'd been unaware of: his mother's Noxzema, the Jeyes Fluid she scrubbed floors with, the paste his father rubbed into his logans every night, all mixed in with the smells of food, fried fish and baked beans and salt-beef dinners. Kyle would not have been surprised to see his parents standing in one of the dim rooms.

He wanted to stay in the parlour, beside the front door, but Gup said the kitchen was safer, being at the back, its window overlooking a closed-in yard. Besides, the old cast-iron stove was still in the kitchen.

It took no time to rip strips of paper from the walls, pull spindles off the stair railings and get a fire going. Everything was better after that. Sitting on the kitchen floor with their backs against walls, feet stretched out and almost touching in the middle of the small shadowy room, they were warm and comfortable.

Kyle and Gup never talked much and that night even Cyril was quiet. Every now and then one of them would say a few words that showed they were all thinking about the same things: "Shifty Benson's pipe . . ." "Look this way, sir!" "All them tires! Gone!" Each phrase a code that sent all three into uncontrollable laughter. In between they lay back, watching shadows on the ceiling, listening to the house, passing the food and the rum bottle from hand to hand.

It was very late. When the fish and chips were gone, the bottle stopped circulating and they drifted towards sleep. Light from the open grate flickered across Cy and Gup's hands and faces. It came to Kyle that his friends looked childlike, like the boys in a picture his mother had once hung over his bed—street urchins seated around a fire. In the picture a robed man with white wings floated above the head of each boy. When Kyle asked his mother who they were, she said guardian angels. She said everyone had one, only you can't ever see them. As his eyes began to close Kyle wondered if there were angels in the kitchen, or if they'd given up and gone home, wherever home was—heaven, he supposed.

"I don't want'ta go off by meself," Cyril suddenly sniffed into the prolonged silence. No one answered and he began snivelling about how lonely he would be in Scotland, how he hated strange places, specially when his buddies were not around.

Kyle was only half listening; he figured Gup had simmered down, probably fallen asleep. He was near sleep himself and wished Cy would stop complaining. He wouldn't though—Cyril would go on and on, work himself into a state and end up bawling. It had happened before. It really got on Gup's nerves.

Cyril was just getting around to telling about the hard time he had the year his father made him go to C.L.B. camp when Gup leapt to his feet, threw himself across the room and landed astride Cyril's chest.

"Shut up! Shut up! Shut up, ya bloody little fag!" Gup grabbed Cyril's shoulders, hauled him up into a sitting position and began pounding his head against the wall.

"What—the—fuck!" Between each word the back of Cyril's head banged into the wall. He was reaching out, clawing without effect at Gup's hands.

Kyle got up slowly, blinking. Cy and Gup seemed locked in some kind of see-saw game, their upper bodies rocking, Gup pulling back and Cyril coming with him, then Gup pushing forward. Cyril's head slamming into the wall. Back and forth, back and forth, their faces appearing, then disappearing in the pale glow from the stove.

"Stop him!" Cyril croaked, staring into the darkness beyond Gup.

Kyle crossed the room in three steps. Yelling "Stop!" he grabbed Gup's shoulder. Just at that moment Gup let go, and

Cyril dropped like a sack of flour, fell back against the wall, then slid sideways onto the floor. The other two lurched backward and landed out in the hallway with Gup on top.

Kyle's head banged into the newel post, his face pressed into Gup's jacket, the stink of Gup's sweat filling his nostrils. He pushed against Gup's body. "What the fuck was that all about?"

Gup hauled himself to his feet, but Kyle stayed where he'd fallen. Had the frigger gone off his head? They'd had fights before but never like this. "What the fuck was that for?" he asked again.

Gup ignored him. Kyle watched as he walked back into the kitchen, picked something up from the floor and squatted beside Cyril.

Rubbing the back of his head—there was no blood—Kyle stood up and went to where Cyril lay. His friend's eyes were closed; his nose was bleeding but he was breathing, loudly through his mouth. Gup had two fingers in the open mouth, Gup was holding Cyril's cheek taut as he smiled and carefully skewered the Foresters pin into flesh—

"STOP!"

Kyle says the word out loud and feels as if he is shouting. But in the encasing darkness his voice sounds small and tinny.

Think about something else, he tells himself. Think about something good—them summer days we hiked out to Cape Spear, days we'd roam around town, hitching rides on streetcars and delivery wagons. Think about all the times we got into the Nickel for free, that time we swiped caplin off drying racks out in the Battery or the day on Long's Hill when we hooked a whole carton of Player's off chummy's handcart. And remember that time we rode a farmer's long cart all the way into Freshwater Valley—late Saturday afternoon it was—the farmer dead drunk, sprawled off on his cart. . . .

He can see the narrow dusty road, hear the turning wheels, the quiet snoring of the farmer, the slow *clip-clop* of the tired horse when they reached the long run. Him and Gup and Cy— three of them together, sitting up on the seat like kings, no need even to touch the reins because the horse knew the way, and ahead of them the sweeping rise of Kenmount.

Remembering that ride, all around them the woods and farms and fields outlined against the orange sky, Kyle moves ever more slowly, feeling his way into darkness, unaware that he is weeping.

IV

The day they found the tunnel the boys were hiding from Mr. Norman, as they often were during summer holidays. The verger was always hounding them to do some job—chop splits, scrape and varnish the church floor, clean bird shit off the pews. If he couldn't think of anything else he'd be after them to rack the pebbled area out front.

Crouching in a corner of the furnace room, hidden behind a stack of discarded pit-props, they could hear Cyril's father thump around upstairs, grumbling that they were useless, predicting all three of them would come to a bad end. They waited, knowing Art Norman's temper would die down, that soon he would lock up and go home. Since the boys could climb out through the coal hatch, they were then free to stay in the warm furnace room as long as they wished.

When they heard the hatch door drop into place they started to giggle, began pummelling one another, rolling on the ground. Their roughness must have dislodged the jerry-built wall, suddenly they fell, rolled over the edge, dropped three feet (it seemed farther then) and found themselves in another place.

That was six years ago. They were younger and first off they were shit-baked—even Gup. "Fuckin dark," he muttered, as they lay there listening in the silence. It was dark and the air felt different, not just cooler—moving, invisible fingers brushed past, wisping the hair on their arms, touching the back of their necks.

"Jimmy Hann up the Brow heard tell there's ghosts down here under St. Mary's," Cyril said.

"That so . . ."

"Heard tell from who?"

"From his mudder. She told Jimmy they used to bury bad people up alongside St. Mary's—outside the fence—murderers and such like, people who weren't holy enough to go in the churchyard." Cyril paused. "Betimes they comes up, wants ta get inside." He was whispering.

"Jimmy Hann's mudder's cracked, b'y." The words hadn't come out as loud as Kyle intended.

"She's the old witch set her crackie on us once. That time we was in her yard getting crabs," Gup said. He was fudging through his pockets, searching for matches and a butt. "Dog turned up dead the next day." He flicked the match against his thumbnail.

"Yeah!" It was no longer dark and they all laughed.

Kyle remembers the laughter, the sudden sense of safety as they squatted in a tight circle, passing the butt, the glow threading between them, the tunnel all around and the church overhead. After a while it hadn't seemed so black, and they'd continued on, feeling their way, touching both sides of the tunnel. They had been shorter then, short enough to walk upright without hitting their heads.

Kyle has stopped moving, has been stopped for some time, is leaning against the rock wall, almost dozing, thinking about that day—them coming to the end of the tunnel, stumbling into the little cave. He recalls their glee in the knowledge that this hidden, secret place was all theirs, the excitement of looking around that first time, discovering shelflike crevices between the rocks, finding a small spring, a heap of rotting rags in one corner, a bone, a dead kitten, long dead, brittle to touch, fur like dandelion fluff falling away.

It is the memory of that small body, dry and hollow as a glove, that brought Kyle back to St. Mary's. He will die in this dry quiet place—well away from that oily sea, away from noise and wetness, away from the terror that flyeth by night. In all his life this is the only decision he has ever given much thought to.

Reassured, he continues along the tunnel. It is slow going, his legs are shaky and he must hunch forward to keep from knocking into rocks and trees, unbarked trunks that criss-cross the tunnel at intervals, propping up the church's floor beams.

Kyle knows the tunnel runs back no more than a hundred feet, yet today it seems endless. He is so hungry, cannot stop thinking about food, the meals his mother cooked, regular meals you could tell the days of the week by. Monday dinner would be vegetable soup made from Sunday's pot liquor and roast bone, baked beans and fried potatoes for supper. He moves forward, recalling the order of suppers in the Holloway house, five steps for each meal: five steps, macaroni and cheese on Tuesday; five steps, corned beef and cabbage with carrots and mashed turnip and pease pudding on Wednesday; five steps, fried hash with pickles on Thursday; five steps, fish on Friday; five steps, pea soup for Saturday dinner, and, because his mother would be scrubbing all day, whatever she could scravel up for supper, maybe fried puddings, or sausages with chips, or fish cakes. Five steps. A roast in the black bake-pot on Sundays, cooking while they were at morning service.

His parents were Salvationists. After moving into town the family began going to the Citadel every Sunday—uneven sidewalks, him in new shoes, knee-length flannel pants, his hair combed wetly back, holding his parents' hands. It was just a fifteen-minute walk from their house to Adelaide Street. People all dressed up, people you didn't see any other time, hurrying along, bells ringing from other churches. The Citadel didn't have bells but there was a brass band, mostly young men, up front behind the mercy seat, playing as people came in. Partway through the service children were sent downstairs where there would be mission stories and songs played by the Junior Band.

On Sundays everything was different. Back in those first years his Sundays didn't include Gup and Cyril. Kyle told them his father made him go to the Salvation Army, but really he went because he liked the stories and the music, thought he might get into Junior Band if he could. Then, for no reason he can remember, one Sunday morning, when they were halfway up the hill, he pulled away from his parents, said, "I'm not going." When his father told him he had to, he shouted, "You can't make me," and took off.

That night his mother came into his bedroom. He pretended to be sleeping but she flicked the light on.

"You always enjoyed church—why don't you want to go?"

"I didn't enjoy it!"

"You did. I could see you did—you liked the music, and the stories, even the Bible verses . . ."

"I hates that old stuff—what use is it anyhow?"

"For comfort," she said—he remembers how she stood there staring down at him. "For comfort, in case you're alone some long night . . ."

She had said other things, but Kyle had clapped his hands over his ears and closed his eyes. It had seemed forever before she went away that time too.

Gravy with Yorkshire pudding and vegetables went with the roast on Sunday, then cold roast with tomatoes and potato salad on Sunday night. Jell-O and tinned cream for dessert, but his parents saved that for later, as a treat when they came back from the Salvation Meeting. Sometimes the three of them would go into the parlour and if it was winter his father would light a fire in the tiny grate.

For comfort, his mother had said. He wonders if she still goes to church, wonders if the things she hears there will be a comfort when she finds out what he's done—

STOP!

Concentrate on now! That's what the officer on watch had told him that night he got caught lighting a fag. *Concentrate on now—on what you see this second. . . .*

But he is tired now, hungry now—faint with hunger. Sometimes his mother made things especially for him, molasses buns with raisins and cinnamon—

STOP!

The officer must have been one of the decent ones or I'd have been tossed in the brig, Kyle thinks. Never mind the cigarette was safely cupped inside his palm, they were under orders not to smoke topside at night.

Him and Gup were both assigned to the *Maunsell,* an old hulk taken off the Jamaica run, conscripted into war service and refitted as an escort vessel. Below deck you could still smell salt fish and molasses; portside the name *Sea Angel* was already coming up in rust through the thin coat of grey paint. Things overlooked in the refit included lifeboats, although there were two dories that the men said were better than lifeboats for getting off a heaving deck. There was no asdic of course, and no sleeping bunks; sailors had to sling hammocks over pipes and beams. Without cargo as ballast the ship rocked like a tub. Half the green seamen, including Kyle, were violently sick for days. The smell of fish and molasses below deck were soon replaced with more unpleasant smells.

The very first convoy they sailed with came under attack on the third night out. They should have reached the point where they would meet the British escort, transfer responsibility and turn back towards St. John's. But they'd been battling gale force winds all the way and were well behind schedule. It was a small convoy, seven merchantmen with only the *Maunsell* and one other naval vessel as escorts. All creeping through the night at about ten knots an hour, under orders to maintain radio silence and keep pace with the slowest vessel.

Kyle had not expected action so soon, nor had he expected it to begin and end so quickly. One explosion, a burst of flame, the black sea turned red, then golden, like melted glass with a gaping hole at its centre—a hole into which the glowing, twisting wreckage of a ship vanished.

The *Maunsell* cut speed, tried to hold steady and keep out of the vortex of the sinking merchantmen. Action stations sounded, men running, officers shouting, signals being hoisted, metal scraping against metal as sailors lifted a three-hundred-pound depth charge onto a carrier and others eased the carrier into the barrel of the thrower.

Kyle seemed to be the only sailor without any memory of where his action station was or what his duty was. He held tight to the forward rail, frozen by the noise, by fear too, by the stink of burning oil, by night become day, by the sight of six remaining merchant ships clearly outlined against the bright sea. Leaning over the rail he could see the whole forepart of the sinking ship, could look down into a swirl of men and twisted steel being sucked to the bottom. No sign of their fellow escort ship—gone under, he supposed, or hidden behind the heavy smoke billowing from where flames had been seconds ago.

Above the din Kyle could hear Gup screaming, "Get the fuckers! Let go the guns!" Someone shouted at him to shut the hell up. Gup ignored the order. Infused with energy he kept racing about, repeating over and over, "Get the fuckers!" Coming upon the depth charge crew he grabbed one man by his sweater. "Let go the friggin depth charge, why don't ya?"

"There's no bloody target, ya stupid git!" the man snapped. He was one of the team standing ready to fire the thrower that would hurl both carrier and depth charge over the side. He gave Gup a mighty shove.

Kyle saw Gup stumble backward and snarl something. He half expected his friend to push the release on the thrower. Instead Gup whirled around, staggered across to where Kyle was standing and began heaving anything that might float into the water. Whether the object hit a drowning man, or gave him something to cling to, did not concern Gup. Three seamen got pulled in, one alive and two dead. Kyle watched Gup bring one of the dead men in, hauling him over the side by his legs, seeming unaware that the body had no head.

It was all over in minutes. Kyle was thankful no one but Gup had noticed his fear. "Jesus what a sight! Had a mind to kick you in the arse—only I didn't have time," Gup told him, laughing as if it were all a game, no more than smashing school windows or heaving snowballs at the cop on Prescott Street.

Gup was never afraid, never had those moments of private terror, that paralysis of fear that overcame Kyle whenever he thought of what happens at the meeting point of flesh and metal. Gup looked forward to leaving port, wanted to come under attack, as if he had no memory of what had happened last time. He wasn't the only one either—there were always a few loudmouths going on about how they were sick of being stuck ashore, fed up with St. John's, wanted to get out where the action was.

This bravado baffled Kyle. Everyone knew what it was like outside the narrows. Word was that the Germans had 160 U-boats and that at least 50 of them were permanently in the North Atlantic. The names of Allied ships sunk off St. John's were scrawled on the wall of the mess hall at Buckmaster's Field. Senior officers kept ordering the list scrubbed off, but it always reappeared, the latest death toll chalked across slime-green walls.

After the attack, their little convoy had just steamed on, zigzagging through the night. The next day they ran into sleet and dense fog, which seasoned hands said would hide them from stalking U-boats. Such talk did not reassure Kyle. He was sick with fear, his jaws and neck hurt, he was plagued by stomach cramps and spent most of the day in the head. More than anything he dreaded the coming night watch, the vast empty dark, the occasional darker shape looming—a sister ship or something else?

He went on at midnight and almost immediately lost track of time. In fog and freezing rain he had no idea if he'd circled the foredeck five or fifty times. When he saw the mess-boy struggle up the ladder with the old man's teapot he knew it was only two o'clock. He had already lost all feeling in his feet and was shuffling along the slippery deck like a drunk. How could he last two more hours? Would anyone notice if he crawled under a tarp into one of the dories? He could sleep, maybe freeze to death. He considered the notion—his grandfather said freezing wasn't the worst way to die, not nearly as bad as drowning.

On his next round he stopped leeward of the funnel and pressed his back against the iron, lifting one foot at a time to the warm surface. Holding his hands against his face, breathing into his palms. He'd closed his eyes, trying to block out everything except his own body, shivering inside the melton jacket. He was not sure the ship was even moving. Maybe only the sea moved, maybe they were going around and around in blackness, circling that hole, the one last night's ship had slid into. He imagined all the seas in the world washing towards the *Maunsell,* converging below his feet, countless fathoms of water through which a hundred German submarines prowled.

When his hands had thawed a little he felt in his pocket and pulled out a pack of Luckys. He barely had the fag lit when the officer on watch appeared out of the sleety dark.

"No bloody smokes, Sailor!" The Englishman plucked the cigarette from his hand, pulling it backward so the stub burned Kyle's fingers, then tossing it to the deck and grinding it under his boot.

The officer sniffed, as if he could smell fear. "Forget it, lad," he said. "Forget what happened last night. Stop imagining what might happen tonight. Concentrate on now—on what you see this second. Remember what we're here for. Watch the goddamn water! Try to see what's on it. Try to see what's under it. Concentrate on now!"

Kyle is still thinking on the Englishman's advice when he comes to the end of the tunnel. He stops, takes time to pull himself into the present, to concentrate on now, on this moment, this place.

He and his friends had always called it a cave but really it's just a widening where the tunnel ends, where the concrete foundation joins an old supporting wall, coming down to meet, but not quite meet, the jagged, intruding hillside. Kyle stands perfectly still, sniffing the not unpleasant smell of rotting wood and earthen floor, listening to the faint sound of water trickling down rock.

The underground room is bigger than he remembers, bigger than the whole crew's quarters on the *Maunsell*. The darkness here is not complete. From narrow cracks between crumbling mortar and the cliff face, needles of light prick through the dimness—touching his face, dancing on his hands in patterns he can almost remember.

"There!" he says, meaning *here*, meaning he is home, has arrived at the place where death will be quiet and dry—the death he's been moving towards since he became a murderer.

He is tired but it is a relief to stand upright. He takes time, walking slowly around the semicircle, carefully choosing where he will lie down. He's done this before, circling with Gup and Cyril to find a place where they would be comfortable—then sitting for hours, for whole afternoons, leafing through stolen comic books, eating stolen food, smoking stolen cigarettes. Wintertime they would make a fire, a small fire because of Art Norman.

There will be no fire this time—he has forgotten matches, forgotten cigarettes. Nevertheless he finds the circle of old ashes, pulls the tightly rolled hammock from his bag, shakes it and spreads it out near the cave wall. He rolls the canvas bag and stows it against the wall, making a kind of couch in the cranny. Although he knows it is not what he deserves, Kyle Holloway hopes for a comfortable death.

But he must have water, must drink before he can sleep. Following its sound to the deepest part of the cavern, he easily finds the place where water dribbles down the rock face, not pooling at the bottom but disappearing into cracks and crevices. He holds back from drinking, presses his palms against the wet rock, making black prints until all the dirt and coal dust has washed off his hands. The water is a rusty colour, like ponds in the valleys beyond the Southside Hills—brown water draining out of bogs, seeping into spongy earth, percolating down through uncounted years of dead things: root and leaf mould, flesh and bone and blood, the body of that Indian woman Art Norman was always telling them about, the one they buried by the church fence.

With patience Kyle manages to collect enough water to lap from his cupped hands. The smell and smatchy taste remind him of sun-warmed bogs, of summer days spent slogging through valleys of stunted evergreen, splashing in tea-coloured ponds.

When he is finished drinking he goes back to his hammock and drops down. It is then, lying with the duffle bag at his back, curled up like a child, that he hears the first sound—a sibilant, disapproving noise, a single breath released from between clenched teeth.

A snake! he thinks, although he has never seen a snake or heard one either and is pretty sure there are no snakes in Newfoundland. He listens, and when the sound is not repeated, decides it must have come from his own mouth.

Kyle closes his eyes, covers his face with his hands and concentrates on the miles of woods and bog beyond the church and the hill. He falls asleep imagining the three of them moving through those vast empty acres, wandering heedlessly eastward to Freshwater Bay, to Blackhead and Cape Spear—to the very ends of earth.

V

A few times each summer they would get clear out to Cape Spear, to where the headland ended in huge smooth boulders as if giants had rolled bowling balls into the sea. The boys used to argue about what country was on the other side, Ireland or Africa or China—all equally unknown, unimagined lands.

Gup always went out beyond the danger signs and Kyle followed, jumping from boulder to boulder, testing how far they could get before waves roared in, fizzing and hissing around their feet. It was Gup's game. He would shout, shake his fist and swear, daring the sea to pull him under—as it had others, grown men whose names were scratched into rocks along this bit of coast.

Kyle followed Gup, but Cy was afraid of the sea. No matter how much the other two taunted, he stayed well back from the water. Kyle was scared too—more scared than Cyril, he sometimes thought—but too afraid to admit it. He tried hard to keep up with Gup, though he never could get as far out, never reached the place where Gup had twice been stranded, water boiling all around, green fingers slapping at his legs as he clung to the smooth coppery face of the rock, waiting for the wave to recede.

The boys did not get as far as Cape Spear very often. Most days were spent in the low woods and bog beyond The Edge, which was what everyone called the crest of the Southside Hills. They felt completely alone back there, killing each other over and over in childish games of cops and robbers, cowboys and Indians. Later they became trackers and hunters, learned to fish and swim in the black ponds behind the hill.

Kyle's father had no time for the outdoors around St. John's. "Fenced in and fished out," Steve Holloway would reply to his wife's annual suggestion that he take his son fishing on the twenty-fourth. Cyril's father wasn't interested in woods or ponds either. Art Norman rarely ventured beyond the sooty streets of downtown St. John's, his only relationship with nature being the vendetta he waged against birds that invaded his church.

For knowledge of the miles of open land beyond The Edge, the boys had to depend on Gup's relatives, his grandfather and his alcoholic uncles. Kyle was never sure of the uncles' names or how many Gup had—four or five, he thought. They lived all together up on the Brow. Not part of the tightly knit little community but well back, at the end of a woods path that was half overgrown with thistle and alder. The unpainted Gullage shack sheltered Gup, his mother (a gaunt, blue-faced creature whom Gup and everyone else called Daze), his grandfather and a rotation of uncles. Always one or two uncles would be away, sometimes camped out in over The Edge, sometimes serving time in the pen for disorderly conduct or petty theft.

The Gullage men fished and hunted year round, whenever the mood took them. Trout and salmon, moose, rabbit, wild birds, hens and lambs—and occasionally jars of strong alcohol—all arrived at their table fresh from "the woods," that tangled network of trails winding through berry grounds and small stands of stunted spruce; circling ponds, bogs and outcroppings of grey rock. Gup's grandfather and uncles had no desire to pass along their woodcraft. "Ya think I'm some friggin Boy Scout?" was the kindest response Gup received to questions concerning those acres the men considered their private estate.

As they grew older the boys began to follow the uncles, trail them to the best fishing holes, lie for hours behind a bush or rock, watching to see how a line was cast, a snare set, a rifle fired. At least learning these things gave them an excuse to spy on the uncles. In fact, stalking the dangerous, bearlike men became an end in itself, more fun than jumping off train tracks at the last moment, tormenting night-watchmen down at the docks or even stealing from delivery trucks.

Sometimes they would be discovered and booted out of their hiding places. "What ya doin here, ya sneaky little buggers!" and one of the uncles would be kicking at them before they had a chance to scramble up. Once caught they were likely to be sent back to the shack to fetch something the men wanted—a tarp or blanket, a bottle of booze or another gun.

Once they were sent to find a girl.

They knew the girl—not her name but who she was. She lived on the Southside, so they'd seen her around school. The uncles had noticed the girl on their way in. They told the boys to go get her, said she was all alone, picking berries just in back of The Edge.

And that's where they found her, squatting in moss, picking partridgeberries. There was nothing special about her, sticklike arms and legs, straggly brown hair. She was wearing boy's boots and a faded print dress, and dropping berries one by one into a string-handled tin, as if it didn't matter how many she picked, as if she and the berries were the only things in the world.

"Thousands more in back," Gup said when they came up, startling her so that she stood right up, shading her eyes with one hand, staring at the boys without smiling.

She was older, about fourteen, and would have known who they were, would have heard tell they were hard cases. A stupid girl she must have been, to follow so heedlessly.

Gup had grown tall that summer, so he and she were about the same height. They trotted along, the girl nattering about how come she was wearing her brother's boots, how she liked berry picking and hated school—though there was one teacher who was nice. Kyle and Cyril trailed behind, exchanging grins, surprised at Gup who was walking right alongside the girl, scowling but making noises like he was interested in the boring stuff she was saying.

Four of the uncles were in the woods that day. When the girl saw the men she dropped her tin and tried to run. Kyle and Cyril caught her under the arms and Gup grabbed her ankles. Her boots fell off. Suddenly it seemed like a grand bit of fun and the three of them were laughing fit to kill, swinging the girl as if she were a young child. She wasn't very heavy. They carried her over and laid her down in front of the uncles.

"See? Lots of berries," Gup said.

It was true—dark red partridgeberries shone in the bright moss, made wine-coloured stains on the faded cotton dress that had runkled up showing the girl's underpants. She made small gasping noises, scravelling to get to her feet until one of the uncles bent down and grabbed her leg. Kyle noticed how the man's fingers wrapped clean around the girl's ankle.

The other men barely glanced at the girl; they stepped around her and stood facing the boys. "Now. You three—get the fuck outta here!" one said.

Kyle and Cyril backed off but Gup didn't budge. He was tall even then, but scrawny compared to his uncles who were big, overweight men. Cyril was still giggling, nervous now, rocking from foot to foot. Kyle hissed at him to shut up. The uncles had been drinking. He was expecting them to punch the guts out of Gup and probably take a crack at him and Cyril too.

Then one of the uncles hauled out some money and pushed it into Gup's hand. "Here—here's a dollar for each o' ye."

The oldest uncle, the one Gup said once killed someone in a lumber camp, made as if to grab the money back. "Fuck sake! That's more'n we'd pay down behind the post office!" But when Gup jammed the bills into his pocket, the man didn't go after them. "All right," he said, breathing hard as if he'd been running. "Okay—just remember that money makes ye lot accessories after the fact." Seeming to like the words, he repeated them: "Accessories after the fact—that means if ye little shaggers breathes one word of this ye'll be hauled up before Judge Furlong." The man jabbed a finger into Gup's shoulder, but it was Kyle he was staring at. "Your old man works longshore, don't he?"

Kyle had nodded or shaken his head—he wasn't sure which. The men all had knives tucked into their belts. One had a rifle slung over his shoulder. But it was their hands that frightened Kyle most, large hands opening and closing at their sides, like animals barely held in check. They could kill us, he thought. They could push our bodies into a pond and no one'd ever be the wiser. Kyle didn't think that Gup's kinship with the men would save them. He could smell something like burning garbage—it might be fear oozing out of him, or maybe out of Cyril or the girl.

The girl was flailing about. Not making a sound now, using all her energy to twist and kick, trying to claw at the hand holding her down. She was stronger than she looked. The man smacked her across the face and grunted, "Get rid of them little fuckers!"

The one who'd passed out the money nodded. "Get the hell outta here—and no hangin around in the bushes or we'll have the skin right off yer arses . . ."

He shouted something else but the boys had taken off, pushing past one another, falling over rocks, racing down the dip of the valley, up to The Edge then down the other side, clattering into the church—not stopping until they flung themselves into the tunnel, until, scratched and shaken, they reached the cave and safety.

Safety—the safety we always found down here, Kyle thinks. Then he hears the sound again, a hissing that becomes louder and louder, that grows until it fills the cavern like water or night, vibrating along the rock walls, ricocheting around him, filling the cleft in which he huddles.

When the sound ends he stays still, his body pressed against the rocks, waiting for what will follow.

Nothing follows. Or nothing he can understand. Yet below the silence there is something—a low mumble, a muted mournful vibration that goes on and on. It could be wind, or birds— probably pigeons cooing, picking around the foundations where there is a little heat, and worms too in the soft earth where the old graves used to be.

The mumbling fades and after a long while is gone. Just when this happens Kyle is never certain—there is a residue, a shadow of that keening in his head, so he can never know what he heard and what he imagined. He only knows that after a time it is gone and he becomes aware of a pain that radiates up from his gut into his chest, then moves to settle behind his eyes.

People talked about the missing girl. She'd been seen going aboard a Portuguese ship, seen down on the Southern Shore, at a dance hall out in the Goulds. Maeve Holloway said none of these stories were true. A neighbour knew someone on the police force, and the girl had simply gone berry picking up on the Southside Hills, just as her family said. The poor youngster had probably fallen off a cliff; sooner or later her body would wash up. "Let that be a lesson to your crowd not to go gallivantin in over The Edge," his mother warned.

For weeks search parties tramped the Southside Hills. The uncles helped. The girl was never found. After a time she joined other nameless spirits who haunted the hills. People on the Brow still claim to see her, one of many ghosts that appear on foggy nights—godless savages and unbaptized infants, along with pirates and other villains hung by Deadman's Pond, all buried without benefit of clergy outside the fence of St. Mary's old graveyard.

Gup and Cy never spoke of the girl again, and Kyle never said a word about the nightmares from which he woke in a sweat, hearing the sad whimpering squeaks she made when she knew she couldn't get away and the sound of her tin pail banging against the drainpipe outside his bedroom window.

He's been lying awake for a long time, all night perhaps. It is day—some day, he doesn't know which—no sunlight seeping in but he can see a little, make out the circle of white ash beside his sleeping place.

The pain in his head has become a faint throbbing but his throat hurts terribly—he needs water, needs to piss too. Apparently people stop shitting when they stop eating; if he could only stop drinking, he wouldn't need to piss either. He could just lie here quietly and dry up. It's going to happen anyway in the end, when he gets too weak to stand. He wonders if it's going to hurt much, all the fluid inside him drying up, the wetness in his eyes and mouth, blood too, he supposes—everything inside shrivelling, his body shrinking. Dead things take up less space.

Kyle reminds himself that he already worked this all out, that he's doing the best thing. Once he could face anything, thought he could face anything. He could have too, so long as the three of them were in it together—so long as he wasn't thinking. When had the thinking started? Now he's alone, alone and thinking, and everything frightens him—especially the knowledge that he will have to remember Gup day after day, see Gup's eyes in that instant when he knew—when they both knew.

No! Kyle thinks. I wants to be dead—be over and done with all the thinking, all the remembering, all the being afraid. Still, he is beginning to wonder if he could have figured out a better way of going about it. Perhaps, even now, he can speed death up by just lying here, not going to the water he can hear dribbling down rock in the cave's far corner.

He holds out for as long as he can, how long he doesn't know—time has fallen off the pegs of seconds, minutes, hours. In the end he gets up and does what he has to do. When he's finished he returns to stand irresolutely beside his sleeping place. Searching for some reason not to lie down he remembers the names, recalls the afternoon in late summer when they carved their names in one of the tree trunks supporting this place. You had to lie on your side with your head twisted awkwardly upward to cut into the overhead beam. He remembers the good clean smell of wood, chips flicking away from the knife tip down on your face.

He begins to circle the cave, bent forward, running his hand along the rough pit-props that are pounded into the earthen floor angling out to the walls. He takes his time; it's good to have something to do, some little thing that pulls your thoughts away from fear and death. He's gone almost around the semicircle when he finds it, just a few feet from where he's been sleeping.

Kyle eases himself down and under the tree trunk. It is bigger than most, has been planed down on one side. He lies on his side so that he can run his palm along the smooth plank, which is pleasant to touch, warmer than rock. His fingers find gouges in the wood, trace a line of letters that waver down the unevenly planed surface of the tree.

Pausing at each letter his fingertips move tentatively back and forth across the last name, *N, A, M, R, O, N* . . . Norman Cyril. Then Holloway Kyle. Then, quickly to the beginning, to the large deeply slashed *V*—Valentine—Gullage Valentine! Kyle has forgotten, or perhaps had never noticed, that Gup carved his real, much-hated name into the tree trunk that day.

Valentine Gullage. Who could have given Daze's baby such a name? Daze herself? One of her brutish brothers? Kyle lies in the now-quiet dark trying to puzzle it out—cannot, and falls to remembering his first school day in St. John's, in that narrow, darkly varnished room with four lines of brown desks bolted to the brown floor. Each desk designed to seat two children.

Children had entered the room willy-nilly, or so it seemed to Kyle, but it was clear that most knew where to go. The desks quickly filled, girls seating themselves on the window side of the aisle, the boys on the side nearest to the door. Kyle and two girls were left standing at the back.

"Find someplace," the teacher-woman called from her platform at the front. "Fit in there—and there." She waved vaguely. Her hands, whiter and limper than any hands Kyle had ever seen, fluttered like tired gulls before alighting on her fountain pen. She uncapped the pen and opened the big book he knew was called the Register. His mother had told him his name was on the Register—it was why he had to go to school.

While he was watching the teacher, the girls had managed to squeeze into two already full seats. He waited and waited but the teacher continued to study the Register, counting names with the tip of her pen. He'd walked to the nearest desk and made as if to sit. As his breeks touched the edge of the seat, the boy nearest him jerked sideways and Kyle landed on the floor with a thump.

Stunned, he sat there, watching from the floor as the teacher, in one graceful movement, rose from behind her desk, descended from her platform and swept down the aisle. Using both hands, no longer limp but iron fingered, she yanked the end boy from his seat, lifted Kyle off the floor, pushed him into the middle, and jammed the other boy back in place as if he were a sandbag.

The woman returned to her desk and began calling out, never raising her eyes from the Register, names popping out of her mouth sharp and quick. By never taking their eyes from her face, by concentrating, each child was able to whisper "Present please" at the appropriate second. But when she called "Valentine Gullage," there was no answer.

"Valentine Gullage," she repeated, her voice rising on the last syllable.

Silence.

The teacher looked up. "Which one of you is Valentine Gullage?" Her eyes searched desk by desk, the green fountain pen jabbing the air, counting heads. Then, "You! You at the back! What is your name, young man?" The pen pointed at the boy she'd rammed in beside Kyle.

The boy raised his head. For a long minute he stared at the teacher, at her pen, at the row of pearl buttons down the front of her black sweater. "Gup," he said, "me name's Gup Gullage."

"Valentine Gullage," the teacher said.

"Gup Gullage," the boy said, his voice dead flat, without expression.

"Valentine!"

"Gup."

The other students watched, wide-eyed, hands folded on desks. Only their heads moved, swinging back and forth from pupil to teacher.

"Valentine!"

"Gup."

After several exchanges the woman placed her pen on the desk. She picked up a ruler, positioned it carefully across the register page, picked up her pen and drew a long line. She called out, "Kyle Holloway."

Kyle turned to stone.

"Kyle Holloway." The teacher was looking at him, glaring at him.

"Present please," he squeaked, and the one named Gup gave him a vicious root in the ribs.

Kyle lies below the supporting tree trunk, tracing the three names, remembering that first day, remembering the afternoon they carved their names. Cyril wanted to put in their birthdates and the year, like on headstones. But it was too hard. Every few minutes you had to trade places because your arm would have gone dead, and besides, they only had one knife—Gup's knife . . .

And he is back there, back at the place he always comes to—the tilting deck, the darkness, the wires singing overhead, the knife—always he is back there, over and over again. Kyle wonders if it will stop when he dies, or will it go on forever, his mind running in circles like a rat in a bucket, doing the night watch for eternity. It occurs to him that he might already be dead, might be a ghost. Do ghosts know that they are ghosts?

According to Mr. Norman there are no such things as ghosts. Ghosts, like birds, are unwanted intruders. Talk of such things irritates the verger, who maintains that not even ministers believe what they preach. "If they really thought there was such a thing as life after death, you think they'd have built the church extension right in over them old graves?" he once asked the boys.

Kyle's mother never spoke of ghosts but she certainly believed in life after death. When he was small she was always telling him stories, reading *The War Cry* out loud to him and his father, holding up the coloured pictures—people in strange getups, blankets pulled around their shoulders and sandals on their feet, naked people in gardens with all kinds of fruit and flowers and birds, with winged creatures overhead like those in the picture above his bed. His mother said angels were not like ghosts. God had made angels to watch over people, she told him. God made people too, but after that he was sorry and tried to drown everybody.

"Why had God decided to make away with people by drownin 'em? Couldn't he just have unmade them?" Perhaps the answer had been in his mother's story, but Kyle cannot remember.

Later, in school, teachers must have told him these and other stories about where people came from, where they went, but by then he was not hearing a word grown-ups said. He is sorry now. Huddled in that narrow space between earth and rock Kyle wishes he had listened more. Maybe that was what his mother had meant about comfort—it must be a comfort to believe you were created by God, cared for by angels with bright wings.

"Listen to me, Dogman!"

Listen to me. No God made you! There was no garden, no creatures with white wings. Listen and hear how you came to be.

This story happened in Old Time. After Perfect Time when the Great Spirit spoke to people directly, but in that time when creatures who walk upright were still all of one family.

In that time a beautiful girl refused to marry the man her father had chosen. Her father, who was a powerful shaman, became very angry. In the heat of anger he called upon Nakhani the evil wolf spirit to punish his disobedient daughter.

Nakhani, who had long wanted to mix wolf blood with the blood of people, agreed to the man's plan.

Nakhani waited until the coldest full-moon of winter. On that night seven wolf-dogs, who had betrayed their kin and gone to hunt with men, heard Nakhani's voice calling from deep in the forest. The wolf in them had no choice but to obey. They slunk away from the camps of men, ran like smoke through the white night until they came to the Middle World where Nakhani, together with all evil spirits, lives.

When the wolf-dogs had gathered, Nakhani swept a spell over them and all seven froze in a circle of moonlight. Then Nakhani hunted down a deer and flung its carcass into the middle of the circle. In that moment the wolf-dogs came to life, fighting over the meat, snarling and tearing at one another. For hours they fought, claws slashing through fur and flesh, fangs ripping throats. Every animal in the forest hid, the snow steamed with blood and the moon moved slowly, slowly through the frozen sky.

At dawn only the wolf-dog Euano remained alive, a huge white beast with powerful shoulders, and eyes so cold that even Nakhani shivered when he looked into them.

With his magic Nakhani transported Euano to the opening of the shaman's tent. The shaman looked into the wolf-dog's eyes, and knowing its nature yet bid him inside where his daughter slept. Then the shaman turned his back and sat in the doorway of his tent. There he sat, smoking and staring outward all through that day and all through the night that followed. And all that time Euano raped his daughter.

At dawn on the second day the wolf-dog disappeared into the forest. The shaman returned to his tent and slept. His daughter slowly crawled down to the shore and washed herself in the Great Water.

After that the girl went about her work without a word. Through the rest of winter and spring she did not speak. Summer came and she gave birth to two babies, one a girl, one a boy.

When the young woman looked at her newborn children she saw that their skin was white as the skin of grubs, not the pleasing colour of people. The bodies of the babies, though furless, were poorly shaped, and their faces had the yellow eyes and features of the wolf-dog. A great rage came over the woman. She picked up a hatchet and cut off her father's head. Then she chopped off his feet. She pulled the bloody moccasins from her father's chopped-off feet, placed a child in each moccasin and pushed the wolf-dog babies out into the Great Water.

Driven by wind and tide, the moccasin boats drifted away from our island. They drifted across water and into the mist where no birds fly and no fish swim, carrying the wolf-dog babies, who slept and woke and lapped up the blood of their grandfather.

On the other side of the vast water these wolf-dog creatures washed up. They were in another land, and in that evil, unhappy place they bred, became Euano, became you—murderers, rapists who have overrun the earth.

Kyle heaves himself upward, smashes his face against unseen hardness and falls back. "Fuckin Christ!" The sound of his own voice calms him a little. When he is done cursing he lies still and listens. But all he can hear is his own breathing—that loud gasping sound again. He has lived all his life without ever noticing he was breathing—now he seems to be doing it wrong. He shuts his eyes, wraps his arms around his body and waits for the shivering to stop.

He must have fallen asleep, must have been having a dream—worse even than the ones he used to have about the girl. And he's wedged himself into the crevice, pushed his body back until he is half encircled, lying below the tree trunk they cut their names into. Only now the place is damp, something dripping down his chin and neck. He licks his lips, tastes salt, thinks sea water—the ocean oozing through rocks.

God's sendin the ocean to get me! As soon as Kyle thinks this, he sees how necessary, right and just it is. He waits, imagining a wall of grey-green water filling the church basement, rushing down the tunnel towards him. The image is so real that minutes pass before he realizes that what he is tasting is blood—his nose is bleeding for Chrissake, and not a little bit either.

He dabs at the blood with his sweater but more comes, dribbling into his mouth and down his chin. Cautiously he reaches up, and using the tree trunk he banged into minutes ago he pulls himself upright. He is shaking but manages to stand, and supporting himself against the rock wall he waits for the bleeding to stop.

You're half-cracked, b'y. Ocean can't break through the Southside Hills, no more'n someone can be talkin in an empty tunnel. He's never had such thoughts before, never imagined God was after him, never heard voices. He discounts the berry-picking girl—he always knew she was only a bad dream. Can he be going mad?

He considers madness. He has seen raving mad sailors dragged from the sea—men blinded by fire, limbs missing, metal splinters embedded in their faces, flesh hanging in white strips—but it was their loss of sanity that horrified Kyle most. The medics injected something into the men who screamed, covered their burnt skin and bloody flesh with pads of white gauze, keeping the wounded quiet and the wounds out of sight. It did not always work. Sometimes the screaming would start again before they made port.

VI

After the officer reprimanded him, Kyle did not lose his fear, but he did learn to control it—at least when they were not under attack. Twice in the weeks that followed he was the first to spot U-boats; once by the telltale oil slick, and once, in full daylight, when he glimpsed the black tip of a conning tower, the frill of white froth just as the sub dived. Much to Kyle's relief neither sighting led to an attack.

Sometimes, lying in his safe crevice of rock, Kyle tries deliberately to recreate the fear he lived with then, that cold weight inside his stomach—always there, moving like a bird, fluttering up to his throat a hundred times each day—when a shadow rippled over the water, when he heard Gup's laugh, when someone mentioned wolf packs, submarines, U-boats. Recalling these things makes what he now fears seem smaller.

Below deck all hands talked about submarines—their shapes, their size, their equipment. They said U-boat commanders received all the routing instruction sent to convoys, knew where every one was. U-boats had the ability to move quickly, swerve, even dive sideways—Kyle wouldn't have been surprised to hear they could fly. Even with the second-hand asdic the *Maunsell* had acquired, subs were almost impossible to locate. Not only was the asdic fixed dead ahead—when any stunned-arse could see it should be mounted on a swivel device—but it was set off by fish, seaweed and variations of water temperature more often than by enemy ships. Because of this, Kyle's keen eyesight was an important skill, but not one likely to earn him a promotion unless a hit was credited to his sighting.

Gup, on the other hand, moved up and then down, from ordinary seaman to able-bodied seaman, twice in four months. Officers began watching the young man much the way they watched the depth charges that kept popping out of their wooden cradles and rolling around on deck.

"We'll need that crazy bastard one day!" Kyle heard the first mate tell another officer the night Gup started a fight and got thrown in the brig for twenty-four hours.

The day came in August, on a calm sparkling sea just outside St. John's Harbour. The *Maunsell* was one of four escort ships assigned to sweep ahead of a Norwegian tanker outward bound. Having been cleared by a minesweeper the night before, the shipping lane was presumed safe. Nevertheless, because of the tanker's cargo—rumoured to be high-octane fuel below deck, and in clear sight, twenty fighter aircraft, wings folded, secured to the for'ard deck—the Norwegians had to be escorted to the relative safety of deep water, where they were to rendezvous with a large convoy coming from Halifax.

Watching the two outside vessels begin to veer off, Kyle felt immense relief. The water was getting on to a thousand fathoms, and soon all four escort ships would turn back. They would make port before dark. Since he wasn't on duty, Kyle decided he'd go ashore, try to get a bunk at Buckmasters for the night.

Then the *Maunsell*'s signalman yelled, "Mine amidship! Off starboard!"

Orders were shouted down the blower and the *Maunsell* cut her engine. Signals went up, and one by one each vessel in the convoy stopped. It took almost fifteen minutes to discover that none of the ships had a rendering-mines-safe officer aboard.

"Bugger that," the officer on deck said mildly, as if it was only what he expected. Everyone knew that mine disposal officers were regularly blown up and it took months to get a trained replacement. Like most Royal Navy ships, the *Maunsell* had never been assigned one.

After a flurry of signals the men aboard the *Maunsell* watched the Norwegian tanker and three of her escort ships drop astern, watched as the ships slowly, slowly manoeuvred in tight circles until their bows pointed back towards St. John's. Then, holding as close as possible to their outward-bound lane, all four started back to port. The *Maunsell* was left, holding steady about two hundred feet from the rogue mine.

By then the captain and first officer were on deck, along with the bosun and many of the crew. When the first officer asked if anyone had experience defusing mines, the bosun said he'd seen one taken care of.

The officer waited. When nothing more was forthcoming he snapped, "Well? Are you going to tell us how to defuse the damn thing or not?"

"Can't be defused proper without a trained man." Bosun Hoskins chewed thoughtfully on a wad of tobacco he always had tucked in his cheek. "Thing is, you never know what's inside the buggers."

"But you said you'd seen it done . . ."

"Said I seen it taken care of," Hoskins said. He was a Newfoundlander and well aware of his own officer status.

"Jesus, man, tell us what you saw!"

"I saw a man let down in a lifeboat—he netted the mine, towed it out of the shipping lane and blew it up."

"Blew it up! In the water?"

"He towed it onto a beach, backed off a good way and shot at it. It blew up."

"Frig, anyone could do that—I could do that," Gup snorted, and a kind of cheer went up from the three men who had lately become his followers.

The men reminded Kyle of the uncles, although they were small and quicker on their feet. They egged Gup on and stood behind him in fights. Kyle was not part of this gang and it seemed to him that Gup was now treating him differently, looking at him the way they had once looked at Cyril.

Hoskins had a strong dislike for Gup and his hangers-on. Not only was Gup the ship's prime troublemaker, he also ran a crap game at which the bosun regularly lost a good part of his pay. He stared at Gup for a long minute. "So, Gullage! You think you're up for it, do ya?"

"Sure am, old cock!"

Kyle saw the captain nod to the duty officer. He tried to catch Gup's eye, but his friend turned away, went and leaned over the side, looking as if he might jump in after the rogue mine.

"Some of these buggers are electronically controlled, but I'd say this one's acoustic—preset to detonate by sound," Hoskins said.

No one asked the bosun how he knew this. He went below and came up presently with a net bag attached to a gaff and an old hunting rifle, very like the one Gup's uncles owned.

"All ya got to do is net the mine and tow it into that little cove." Hoskins waved vaguely towards Freshwater Bay. "I hear tell you're a good shot, Gullage. Just land her in there, back off a good ways and let her have it with this 'til she blows." He passed Gup the rifle.

Kyle was one of the men ordered to launch a dory, and straining above the noise of the winch he could hear the second officer, carefully repeating the bosun's plan to Gup. Clearly uncomfortable with the sketchiness of the idea, the man added a few warnings of his own: "Be very careful, this one could very well be attached to others we can't see—mines anchored a few feet or so beneath the surface."

His eyes still on the bobbing mine, now within yards of the ship, Gup gave no indication of listening.

Annoyed at the sailor's inattention, the Englishman raised his voice. "Do I understand, Gullage, that you have volunteered for this undertaking?"

Gup turned around and shrugged. "Sure," he said, grinning. He slung the rifle over his shoulder and took the long-handled net Hoskins had rigged up. Without a word or glance at anyone on deck, he hoisted himself over the side, climbed down the rope ladder and jumped into the dory.

It took him a good half hour to manoeuvre the evil-looking black kettle into the net bag, even longer to pull off from the Maunsell. Once he hit the hull so hard that one of the English officers muttered, "Stupid bastard's going to blow us all up."

But the tide was on the turn, and when he did get clear of the ship the dory was carried shoreward despite Gup's poor oarsmanship.

Standing along the rail with most of the crew, Kyle thought what a peaceful sight it was, a man rowing into the snug sparkling cove. "What became of that guy you saw blow up the mine?" he asked.

"A big rock flew down into his boat, went right clean through her," Hoskins said.

"What happened?"

"What ya think happened? She sank."

"What happened to buddy?"

"He drowned." The bosun looked thoughtful. "Seems the stunned bugger couldn't swim."

"Gup swims real good."

"Be all right then, won't he?"

"Take care unloading her! Find a nice sandy spot!" the duty officer shouted after Gup.

Gup didn't acknowledge the order, perhaps he was too far away to hear.

What odds, Kyle thought: to find sand in Freshwater Bay, Gup would have to carry the mine over half a mile of large wet boulders into the little inlet beyond the barachois. Kyle was not expecting Gup back. If he didn't get blown up, he would take off, disappear into the hills, forget he'd ever been in the Navy. If anyone could live off the land it was Gup. Kyle wondered how many bullets were in the rifle. He wished he'd said something before Gup pulled away, had called something down to him. For a moment he even wished he were in the little boat, two of them rowing into the familiar cove—but no, not with death dragging behind.

Gup did come back. He was cheered on board, even by men who didn't have much use for him, and hoisted onto the shoulders of two of his buddies. Got a sleeve patch out of it, got made a leading hand.

One of the higher-ups must have heard of Gup's bravado, because the *Maunsell* began to be sent out regularly to hook in mines the sweepers had accidently cut adrift. Gup repeated his performance seven times, always in the same offhand manner. Some hands thought he should get a medal, more said he was going to get the whole crew blown to kingdom come.

Even Gup's three cohorts grew weary of his leaving and returning without incident. Only the bosun and Kyle faithfully saw him off every time. When he could, Kyle would stay on deck and try to keep the dory in view. Sometimes he would see a spout of smoke, water exploding into the sky, but not always— though Gup was a crack shot and said that the mines always blew. Kyle got the idea that Gup might be saving the mines, stashing them away. He imagined the war over, and him, Cyril and Gup blowing up cliffs out in Freshwater Bay.

Gup's rowing didn't improve. Every time the returning dory banged into the hull, the hands waiting to winch the boat up would gleefully shout, "Refit! Refit!"

By then Gup had the run of the ship and rarely bothered to show up for muster. Still he didn't lose his patch. The officers now turned a blind eye to his rowdiness and drinking. Gup had become a legend, an expert—not by quietly defusing mines as a trained man would, but by blowing them sky high in uninhabited coves and bays. Stories went around town; someone had seen a fish flake explode out in Flatrock, hundreds of dead fish falling from the sky on Maddox Cove. People recognized Gup, joked with him, offered him drinks in taverns. Word had it that Hoskins was making book on how long it would take Gup to blow himself up.

Kyle began to see that the ship was like a larger, better school-yard. Gup was in his glory, nothing could touch him. Shooting mines suited him better than anything he had ever done. He would climb down the side and climb back wearing the same manic grin. "Fuckin good what!" he'd say whenever he found

Kyle waiting. The words warmed Kyle, made him remember how it had been to be Gup's friend; how nothing anyone said to Gup made a blind bit of difference. He remembered how Gup would stay on the railway tracks until the very last moment, how he climbed five stories on fire escapes behind the Newfoundland Hotel. Best of all was that great trick Gup did with bottles; tossing one bottle high into the air, then, just as it started to fall, throwing a second bottle at it. Two bottles colliding in mid-air, glass exploding like sunshine, spraying out, everyone in the schoolyard ducking, Gup giving off that wild laugh—a high, insane guffaw. That laugh, the lifted arm . . .

The man in the cave moans, calls out, "Stop!" But nothing stops, not memory or thinking or breathing, nor the low, persistent grumbling that is always there—sometimes loud and angry, sometimes low and monotonous, like that underwater rumble the sea makes. The sound is continuous, encompassing, the background to Kyle's sleeping and waking and to all that grey slurry in between.

A dark morning, Grandmother—and this creature slouched against rocks, mewing over small griefs. Is it you, Grandmother, who sent this white ghost—this whimpering thing who desires nothing, who wants only to stop, to forget? Has his world ended? Have his people perished?

Euano! I shout. Stupid Dogman! Why seek to forget? He doesn't answer, doesn't listen, doesn't know that in this place memory is food, is air, is water. What is left beyond memory? Night and blackness and cold and the walls of this desolation where his kind put me.

I thought many townspeople would come to see me buried. They had crowded around me when I lived, had touched my hair and skin, had dressed me in soft cloth, paraded me around their streets, brought me inside their stinking houses, displayed me as they did other strange belongings—dusty flowers and dead butterflies, stuffed birds and the terrible mounted heads of bears and caribou. They had petted me, asked me endless questions, given me coloured sticks, coaxed me to draw my world for them. Surely they would come to see their tame savage put into the ground.

But the hillside was empty—rain and two men, and a wet horse tied to the graveyard gate. One of the men asked his god to forgive me and to accept my pagan soul; the other did not speak at all, only wrote something down in his little book. Then they left, and two workmen, who had been standing well back, smoking their pipes in the shelter of the cliff, came over. They carelessly shovelled wet clay and rocks onto the box that contained my unanointed body. No songs and stories to honour my life—just two rough Dogmen thumping earth down with their heavy boots. Then it was over. They walked away, complaints about thirsty work and the rattling of their picks and shovels seeping back through the grey mist, through the loose earth and poorly made box.

I was dead. Dead and the worms already eating my flesh. Buried without ceremony, without oil and ochre, without belongings or tokens for my spirit guardian. Buried far from our sacred places. Yet in that silent time after the gravediggers left, I was happy, more happy than I had been since that long-ago morning when Nonosabasut and I watched the sun rise over a vast snow-filled valley.

Now I would see him again. It did not matter that we would be spirits—only that I would see his face, see all of you, hear your voices, listen to your stories—know why things came about as they did . . .

I expected it to happen in an instant. That was what you promised me, Grandmother, that when I left this world, a spirit guide would set my feet on the Ghost Path. Ancestors who had watched me live among Dogmen would come for me, would restore me to my people.

I believed. Though I lay dead in my box I was warm with memory—memory inside me like the sun, so bright I knew that wet clay could not contain me. My grave would open, and any moment I would find myself on the Ghost Path, travelling to our Perfect Time, to you, to my people.

The men who buried me are long dead, Grandmother. The box I lay in has rotted away. The worms that ate my flesh have themselves been eaten. The very graveyard has vanished. Dogmen have built their stone church over my bones. A thousand, thousand mornings I have reminded you, yet you have not kept your promise. Why have you not come? Why have none of my kin— my mother, my brothers—come to save me? Are the spirits of our people so content that they forget promises? Is Perfect Time a place without memory?

I am all memory. Nothing else. But even memory can dissolve, leech into earth. I am forgetting your stories, Grandmother, forgetting past time, forgetting our Spirit World. This is what I fear most—that I will forget all, forget even you, forget to call out to you each morning. Without memory everything I was will vanish—Shanawdithit become nothing.

To hold memory I speak to water, to rock, to darkness— speak even to this Dogman. Each day I story-talk, calling back what night has stolen, words lifted on memory, sparkling. Yet they cannot be saved—each night they fall back into the dark river, each night some are lost.

The sailor is jerked awake by the crash of iron against iron, the sound rumbling down the tunnel. Torpedoes! he thinks, torpedoes smashing into the hull. He struggles to stand but cannot. Weak from hunger and bad dreams, tangled in lines of the hammock he's wrapped around himself, he gives up, crouches, waiting for the rock to burst open, the roof to buckle, waiting for fire and water to come roaring in.

Then, between the banging and scraping he hears words, not clearly but well enough to know it is neither the voice of a U-boat commander nor the mad, monotonous voice he has become accustomed to. This is someone speaking English, swearing in a cadence he understands—or will understand after the noise in his chest stops.

"Light, ya Jeezly frigger! Light, I tell ya!" The order is followed by a volley of curses.

Kyle laughs out loud. It's Art Norman! Cyril's old man is on the other side of the passageway, banging and swearing.

Mr. Norman's rational mind never kept him from talking to the ancient, cranky furnace—no more than it kept him from arguing with birds or calling doom down on the heads of Kyle, Gup and Cyril, proclaiming with apparent pleasure after each new folly, "Mark my words, ye three'll hang or end up in the Mental!"

Kyle wants to run down the tunnel, wants to embrace Mr. Norman, to kiss the old bugger, to tell him everything. The impulse is so strong that, without thinking, he manages to untangle himself, begins to get to his feet. Then he remembers. He pulls himself back and lies down again.

A hundred times Kyle has watched the verger get the church fire started. He knows each step: crumpled newspapers and shavings piled on, then splits and wood junks; then, after a good wait, shovelfuls of coal eased onto the bed of hot embers. If the coals failed to catch, the old man would deftly restack and relight the small wood, all the while cursing on the meanness of church sidemen who bought damp splits and slack coal.

Kyle crouches with one ear pressed against the rock wall, listening to the familiar sounds, the blessing of a voice that belongs neither to himself nor to the hag who haunts his cave.

He imagines heat and feels more comfortable after the furnace is lit, more and less comfortable because he begins to think about food again, about the thick cheese sandwich Mr. Norman will eat while he's waiting for the junks to burn down, the possibility that Cy's old man might leave a piece of bread or an apple core.

Although his stomach cramps and saliva dribbles down his chin Kyle doesn't move. Long after the noises end he holds back—sidemen sometimes come down and check to make sure the fire is properly stoked. He must not go into the furnace room until the service is over and the church safely empty. He weeps, thinking of food on the floor of the furnace room, mice nibbling it. But he waits.

VII

He waits, watching pearly strands of light moving along the walls, revealing rock colours he's never noticed before. Pulling his thoughts away from the possibility of food, he concentrates on the rocks; some are blue and purple, some red, others are creamy white, marbled with pink. Beautiful. He supposes rocks are like trees, different kinds have different names. Kyle wishes he knew what they are.

He rests against the hard wall, watching time move, trying to remember beauty—something he'd seen up above, outside in the sunshine, something he'd looked at and known, even then, to be beautiful. Drifting, subsiding into a time before thought, a place between dream and memory, he recalls a mossy valley, three boys falling into greenness, into woods and dappled sunshine.

It was somewhere between Freshwater Bay and Gallows Cove. He, Gup and Cyril were walking through woods and thick brush when the goat path they'd been following disappeared. Suddenly they were standing on the edge of a steep-sided ravine.

Below was a valley no wider than a street, a green fold filled with golden light. They had held back for a moment, for more than a moment, staring down through spindly birch, down into flickering greenness at a place that even to them seemed strange, set apart by time and silence.

Maybe that is where he should have gone. I could still find it, he thinks. If I had the strength to leave this hole I could find it.

The boys all saw the thing at the same time—deep in the hollow lay the green shadow of a truck. No square lines remained— the trunk's corners were all rounded, angles cushioned by layers of plushy moss—but it was a truck, no doubt about that, a large flatbed tipped on its side.

"Jesus!" Cy whispered. But no one moved, each of them, even Gup, momentarily held in thrall by beauty, by the moss-covered truck, its rusting axle sticking out like an arm reaching from a green sea.

Then Gup let out a whoop and all three of them took off, hurling themselves down the steep side of the gorge, falling into the tree-shaded dimness at the bottom, falling into flickering sunshine and the gurgle of water over stones—a sound coming from a small brook that separated them from the overgrown truck.

Moss covered everything; it climbed trees, draped branches, grew even into the brook. Green eddies of moss swirled around their feet as they splashed across to where the huge machine had been overtaken by nature.

They had seen enough gangster movies to know an abandoned truck miles from any road suggested violence. "There'll be a skeleton somewhere under all that green stuff," Cyril said. "The driver'll be sittin in there with a bullet between his eyes.

That's why this place feels so creepy—he's probably hauntin it, watchin us right now!"

"What crap you gets on with!" Gup was already kicking at the cab roof, his boots tearing apart moss as if it were a garment, exposing a rusty frame that he began to stomp on.

Excitement overcame fear and Kyle and Cyril joined in, jumping up and down on the truck carcass. Glass smashing on glass, metal against metal. Exhilarated by the power of destruction the boys hooted and yelled to one another as the rusting frame crumbled like molasses brittle, and screeching birds darkened the sky. Within seconds the forest floor resembled a battlefield, white tree roots lay like scattered bones beside sods of ripped-up green, glass glittered everywhere, iron rust bled into the little brook.

But in Kyle's dream-memory the quiet has returned. The truck frame has reassembled itself, the forest has gone on making moss, recovering rocks and fallen trees. The brook again sparkles between green banks and sunlight falls softly through tall trees. Everything has become as it was. What if that happens? Kyle ponders. What if things mend—go back together? What of bodies—his father's smashed body? Gup's body?

Could his friend's sea-scrubbed bones grow flesh, become once again Gup's wild, raging self? If so he would surely return to this place. The thought chills Kyle—but only for a moment. Gup is not here, he knows Gup is not down here in the cave. If he was I'd be dead too, he thinks, and I'm not, not yet.

Since Art Norman has come to light the furnace it must be Sunday. And since he's not heard the furnace lighting sounds since he hid, this must be his first Sunday here. Can such a thing be possible? It seems so long ago—weeks, months, years even, might have passed since he shut out the sun and crawled into the tunnel. But if it had been months or years he would be dead, long dead.

How much time does it take to die when you have drinking water? He doesn't know—it's one of a million things he doesn't know. The things he doesn't know have begun to sadden Kyle. Thinking, remembering, has made him realize how much of the world he's missed, never paid attention to—the various colours of grass and sea and sky; the stories Art Norman used to tell about old times, shipwrecks and Indians, and how St. Mary's came to be built; those long poems his mother used to read out loud; that poem about arrows that the old minister read; the rocks all around, the names of which he will now never know.

When the slits of light indicate it is well past noon he feels safe enough to leave the cavern. Slowly, moving like an old man, he creeps down the passageway, fumbles for the opening and climbs up and out into the furnace room. The room seems huge, the space unnatural, even frightening. He sees at once there is no food. He can smell bread and cheese and tea, but nothing is left, not a crumb. He stands for a time staring at the dirty walls, the looming coal-pounds, the dark corners of the large, empty room, before moving to ease himself down on the little stool in front of the furnace.

Art Norman will not come back to St. Mary's today, will not return until next Sunday. The verger has given up his careful polishing of dark wood, his chastising of boys and birds. Already he is in his taxi, carting old people to Sunday tea and delivering well-heeled businessmen to their weekly card game at the Newfoundland Hotel. Or he may be driving servicemen and their girls back and forth between the USO and the K of C, to ice rinks and the roller rink, taking them to restaurants, to the back doors of pubs, to seedy boarding houses, on innocent country drives or to supper at the bungalow in Bowring Park. It is pleasant to sit beside the warm furnace and imagine all the amusements on offer in St. John's of a Sunday night.

It was Sunday night when he and Gup ran into Art Norman, the Sunday of their last long leave. The *Maunsell* had finally landed in dry dock—not through Gup's efforts but because one of the officers had done a rotten job of docking in the crowded harbour. A fast, badly calculated turn had slammed them into the bow of a Canadian frigate, sliced the *Maunsell* from stem to gudgeon. Every sailor on deck had doubled over with laughter, and joyous shouts of "Refit! Refit!" echoed off the Southside Hills. The crew got six days shore leave out of it—God alone knows what the officer got.

Kyle and Gup spent most of their last day ashore in Dobys' out by Mundy Pond. The Dobys ran a combined whorehouse and bootlegging business. It was a good place, women and booze and Mrs. Doby serving up corned beef and cabbage for a dollar extra. Around midnight they had staggered out of the place and flopped into the back seat of a waiting taxi.

Muttering, "Down to Water Street," Gup put his head back and closed his eyes.

"Some sight you two are—pissed to the gills!" The driver scowling over his shoulder at them was Art Norman. "By rights I ought to take ye over to Buckmasters and dump ye out by the gate. Them Canadian MPs got it in for Newfoundlanders— they'll sober ye buckos up fast enough."

"Fuck Canadians." Gup's laugh turned into a retching gulp.

"Hold onto yer guts! Here—keep this up under your face." Mr. Norman pushed a copy of yesterday's *Morning News* at Gup. "If ya throws up over my car, I'll have ya up on charges— swear to God I will!"

Instead of taking them downtown or to Buckmasters, he'd driven them to his flat down off Tank Lane and set about trying to sober them up.

"S'pose you heard about Cyril?" Art Norman asked after he'd made them drink some godawful mixture of tea, molasses and liniment. Kyle and Gup ignored his question. They had not spoken Cyril's name for months, not since they left him unconscious in the house on Boggan Street.

The morning after the beating, the thought that Cy could be dead had suddenly occurred to Kyle, frightened him. Without a word to Gup he went back to the house. The place looked worse in daylight, torn wallpaper stained with soot and greasy fingerprints, splintered stair railings, a smashed rum bottle, and the stinking remains of their fish and chips littered the kitchen. But the place was empty—a little blood spattered on the worn canvas, that was all.

As much as he'd wanted to be away from the awful house, Kyle had to sit for a time with his head on his knees, weak with relief that they hadn't killed Cyril.

Not long after that, he and Gup had shipped out, found themselves aboard the *Maunsell* somewhere east of Cape Spear, the nearest land a thousand fathoms below the hull, their lives so changed that the past might never have been. Had they forgotten Cyril so completely that even seeing his father, even sitting in his house, had not brought him to mind?

Mr. Norman was used to their silences. He began to tell them about some camp in Scotland where Cyril had been sent: ". . . but he pure hated bein stuck in the woods with some limey tellin him how to chop down trees. Can't say I blames him—a stunned thing to go overseas for. That's all over now—he got himself transferred to the Royal Navy same as ye."

It came to Kyle that something about Art Norman had changed; he seemed rougher, a different sort of man from the bird-chasing verger of St. Mary's. He'd glanced over at Gup, pale and red-eyed, half lying on the sagging daybed. Gup had drunk a lot—for most of the day he'd been in one of the Dobys' back-rooms with two girls and a supply of rum—he didn't seem to be following the story about Cyril.

"Twelve other Newfoundlanders got reassigned along with him," Mr. Norman was saying. He pulled an envelope down from behind the radio, held it up so they could see the Royal Navy crest in the corner. "According to this they're all aboard the HMS *Hood* right this minute."

There was another bit of silence. Kyle watched Cyril's father tuck the letter back behind the radio. Mr. Norman went and sat in a rocker that was wedged between the stove and the daybed.

"So! What ya make of us now, Skipper? All of us off fightin for King and country." Gup gave a snorting laugh. "Looks like we're not gonna hang or end up in the Mental after all."

Though bloodshot, Gup's eyes looked innocent, his face open and happy. Watching his friend, Kyle realized that Gup might have forgotten he'd pounded Cy's head into the wall, forgotten about calling him a fag and pushing the pin through his cheek.

Perhaps he's forgotten every single thing we ever did—all of it, Kyle thought. It would be nice to be like that—have no past, have it all gone each morning. Even then, he wished he could do the same.

Mr. Norman was sizing them up. Gup sprawled on the daybed, Kyle slumped on the kitchen chair with an enamel pail in his lap.

"We'll see. Ye're not dead yet, are ye?" he said. Art Norman was a little man, almost bald—short and scrawny but strong. He leaned forward and grabbed Gup by the wrist, forcing his arm back against the worn upholstery, holding it there as he stared into Gup's face. Gup kept on grinning his crazy grin, but Kyle could see that he wasn't able to pull his arm back.

He knows, Kyle thought. He knows what we did to Cyril and he'd like to murder us right now, right here. He could taste the poisonous drink in his mouth, wondered what Art Norman might have mixed into it. His stomach heaved but he swallowed and quietly eased the pail down on the floor. If the old bugger starts in on Gup, I'm takin off. The thought shocked him—of course he wouldn't abandon Gup. Still, he measured the distance between himself and the door.

"Not dead yet—and while there's life, there's hope," Art Norman said, and let go of Gup's arm. He leaned back in the rocker and stared into the young man's face, then he turned and did the same to Kyle's. "There's not much war's good for. Still, I hear tell it can turn the likes of ye two into half-decent men—sometimes does the opposite, of course, turns decent men into brutes."

He didn't say another word. After a few minutes he got up, pulled on his jacket and drove them back to their billet. As he dropped them off outside the gatehouse he repeated, "Ye're not dead yet—neither one of ye."

Sitting on Art Norman's stool, Kyle thinks about the man's words. Then they had sounded like a curse—they still do. He had remembered that later, when he saw BATTLE CRUISER HOOD written in big black letters on the mess wall at Buckmasters. The *Hood* was gone—with only 3 survivors out of the 1,419 men on board. The dead including 19 Newfoundlanders, 13 of whom had just transferred to the Royal Navy from the Newfoundland Overseas Forestry Unit.

Poor, harmless Cyril lost—no, drowned. Gup was drowned too—no, murdered. But maybe Gup drowned? Suppose he'd been alive, still alive when his body slid across the tilting deck, alive when he hit the oily black water, when he fell among those other bodies, the live ones still calling out, reaching. That would be worse, even worse—STOP!

Kyle had seen the *Hood* once, she was a beautiful ship. Her sinking was a terrible blow; people around town said she'd gone down in minutes. Talk at the Belmont was that over three million gross tons of merchant shipping had gone to the bottom in six months, that the Germans were putting out new submarines weekly, while our ships were being sunk far faster than they could be replaced. And everyone knew that both naval and merchant seamen and their ships were grossly overworked. Despite this, there was an unreasonable sense that things would get better in the new year. In early December when Kyle and Gup made their last trip, even Kyle had felt that faint tug of hope. As Henry at the Belmont said, *How could things get worse?*

By then Kyle had learned to steady himself, to feel more confident about his shipmates and about the ship. Officers and men on the *Maunsell* had melded into a unit; signalmen, gun crews and depth charge teams knew the drill, men in the wheel-house knew how the ship handled, men in the engine room had learned to stoke the furnace without making give-away smoke.

Even an ordinary seaman could see that the North Atlantic Convoy was larger and better organized than it had been eighteen months ago. Ships and equipment were being improved, the *Maunsell* now had proper lifeboats, and asdic apparatus had been installed in a little hut on deck. One captain would now be designated as senior officer of each escort group, another would be commander of the convoy; formations, evasive manoeuvres and signals had to be worked out before each convoy left port. The Admiralty had finally gotten note of the speeds of all merchant-men and were able to allocate each ship to a fast or slow convoy. The speed of slow convoys—ONS, Outward North Atlantic Slow—was seven and a half knots.

By that December the *Maunsell* had engaged with U-boats three times without making a sure hit. Three times Kyle had con-trolled his fear enough to respond as well as his crewmates when action station was called. The asdic could pick up the distinctive *ping* of a submarine. With luck the beam could keep contact with a U-boat until they were the necessary one hundred feet from target. But the North Atlantic was often stormy and depth charges could only be fired from the stern—fast manoeuvring was needed to get into position to fire before the submarine dived or altered course. More manoeuvring was necessary to get the firing ship outside of what was called the depth charge's "area of effectiveness" before it went off.

They were just two days out from St. John's when it hap-pened, eastbound for Londonderry with twenty-two merchant ships and six Navy escort vessels. It was a clear cold night. Kyle was on deck, not on duty, just looking, taking comfort from the silence and from the many grey shapes moving in orderly for-mation across the moonlit ocean.

Four of the escort vessels were zigzagging ahead of the con-voy. Four columns of merchant ships followed, a pattern of 5, 6, 6 and 5—with the designated eight hundred yards between each ship and one thousand yards between one column and the next. The *Maunsell* and her sister escort the *Jed* were bringing up astern on the outer edge of the outside columns. In storms it was not possible to maintain such precision, but that night the sea was smooth—and dangerous.

Neither Kyle nor the men on watch saw the track of the torpedo. The *Maunsell* shuddered and they heard the thud of an explosion, followed by a vivid flash and a geyser of water that flooded the decks, knocked a depth charge out of its cradle and ripped one side out of the newly constructed asdic hut. Two men came near to being washed off deck and Kyle was swept against the wheelhouse. All three managed to hang on, right themselves and keep the depth charge from going overboard. The vessel seemed to pause, then continue on, water sloshing across her decks. The torpedo must have rippled along her side, Kyle thought. Probably dented our plates without doing any serious damage.

The *Maunsell* began picking up echoes indicating that the submarine had moved in between her and the column. They were about three thousand yards astern the nearest merchantmen. Action stations had already sounded, the torpedo crew had restored the loose charge to its place and signals were going out to the *Jed*. As Kyle made his way across wet decks and splintered wood he could feel the *Maunsell* altering course.

With their asdic trained on the U-boat's echoes, the captain brought them around between the sub and the merchant ships. The gun crew stood ready at the four-pounder in case the U-boat surfaced. The throwers were being loaded as the *Maunsell* came into position—then the torpedo men let go, dropping three charges, two set to explode at 100 feet, the others at 250 feet, in what was calculated to be the U-boat's path.

Five minutes after the depth charges exploded, the surface of the water was as calm as it had been before the attack. Every man on deck searched for some sign that they'd hit the submarine, but there was nothing—no bubbles or scum, no floating wreckage. Worse, they had lost asdic contact with the U-boat's echo. To drop more charges would put the *Jed*, now on their starboard side, in danger. After making a sweep on either side of the last bearing, the *Maunsell* began to manoeuvre back into formation.

They had just resumed station when their asdic picked up the U-boat's beep, and at the same instant the merchantman directly ahead of them was hit amidship.

The *Maunsell* repeated its original manoeuvre but in the opposite direction. They turned and increased speed at the same time, the ship shuddering as if about to come apart. From his action station beside the port lifeboat, Kyle could see a huge sharklike shadow below the surface of the water. The asdic held contact and they stalked the submarine in a wide sweep away from the convoy. Kyle had not seen Gup for hours, but recognized his mad yell when the *Maunsell* dropped a ten-charge pattern at the intersection point.

This time there was no doubt they had a hit. Frothing bubbles and a spreading circle of black oil came to the surface. Then the U-boat's bow came out of the water and the *Maunsell*'s gun crew let go with the forty-pounder. When the sub's conning tower blew, seven men pulled themselves out, jumped and began to swim away from the sinking U-boat.

There was noise then too, noise everywhere, the echo of explosions, the screech of throwers being reloaded, the creak of the hull, the barking of megaphone orders and a sharp ominous ringing in wires that supported the *Maunsell*'s funnel. Kyle remembers the wires, only inches above his head, remembers the ship wallowing as they took on water.

Trying to fight the onrush of fear and seasickness, he'd concentrated on his duty, had begun to review the steps needed to release the lifeboat for which he was responsible. When he saw Gup striding towards him, he felt immensely relieved.

To shoot off her depth charges the *Maunsell* had pulled broadside to the waves and now rocked like a washtub even in the calm sea. The ship crested on each wave; she rolled larboard and the moonlit sky vanished, swinging back into view as she righted herself.

"We got a fuckin great hole back aft," Gup shouted. He stood, legs apart, grinning down at the five Germans who were still afloat, floundering in the heaving sea.

Each time the *Maunsell* dipped there was darkness, and when she rose the moon reappeared, reflecting off the drowning men. They were visible for an instant on the crest of each swell, arms rising a few inches above the oil-heavy water—black angels with iridescent wings, large human eyes, white teeth circling human voices, screams of *"Ach Gotton!"* Human terror rising above all other sounds.

Farther along the deck a young officer was throwing a life-line towards the Germans. By then escort ships knew it was dangerous to hold position long enough to take prisoners. *The law of the sea's changed, lads—they started it and it's dog eat dog from here on,* a first mate had told them months before.

But Kyle was remembering a story about the German captain who, before blowing up some merchant ship, set the crew adrift in a lifeboat, gave them a compass, food and water. He tried to recall where he had heard that story, considered undoing the lines that would drop the lifeboat over the side. Instead he hauled a life preserver out of the lifeboat and heaved it as far as he could towards the drowning men.

In the next splash of moonlight Kyle saw that both his and the officer's lines had fallen short of the Germans. But they had been seen and men were flailing towards the white circles. Then one man lunged forward, wrapped his arms around a preserver.

Realizing it was the one he'd tossed, Kyle quickly tied the rope to the railing. He saw the man rise and fall in the oily soup, then blackness dropped again.

"What the fuck ya think you're doin?" The moon returned, shining on Gup's wild face, on the knife he'd raised, ready to slice down through the rope to which the drowning man clung.

Instinctively Kyle's hand reached forward. He yanked the knife from between Gup's fingers—blood spurting. Kyle's arm rose, came down. The knife slipped smoothly into Gup's neck, just above his sweater. For one awful instant their eyes met. Then Gup's body hit the deck, slithered like some huge fish below the rail and into the moon-drenched, oil-drenched sea. The *Maunsell* lurched into darkness, water rushing over the stern, knocking Kyle backward into the well-deck, into oblivion, into safety.

Kyle topples off the three-legged stool onto the furnace room floor and curls up as if he were a child. He lies bawling, his face pressed into the dirt and grit, stays there for a very long time. Eventually he stops crying, stops whimpering. When he begins to feel heat, to realize where he is, he has to fight the urge to rush out of the church, to run into the street yelling his guilt.

"I must not—must not," he repeats over and over. If they know what he's done they will arrest him and put him on trial. They will either hang him over that black pit beside the court-house or send him away to the Mental. He pushes himself up onto his knees, then to his feet. He will not hang and he will not rot in the Mental—he will die just as he's planned, in the soft darkness of the cave. Holding that thought, he hauls himself towards the hidden opening. Pushing aside the stakes, he eases his stiff body back down into the tunnel. He moves forward slowly, stumbling against clay and rock and tree trunks until he reaches the cavern.

He goes directly to the trickle of water, drops to his knees and, leaning against the wall, puts his lips to the brackish water, licking it from the rock, filling his parched mouth. When his thirst is quenched he pushes himself up and begins to pace; shuffling like an old man he circles around and around.

Darkness flows in over dimness and still he paces, walking in a well of darkness—darkness and the low persistent murmuring that envelopes him like an ocean.

BOOK TWO

THE SAVAGE

VIII

Dogmen do not tell stories as we do. Even Cormack, that foolish man-child I learned to trust, would became angry when I did not tell stories his way. He would tap my head with his marking stick, shout, "Do not repeat! Tell things in order! Tell things straight!"

Dogmen believe in order and in the power of straight. I who trod their straight paths and lived inside their straight walls for six weary winters know this. Cleaning their stinking chamber pots, scrubbing their floors, tending their children, I learned more of Dogmen than Dogmen ever learned of me. Dogmen breed and bleed, eat and shit, they are born, love, feel joy, they feel pain and die just as people do.

Yet they are not people. They do not know earth as we do, do not see that earth is owned by others—by animals and animal spirits, by the spirits of all things that live and have lived in this sweet world. Dogmen know nothing of good Ash-wa-meet, of Old Caribou and Crow and Firewoman, of evil Aich-mud-yim and Nakhani. Having no shadowdancers, Dogmen have not been told of all the good and wicked spirits who guide and beguile us, who give us food, who lead us into green valleys, who trick us, twist our lives, pull us down dark and tangled paths.

Dogmen think to make order from life as arrowheads are hacked from flint, but lives have no order, follow no lines. Again and again we circle back, return, repeat, mix parts from one life into another life, one time into another. Even now, even in this dismal place, I live in more than one time, more than one life. Our stories cross over and break away, drift into a future we cannot see, will never know.

Do not think I trade my story for yours, Dogman! I speak to hold memory, to hear words, to make time pass. Since you are listening I will try to speak straight, the way I would to a child, the way Hebbosheth spoke to me—although I am not a shadow-dancer, not the storyteller she was.

My life did not begin in Perfect Time, not even in Old Time, but in the time my people called Evil. Much of Baetha had already been taken from us; all our great salmon rivers, our deepest bays, many of the wide beaches where seals come in spring. The distant eastern coastline, sacred cliffs where as a child Hebbosheth watched the sun rise from the sea—all this belonged to Dogmen long before I came into the world.

A child knows nothing of such things. My first memory is of safety, of being held against my mother's body, smelling her skin, each of us surrounded by the other and by the warmth of fur. I existed inside circles of safety. At the centre of all circles was our fire, banked down each night, a small bright glow under blackened logs. Around the fire my family slept: Nodurra, my soft, milk-filled mother; Washomish, my father, who was tall and wise; my two older brothers Ianamish and Longnon—us five together with my father's grandmother and my mother's sister and her family. All of us enclosed inside the circle of pine posts and caribou hides that was our mamateek.

I remember lying curled against my mother's body, half asleep, listening to rain, imagining rain falling on our circle of mamateeks, rain falling on the river, on trees that enclosed the river—a forest of trees stretching around and beyond us, all the great land of Baetha, and me warm and dry at its safe centre.

I had lived no more than three winters when I was taken from that safe place and told I would have to sleep beside Hebbosheth. "The Old One will care for you when the new baby comes," my mother said.

The words made no sense. Although she had always lived in our mamateek and was my father's grandmother, for me Hebbosheth was no more than a voiceless shadow at the other side of our fire. I screamed that I would not go, shouted and clapped my hands over my ears—even then I refused to hear what did not please me.

My mother would not take back her words. The baby was born, and I, who had slept from birth inside her tunic with my mouth around her breast, was bedded down beside the milkless Old One.

In our mamateeks we sleep like sunrays with our feet near the fire, our heads not far from the sloping walls. Our sleeping hollows are comfortable, padded with dry moss and springy evergreen boughs covered with furs. But the Old One's sleeping place was far from my parents,' on the side of the circle where my Auntie Santu slept with her husband and children. The Old One's hollow felt strange; her boughs were not properly arranged, her bearskin coverings did not fall snugly around me.

That first night I lay still until everything was quiet, then I crawled out and crept around the bodies of my sleeping relatives to my parents. Determined, and angry at the baby brother who had taken my place, I wormed under the coverings and tried to burrow my way to my mother's breast.

Father peeled me away. He carried me, kicking and yelling, back around the fire and silently passed me to the Old One. She took me as if I were some small wild animal, wrapped her arms around me, pinned my flailing arms to my sides. I cried all through the night, but no one came.

"Do you remember the child who scratched your face, hated you, who wept for her mother? I will call her up for you, Grandmother—and for this Dogman if he cares to listen . . ."

On the second night I told the old woman that I hated her: "You are bony and you smell bad!" I screamed these and other unkind words at her. But she only grunted and held me tight with my back pulled against her stomach so that I could neither scratch nor bite. I shut my eyes and howled like a wolf until my father came.

He took me outside. Cradled in his arms I whirled through air—night and stars spinning above me, night cold on my skin, in my hair, night pulling me into sky, like Firewoman when she left earth. Then Father stood still, everything stopped and all I could hear was our breathing.

He carried me back into our mamateek. Without speaking a word he passed me again to the old woman.

That was my first parting.

Although she was without a husband herself, when her son and his wife died Hebbosheth raised her two grandsons—Washomish, my father, and his brother, Adibish, who is the father of my cousin Demasduit. I have heard my mother say of Hebbosheth that she was old as trees and stubborn as rocks—my mother was right. Of all the people in our meotick, Hebbosheth was the oldest, the healer, the one who had once been a shadow-dancer, the one who still sat within our Circle of Elders. She was therefore to be honoured. I knew little of such things then, but even I knew I should not have spoken to an old person with such disrespect.

I stopped crying but continued to make small gulping sounds, refilling my body with air my screams had pushed out. When she felt it was safe to do so Hebbosheth released her grip on my arms and began patting my head with one of her bony hands.

"Sleep," she told me, "close your eyes and lie still, lie still and I will hum you to sleep." But her humming was dreary, and because she rubbed bear grease into her swollen fingers her hands smelled. It took a long, long time for me to sleep.

I cried softly on the third night and again on the fourth. That was the night she stopped humming and began to story-talk. As she talked she patted my head, patting out a kind of rhythm to her words, a story of how our people came to the Great Island. I had never before listened to the Old One's voice. It was low, husky from all the fires she had sat beside, all the words she had spoken, the many pipes she had smoked in her long lifetime.

I will tell it to you, Dogman, the first story I remember. Do you want to hear it, want to know how my people came to this great land we call Baetha?

Former People lived in Perfect Time, in a world without pain and without danger. Because Great Ash-wa-meet supplied all their needs there was no hunger and no winter.

Then, that evil spirit Aich-mud-yim sprinkled greed on their heads and the people turned to quarrelling. Strife spread like fire in dead trees. In the end only a few remained peaceful and of one mind. Perfect Time was over forever.

Those few peaceful people left the quarrelling ones. They sailed towards the sunrise in a canoe they had made from a hollow tree. This canoe was big as a whale. Day and night they paddled, moving through a hundred moon cycles, through times and seasons. They passed that line where sky comes down to earth and touches it, passed through mist, through sun and rain, paddled until they came upon a green island that lies at the centre of time.

It was then, at the moment when these people came ashore, that Old Time began.

At first they thought they had returned to Perfect Time, that beautiful Spirit World beyond the Ghost Path. They had not died, had not, as far as they knew, travelled along the Ghost Path, but because they were innocent and happy and because it was summertime, the People thought this.

Then winter came. The ground froze, ice glittered in the air, snow covered all the plants. Even the sea froze. These few Former People had never known cold, never seen snow, never killed any living creature. They had no coverings, no fur clothing, no tents or sleds or snowshoes. When the summer food they had gathered was gone, they looked out over the white, empty land and saw that people could not live here. Then they looked at the frozen sea and knew that they could not leave. Weeping, they crawled under their overturned canoe and prepared to die.

Under the canoe the People became very cold, so cold that the breath inside their bodies turned to ice. One by one Former People began to die. They all would have died, but at that moment Old Woman saw steam seeping in under the canoe—warm steam, smelling of berries and woods and the green moss that grows in the shadow of old trees. This scented steam filled the overturned canoe with vapour, making it like the huts our people build to bathe in and for those who have breathing sickness to sleep in. Soon all the people under the canoe were feeling better. Even the dead ones, taking the sweet air into their bodies, came alive.

Old Woman, she who was the first shadowdancer and the long-ago ancestor of Hebbosheth, told the people under the canoe that Ash-wa-meet the Great Spirit must be outside. Who else, she asked, could save people with his breath?

For a long time they sat quietly in the warm dark, listening to Great Spirit circle, brushing softly against the side of the huge canoe, and except for their hunger they would have been happy.

Then, "Come out!" said a voice—a deep, commanding voice that frightened them.

All together, each one whispering a prayer to his spirit guide, they pushed back the canoe. And there, towering over them, stood Old Caribou, the largest animal anyone had ever seen. Not one of those Former People moved, not even Old Woman, not even the smallest child moved. Like newly hatched birds they sat and listened while Old Caribou told them everything they must know to live in this cold place.

The forest only seemed empty in winter because they had not learned to see, he told them. Bear and caribou, fox, martin, lynx, wolf and rabbit turn white or hide themselves when snow comes. In ponds and rivers salmon, trout, beaver and muskrat build homes and bury themselves in mud. Around the coast, below its frozen surface, the sea is full of life. Soon whale families would chase fish by the thousands into the bays of Baetha. Every spring great waves of caplin would roll ashore, followed by cod and herring, lobster, shrimp, crab and uncounted other sea creatures. Seals too would come up onto the sea ice in spring and fat white bears, following the sun, would float ashore on ice pans. In summer the woods and barrens would be full of birds, in autumn geese and ducks would fly overhead in flocks so vast they would blot out the sun.

Old Caribou explained all this to the poor naked people; how they must watch animals, learn their habits, become cunning, learn to track and kill in order to clothe themselves in skin and fur, learn to eat the flesh of birds and animals—even his own relatives, the caribou, they must eat.

Hearing this the People were sickened. How could they eat flesh? Feed on creatures who themselves have spirit helpers, creatures who beyond memory had been guardians of the People?

But Old Caribou stood there with his breath smelling of summer and patiently explained everything the People must know, telling them that animals and birds, and indeed trees and plants must only be killed out of necessity. Living things must be taken with ceremony and with great care, a few at a time, many others being left to live and reproduce. Only in this way would there always be food and shelter for the People.

After a time, because he was so big and his voice so deep, and because they were very hungry, our people realized that everything the huge animal said was true, that his commands must be followed if we were to live through winter in this land.

"This is Old Caribou's greatest gift," Hebbosheth whispered, "and like all gifts it holds pain as well as pleasure."

His great gift and our great peril is that people must live on death, on the dead flesh of our fellow creatures. All the animals we kill in order to eat and to keep warm, all have spirit helpers just as we have. These spirits do not perish with the body, therefore they must be appeased. The bodies of animals must be used with the same dignity we give the bodies of people. Creatures who die to feed and clothe us must be thanked for giving us life, their blood and bones treated with ceremony, nothing wasted.

That is the first story Hebbosheth told to me. It is a story shadowdancers have passed down through countless generations of the People.

Only Dogmen do not know such things. Dogmen have no respect, they tear the earth apart. They hack off heads! Discard bones!

"Be still and listen," Hebbosheth would say when she grew tired of whispering into my ear.

At first all I could hear was the coughing and turnings of my older brothers, and my mother suckling the new baby—a sound that filled me with sadness. To keep me still the Old One would show me how to fold back the fur coverings, push aside the evergreen boughs and press my ear to the earth.

She listened too, speaking into my dreams the secret names of birds and animals—mink and weasel, beaver and otter, ptarmigan and owl, crow and hawk and eagle—identifying the sounds of night hunters—the low pad of wolf, lynx and fox who grow fur on their feet in winter, the dawn *click* of caribou hoof on ice, the muffled *thump* of hoof on packed earth, the hollow *crunch* of hoof on snow, the brush of antler against tree trunks, the sudden rush of some large animal emptying its bladder.

"When you have learned to hear the sounds of present time you will begin to hear the sounds of past time, words that have been absorbed into the earth," she told me.

Shanawdithit, the Old One said, was the word for listener: "If you were truly named, the bones of your skull will hear the words of Former People. They call to us from the hollow of past time, from future time—even from the Perfect Time that waits for us beyond the Ghost Path."

I was a small child. In the long nights of that winter the Old One took me over, poured her thoughts into my skull, began to remake me to be her. "You are the daughter of many shadow-dancers, the descendant of Miaoth, the great traveller. You will live to see things I cannot see, hear stories I cannot tell, stories no living Person can tell."

Even after I grew used to her, came to trust her, to need her stories before I could sleep, I still found it hard to believe that the voice in my ear at night belonged to the sullen old woman who spent her days cleaning hides and sewing. Some mornings after everyone had left our mamateek I would return and search each sleeping place looking for the night-woman.

Back outside I would see that she was in her usual place, squatting beside frames on which animal hides were stretched. I would go then and sit close to her, sniffing at her tunic, watching the movement of her hands, wondering if these could be the same hands that patted my head at night. She smelled like the Old One and I could see this person's fingers were stiff and lumpy like those of the Old One. After many moons passed I came to accept that the talkative night-woman and the silent day-woman both lived in the same body. Yet I always thought of them as two beings—my Old One at night and Hebbosheth by day.

Despite her stiff joints Hebbosheth was better than any other woman at preparing caribou hide. She could separate fat from skin gracefully, one hand making wide sweeps with her scraping knife while the other caught the thick yellow curls of fat in a birch pan. Have you seen a hide cleaned, Dogman? A lovely thing to watch. After cleaning it is rubbed all over with a mixture of grease and animal brains, the skin kneaded until it slides through your hands like water.

When the hide was ready she would cut and sew it into leggings and shirts, tunics, mitts and the warm, winter footwear she always made from the knee skins of caribou to save making a heel.

When Hebbosheth was done sewing she began decorating the garments—the part I liked most to watch. With a small burnt stick she would draw shells, or leaves and flowers on the shirt or tunic. To finish her pictures she made bright colours from things she found, from ground-up shells, jellyfish and small sea creatures, from the boiled-down juice of berries, roots and crushed flowers and from red ochre, even from her own blood. In her cupped hand she would mix the colour with oil and then fill in the outline she had drawn. In this way she made the flowers glow as if alive. If she was not tired or cranky she finished by biting a neat pattern around the edge of clothing she made.

Hebbosheth did not talk while she worked—no stories, no wise sayings, no explanations of what she was doing. Every little while she would notice me and growl, "Be off!"

I never budged. Often the cripple boy, Godith, would sit with me. We would lean forward as close as we dared to the Old One, watch her hands put a butterfly touch of colour on the soft hide, stare up into her face as she pulled the edge of a tunic or shirt between her lips, amazed that ugly knotted fingers and four yellow teeth could make a perfectly scalloped border.

"Magic!" Godith whispered, but I knew it was not. In secret I began practising on small scraps of hide the Old One set aside for patches.

In the safety of our winter camps, boys Godith's age did not stay nearby during the day. They had their own tracking and hunting games, they snowshoed, played stick games on the frozen river and took canoes out whenever the ice thawed. But Godith had one short leg and walked with a tilted wobble. He could not keep up with other boys—or perhaps he never tried.

Godith was a boy and three winters older than me, and we were not really friends, although he saved my life.

Even then we could no longer go to the easternmost parts of Baetha, beaches where time beyond memory my people had hunted seal. Yet there were hidden inlets and coves and one beach the Dogmen had not come to. The People trekked to that holy beach every spring to hunt seal and to fish. We were safer in our winter camps, yet I always loved those places where the sky and sea meet. The white beach seemed large to me, but Hebbosheth said it was enclosed and small compared to the vast open coasts of her childhood.

During the trek eastward that spring I began to notice the lame boy, Godith, wandering off-trail to stare at ordinary things—moss attached to trees, patterns in rocks, the bleached bones of some bird or animal. Because I too was curious, though more about people than about nature, I began watching him.

About halfway through our journey we came to the head-waters of Great Spruce Lake, where we always made camp for a day or two. We would swim, and clean ourselves and our belongings. By then our winter food would be almost gone, so our men fished upriver for trout and salmon while women gathered the herbs and pale spring ferns that grew so abundantly in that place. In a nearby ochre pit old people refilled the little bags they always carry with them for ceremonies.

On our second morning beside the lake I saw Godith walk into the woods. I, who was always careful to carry food, snatched one roasted caplin from my mother's store, folded it into my sleeve and tracked off behind him. It was not hard to do. The other boys were right—Godith did not move swiftly and silently as they did. We walked northward all morning, following a stream that branches off Great Spruce Lake. Each time he stopped, I stopped, watched him press his ear to a fallen tree, tap a rotting trunk with his fingertips, kneel and sniff at something growing on a rock. A dozen times I saw him crouch to study a flower or leaf, or just the forest floor—looking at nothing. Once he trailed his hand through a stream, lifted out a brown trout, held it up nose to nose as if he were telling it something—then he quickly released it back into the water. Nothing he did had any purpose.

It was early spring but when the sun reached sky's centre it was already warm in the woods. Watching Godith was not as interesting as I'd expected, so I sat on a rock beside the stream and listened as he lumbered away. I would eat my caplin, drink, and then follow the stream back to our camping place by the river.

"I thank you for giving your life to feed me," I told the fish. I was very hungry but I nibbled slowly, making the caplin last. Even now I am warmed by the remembered happiness of that day. Sitting there listening to the sound of water gurgling over rocks, imagining the long warm summer we were walking towards, looking forward to playing on the beach with my friends, to the storytelling, to the wonderful food we would take from the sea, I was a happy child.

I thought then that seasons occupied space, not time, thought winter did not *come* but *was*—that it lived at our great land's centre all year round. In fall, when we travelled inland away from the summer beaches, I could see that we trekked from red marshland, to yellow birch, to evergreen forest, that we paddled into colder and colder lakes until we came to winter. It seemed the same winter we had left moons before. In Baetha's deep heart winter always waited, just as summer was now waiting on our seal beach.

The roasted caplin tasted good. I wondered if its brothers and sisters were already swimming towards our beach. I was just a baby last summer, but this season I would be able to play games in the sand and catch these little fish in baskets as I'd seen older children do.

A shadow passed between me and the sun and I stared up into the face of a large brown bear—a mother bear, I thought, though I did not look to see if there were cubs nearby. I dared not look away from her small, squinting eyes—nearsighted eyes, according to my Old One, who had met many bears in her lifetime and had great respect for them.

I was afraid but thought it best to speak. "Good day to you, Keathut, you look well after your winter sleep." I was hoping to flatter her, but she shook her head and made a swiping movement with her forepaw to show she wanted my fish.

I tossed her the last bit of caplin—but it missed, arced past her shoulder and into the bushes. The bear did not go in search of it; she stood over me and began moving her body, swaying very slowly from side to side like a huge brown tree when the wind blows.

I did not stir. I could think of nothing else to do, and we stayed like that for some time.

Suddenly, beside the bear's head, a stick appeared—a long thin tree branch with my scrap of roasted fish stuck to its point. The stick prodded the bear's ear, moved to her cheek, then pulled away. The animal sniffed, turned her snout towards the food, slowly turned her body. She began moving towards the fish, kept on moving as the stick moved, away from me, until both it and the bear had blended into the shadows of the woods.

I stayed on the rock, not budging until I heard crashing in the underbrush. Thinking the bear had returned I jumped up and, because my feet had fallen asleep, toppled backward into the stream. Godith appeared, quickly pulled me out of the water and hurried me back to our camping place.

Neither of us said a word to anyone about the bear, but for the rest of that trek, and sometimes through the summer, we talked—rather, he talked and I listened. This boy, whose voice was never heard around our tents, would talk endlessly if I just sat beside him listening.

It was Godith who taught me the stars. At dusk we would find a place in the sandy dunes well beyond the campfire. Hidden there we would sit and watch sunset through the grass, see the sky ripple into blues and pinks, glowing like the inside of a mussel shell. Then the blue deepened and Godith would name each star as it appeared. When the sky was filled with stars we would lie on our backs looking up, watching for stars that shot through the sky like arrows. Godith would point out star creatures and tell me stories about wolves and bears, seagulls and whales, and even people who had been changed into stars. He told me their secret names: Adanishit, the evening star, and Shewthake, the morning star, Adibish, the lynx star our shadowdancer was named for, and Osepa, the seagull star whose wings you could see shimmering out if you half closed your eyes. There are others but they have seeped from memory.

I never told Demasduit or Kasathi about Godith's saving me from the bear or about the times we were together—it was a separate thing only he and I knew. Once I did ask the Old One if Godith was a listener like me.

"Godith is just a nosy little boy," she said. "Every meotick has at least one. They often die young."

It was then, I think, that the Old One told me about our ancestor Miaoth who sailed all around the Great Island, who tied his canoe to a blue iceberg and was pulled through white air and white sea into the land of Seal People. Miaoth learned many things from these northern people who are our cousins. With their help he returned safely and became a great shadowdancer and a shaman within the Circle of Elders.

As always, Hebbosheth had been patting her singsong words out on my head. When she got to the end of her story her hand paused. "Perhaps your friend Godith will be one of the curious ones who live. Perhaps, like Miaoth the great traveller, he will become wise and find out useful things."

Children are strangers on earth, they all listen. How else would we learn to live? I could see that listening was not a special talent as the Old One would have me believe—not something that needed teaching. I would never have said such a thing to her of course. I wanted to be her special child. Just as I'd once depended on my mother's milk, I now depended on the Old One's hand patting my skull, her voice whispering me to sleep each night.

In all our meotick the only girls near my age were Kasathi and Demasduit. We each lived in different mamateeks but we spent most of our daylight time together. Demasduit was also my cousin, the daughter of Adibish, our shadowdancer who was my father's older brother.

"Why do you think our fathers live in separate mamateeks?" Demasduit asked one day. We had just come back to our winter place, were already tired of playing with the old game pieces our parents let us use.

I thought my cousin was teasing me, a thing she often did just to pass the time. I muttered, "I don't know."

I hardly understood her question. *Mamateek* is our name for the birch and hide tents we sleep in. Many mamateeks make a *meotick*—people who travel and hunt together. Our meotick had eight mamateeks. One was for unmarried hunters who had grown too big and restless to live peacefully in the tents of their parents. My older brothers Ianamish and Longnon now lived with these young men. I was sad when my brothers left our family mamateek, but my father said they would return when they found wives. These young unmarried men hunted for themselves and for five childless old people who lived together in another mamateek. In the remaining six mamateeks, families like mine lived—parents and children, grandparents, aunts, uncles and cousins, all sleeping around one fire. The adults worked together by day, smoked, story-talked and played dice games at night.

"Do you not think it strange for brothers to live in different mamateeks?" Demasduit persisted.

When I considered, it did seem strange. All other brothers in our meotick, along with their wives and children, lived together in one mamateek.

"There are this many in Shanawdithit's mamateek, her Auntie Santu's family and the Old One—maybe that mamateek is very crowded." Kasathi, who wished things always to be pleasant, held up her hands to show the numbers.

"But my father is the oldest son," Demasduit said, "so why did he not stay in the family mamateek with the Old One? Shouldn't your father have been the one to leave if it was crowded?"

Kasathi and I shook our heads and waited. My cousin was born two winters before us; she was tall for her age and very beautiful, lips red as if they'd been stained by berries and eyes the colour of seaweed. She was smart too, smarter than we were, and I had noticed that she usually knew the answers to questions she asked. Kasathi almost always gave in to Demasduit, and sometimes I did also.

We three were huddled in a circle below the wide branches of a pine tree that grew just behind Demasduit's mamateek. It was our special winter place, snowless and so private we could have been in our own small tent. The air smelled of evergreen and in the long silence that followed Demasduit's question two small birds came to root in the cones and pine needles around our feet.

Demasduit was staring at me, still waiting.

I could not understand why this thing about our fathers was so important. "You are the only child of your parents—it would have been easier for them to move," I guessed.

"This happened when both our fathers were unmarried, long before I was born, before any of your brothers came into the world," she said.

"Even Ianamish?" I loved my eldest brother dearly. On long journeys he sometimes carried me on his back. I tried to imagine a world without Ianamish.

"You two are just babies—I will explain when you are older, when you know about men and women." Demasduit stared at me as if something was my fault, but when she spoke her voice was not angry. "Our fathers do not love one another as brothers should—but that does not matter to us, does it?" She smiled, and I forgot the cool, haughty look she'd turned on me a heartbeat ago.

I shook my head. It did not matter to me—my father sometimes answered my questions about animals but I had never even spoken to my uncle.

After that I thought often about Demasduit's question and about my Old One who had made her life over so that she could care for her grandsons when their parents died. I wondered if it mattered to Hebbosheth that my father and uncle did not love one another, but two winter moons passed before I found the courage to ask.

IX

My Old One had once been a canoe maker. "It was an unusual thing for a woman. I learned the skill from my last husband. When Odemen died, I had no children to care for and wanted no more husbands," she told me.

"In that time few Dogmen ventured in-country. People could travel greater distances, up the Widest River in the World and to the inland sea with its hidden islands.

"At melt-time it has always been the custom to leave our winter camps and walk to the sea. There were many travel lines then, but all the People would meet, all our meoticks joining to hunt, fish, dance and story-talk by the sea. Young men and women would marry, as they do now; names and spirit guardians would be chosen for the newborn, and the dead would be celebrated and buried in the holy caves along that coast. But back in that time there was one group who did not go eastward to the seal coast when spring came."

She told me then how canoe makers from every meotick would meet at a special place and travel together into the heart of

Baetha. Hauling the worn and damaged canoes, they would paddle up to Eel Lake; passing all the small islands, they would go on and on to the end, would portage far in-country to the Widest River in the World, then paddle westward until they came to the inland sea and the island of tall birch.

I, who had never been farther in-country than our winter camp, wanted to know what the inland sea was like.

"Beautiful," the Old One said. "So wide that sometimes we could not see either shore. We were very few—five old men and Hebbosheth. I was not so old then. We would travel from dawn to dark without speaking, whole days in silence, in dreamtime, watching the bright spray of water around a paddle before it fell back into the dark lake. That same interweaving of water and light over and over again.

"Sometimes birds would follow us, flying low across our canoes. One morning Osepa the white gull flew out of the mist and perched on my shoulder—Osepa was the spirit guardian of my poor dead sister Sanagi. I knew then that she had crossed the Ghost Path and was safe with our ancestors."

My Old One's voice became a chant as it always did when she spoke of past times. "Late on the fourth day we would come to a little cove on the island of birch trees—trees used for generations of canoe makers. Sometimes a great canoe maker would cut his mark into the trunk of one tree—a small canoe or arrow, a star or some bird or fish. We would never take bark from these special trees and so they grew tall, so tall that clouds hooked on the top branches hiding the nests of eagles and cormorants.

"We stayed on the island in the lake all summer, mending old canoes and making new ones. Taking bark from a tree must be carefully done; if too much is taken the tree will die. I learned to strip bark from a tree in one piece—so smart! Already shaped like one half of a boat and soft as hide after it was soaked in water a day or so. I could make a canoe in the days of one moon—lay down the long bottom line, then shape bark up around black spruce ribs. I'd lash my canoes with strong roots of spruce and strips of hide, caulk all the seams with a mixture of spruce gum, bear fat and animal hair, then set her in the river to plim. On every canoe I ever made I marked a new moon— there is still one canoe in our meotick with my mark on its bow.

"At night we made a fire on the beach. Birch trees white as spirits towered above us while we smoked and told stories. The others would forget I was a woman and make men's talk, reaming off half-remembered resentments against long-dead fathers, unruly sons and wives, untrustworthy shadowdancers."

From these summers with the canoe makers Hebbosheth learned many secret things about the People. She discovered that we had not always listened to good spirits and had sometimes followed bad leaders. Meotick had fought meotick over the best caribou runs and we had bickered about the proper way to conduct ceremonies. We had even fought the good Seal People, who were our kin and should have been our friends, and had finally driven them into the frozen half-world beyond Baetha.

"When we had spoken all our past griefs and settled on who was at fault, we rolled furs around our bodies and slept as only children sleep—knowing we were the only canoe makers on the earth."

Each canoe maker was from a different meotick and two were themselves shadowdancers. Once in a long time one might tell a new story, but more often it was an old story told a different way. "These are the stories I once told your Uncle Adibish, the stories I now tell you," she said.

Whenever my Old One repeated a story she would tell me who she had first heard it from. In this way I came to know the names of five old men who died long before I was born: Wiksona, Shansee, Awoodet, Tapathook and Shawwayet.

Years later I chanted these names for Cormack. I lied, told him they were the names of different tribes, warned him that Dogmen should never go in-country where each tribe had a hundred warriors, each warrior willing to fight to the death to save our hunting grounds. If only it had been so . . .

My Old One left those happy summers behind when she took over the care of her grandsons—Demasduit's father, Adibish, and Washomish, who became my father. The boys, born just four seasons apart, were still babies the winter day that their parents went off to check snares and did not come back.

After the time when Demasduit spoke of it, I began to watch my father and his brother, Adibish. The two men treated each other with grave courtesy but neither went into the other's mamateek or sat by the other's fire. They hunted in a group with other men but never worked together when raising mamateeks, repairing caribou fences, netting seabirds or night fishing— things kinsmen help one another with.

One night after she finished talking, I dared to whisper Demasduit's question into the ear of my Old One. "Why is it that my father and my Uncle Adibish do not love each other as brothers should?"

"Who says this?"

Her voice was so sharp that I did not answer, but she repeated the question until I whispered, "Demasduit."

"And if I tell you, will you tell Demasduit?"

It was late and the air in our mamateek was heavy with woodsmoke and sleep, with the sound of my father's snoring. Far off a wolf howled, and nearby I could hear the rustlings of rabbit or ptarmigan. Yet the Old One and I were completely alone.

"Do you say I must not tell?" My head was already heavy with secrets. I wondered how many it could hold.

"Nothing I tell you must ever be told outside!" She made her hissing sound. "Not before I have placed my feet on the Ghost Path."

Until that moment I had thought of the Old One herself as a spirit, kin to Old Caribou or the Great Shaman Annooee, whom she spoke of so often, like Firewoman, or Mossessdeesh, the boy runner. The dreadful knowledge that she would die caused me to miss the first words of her story.

" . . . to my oldest grandson, Adibish, I told all the stories the canoe makers had told me. He was far-sighted, serious. I talked to him as I do to you, knowing long before he did that he would someday become our shadowdancer.

"Your father, Washomish, was more carefree. People liked him—a child with a quick smile and a quick temper. My grandsons were very different but they played well together. I never heard them argue—until they saw the girl Doodebewshet.

"Her family was from a different meotick—we only met in summertime on the white beach. One summer she was a plain, breastless child running with a pack of little ones, the next year she was the most beautiful creature any of us had ever seen. Danger attends such beauty. The shadowdancer in her meotick said the girl had been sent from Perfect Time to show us how people had once looked.

"Many men among our people would have taken Doodebewshet as a wife, but her parents guarded her closely. It was only my foolish grandsons who did not hide their desire. They were both very young then, not hunters or warriors or runners, or anything else—just untested boys, neither of them ready to take a wife. Yet for three summers they followed her about, vying for her attention. People watched and some laughed, but I was saddened to see their brotherly friendship dying. Doodebewshet herself seemed well pleased to have my two young cubs at her bidding.

"When Doodebewshet, or even her father or brothers, were nearby, my grandsons would take unnecessary risks to attract attention. At first I hoped this rivalry would end when summer drew to a close. It did not. Even in winter, when the girl was in a distant camping place, Adibish and Washomish threw insults at each other, tormented each other into competition over small, often dangerous things—who would be first to taste some strange plant, venture out into a blizzard or walk to the middle of a river that had just caught over.

"Adibish was foolish enough to come asking me, his grandmother, to take my staff that holds the newborn moon, to hold it up to the sky and draw down a charm to make Doodebewshet want him for a husband. I was disappointed in both of my grandsons, but especially in Adibish, who had always seemed to me more steady than his brother. I was not only their nearest kin but also their shadowdancer. Though I knew they would not listen, I talked to each of them, told them where such foolhardiness would lead.

"In the winter I am speaking of, the herds came late but there were many, many. When runners brought news of the caribou coming, they told us they had never seen so many animals—a sea of grey spreading out across the frozen marshland. Hearing this, our hunters went into the steam house to cleanse themselves and talk with the spirits. All night they stayed there, smoking and performing rituals necessary to honour Old

Caribou, showing our respect for his people, explaining our need to use the bodies of his kinfolk as food, asking forgiveness for the killing they were about to do.

"Neither Adibish nor Washomish were yet hunters. They were stationed among the beaters waving tree branches about, trying to herd the lead caribou into our fenced pathways where the others would follow. Although young people and women are beaters it is still a job that requires skill. If done carelessly the lead animals will veer away, the herd will panic, break down wide swaths of fence and scatter before they get to the killing place where our hunters wait.

"It is Old Caribou who leads his family to our fences. Often he is hidden in the great movement of animals. In all my lifetime I have seen him only twice—larger than all the rest, moving like a great shaman, head up, his wives and children all around. Even a child who has seen just one hunt knows that these first caribou must go quietly into the fence and leave quietly; they must not be hurried or hurt in any way. Only if we permit Old Caribou and his close kin to live will they return year after year to our camps. This is the covenant made in past time between the People and Old Caribou.

"He may have been goaded on by Washomish, but it was Adibish who struck one of the lead animals. Not only struck it, the foolish boy prodded its hindquarters with an arrow. The animal swerved as if making for the distant edge of forest. As it came broadside to the beaters, Washomish lifted a spear he had no right to carry, and sent it straight into the side of the huge beast. The wounded animal roared, pawed the ground—then it staggered and fell, blood gushing from its side."

"Was it Old Caribou?" The thought that my father may have killed Old Caribou frightened me. So many of her stories were about the great animal that I considered him a relative, like one of the husbands she often spoke of but seldom named.

"That was what we all feared. I and other shadowdancers performed all the necessary ceremonies. We asked forgiveness of the animal, kept its head at the centre of our circle all through that hungry winter. In spring we took the head along with our own dead to the sacred cave that is beyond the holy beach. It was not until the herds returned the following fall that we knew my grandsons had not killed Old Caribou."

The Old One stopped talking then and would not go on, although I knew she was not sleeping. Two sunsets came and went before I could make myself stay awake until the old people put away their gaming pieces. I waited and waited. At last everyone slept and she continued the story of rivalry between my father and Demasduit's father.

"When the big animal went down, the herd panicked and a headlong rush of young bucks flattened our fencing. They ran in all directions, banged against one another and against the fear-stricken does who were shouldering their young away from the beaters and back from the wide entrance to our fences.

"The old stags stopped still for an instant—snorting air, their massive antlers pointing this way and that, searching for the enemy. Then they too turned and thundered back the way they had come, back into the safe hills, leaving only the vast empty marsh, torn turf and the piles of steaming shit.

"In the confusion an old man named Jalamish, who had once been a shadowdancer, was trampled. He recovered, but his legs were so crippled that he could not stand upright. Only two caribou were killed. We all went hungry that winter.

"Never again did my grandsons agree on anything. In time their quarrel became part of the large quarrel that goes back to my brothers, to my father, to my father's father and his brothers—back through generations to the Great Shaman Annooee."

That great quarrel was to take my life, take the lives of all my people. Then, it did not seem important enough to ask about.

I only wanted to hear the rest of the Old One's story, to find out what had happened to the beautiful young girl. Since my mother was Nodurra and Waunathoake was the name of Demasduit's mother, Doodebewshet could not have married either of Hebbosheth's grandsons. But I was learning never to question the Old One, so I lay still, trying to control my curiosity.

After a time she continued. "Adibish and Washomish were both called before the Circle of Elders. In my lifetime I had not heard of such a thing. Since I myself was of the Circle this was a matter of great shame to me. One cannot leave the Circle, but I could no longer be the shadowdancer of our meotick.

"After consideration the elders decided that the old man who had been crippled by the crazed animals could choose what punishment would be given out to my grandsons. Jalamish ordered Adibish, who had hardly spoken since the day of the hunt, to move into his mamateek and care for him for the rest of his days.

"Jalamish told your father, Washomish, to move out of my mamateek, to go into the tent of the young hunters and remain there, learning their skills all winter. When spring came Washomish was to leave our meotick and go far in-country. He was to live there alone until he received forgiveness from the caribou people—until he learned patience.

"My mamateek seemed empty without my grandsons. I would have wished to go back to the island inside the lake but the old canoe makers had all died—also the joint stiffness had gotten into my hands. I could no longer paddle all those hours, would not have the strength to fold the bark and sew it together with good spruce root the way I once did."

The Old One held her hands up and even in the dim firelight I could see how her fingers had thickened and were themselves like tree roots.

"It was a sorrow to me then, but now I am content enough with this narrow life. I have learned to work with the skins of animals." She snorted. "And now, when I should be given a quiet death, I am compelled to teach a small ungrateful child the stories of our people."

I had little sympathy for Hebbosheth or for my uncle and father. "I think Jalamish was right to make my uncle care for him—their punishment was not great for all the trouble they caused."

"You have a hard heart, Shanawdithit," she said, but I thought she sounded as if my hard heart pleased her. "Yet you are right, Jalamish's punishment was not unjust. I knew him to be a wise and kind man; in the end he passed his knowledge on to Adibish and made him a shadowdancer, which is what I had wished. And Washomish, when he returned from his season with animals, had become a good tracker and hunter—he has not yet learned patience but he is more in control of his anger."

Her approval gave me courage and I dared to ask, "But what became of Doodebewshet?"

"I told Jalamish that the girl had encouraged strife between my grandsons and he commanded them never to approach Doodebewshet again. Since she is not of our meotick I do not know her well but I do know she has had many troubles in her life, and that even now she is beautiful. Three summers after the story I am telling, she became the wife of Sabasut, the grandson of Osagana. By then your father had already married Nodurra.

Adibish did not return to my mamateek and he did not take a wife until he was almost old—but that is not unusual for shadow-dancers. I think Demasduit will be their only child."

Stories are powerful things; among my people those who tell worthy stories are honoured. It was therefore a hard thing for me, a vain and envious child, to keep my promise not to repeat this story to Demasduit.

My cousin was herself a good storyteller. She liked to tell Kasathi and me things she heard her father speak of inside their mamateek. I thought Demasduit should not have done this—Adibish was not only her father, he was our shadowdancer, his magical power our link to the Spirit World. I could not have explained it but I sensed that the things she told us took away some of his power. Yet we listened, Kasathi and I, we always listened to everything Demasduit said.

One of the best stories Demasduit told us was about how Crow tricked Firewoman into giving the People fire. Fire made light and heat in our mamateeks; it cooked food and made the steam that cures winter's breathing illness. Without fire we would have no shadows, without shadows there could be no shadow-dancers, and without shadowdancers we would have no stories. Without stories the People would be adrift in time.

When the long dark nights of midwinter dropped down on the forest we would all crowd into one mamateek. We would sit close together, watching the fire, watching the shadows, listening to stories from past times, learning how we must act towards one another and towards all living things.

Even if you were the first to come, Shadowdancer would already be there, hunched beside the fire with the skin of Keathut the bear over his shoulders, the horns of Old Caribou on his head. He would sit smoking his pipe, waiting until all the People had settled tight against one other, old ones huddled nearest the fire, small children curled into the laps of their parents.

If a hunter had been careless with ceremony, if he had inflicted needless pain upon animals, if a woman had wasted the skin, flesh or fat of animals, if a child had used trees or rivers, or the bones of some animal disrespectfully, these things were all known to the shadowdancer and would be woven into his stories.

Though innocent of such acts, I feared the crouching figure—more than feared him, the sight of him made cold stones rattle inside me. We never spoke of it but I thought the Old One shared my feeling. She and I always sat beyond the circle of heat, well back from the shadowdancer.

His body would be still, still, then his hands would begin to move, weaving shadows, making shapes that slithered in and out, around and above us on the skin walls of the mamateek. The shapes flickered, then danced as Shadowdancer began to speak. He told us about Perfect Time when only Ash-wa-meet and other good spirits lived, when the inhabitants of earth, sea and sky were all one people and talked daily to one another and to that Great Spirit who created all things.

As the story continued, people in the circle would begin to hum and the shadowdancer's body would slowly, slowly unfold until he was standing—half man, half beast, a spirit creature come inside our mamateek—moving around our fire, his huge shadow dancing behind us along the wall. No matter how far back I had pushed myself, Shadowdancer's bear-claws reached towards me, his great horns pointed at me. The hump of his back rose almost to the smoke hole, and I would shiver with fear. At such times Adibish was not my uncle or Demasduit's father, he was the link between my small world and the vast Spirit World that surrounded me and all my people.

Hearing the shadowdancer's stories from the time we are small children, they become part of our memory, part of our dreams, part of our spirit-vision, teaching us how to conduct ourselves in life, so that in death we can walk quickly across the Ghost Path and join our ancestors in Perfect Time.

One of the things we learned from stories is that the spirits of all men and all animals live in the skull—this has ever been so, from that first day when Great Spirit Ash-wa-meet breathed life into the mouth of Crow. The spirit of every living thing will stay in its skull long after the creature it inhabited has died. The spirit waits and grieves until the body it was part of has crossed the Ghost Path into Perfect Time.

For this reason heads of all the animals we kill must be treated with respect. This is especially true of caribou heads, which are to be washed and combed. Necklaces made from the carved finger-bones of bears must be strung around their necks. While shadowdancers chant songs, the heads of all the caribou we have killed are set up on poles around our camping place. If any in our meotick should die during the winter the bodies are placed on platforms as near as possible to the caribou heads.

All winter these caribou heads look down at us and at our dead; they accept our whispered thanks each time we pass. At night those bear-finger necklaces clatter and dance in the wind. "Bones talking," my Old One said, "reminding us that all life depends upon the death of other creatures." Another time she said the sound prevented the evil Aich-mud-yim from stealing the spirits of our dead.

Long before the shadowdancer finished, I would have put my head down on Hebbosheth's lap. Covering my head with her bearskin I would fall asleep in the soft, spirit-filled dark. I wonder now if I missed parts of my uncle's stories—things I was meant to know.

I was still very young and cannot remember Adibish our shadowdancer or Hebbosheth ever speaking of Dogmen—though they often told of malevolent spirits such as Aich-mud-yim, the sea monster, and Nakhani, the bloodthirsty wolf spirit. In our stories these evil beings fought continually with good spirits, but the good spirits were always stronger because Crow, who was very clever, was on our side.

Knowing myself protected by all the good spirits I slept, innocent enough to think my world the best world, to think the time I was born into the perfect time, to feel safe. How could I know my people were living in that tiny stillness within the storm's eye?

X

In our winter place it is nighttime I remember most—night and firelight and the stories of Hebbosheth and of our Shadowdancer Adibish. But there was daytime too, brief sunshine when Demasduit, Kasathi and I hid under trees to whisper and giggle as all children do.

When Demasduit's proud talk made me angry I would have to fold my hands between my knees and press my lips together. This kept me from matching her stories with the stories Hebbosheth told me. If my anger kept burning I would leave and find Godith. Listening to his quiet talk, about stars and clouds and why the sky moves even when there is no wind, always calmed my mind.

If Godith himself was hiding, as he often was, for he liked to be alone, I would find a quiet place where I could sit and make pictures. I made pictures without thinking, using coloured stones and burnt sticks, drawing on scraps of hide, scratching shapes into bits of antler and animal bone and burning patterns of leaves and flowers into the wood we used for fires. In summer I drew on rocks and shells, even on mud and wet sand.

Every night while the Old One talked, I traced with my finger into darkness, outlining the animals in her stories. I learned how to make pictures that looked like plants and animals and fish—even like flying birds, which is the hardest thing. I drew so well that Godith could tell one bird from another, male from female.

Sometimes I story-drew for smaller children. This annoyed Demasduit, who could not make pictures. As I got older I made patterns on my father's bone gaming pieces and around my mother's birchbark containers. I made three sets of bone and shell beads, each set inscribed with a different flower; forest lilies for Kasathi, roses for Demasduit and, for myself, purple iris, a flower I loved despite the stink. Whenever I found something to make marks with, I saved it in a small pouch that I wore on a cord around my neck.

I had been making pictures for a long time before the day when Hebbosheth noticed. We were walking towards the coast and because our food supply was almost gone we stopped beside a salmon river. The men had taken canoes upstream to where it was more likely they would catch jumping salmon; women and children were gathering spring ferns or standing knee-deep in the river holding spears in the hope a stray fish might swim by. I found a salmon-coloured marking stone, sat down and began to draw a salmon on a flat black rock that I lifted out of the river.

"It is not wise to make such lifelike shapes," Hebbosheth said when she saw what I was doing.

I laughed, partly from surprise at hearing the Old One's voice in the daytime. "Can drawing a salmon be more dangerous than eating its flesh?"

"More dangerous!" she muttered. "Much more dangerous."

"Why?" Always I wanted to know why.

"You are not a hunter, you have performed no hunting cere-monies—yet you have pulled the body of this fish into our time." She knelt beside me, tapping my drawing with one of her clawlike nails. "But all you have is a body. Its spirit is left behind in Perfect Time. Because you have done this, the fish spirit is unhappy and untrustworthy."

"Maybe I will learn to draw so well that the salmon's spirit will come and join its body."

"Never!" She looked around as if fearing someone might have heard, then hissed, "Never play games with the Spirit World, Shanawdithit—do not even speak of such things. Those who have power to draw creatures through time let loose rest-less and unhappy spirits. One who creates such creatures must quickly destroy them."

"Why?"

"Spirits come to take revenge on the one who snatched them from Perfect Time—to interrupt the life of those who inter-rupted their life in the Spirit World."

It was a warm day, well past melt-time, both of us kneeling in a sunny spot, but suddenly I felt chilled, as if the salmon appearing under my fingers had been frozen, the way my father sometimes froze fish into river ice.

"Feel the cold?" I said, and reached out and touched the Old One's cheek with my icy hand.

She pulled my hand away from her face. "The messenger of death comes to all. To some he comes twice—once to warn us and once to take us." She was holding my wrist, my open hand pressed against her thigh. Before I could know what she was about to do, she'd cut my palm with her little flint.

I gasped and then began to sob.

The Old One held my bleeding hand over the rock, letting my blood fall onto the salmon picture. When it was smeared with blood she held up the stone, lifted her head, and speaking quietly, as if to the sky or to the river, said, "I call on all restless and seeking spirits to accept this sacrifice from our foolish child. I, Hebbosheth, ask that you forgive her thoughtless act and not interrupt her young life." She threw the stone far out into the river.

Afterwards she pulled open her leather pouch, unfolded one of her little packets and put salve on the cut. "Water-lily root," she said, when I asked about the yellow paste.

For several heartbeats she held on to my open hand, touching my palm with her fingertips. "You have been warned. Take care what you call into being, Shanawdithit. Those who create are always punished." Then she sighed and gave me back my hand.

The Old One, who was like Crow for repeating things, never repeated that warning. When I asked (and I often did, for I had a scar on my palm to remind me) what was necessary to call a creature back from the Spirit World, she would say, "Hush!" or pretend not to hear.

Five moons later, Godith vanished.

I remembered the death warning then and wondered if the salmon spirit had mistaken him for me. It might be possible; we were the same size and each often alone in some hidden place.

It happened in late summer, the season of deep blue skies, of night frost that melts at sunrise, a time when the People turned their backs on the sea and moved inland to our winter camps. Already we were packing—making bundles of dry seal, of salmon, caplin and cod the women had smoked, layering eggs and mussels into moss-filled baskets, rolling flint tools inside sealskins.

Soon we would travel northward through marshland into birchland, taking our time, moving towards evergreen country. I was looking forward to the trek in-country, where biting insects were gone now and my belly would always be full. We would gather even more food as we went—circling around mountains, trekking through bog and marsh where the ground was red with partridgeberries, over the barrens where blueberries, mintberries and many of the herbs I helped the Old One gather grew. As we moved into birch country the light would change, filtering down through yellow leaves, making even our voices seem softer.

The season Godith was taken, the season I first heard of Dogmen, we stayed on the beach long after all other meoticks had left. Our runners and trackers searched over hills and marshland looking for the boy. They took canoes around the coast, into caves and inlets.

Each sunset I waited in the grassy fringe by the beach, in the place where Godith and I had watched stars. The tall grass around me became brittle, soon it would freeze. I listened to the shivering grass and wondered if it was the same grass each year—or did new grass grow every spring? Godith would have known, but he never came and I never found out.

Then, in one of our message trees, a tracker found the small whalebone amulet Godith had been given at his naming ceremony. Searching the ground around the tree they discovered bent bushes and the footprints of more than two Dogmen.

Mishatut said her son might yet escape and come back to the beach. She begged us to stay, but it was already cold and Adibish told us that we must get in-country before the rivers froze, must reach our winter camp before Old Caribou brought his family down from the hills. So we left. The mothers wrapped their arms around Mishatut and forced her to come with us.

That winter our shadowdancer added Godith's name to the names of others who died. We chanted a song for him around our fires—an old song, changed only a little for Godith. I wished they had put in something about stars but did not say so.

> Your feet are on the Ghost Path,
> do not stumble, do not stray,
> dark comes light as night comes morning,
> moon comes sun to guide your way.

When a small song is sung over and over it will take away fear and hurry a dead child along the Ghost Path towards Perfect Time.

After Godith was taken, our meotick filled with talk of Dogmen. Everywhere there were signs of their presence—footprints seen and shots heard. My brother Ianamish had his cache uncovered and his arrows taken. Our hunters told of ancient trees that had been cut down with iron axes. Dogmen's traps were set near beaver dams, and just a day's journey from our winter place runners found the bodies of slaughtered birds and animals that had not been treated respectfully. Inside our mamateek I continually heard such talk between my father and brothers. Outside, when Demasduit, Kasathi and I were together, we frightened one another with terrible things Dogmen had done or might do.

Yet, until that day when we overheard my father and Demasduit's father shoot words at each other, I thought Dogmen existed only in stories, that they were creatures like Aichmud-yim and evil Nakhani who lived beyond time, not beings who could come into my world.

Our fathers were behind Adibish's mamateek, talking so quietly that no one should have heard. But we three were in our secret place right beside them and Demasduit's father must have raised his voice a little. "There are many good Dogmen and a few evil. You only make things worse by repeating women's talk!"

The wide evergreen branches hid us, but when we peered out we could see the men clearly and hear them too.

"Dogmen have torn down all the caribou fences north of Ecshamut's winter place. This is not women's talk, this comes from the message tree beyond the marsh." Father held a rolled strip of bark out to his brother.

Instead of taking the message, Adibish reached forward and laid his hands on my father's shoulders. "Ecshamut's fences are never well made. It may have been wind or animals."

"You have ever been good at deceiving yourself!"

"It is you who deceive yourself, brother. Always you see evil, always you look at the world through the fog of anger."

"And you? You see all things through a fog of pride!" My father wrapped his fingers around Adibish's wrists and jerked his brother's hands away. "Every season these Dogmen become bolder. Now they take our children, tear open our storage places, steal our food, our skins and paddles—my son's arrows . . ."

Beside me, Demasduit pushed air out between her teeth, whispered, "Your father should not touch our shadowdancer in that way!"

Kasathi and I looked at each other; we were afraid, did not want to hear. But there was no escape without being seen. Like First People hiding under their canoe, we sat motionless, peering from green shadows out to the light, watching two men face each other with such contempt that even we recognized it.

"What would you have us do?" Demasduit's father did not sound like the giant who shadowdanced around our fire.

"We should track down any Dogman who harms us—we should have found the Dogmen who took Godith."

"And?"

"And killed them!"

"You know it is a deep evil to kill creatures who walk upright as we do."

"These creatures took one of our children. It is only just that we kill them."

"Use your mind, Washomish! If we kill two Dogmen, they will kill many more of us. From Old Time we know this—they have thrown fire at us, burnt our mamateeks, killed women and children."

"This is not the song you and your friend long chanted about Dogmen being like us, being People—People we could share Baetha with!"

"Many Dogmen are people like us. Only a few—the eggers and the furriers—do the killing. Sabasut and I have known this since we were young."

"Since you and Sabasut guided a Dogman in-country . . ."

Adibish took a step backward. "That Dogman was good, a trustworthy man—his People wanted to live in peace with us."

"Trustworthy!" My father spit the word. "For bringing a Dogman near our camps you and your great friend Sabasut both should have died—would have died if our grandmother had known of it. Instead you both crawled under Osagana's wing and became shadowdancers."

"Sabasut has said—,"

"Sabasut has said! Sabasut has said!" my father interrupted. "Sabasut speaks too often, has grown proud and sure of himself, would be our shaman if the Circle permitted it. Your friend wishes to rule over us as his mad grandfather did." Father sounded so angry I thought he would strike Adibish.

I recalled what my Old One had told me about this Sabasut. He was the young man she said had married the beautiful

woman, the girl named Doodebewshet, the girl these two arguing ones had both once loved. How then could Sabasut be a
friend of Adibish?

When I listened again, my uncle was speaking more calmly,
saying things had become more peaceful since their childhood.
"Perhaps we are learning how to live with Dogmen—there have
been many seasons now without any killing . . ."

I have noticed that anger is different in different people.
Demasduit's anger was haughty and sweet, measured—if you did
not know her you would not guess it was there until it bit you.
My anger is hot, wild, unthinking. My mother's anger smouldered,
banked down with chips of resentment. Such small things did not
anger Hebbosheth; she carried one large anger inside her like a hot
stone that she could never lay down. I think our father's anger was
more like mine—it sparked, burned bright and died quickly.
Ianamish, Longnon and I knew this, knew that when our father
was angry we had only to keep out of his sight for a time.

Father's anger against Adibish was different from his anger
against me and my brothers. Watching his face that day, I could
see it had not died, not in all the years since their first falling-
out. Words rushed out of his mouth as if something inside him
had tipped over. "Without killing! Without killing with their
muskets perhaps! They are starving us instead, taking over our
hunting grounds, blocking us off from the best seal beaches,
from the salmon rivers, from places where whale come in—
forcing us to abandon familiar travel lines."

"There are many travel lines in Baetha."

"Are you blind?" My father was still holding the message,
and now he flung the piece of bark on the ground. "Once I would
have gotten Ecshamut's marks between sunsets, now it takes four!
As we lose our old travel lines we lose marking places—ancient

trees and rocks under which our runners once left messages are already forgotten. How will our children's children know Dogmen are coming towards their camping places?"

"We have managed on what is left."

"What is left gets ever smaller! We are like the caribou. Once we owned the earth, now we are lured between fences to our death, betrayed by our own shaman and shadowdancers!"

"You listen too much to the Old One."

"And you have not listened enough! Have you and Sabasut deceived yourselves into thinking Dogmen are now content? Will they let us hunt in peace in our winter camps? Will our children's children be free to catch fish in the few coves where Dogmen have not built their stinking huts?"

Beside me, Kasathi had placed her hands over her ears and curled her face into her lap. Demasduit and I were crying silently, tears of fear and shock dripping off our chins. We had never heard such bitter talk, never dreamt brothers could be so disrespectful of each other.

When Adibish did not answer, my father turned and walked away. Our shadowdancer started to follow his brother but then he stopped, came back and went into his own mamateek.

Then there was silence—like the silence in a forest when two bull caribou stop fighting.

After a time Demasduit and I wiped our faces with the fringes of our tunics. Demasduit tapped Kasathi's shoulder until she took her hands from her ears and sat up. We did not look into one another's eyes. We were not only frightened by what we'd heard—we were ashamed.

"Our spirit guardians will protect us." It was Demasduit who said this, but her voice sounded less confident than usual and I was not comforted.

That was all. After a while we crawled out from under the tree and went quietly to our own mamateeks.

That night, after I'd whispered what we heard into my Old One's ear, she told me her grandsons were fighting an old argument. "Generations of our people have argued bitterly over the killing of Dogmen." She sighed. "And you will do the same, Shanawdithit, you and your children's children—if time should last that long."

Hebbosheth told me then of her own grandmother, she who had been able to remember a time before Dogmen. If I turn this story backward, if I weave down past Hebbosheth's life into the life of that grandmother, then I can tell of how your kind came to Baetha.

Generation after generation my people took life from the sea and the forest. We followed all the rituals and used every good thing Old Caribou told us of. Sometimes we saw Seal People on our beaches. They were our cousins, yet they did not look or smell like us, did not have our ceremonies, did not speak our words or hunt like us. Because of this we hated them. In time we drove the few that remained north into the white country where they belong. After that the People shared Baetha only with the animals and with our Spirit Guardians.

Shadowdancers had long warned us that the sons of Nakhani would not always be content in the unhappy place to which their blood-soaked ancestors had been banished. But we grew fat on our summer beaches, lived warmly in our winter mamateeks and began to forget the old story of an evil wolf spirit and his dog-children.

The dead ones came first. In that time when my Old One's grandmother was a young woman, Dogmen floated ashore on bits of wood. Sea-washed and white as slugs they were, with seaweed streaming from their hair, growing from the tips of their blue fingers, from holes where their eyes had been.

Later, living Dogmen came. Only a few at first, walking down from boats so cumbersome we knew why many had drowned. They came ashore without caution, as children would, never dreaming that hunters watched every step they took, that our arrows pointed at their hearts. They filled water barrels in our rivers, cut down our trees, wantonly killed great numbers of animals with the evil fire-sticks we learned to call muskets.

Some wore blue jackets. The blue jackets had a ceremony; they would come down from their ships, stand together on a beach, speak strange words, beat loudly on something that looked like a skin frame and then go back to their boats. Often these Dogmen would leave behind a stick with a coloured skin tied to it. They would sail away, and not be seen in that place again—or not for many seasons.

Although they were not as useful as iron nails and the bits of rope and sail Dogmen left behind, these thin coloured skins were greatly prized by our women. When I first came to sleep with Hebbosheth she still had one of these skins tucked beneath the furs in her sleeping place. I liked it because of the colours, white and blue and red as bright as berry juice—prettier than my rabbit sleep-cover. But the Dogman's stuff was neither soft as my rabbit nor warm as seal or bear coverings. When it fell apart, Demasduit, Kasathi and I tore the red bits into strips to weave into our braids.

For a long time the People told stories about the stupidity of Dogmen. They are mysterious, unpredictable, live by no fixed codes. Because of this their habits were not consistent as the habits of animals are. Yet we always knew when Dogmen were coming towards a meotick. Any tracker seeing a Dogman would leave a sign in the nearest message tree. Our runners checked such trees each time they passed, moving news of their coming from meotick to meotick well ahead of the plodding savages who had not learned how to send messages, build swift canoes or use snowshoes.

Dogmen themselves refuse to follow signs. Even when our people tried to save one from starvation, a Dogman could not find animals, follow a trail, predict storms or find shelter. Our trackers spoke of their arrogance, their lack of humour, their blindness, told of encounters with Dogmen who seemed to have no civilized habits, no knowledge of how to greet guests, the honourable way to exchange gifts or share food. My ancestors laughed at those first Dogmen.

"They are like early people before Old Caribou taught us to live," some said, thinking Dogmen harmless, thinking they would die of their own stupidity.

"That was our mistake," Hebbosheth told me. "We should have used our skills. Should have shot them down as my father and brothers would have had us do—one arrow for each as they came ashore."

But our shadowdancers, who still knew the stories and songs from Perfect Time, forbid such killings. These men told the People things that must never pass from memory, reminded us of times when we had not been faithful to Old Caribou's laws, of our brutality to the gentle Seal People, of how we had taken Dogmen's tools and used them, times when, in our greed, we had killed more animals than was necessary. Again and again they told us that it is always evil to kill creatures who walk upright, creatures to whom we are distantly related and whom therefore we cannot eat. One shaman even said that Good Ash-wa-meet had sent Dogmen to punish us because we had driven the Seal People, who are our kin, into that place where it is always winter.

Since our hunters and runners had observed that Dogmen, having no spirit guardians, are changeable as wind—one season wanting to be friendly, the next season killing us with fire-sticks—these shadowdancers easily convinced the People that it would be unwise to approach such creatures in friendship or in anger. It was the Shaman Annooee who commanded us to never trade with Dogmen, to never again use their tools or weapons. This long-dead shaman said that we must leave all the places Dogmen moved into.

"Now it is too late!" Hebbosheth said. "Having learned the sea path to Baetha they will never return to their own unhappy place!"

By the time she came to this part of the story she was angry, hissing words into my ear, listing people and things and places the Dogmen had taken. "They steal even from the dead! Scattered my sister's bones, stole the small doll my father made for her, tore the burial robe I wrapped around her body." It was the only time I ever saw my Old One weep. Tears and words fell on my head, filling my skull with a sorrow that I will never be free of.

After the day I heard Adibish and my father argue and the night my Old One told me about Dogmen, I became fearful. I would lie awake listening for Dogmen, sleep dreaming of Dogmen and wake expecting to find my family dead. For a season I never walked into the forest, staying all day within sight of our mamateeks.

Yet that winter and two others passed without a Dogman coming near us. Nothing seemed to change and slowly I began to feel safe again, even happy. Is it not a strange thing, how we can be happy inside our own lives even when the world is dying?

Nothing in my world seemed different. I still brought sticks to the fire, drew pictures and listened to the Old One at night. During this time she showed me how to bite patterns into hide and began to teach me about the cures she carried in her leather pouch.

Winter and summer Hebbosheth and I gathered roots and leaves, buds and berries. She bundled them, dried them and pounded them into powder, which she then folded inside bits of eel skin. The Old One carried many of these little twists in a pouch around her neck. She smoked some of the dried herbs in her pipe; from some she made hot drinks, but most she used for curing broken bones and various sicknesses. Whenever she helped someone she would tell me what plant or animal the cure came from and how it should be used. Some powders were dangerous if more than a tiny amount was swallowed; others could heal cuts, drive pain away and even help women in childbirth. She promised me that someday she would give me the leather pouch.

In wintertime I still sat with my friends every day, hidden in our secret place, playing dice games and talking of what we would do when we became women. I remember telling Demasduit and Kasathi that I would be a shadowdancer, knowing at once from the smile Demasduit gave me that my bragging had been unwise.

Two cycles of seasons came and went. Babies were born and two died; women nursed infants, cooked, gathered firewood, sharpened cutting tools and mended garments with their bone needles. In winter the snow was deep and game not so plentiful as in former times, but after the caribou passed we had meat and our hunters always found a few winter ducks and ptarmigan. Boys pulled fish through holes cut into the river and girls gathered frozen rosehip and spruce twigs and berries from under the snow.

When melt-time came we would be hungry, but then we trekked to the beach where we could take summer food from the sea and rivers, from the surrounding hills and marshland. When we left the beach we would be loaded down with food—glad, when we came to the mouth of Great Spruce Lake, to pack our bundles into canoes and paddle once more in-country to our winter place. Whole seasons went by when no one went hungry, seasons when we spoke less and less of Dogmen.

I had lived through seven, or perhaps eight, cycles of seasons the winter Ianamish and Longnon gave in to my pleadings and took me with them to check our family's traplines. It was the farthest I'd ever been in-country from our winter place. The day stays in my memory for that, for the beauty of sun on snow and for the happy company of my brothers.

By then I could walk all day on snowshoes and was not nervous, not even when I saw Nakhani the wolf. The day was dimming, light drawing in and I saw only his eyes, grey and evil, looking steadily at me, hating me. He was very near. I tugged on Ianamish's sleeve. We stopped and the wolf stopped too, became a shadow skulking under snow-covered trees. That was all I saw. My brothers pushed me between them and turned, one facing the trees, the other facing the bank sloping down to the river.

"There are three," Longnon said; he already had an arrow fitted in his bow.

"Leave them be," Ianamish told him, and keeping together we edged down the bank and out onto the ice.

With Longnon standing guard, Ianamish pulled off my snowshoes, looped them to his belt and swung me up on his shoulders. We were not far from our meotick, and once out on the wide frozen river we made good time.

When I saw that the wolves were not following I relaxed, began to look around, to enjoy the sound of ice crystals scrunching under my brothers' feet. Sunset turned everything salmon colour, then purple and then deep blue; ice and sky became the same cold blue and suddenly I was afraid. But then, beyond the blueness, I saw smoke rising from our mamateeks, smelled sliced bibdid, red berries bubbling out over hot stones, a caribou haunch turning above our fire.

"Baetha," Longnon said softly. It is our word that means both country and home.

My brothers walked faster. I wrapped my mitts tightly around Ianamish's neck, rested my chin on his black hair and was happy again.

XI

The seasons passed and I grew taller, but nothing changed between my father and my uncle. I fancied that Demasduit's father grew more confident. He story-danced as he always had, his shadow leaping along the walls, so large and strange that I always forgot who he was. My father, as he always had, hunted and fished winter and summer; sometimes he sat near our fire carving bows or spoons or wooden bowls. At night I listened hard to grown-up talk and watched fingers flick carved bits of bone across my mother's game hide. The hide was a beautiful thing—Hebbosheth had marked it all out with colour, showing seasons and spirit signs. I would drift into sleep, wake and sleep again to the sound of bone game-pieces clicking through the night.

On such nights I forgot about Dogmen and felt safe, snuggled down beside my Old One, taking sips of her spruce tea, breathing the comfortable smells of our mamateek: the earth floor and the pipe smoke, the wintergreen of boughs that covered our sleeping places, the thick seal oil my father and brothers used to clean their arrows, the bear fat people rubbed into sore hands and feet, the roasting meat and drying hides, the baby smells of milk and soiled moss, the people smells of sweat and sex.

Then came a spring when a runner from Ecshamut's meotick brought news that a young couple had been killed with a musket. They had been alone, duck hunting along Eel River, and Dogmen had killed them from across the water. The runner told us that Ecshamut and his son had tracked the Dogmen and killed them both, had stuck their heads on poles near the place where the man and woman died.

"When Dogmen learn of this they will want revenge," my father said, and Adibish seemed for once to agree with him.

That spring, fearing the old travel lines would be dangerous, our shadowdancer led us inland before circling back out to the coast. This made the journey from our winter place longer than usual, and we were still in wooded country when the biting flies arrived. I rubbed mud on my face, arms and legs, yet by the time we came to the coast my skin was covered with bites. We were very hungry, some so weak they were being carried. Even Hebbosheth had to be carried in a sling by my older brothers.

We crossed the familiar-scented marshland in a long straggling line, climbed up rolling dunes of sand and down again to our hidden beach, expecting to find other meoticks already there. But the beach was empty—although our journey had taken longer than usual, we were the first meotick to reach the place. People were worried that something bad had befallen the other meoticks, but Adibish said there was little we could do.

"Our first duty is to feed our own people," he told us. "Later, when they have rested, I will send runners back to look for the others."

Ice pans still drifted in the bay and we could see seals just
a little way off. Quickly, men pushed three canoes into the
water, speared three old grey ones and dragged them ashore. A
fire was built, the seals were cleaned and small pieces of liver
passed around. While seal flippers roasted above the fire and
seal carcasses cooked in the sand under the fire, we chewed on
the raw red meat and gave thanks to Ash-wa-meet and to the
animals we were eating.

It was still day and we children jumped and danced near the
fire. The smell of food cooking made me giddy, the sun, the endless blue sweep of sea, the glittering half-circle of white sand
dazzled me. At the water's edge I washed the mud off my face
and splashed my arms and legs until my fly bites stung and I
was shivering with cold. Then I raced back to the fire and food.

The knowledge that my friends and I could play in this beautiful place all summer gave me such joy that I did not remember
Godith, forgot Dogmen—could not have wished for a more perfect world. In my happiness I did not even notice our runners
returning to the hills, did not see young hunters leave the beach
to take turns guarding the higher dunes and the fringe of forest
beyond the marshland.

By the third sunset of that season the other meoticks, all
having taken new routes to the sea, had arrived safely. The beach
was filled with movement and the sounds of people calling out
to one another, admiring new babies, sympathizing with those
who had brought dead with them, cooking, setting up tents,
spreading out their belongings—everyone rejoicing that winter
was over, that we had all come safely to this holy place.

Although we were more secure inside our shadowy winter
forest, I loved the summer headlands best, places where sand
and smooth rock reached out to open sea, the smell of salt air

and the sea sounds. I have always loved light. Earth and sky are brighter out on those points, filled with sea light. It was in that light I first saw Nonosabasut.

Kasathi, Demasduit and I, along with other little girls, had slipped off our tunics and were running naked—playing the game we called Teasing the Sea, scampering between sun-warmed tidal pools, squealing each time icy water frothed in over our feet and licked around our legs.

Then a waved slapped into me and knocked me down. Shocked by the coldness I lay there. Water washed over me, filled my mouth, my eyes, turned the sky above me pale green. Through the wet greenness a boy appeared, brown-skinned, perfect. The most beautiful creature I had ever seen, or ever would see, running straight towards me. And I, my head already filled with spirit stories, thought him a spirit come from Perfect Time.

I did not want the spirit-boy to pull me from the sea like some half-dead fish, so I struggled up and planted my feet squarely on the spongy sand. Gulping salt water I held my arms out to him. But the boy ran past me into the sea, hit the water head first, swam out and snatched some other child from the receding wave. Splashing in to shore, he set the sobbing girl down on dry sand, then raced away—back to where the boys were playing stick and rock games with sling-sticks.

It was all over in the time it takes one wave to roll in and out, but the memory of that green and golden boy shimmering in the sun—that of all the memories I hold inside me will be the last to leave.

Although the seals had already gone, our people would stay on our beach all summer, making flint tools, gathering and smoking meat and fish, picking berries, collecting eggs. As I watched the boy run back to his friends I thought of all the long summer to come, and felt content. *There will be time,* I told myself. Time for what I could not have said.

I left the children and wandered over to where my mother and the other women were preparing food for that night's feast. I was a greedy child who loved to eat, especially summer food—new things that had not been smoked or frozen; marsh-berries shining like small suns, sweet pink mushrooms, new eggs and sea grapes, the crunchy seed of seagrass, rose petals, and the tangy spring leaves of dandelion, rape and cress. After the hungry season, now food was suddenly plentiful: lobster and salmon and many kinds of fish, together with ducks and seabirds the women would stuff with pine cones and seamint before roasting.

When four deep pits had been dug, I helped the women line them with seaweed and lay in the strips of seal meat we had sprinkled with spicy green beach-peas. We covered the meat with more seaweed and flat stones. Then we set a good fire atop each pit.

The beautiful boy and his friends had moved far up the beach to play their stick game. I did not go where he was, but stayed around the pits for the rest of the day. It is necessary to watch this kind of cooking closely, building the fire up or cooling it down, moving stones that cover the food, adding layers of fish, mussels, shrimp and lobster that do not take as long as seal or duck meat to cook—and talking, for around the fires women are always talking.

The day was sunny and one of my brothers had tied a caribou hide to poles so that Hebbosheth could sit in its shade well away from the fires. At midday, when Mother sent me to her with food, I thought to ask about the boy, whose name I had already discovered was Nonosabasut. But the Old One grunted so crossly when I put the tea and roasted seal down beside her that I was afraid to ask, and just stood quietly with my hands folded over my fat stomach, the sun warm on my bottom.

She was making something that looked like the snowshoes our hunters wear on their feet in winter, only the frame was wider at the back and pointed at the other end. I asked what the thing was.

"A salmon hawk," she said without raising her eyes from the pattern she was making inside the frame. Hebbosheth was never free with words during the day and even at night did not like questions.

I stayed a long time watching her fingers weave sinew in and out, considering if I dared ask which meotick Nonosabasut belonged to, who his parents were.

At last she looked up. Our eyes were level, our unsmiling faces staring into each other. She was so old! Her face was grey, creased like worn caribou hide. She knew there was something I wanted to ask. "Tonight you will hear many shadowdancers," she said.

"I know that." I had spent all my summers here and well knew there would be a great feast when all our meoticks came together on the beach.

On this first night the feast would be for the dead who had come with us from our winter camps—young men carrying the ochre-painted, hide-wrapped bodies between them in slings. Tonight all of us, the living and the dead, would gather in a circle around one great fire. We would feast, and I would taste food I had not eaten all winter. Many shadowdancers would tell stories, then friends and family would sing a spirit song for each of the dead ones, including the man and woman from Ecshamut's meotick who had been murdered by Dogmen.

It would take a long time. Demasduit bragged that she always stayed awake until the very end, and this year Kasathi and I had promised each other we would do the same.

I was suddenly angry at Hebbosheth. Why should this grim old person hold power over me? What difference if she wouldn't talk to me? I turned away from her and ran towards the firepits. Halfway there I stopped, looked back and screamed, "You never tell me anything about now! Only dead things—things about past and gone times!"

Waves roared in along the beach, children squealed and called to one another, so I did not think the Old One heard. But she looked up as if startled, stared at me and then went back to the work in her lap.

Before that sunset I knew Nonosabasut was the son of Sabasut, the shadowdancer my father had spoken of so harshly. His mother of course was Doodebewshet, the woman my father and my Uncle Adibish had come to grief over. She was still beautiful. The small girl Nonosabasut had saved from the sea that day was his sister, Ashei—she who would always need saving. Between him and Ashei there was a brother named Tomasuth, also pleasing to look at but not as handsome or graceful as Nonosabasut.

This much I learned from listening beside the cooking fires. I heard something else too, a change in the women's voices when they spoke to Doodebewshet, as if something separated other women from Nonosabasut's mother, even when they were side by side doing the same work. The only difference I could see was Doodebewshet's beauty and her silence—and how her eyes were always searching for Ashei. Other mothers did not give such attention to children once they were weaned and Ashei was as old as me.

The shadowdancers—Adibish, Sabasut, Ecshamut and Thebush, one from each meotick—all storydanced around our fire that night. Each spoke in the same growling chant and all had ochre-painted faces. Each shadowdancer wore a fine collar of eagle feathers, a tall headdress of caribou antlers; each had a long shaggy bear skin draped down his back and hands covered in bear claws. Their own wives could not have known which man told which story—who was Demasduit's father and who the father of the boy Nonosabasut?

They all told good stories, but for me only one story was important that night—the night of the day I first saw Nonosabasut. The story was about his parents, although I did not know that then, thought it just an old story from past time. I never learned if the story was new to Nonosabasut that night, perhaps it was.

I had often watched Demasduit when Adibish was story-dancing, often wondered what it was like to know the man behind the caribou head was your father. That night I watched only Nonosabasut. He listened to every story with the same attention, leaning forward with his eyes on the shadowdancer's face, as if breathing in the words.

When the feasting ended, the old ones sat nodding over their pipes. Most of the children had fallen asleep—even Demasduit. Even Kasathi, who had promised to stay awake with me, was asleep before the last story was told.

"This story happened in the time of Osagana, the great shaman who was my teacher," the shadowdancer began, and I knew then that the man speaking was either my uncle or his friend Sabasut.

"In that not-too-distant time, many of our People had dis-obeyed Ash-wa-meet and were once again going where Dogmen lived, taking the iron tools Dogman left about and using them. Osagana repeatedly reminded the People that such things were forbidden, had been forbidden since old time when Dogmen first came to Baetha. In that long-ago time a shadowdancer named Annooee saw that sickness follows the possessions of Dogmen, that our people became ill after trading with them.

"Many generations of our people remembered Annooee's wisdom. Then they forgot, and little by little started once more taking things from Dogman camps, leaving arrows or a caribou in exchange. Sometimes our young men even went into coves and burnt the heavy boats Dogmen left behind so that we could have the iron nails that were so useful.

"All the eastern beaches already belonged to Dogmen. They had attached their wooden buildings to the earth in every cove and bay except this one. Then came a spring when we saw Dogmen boats moored in this very bay. We watched Dogmen come ashore and begin building their platforms on this beach also.

"For three summers our people watched the Dogmen hunt and fish here, filling their boats with our food. Our people did not harm the Dogmen but waited in hunger for the boats to leave. It would already be cold then, the seals long gone, and we would have only a few days to gather what we could before returning to the forest.

"For three winters we lived without seal oil or seal meat, with only a little of the many things we need from the sea. Our people went hungry. Many died, especially children—and we could not even bury our dead properly because we were cut off from the holy cave.

"During that third hungry winter shadowdancers in every meotick met with the Shaman Osagana. They fasted for many days, and on the last night of the darkest moon of the year, along the edge of a freezing river, all our people burned herbs and hummed sorrowful songs. Shadowdancers rubbed themselves with oil, then plunged into the cold water carrying blankets and pots, axes and nails and little ticking things—everything of the Dogmen was buried in the river. They then held cleansing ceremonies and promised never again to touch the belongings of Dogmen.

"The very next day two young men returned from the hills with a little bear cub they had found. Osagana, who had been waiting for a sign that Great Spirit Ash-wa-meet had forgiven us, touched the bear's snout. 'Welcome to the tents of our people, Little Bear God,' he said.

"One of the young men who had found the animal took the little visitor to his own mamateek, where he kept him warm and fed all that winter. The bear cub became a child of the meotick, playing freely with other children and sleeping with the young man's family at night.

"That spring, before the People began their eastward trek, the Shaman Osagana told them that the time had now come for the Little Bear God to start on his return trip to the Spirit World.

"The bear was tethered to a pole, a necklace of carved pendants was hung about its neck and prayers were made to our visitor and Keathut the bear spirit: 'Oh, Divine One, you who were sent into our world to show acceptance of our offerings, we thank you for living among us. Thank you for the wisdom you have brought to our people. Please, speak well of us in the Spirit World, and when you are restored to life, come again to honour our tents.'

"After this, Osagana took his bow and pointed it at the Little Bear God. He shot one arrow over the animal's head, into the stake to which it was tied. Then he passed the bow to his grandson, the man who had taken the cub into his own mamateek.

'From this day on, you will be our shadowdancer,' Osagana said. 'May your arrow fly straight. May no blood fall. May your quiver always be full.'

"The young man sent the arrow into the heart of the Little Bear God in such a way that not one drop of blood spilled on the earth. And from that moment on he was a shadowdancer.

"The bear's head was removed and placed reverently on a pole so that the Divine One could be part of the ceremony, see the dancing, share the parting feast and have gifts placed before him.

"'Oh, Little Bear God, we give you carved antlers and birch cups—take these gifts with you to the Spirit World. Do not pause to look back. Go quickly and tell your ancestors of our kindness. Tell them we no longer touch the belongings of Dogmen. Tell them how we have honoured you, have nourished you with our milk, given you our food, kept you warm in winter. Ask good Ash-wa-meet to deal kindly with us who have dealt kindly with you. If you say this, Little Bear God, your ancestors will be happy and will bless us.' This the Shaman Osagana asked of the visitor.

"And that spring, when the hungry people crossed the marshland, when they climbed over the last sand dune and looked down on this beach, it was empty. The Little Bear God had brought our message to the Spirit World. Dogmen and their ships had left this place, the sea had swept away their fragile platforms. And they have never returned here, not for all the summers that have come and gone since that day."

It was the last story.

We called out our thanks to Ash-wa-meet and then poured water on the ceremonial fire. Men lifted our dead, carried them to the sea and placed the tightly wrapped bodies in canoes. Shadowdancers paddled the canoes, moving silently out into the quiet cape, taking our dead to a deep sea cave that only they know. From such holy places it is possible to step quickly onto the Ghost Path.

When the last canoe had vanished around the dark headlands, people left the beach, wandering half asleep to their summer shelters among the sand dunes. Only Hebbosheth and I stayed, standing on the edge of white foam, staring into blackness.

"Now, Shanawdithit, if you stay awake I will tell you that story again. I will tell you differently, tell you how it truly happened," she said.

I knew from the way Hebbosheth spoke that she was very angry, but not at me.

She took my hand and led me back to the small half-tent my father had made just for us. When we were settled comfortably inside, the Old One told me this story.

"Doodebewshet, the beautiful young woman my grandsons argued over, never belonged to our meotick but to the meotick of Osagana the shadowdancer, who became a shaman and was treated as a great spirit long years before he crossed into the Spirit World.

"After my grandsons, Adibish and Washomish, scattered our caribou herd, they were compelled to leave my mamateek and told never to pursue the girl again. Your father, Washomish, married soon after, but your Uncle Adibish spent many seasons living with the old man Jalamish who had been made lame by the foolish actions of my grandsons.

"Sometime in those years Doodebewshet became the wife of Sabasut—Sabasut, whose story you heard tonight from his own lips. It is unseemly that shadowdancers tell stories from their own time." Hebbosheth made a sharp hissing sound and stopped talking.

I sat still and did not ask why—I was remembering the words I'd shouted at midday on the beach. My anger was gone, leaving fear and the knowledge that was at its root—that my Old One was not a spirit but a weak old woman who would die and leave me.

She spoke differently that night, not in the singsong chant she used when storytelling past time but as if she were simply talking. She could not pat my head as she usually did, for we were sitting side by side in the tent's opening, chins on knees, looking out across the dark empty beach. Only the sea moved, a line of white foam swishing softly around the crescent of sand, vanishing at the far curve just as a new wave began—on and on, one wave beginning as the other ended.

"Is it the same wave or a different wave each time? What do you think, Shanawdithit?" she asked, and I shook my head.

"Stories are like that, flowing around different lives, moving between different times, maybe even between different places. The same story may have happened in past time, may happen again in future time." She paused. "Perhaps then I am unfair to Sabasut, perhaps the story he told tonight happened before, before my time or his time—in another time.

"Yet I will tell you truly what happened in my lifetime, when, with my own eyes, I saw a Little Bear God come into the mamateeks of our people.

"Before the old man Jalamish died, he came to love Adibish like a son. Jalamish wanted my grandson to have deep knowledge of all matters concerning the Spirit World, and so he told the young man to spend two circles of seasons in the mamateek of the Shaman Osagana. Adibish might have learned better things in my mamateek, but Jalamish did not have the same regard for me that he did for the Great Osagana.

"During those seasons Adibish and Sabasut, who is the grandson of Osagana, became like brothers. It did not seem to matter that Adibish had once loved the woman who was now Sabasut's wife. Osagana's grandson and my grandson were the same age, were young men training to become shadowdancers in their own meoticks; both were Osagana's students and lived daily in the circle of his charm, both believed every word the great shaman spoke.

"Things were as Sabasut told us around tonight's fire. We had been kept from this beach for three summers, had no seal oil for our lamps, were starving for lack of sea food and seal meat. That winter the Circle—all our shadowdancers and elders— were called to Osagana the shaman's meotick. Because I was still one of the Circle and because interfering spirits guide my life, I sat at Osagana's gathering that day.

"I will tell you, Shanawdithit, that I was one of those who wanted to drive Dogmen from this holy beach by force. When spring came we could send a large hunting party ahead to this place. With our canoes it would not be hard to cut nets at night. Burning arrows would set fire to Dogmen boats. We could kill any Dogmen who remained.

"Many nodded when we told this plan. But when Osagana stood and began to speak, he reminded us that beyond memory, our ancestors had done these same things to Seal People. We had destroyed their boats, broken their harpoons, even killed them— until every one had vanished into that cold northland that is always winter. Osagana said that Dogmen had been sent to us as punishment for refusing to share Baetha with the Seal People. He spoke powerful words, called our plan evil that would beget evil. The Circle agreed with him.

"'We bring all evil on ourselves,' Osagana told us. Even the loss of our sandy beach had come about because we had forgotten Great Annooee's words and had used tools made by Dogmen.

"Then Osagana called to the People to bring everything that had ever been touched by Dogmen out of their mamateeks. And they came with bags of nails, with fish hooks and buttons and kettles and axes, with iron rods and cooking pots and traps and pieces of sailcloth—but not fire-sticks, for even in those days the People never touched Dogmen's evil weapons.

"These things were gathered in bundles, wrapped in sailcloth and taken by shadowdancers out into the river, just as we were told tonight. After all the Dogmen tools were drowned, Osagana and all our shadowdancers went into a steam-filled tent to perform cleansing ceremonies and to ask Ash-wa-meet and the good spirits to forgive us. The rest of us sat outside. We chanted sorrowful songs and waited all night for a sign that we had been forgiven.

"We were still there the next morning. Our shadowdancers came from the steam house looking tired and dejected—no message had been received from the Spirit World. It was then, as we sat on the ground waiting for our leaders to speak, that the two young men, my grandson Adibish, and Sabasut, the grandson of Osagana, came out of the forest with the bear cub.

"I saw the sudden joy on Osagana's face. 'Welcome, Little Bear God!' he said. Then he went and took the bear cub into his arms. Holding it up so that we could all see, he placed a bowl of food under the animal's snout.

"This did not please the Little Bear God. He slapped the bowl away with his paw and whined.

"Darkness passed over the shaman's face. His eyes swept around the circle of people, daring us to laugh. No one laughed. We were cold and tired. We sat and waited, staring blankly at the Great Osagana and the dirty, matted animal in his arms.

"The only person not looking at the shaman was Sabasut's wife, Doodebewshet. She was nursing her first baby, the tiny girl-child she'd given birth to only days before. The Shaman Osagana stared at Doodebewshet and her baby. I knew his words before he spoke. 'The wife of my grandson Sabasut will take the Little Bear God to her breast and make it feel welcome.'

"Doodebewshet's head jerked up. 'No!' she said, loudly, as if it had burst from her insides. But Osagana told her to be silent.

"Osagana would die just three seasons later, but that day he had great power. He was still handsome, the best looking man among all the People, tall with broad shoulders. Osagana had the ice-blue eyes that are so unusual among the People, eyes that seemed to see into your skull—and a deep voice that made all his words sound wise. I watched the little bear squirm in his arms and hoped it would shit on him.

"Then, in front of us all, Osagana the shaman commanded Sabasut to compel Doodebewshet to suckle the bear cub. 'From this day the Divine One is to be given all the milk it can take—the girl-child can drink only after the Little Bear God has finished.'

"Doodebewshet turned her face not to her husband but to my grandson Adibish. She did not speak but it was clear she was asking him to stop this thing. No one spoke; everyone was watching your uncle. He was still young then and without a wife of his own. Doubtless Doodebewshet would have gone with him if he had offered her protection. I do not know what would have happened if he had. Beyond memory our people have never fought with one another, but in that moment I feared it. I looked around, counting how many were there from our meotick.

"Adibish stared back at the young woman. Even with the strain of childbirth still on her face she was beautiful, with great dark eyes, and dark hair falling over her shoulders, half covering the baby she clutched to her body.

"My grandson Adibish turned from her and took the Little Bear God from the old shaman's arms. He carried it over to Doodebewshet and, holding the cub with one hand, he reached under her hair and jerked the baby away from her. Then he pressed the bear into her arms.

"The woman cried out and pushed the bear away. But by then Osagana and Sabasut were standing one on either side of her. The shaman held Doodebewshet's arms, but it was her husband, Sabasut, who pressed his fingers around her nipple and forced it into the bear's mouth. Adibish held the crying baby while Sabasut kept the animal's mouth wrapped around the young mother's nipple until her milk began to flow down over the black snout of the bear.

"After that, every time the animal wanted milk, the old man and his grandson arranged the woman as if her body were an oil-filled seal paunch. They held the bear cub, moving him from breast to breast. My own grandson, your Uncle Adibish, circled around them with the baby in his arms because her crying made Doodebewshet's milk flow faster.

"It is to my shame that I was afraid to speak out against this ugly thing.

"It was said that after several days Doodebewshet began to accept the bear meekly, taking her own child only when the cub turned his snout away from her breast. By then I had gone back to our own meotick, but the thing was talked of by women for many seasons.

"The Bear God grew round and sleek, his fur glistened. He was petted and admired, played with by the children. Sabasut left his wife and went to sleep with the Little Bear God in the shaman's mamateek, bringing the animal to his foster mother whenever he whined for food.

"While the cub nursed, the baby cried—always cried—as if she knew her milk was being stolen. She did get a little milk but it must not have been enough, for she died in mid-winter, still without a name.

"It was feared that Doodebewshet's milk might dry up then, but Osagana made a mixture of bear grease and the crushed leaves of mint, and the women rubbed this into Doodebewshet's breasts, massaging her sore nipples until milk flowed as plentifully as before.

"Sabasut, as he told us around tonight's fire, became a shadowdancer on the day his arrow killed the Little Bear God. Also on that day he was free to return to Doodebewshet's sleeping place.

"During the winter that followed, Sabasut and Doodebewshet had their second child, the boy Nonosabasut you have been watching all day." For the first time since she had started talking, Hebbosheth turned her face to me. "Nonosabasut's eyes are like the eyes of his grandfather Osagana.

"The prideful and haughty spirit that told Osagana he could never be wrong dwells in Sabasut's skull, as it does in the skull of his son Nonosabasut," she said.

And with that she rolled her bearskin around her, lay back and went to sleep.

———

I paid little heed to my Old One's warnings and spent much of that summer watching the beautiful boy. I was curious about his family also, especially his mother, Doodebewshet. Although I tried to forget Hebbosheth's terrible story, I could not, and I never looked at Doodebewshet without remembering she had nursed a bear cub. In time I came to believe that part of her spirit had been stolen, not by the Little Bear God but by the cruelty of those three men—Osagana and Sabasut and my Uncle Adibish.

One morning near dawn, when I was making water, squatting in tall grass behind our tent, I saw Doodebewshet and her daughter walk down to the place where our canoes were tied. They did not speak to each other, carried nothing and hurried as if late for something, though day had not yet begun. At the water's edge Doodebewshet pulled a small, one-paddle canoe towards her and they climbed in. More quickly that I would have expected, she paddled far out into the smooth water, around the whale-shaped headland and out of sight. No one else was watching, and later, when my mother brought word that Doodebewshet and Ashei had gone off by themselves, I did not tell what I'd seen.

I remember the stubborn silence of Nonosabasut that day, remember Sabasut's hard secret face when he had to send trackers out searching for his wife and daughter. Long after sunset, men brought Doodebewshet and Ashei back from the bird island where they had gone ashore. I listened but heard no one speak about why these two acted as they did. Neither did anyone speak of why people from all meoticks gave such attention to Sabasut's feelings and his words—much more attention, it seemed to me, than to the words of other shadow-dancers. After many days of watching and listening, I asked Hebbosheth why the Shadowdancer Sabasut and his family were treated differently from all other people.

"Why do you think?" Hebbosheth asked.

It was a soft misty day in early summer, waves of caplin were rolling up on the sand, and all around us women and children were wading into the sea, scooping up baskets of fish.

"Because they are different from the rest of us," I said. I was watching Nonosabasut and Tomasuth. The brothers were racing to see who could collect the most caplin, laughing, holding baskets of glitter against their bodies, streams of sea water splashing down over their brown legs.

My Old One had not mentioned Nonosabasut since the night of the bear story. I longed to hear his name spoken, to find out more about him and his strange parents. At that very moment, his mother began to shriek and everyone stopped what they were doing to watch her.

"Some trickster spirit has gotten into Doodebewshet's skull," Hebbosheth said.

Nonosabasut's mother was pulling on Ashei's tunic, dragging her daughter back from the water, screaming that the child was about to drown. Although their sister was clearly in no danger, Nonosabasut and Tomasuth put down their baskets and ran to their mother. All four left the beach, the boys holding Doodebewshet's arms, Ashei trailing behind, drawing toe patterns in the wet sand.

"You think that family beautiful?" Hebbosheth asked.

I heard the scorn in her voice and truly it did look foolish— two sons supporting their weeping mother, coaxing her up to their tent. Such noise for something my mother would not have heeded.

I did not answer my Old One until the boys came back to the beach. "But they are beautiful—especially him . . ." I nodded towards Nonosabasut. He and Tomasuth were again gathering caplin, but without joy, as if it were only a thing they must do to live.

"This him you speak of is the oldest boy?"

I nodded. "Nonosabasut," I said. His name was like a name I had always known; it was like laughter.

"As far back as I can remember, before I can remember, beyond the Shaman Osagana's time, the ancestors of Nonosabasut have been listened to. Sometimes we mistake beauty for wisdom." The

Old One was looking at me thoughtfully—perhaps sadly, as if she knew I would not do her bidding. "It would be best if you do not speak of that family to your father."

Then she clamped her lips shut, turned and walked away.

I stayed on the wet sand watching Nonosabasut, and caught a few slippery caplin in my hands, tossing them carelessly towards land until Mother came to rebuke me. She told me to leave the beach, to go to the fire and turn the caplin that were hanging on roasting racks.

Mother was unwell that summer, but I did not see this, just as I did not see the new grimness in my father's face or notice the long absences of my older brothers. I was young and without care. I would wish such summers for every child—but the children of my people were never to have another.

When the days shortened we all left the beach together. Four meoticks of the People with our shadowdancers, Ecshamut, Thebush, Sabasut and Adibish, walking ahead, each holding a stave with his mark on top.

"How many people were there?" The Dogman named Cormack asked me this again and again.

But I could not tell how many. "Many," I said, "more than I have fingers and toes. More than I have hairs on my head!"

I cannot tell numbers, but that autumn many of us left the seal beach to walk into the green heart of Baetha. It had been a plentiful summer and every person was carrying something. Young men walked in twos, balancing canoes on their heads and holding sleeping rolls in the crooks of their arms. Older men carried spears and arrows and long staffs from which things hung: stone oil-lamps, animal bladders filled with seal oil, skins and furs and clothing. Women and children carried baskets filled with berries and eggs, bags of herbs, strings of seabirds—turr, puffin and gannet—bundles of dried seal meat, smoked salmon and cod, roasted caplin and many new flint tools.

Dogmen say we were dirty and unhealthy—they lie. We were brown, healthy people with white teeth, tall men with broad shoulders, round-faced women and fat babies, wilful girls like me and my friends, laughing boys like Nonosabasut and his brother, Tomasuth. Even Hebbosheth, who had been unwell when we came to the beach, looked well.

We all stayed together until Great Spruce Lake—the place I called Godith's River, where he saved me from the bear. From there each meotick took a different travel line into their own winter place.

I watched Nonosabasut walk away from me into the forest. He did not look back, did not know Shanawdithit was alive on earth.

XII

So it started. I tell you my own life now, Dogman, tell of the days and seasons I spent waiting for Nonosabasut, listening for his name, measuring time against how its shadow fell on him—while our world closed in, became small, became cold and hungry.

When we came to our winter place that season we found our caribou fences torn apart, just as the fences of others had been destroyed other winters. My father was enraged; many were, but there was nothing he could do.

Quickly the men set up poles for our mamateeks, the women sewed the six or eight caribou-skin walls tightly around the poles and fixed long strips of birchbark in place. There was no time to do more. As soon as our mamateeks were up we began to repair the long runways our ancestors had built. It was hard work and even old people and children were expected to help.

Demasduit, Kasathi and I worked together, fetching and carrying sticks and strips of sinew, stripping twigs and weaving them into breaks. Our mothers had made sealskin mitts for us, but before the first day was over our hands were sore and our wrists bleeding. No one complained, for we all understood how important it was that our fences be ready when Old Caribou led his relatives down from the hills.

When it became dark we children were told to go into our mamateeks and sleep, while older people, men and women alike, made bushfires and worked on through the night. One morning when I woke, my mother was crying, holding a dead baby girl that had come out of her body too soon. The tiny white thing would have been a sister for me. Hebbosheth said the baby must have not wanted to leave the Spirit World and had now returned there.

On the night we finished the fenceways, Firewoman danced. Firewoman comes only once or twice a season, always on clear, cold nights in the first moon of winter. Some winters she does not come at all. Because she is a messenger from good spirits, our people are always happy to see Firewoman. We wrap ourselves in furs and settle down outside to watch her dance.

It is a lucky and blessed thing to be joined under Firewoman's skirts, and couples often wait until she comes to hold their marriage ceremonies. On this night my Auntie Santu's son Manus was to wed a girl-woman from the Shadowdancer Ecshamut's meotick. The girl's name was Amet, and she had come to live in our meotick since the summer when they became betrothed. My cousin Manus was a good friend of my brother Ianamish, but I knew him only a little. He was as serious and silent as Amet was talkative and silly—not silly perhaps but foolishly happy— seeming nearer to Kasathi's, Demasduit's and my age than the age of a woman ready for marriage.

And so, beneath the swirling, whirling skirts of Firewoman, our shadowdancer called on Ash-wa-meet to watch over the couple standing before him. Adibish spoke for a long time, but I remember only what he said at the end.

"Be joyful," he told Manus and Amet. "Give one another joy, take joy from one another and from the world around you. This is what Good Ash-wa-meet wishes for all her children."

I remember his words because they surprised me, so different an image did they give from the way I'd seen my Uncle Adibish act, so at odds were they with the dour life he seemed to live with his own wife and daughter. We were surely joyful that night, all of us sitting outside, faces lifted to the sky, giving thanks for the bountiful summer, thanks that we'd finished mending our fenceways before Old Caribou led his family down from the hills, thanks for the healthy young people standing beneath our shadowdancer's feather-trimmed stave.

So as not to offend her, we never go to our tents until Firewoman has folded her wings and given that last flick of her hair, the last pale swish of her skirt. That year, as always, not even the youngest children went inside. Because this was a special night and because we had all worked so hard, each child had been given a stick of dried salmon to chew on. Kasathi, Demasduit and I sat with other girl-children a little distance from the ceremony. We were talking about Amet, who we liked very much, wondering why she would marry such a plain, quiet man.

"There are magical places in Baetha, places where lovers will always recognize each other, always think one another beautiful. Perhaps Amet met Manus in such a place," Demasduit said.

"Um . . ." Kasathi made a polite sound that I knew meant she was not interested, but I asked what lovers were.

"People who want to sleep with each other forever and always," Demasduit said.

"Like me and Hebbosheth," I said.

"Of course not!" My cousin spoke in the haughty voice that always made me feel small and foolish.

"What are they, then?" I was still looking up—we all were, slowly chewing, turning our heads to follow the swirl of red, yellow and green, Firewoman's great wings folding and unfolding, filling the vast northern sky.

"Lovers are young—young men and girls, like Amet and Manus. Two people who think each other perfect, who want to touch each other, want to live together and have babies."

The way I feel about Nonosabasut! I thought—almost said his name, but managed to swallow it back, choking on a bite of salmon. I kept my eyes on the whirling, turning sky and wondered if Nonosabasut and I were lovers. I thought we could not be, since Demasduit had said two people—*two people who think each other perfect*. Can one person alone be a lover? I wanted to ask but was afraid Demasduit would laugh at me.

I pulled my rabbit-fur hood up over my hair and lay back. Above me the whole wide sky danced, colours mixing, moving, feathers sweeping upward, arching over me. After a time the earth under me began to spin, turning slowly around, like a canoe when the river catches it, all our Great Island turning and drifting, spiralling in space until my head and stomach hurt—and I had to go into the bushes and vomit up everything inside me.

When winter came down that season it was cold with sharp winds that drifted snow high over mamateeks. Because we had spent so much time on the fences, our mamateeks were not as well-made as in other winters, seams had not been moss-stuffed, the outer layer of birch bark had not been properly oiled to keep out dampness. Even our days were dark because every skin we could spare from our sleeping hollows was tied to the inside walls, covering the thin, hairless skins of rabbits, which when rubbed with bear fat let sunlight into our tents. With the winds so strong we hardly even opened the smoke hole, so that when I did get to sleep the choking and coughing inside our tent often woke me.

Because Old Caribou had come and because of all the food we had brought from the sea we were not hungry. Yet that was the winter I learned the misery of being always cold.

In mid-winter the Old One became so sick she expected to die. She spent her days in the little steam house my mother built. At night in our sleeping place she shivered, and rattled in her chest. It was hard for me to listen to her rasping voice, yet she never stopped talking, hurrying to tell me all the things I should know before she stepped onto the Ghost Path. She talked on and on, pushing her stories out into darkness and cold, into the ear of this unwilling child.

With the cold and the coughing and the Old One croaking into my ear early and late, many mornings I was too tired to crawl out of my sleeping place. I began to feel sick myself. During those long miserable nights my Old One repeated everything she had ever said, told me again that I would see things she had not seen, go to parts of the Great Island where she had not been.

"Will I go in-country, up the great river to the secret island where you built canoes?"

"You will go farther than that. It may be you will even see the high eastern cliffs where all of Baetha's rivers fall into the ocean—places my own Old One spoke of when I was younger than you are now. I have heard earth voices say your name; it will be remembered long after mine is forgotten. You will see many strange things, Shanawdithit, before you travel the Ghost Path."

She told me that I must always listen to the earth voices and always protect my people. On those nights she frightened me, made me promise things I did not understand, made me promises I thought I understood.

"Remember, Shanawdithit, if you follow good spirits you will swiftly cross the Ghost Path and come to Perfect Time. I will wait for you there—I and all your Ancestors."

Where are you now, Old One? Have you grown weary or do you still wait beyond the Ghost Path? Or was all you told me false? I would think it false—except that I am here still, trapped beneath these eastern cliffs you told me of, still remembering, still calling out to you. Memory my only witness, all I have to show that you were real, that *he* was real, that my people once walked upon this sweet earth.

Winter is not forever. Even that year melt-time came, birdsongs changed, sleeping animals began to stir, river ice cracked and turned tea-colour. The day we prepared to leave our winter place I danced with happiness as I helped my father rub oil into the pieces of skin and bark he took from our mamateek. When the bark was oiled he carefully rolled and tied each piece. In this way our neatly bundled mamateek could be hidden in the forest until our return.

Father was not as pleased as I was to leave our winter place that season. He wanted to stay behind and guard the caribou fences. I had heard him talking to Hebbosheth when he thought I was sleeping. My father wished to live in the hills all summer, he and my brothers. "Every meotick should do the same, leave two or three men to keep watch on our hunting lines, put an arrow into the heart of any Dogman who comes near our fences," he said.

"The Circle has forbidden killing." The Old One sounded weary. "If you truly wish to stay behind, you must say to your brother, Adibish, that you only want to frighten the Dogmen away. This he might agree to."

Adibish and others in the Circle must have refused my father permission to stay, because all our meotick left the winter place together. Even Hebbosheth walked with us instead of travelling the Ghost Path as I had feared during the cold winter. The only dead we carried was my tiny sister who had come into the world too soon. My father had carved a doll smaller even than she was, to keep her company on the Ghost Path.

When we came to Godith's place, the camping spot beside Great Spruce Lake where we always rested for a day or two, washing ourselves and our belongings before we travelled on to the beach, we found the Shadowdancer Sabasut and the people of his meotick already there.

Nonosabasut seemed much taller than I remembered. I was still a child and he was becoming one of the young men in his meotick. During the winter I had imagined us becoming friends. Somehow I would make it happen. On winter nights I made dream pictures of us talking, of me showing him Godith's stars, drawing pictures for him. To hold his attention I would even tell him the Old One's secrets. . . . But now I was afraid even to look at him.

For the rest of our trek seaward, the people of Sabasut's meotick and our meotick walked together. I remember Nonosabasut and his brother, Tomasuth, carrying the body of a child between them, for there had been much winter sickness in Sabasut's meotick—two old ones, a hunter, two women and two children had died. Others were still weak. Doodebewshet and Ashei walked hand in hand like children, both mother and daughter fleshless as boiled bones. The journey seemed long but I was content to look at Nonosabasut and to hear his voice.

"We are here, Grandmother," Father said when we came at last to the crest of the sand dunes skirting the beach. "Look down, we are here." He folded the bearskin back from the Old One's face.

"Here," Hebbosheth repeated. She had been carried for days; the gentle roll of the hammock, the footfalls of men, the smell of bearskin had become her world. Suddenly she was staring into blueness, smelling salt air, hearing the sea's roar.

"I thought never to hear that sound again—I want to die in this holy place."

I heard her say this although I was half asleep, dozing against my brother's back. I was far too old to be carried but I could always get Ianamish to do what I wanted. My arms were draped around his neck, long legs sticking out on either side. I opened my eyes, looked down on the beach, and already I was wiggling free, eager to be the first one to race across the untouched sand to the sea.

Then Ianamish whispered, *"Wait!"*

One word and the world changes. I am below, I am him—a boy hiding in the goose grass that fringes the empty beach. He is sitting comfortably on the warm sand, looking inland, waiting, knowing we will come.

We appear against the sky, a line of silent people dressed in loose, earth-colour skins. We carry things: baskets, bows and arrows, skin-wrapped bodies, fur coverings, long posts, harpoons. Sabasut and Adibish hold the sacred staffs, mothers have babies in slings, men have canoes on their shoulders, one man carries a child on his back, an old one is carried by two men in a kind of hammock made of caribou hide.

On the crest of the dune they all stop. Men with canoes roll them gracefully down from their shoulders, the girl is set on her feet, the hammock gently lowered onto the sand.

Only he could have seen this. Yet it is what I remember—
that, and the quick spark of happiness he must have felt.

Then comes the sharp *"Wait!"*

No one moves. We watch the ocean break, see it froth up
the beach, fold back on itself; see the outward roll, the pause, the
inward rush, the sea's pulse repeating over and over again.

"Dogmen!" someone whispers.

Soft thumps and we are all lying flat on the dune, puffs of
sand rising around us and settling on our sand-coloured skin.
The canoes and some of the children have been pushed backward, rolled into the hollow behind us.

I am shaking, burying my face in the Old One's bear fur, her
clawlike hand reaching out, cupping my head. I close my eyes
and pretend we are in our mamateek, remember stories of former times when Old Caribou saved his people. I think it is time
he made that trick again.

There are no movements, no screams, no cries. I can hear my
heart beating, hear the way-off swish of landwash, the distant
shrill of seagulls.

I lift my head in time to see a crouched figure far below. He
crawls slowly out from the tall grass. His long shadow unfolds
across the sunlit sand, the shadow stands, begins walking
towards us.

I know, can tell at once, who it is. I say, "Godith!"

Before his name drops into our silence, before the Old One
has time to pull herself upright, Mishatut is on her feet, plunging forward, wallowing ankle-deep in sand, joyfully floundering
towards her son, shouting, "Godith! Godith!"

Hearing his mother's voice the boy is reassured. In that
jerking hop his uneven legs mistake for running, he hurries
across the beach towards us.

Faster than I believed possible, Hebbosheth is pushing her-self to her knees, is saying, "Stop him!"

The command is not necessary. Three young men have posi-tioned their arrows and raised bows.

I shout, "No!" I grab at Ianamish's arm so that when he shoots, his arrow veers off, falling weakly to one side.

The other hunters release their bows in the same instant, sending two arrows in a high clean arch above the Old One's head, above Mishatut—who, having reached hard-packed sand, is now running, arms outstretched towards her son.

The arrows outrun her—slice through the sunshine, curve downward and pierce the shape that is Godith. He stops, his uneven legs holding him upright for one intake of breath before his body crumples, his shadow dissolving, spreading dark wings across the bright sand.

A body's length from where the boy lies, Mishatut's hus-band catches up with her, pulls her back. She fights but Ebanthoo is stronger; he holds her arms, turning her away from their dead son. On the hill a woman begins a long drawn-out wail, and one by one others join in, the sound rising, blending with the moan of sea and the cry of gulls. Godith's parents are gathered into a circle of women. The wailing is all around us like wind inside an empty cave.

After a time Sabasut and Adibish walk down from the dune together. They slowly approach the still body. Each shadow-dancer carries a long pole, each wears a caribou skin over his shoulders, large skins that trail in the sand, marking two dark lines behind them as they cross the beach. From the hill I cannot tell which man is my uncle, which Nonosabasut's father.

When they get to Godith they stand, one at his head and one at his feet, calling words I cannot hear into the sky. They take the caribou skins from their shoulders, cover Godith with one and spread the other beside him on the sand. They lay a pole gently on each skin. Then, with shadowdancer magic, they roll the skins, roll Godith into the skins with a carrying pole on each side of him. Sabasut and Adibish pick up the narrow bundle, move it a distance from the black shadow that is blood. They lay Godith down and sit silently beside him in the sand.

Then we come down from the dunes. We do not talk, do not look at one another. People walk in a wide circle around the two shadowdancers, the dead boy, the blood. Later we will pile fire-wood over the clotted sand—when night comes we will light a fire there.

My heart is bitter towards the Old One. I blame her—do not understand—dare not ask. I go and find the place where Godith was hiding, find his footprints, his handprints, the shape of his bottom in the sand. It is the place where he used to tell me star stories. All day I stay hidden in the grass, sit where he sat and watched us come up over the dunes—he must have been happy then, in that moment when his mother called, when he ran forward.

When dark came I was the first one sitting beside the fire. I had not spoken since the killing, had not eaten or had anything to drink. When my mother put a bowl of tea into my hands and sat down beside me I was thankful. My mother's face, the wooden bowl, my own hands holding the bowl, the fire and the people gathering around the fire—suddenly all these ordinary things seemed good and strange and altogether beautiful. That Godith would never again see these small everyday things, that someday I also would not see them, was unbearable. I began to weep. To hide my tears I held the warm bowl against my chest, bent my head and lapped the tea into my mouth.

I could not see Godith's body anywhere. His mother and father walked to the fire between Adibish and Sabasut. Our shadowdancers were ochre-painted and wore caribou antlers on their heads. They eased Mishatut and Ebanthoo down, then sat one on either side as if holding the dazed couple in place.

Gradually all the people of Sabasut's meotick and our meotick came to sit within the circle of firelight. Even Hebbosheth hobbled out of the dark. She did not come to me but silently squatted beside her grandson Adibish. The Old One's face was half hidden by the bearskin she still held around her head and shoulders. Nonosabasut, his beautiful mother, his brother, Tomasuth, and their sister came last and sat across from where I was. Beyond the fire's heat their faces seemed to change shape, floating above the flames. We all stayed like this a very long time without speaking. With my finger I began to make a design in the sand. Once I thought Nonosabasut was staring at me.

One of the shadowdancers invited anyone who wished to, to stand and talk about Godith. This was a hard thing—most people had never looked at Godith, never heard him speak. He had been gone many seasons, some had forgotten him. An old man said he'd been a good, obedient boy. One of the women remembered Godith was born on a clear fall night, in a grassy meadow halfway between the sea and our winter place. Between these faltering little stories, we chanted the song we had made up for him many moons ago when he was taken by the Dogmen.

In one of the long silences I began to speak. Without thinking I heard myself telling the story of how Godith had saved me from the bear. I did not stand but I made my voice as loud as I could. Even the men listened, even the shadowdancers listened. Although I was more afraid of her than I'd been of the bear, I looked straight at the Old One—she who had ordered Godith's death.

When I finished there was another silence. No one looked at me, not even my mother looked at me. Godith's mother, Mishatut, had not said one word all night, had not even nodded to others who had told their memories of her son. Her eyes were open but empty and staring, her head lolled against her husband's shoulder. I thought she had not heard my story, but then her eyes changed, and she sat up and looked directly at me.

"My son saved your life," she said, "yet your Old One took his life."

People turned, searching around the fire for the Old One, who sat so quietly under her bear fur that she herself could have been a bear, a dead or sleeping bear. Then she stirred and pushed back the skin. Placing one knotted hand on her grandson Adibish's shoulder, she pulled herself up. Since morning she had changed, become even older, had shrivelled like a dry root.

People were so alarmed at her grey face and shaking body that they began to make soothing noises. Mother went to her, picked up the bearskin and wrapped it around her shoulders, coaxing her to sit down. "There, there," everyone was saying. "There, there." Even me, even Godith's father, Ebanthoo.

Father stood up. "It is Dogmen's evil, not ours—nor yours, Grandmother—all people know this," he said. But he was staring across at Adibish and Sabasut as if they were to blame.

Hebbosheth pushed my mother away. "Sit down, Washomish," she told my father, and he did.

"All people know. Then all people forget," she said. She studied each one of us, her fierce eyes moving from face to face around the circle.

"My name is Hebbosheth, daughter of Ozeru, wife first of Sosheet then of Odemen—once your shadowdancer, now a keeper of shadows, keeper of words, keeper of things we might forget."

This way she began the story I will tell you now, Dogman. It concerns your ancestors as well as mine.

While Hebbosheth spoke there was no sound, no cry of gull or child, no pounding waves, nothing but her rough voice laying down words before us like stones.

"My parents had five sons but only two daughters. My sister, Sanagi, was born first, then there were two boys before I came into the world and three other sons after me.

"My sister hunted with my father and brothers, and was like a wolf for braveness—still she was a pretty, laughing girl. Sanagi could make even me, a child who listened too much to Dogmen stories, see the world was a beautiful happy place, think it a safe place.

"Yes, even then there were Dogmen, even then we had moved into Evil Time. Dogmen would come into our forests to hunt animals, sometimes take people away, sometimes kill us outright, sometimes burn our mamateeks, leave men, women and children to freeze. Winter and summer our runners brought news of such things, but my father and brothers guarded our meotick well. When Dogmen were nearby we moved quickly— once my father killed two Dogmen who were shooting fire at my brother's canoe. In this way we escaped Dogman's evil for all the seasons of our childhood.

"Sanagi was almost a woman, waiting until her moon blood came so that she could marry Sosheet. He was of a different meotick, a young man she met each summer on the beach. Even I, who thought my sister should never leave our mamateek, could see they were well-matched, always laughing at things only they thought funny.

"But that summer, while she and three of our brothers were gathering birds' eggs on one of the islands out beyond the bay, they found a fishing net Dogmen had left hanging in trees. Thinking it a useful thing, they cut the net loose and took it with them. That night they were set upon by many Dogmen, who killed two of my brothers and dragged Sanagi into their boat. We were told this by my youngest brother, who lived long enough to return to this beach. Men from our meotick went to the island and brought back the two bodies, but the Dogmen and their boat had gone and there was no sign of my sister.

"Our mouths filled with sorrow. My mother cried out in her sleep and no one ever again laughed in our mamateek. Two winters passed, and the next summer I was promised to the man Sosheet, who was to have become Sanagi's husband.

"When fall came we married at the winter place of my husband's family, which was in a remote valley many days' journey from my parents. The mamateeks of my new family were set in a place where wind swept both down from the hills and across from the water. Sosheet was a kind man, but it was Sanagi he had wanted and I was not like her.

"Our son was in my belly when runners brought word that my sister had returned to our parents. The message said she had walked out of the forest pulling a Dogman's sled loaded with soft blankets, with axes and pots and beads and magical shining circles you could see your own face in. Sanagi seemed unharmed. She had been saved from the Dogmen who killed our brothers by another Dogman, who had fed her and cared for her for two circles of seasons.

"That Dogman, together with three others, returned Sanagi

to the forest, walking with her almost to the mamateeks of our family. Before leaving my sister, they told her to go quickly to her people. 'Go and tell them how we have fed you, clothed you, treated you as our daughter. They will rejoice in your return and in these gifts you bring. Do this and tell them our people wish to live peacefully with your people.' The Dogman who had been kind said this to my sister.

"Deep winter had already set in when we heard of Sanagi's return. I would have gone to her then but Sosheet said we could not travel to my father's meotick until the river ice broke.

"I longed to see my sister. It would not matter that I had married her husband, not even matter that his child was inside me—if she wished it the man could be her husband, the child her child. All would be made right when I saw her, heard her laugh.

"Each morning I went down to the frozen river and walked out onto the ice, willing the grey-white surface to change, to lighten into sparks of colour, to crack and sag, to become water. My sister's spirit guardian was Osepa the seagull, and one morning a cloud of white gulls flew low over the river, riding on air, a blizzard of wings swooping and circling just above my head. Then they swirled into the wind and vanished across the river. This was a sign that the water would soon open, that I would soon see my sister.

"My husband's people said that travelling to my sister was a dangerous and unnecessary thing, especially in springtime—a three-day paddle downriver through rafting ice, then a half-day trek inland to my father's meotick. But I persisted. In the end, since I was already fat and awkward, Sosheet's oldest brother, Yaseek, agreed to come with us.

"The ice was gone by then and the trip downriver was pleasant. On the fourth day we came ashore, left our canoe beside the river but took the paddle and bows and arrows. I had never come this way before. There was no travel line to follow and we spent the day pushing through tangled evergreen, tripping over rocks and twisted roots, floundering knee-deep in snow because this was a sunless place, so dark and silent I thought no man or animal had ever set foot on it.

"Long before we reached the winter place of my people, before we even saw our mamateeks, a terrible dread had come over me. There were no bird sounds, no animal noises, no smells of campfire—there was a smell, though. We caught the stink long before we came into the place of misery and death, before we saw the pieces of human bodies that animals had dragged about, moss already beginning to cover the white chewed bones of my people, green inside their skulls.

"'Do not touch anything!' Yaseek whispered. 'There are evil spirits all around us!' He went back to the edge of the forest. There he lit his pipe and stood watching my husband and me, calling out to us that we were walking through Dogmen's evil, that we must leave quickly.

"Still I thought someone might be alive, already I was moving towards my father's mamateek, picking my way through the decay.

"'This happened moons ago,' Sosheet was saying. 'Everything you see has frozen and melted.' He pointed at the scraps of coloured cloth, the bright beads and bits of smashed mirror that shone like stars from the slime of rotting seal and caribou meat.

"Yet he walked ahead of me. With the canoe paddle he lifted the caribou skin, then pushed aside the birchbark and tree trunks that were wedged against the opening of our mamateek. My husband put his head into the hole he'd made. In a heartbeat he pulled back. 'They are all dead—do not look, they are dead.'

"'I *will* look!' I was wild with grief and would have forced my way into the mamateek had Sosheet not held me back.

"'Look if you must, but do not go inside.' He was blocking my way, still holding the paddle across the opening, but I bent my body forward and looked.

"My family, all dead. Four bodies wrapped in caribou hide in a circle around the dead fire. My sister, Sanagi, my mother and our two brothers, placed in their own sleeping hollows. My poor father's body lay where he had fallen, while pushing tree trunks in place, trying to make fast the opening against the animals he knew would soon come.

"I saw nothing else. I fell forward, would have dropped down on my father's body but Sosheet caught me. He carried me back to the trees where Yaseek still waited.

"I lay on the ground and watched the two men pile dead boughs around the circle of mamateeks. They lit fires and then we turned away, pushing as fast as we could through trees and shrub towards the river. Behind us sap hissed and cracked, sparks leapt from treetop to treetop, Firewoman danced after us, cleaning the earth, licking at our heels."

Hebbosheth had not moved since she stood up, and now she began to sway, rocking back and forth. "All my people, all my father's people, all the husbands and wives, the babies and old people—all dead. Killed by the evil unseen spirits that Dogmen had hidden in their gifts.

"That night my first child was stillborn. The next winter Sosheet walked into a white blizzard and did not come back. I was alone—all my people, all my father's people . . ." She chanted over and over, caught in a net of words until my father went to her.

"That is the story, Grandmother—it is enough." He took the Old One's hand and led her to where Mother and I sat.

"It has happened before. Everything has happened before." Still standing, she searched the circle until she saw Godith's parents. "That is why we had to kill your son—Godith's death saved us from Dogman spirits!" She said this loudly and sat down. Then she pulled the bearskin around her so that no one could see her face.

Before anyone could gather their thoughts, my uncle stood and began to talk. Holding the long staff of Ash-wa-meet with its spray of eagle feathers tied to the tip, he seemed able to touch the stars. I thought he would say something I would remember forever—but he did not. He did not even look towards the Old One, or speak a word about her story, only told us that he and Sabasut would make a new song for Godith.

"Sabasut and I will begin the song this night as we take Godith's body to the hidden cave. It will be a hero's song, a song befitting one who saved his people, one who stood without fear before Keathut," he said.

When Adibish finished, he and the Shadowdancer Sabasut threw herbs into the fire. Sparks flew up and we were enclosed in the sweet smell of marshflowers. He then ordered the young men who had shot Godith to place their arrows in the flames.

My brother Ianamish, who had not shot Godith but had tried to, also went to the fire. The hunters set their arrows carefully upright, each one supporting the other like poles in a mamateek. Adibish and Sabasut stood in the circle beside the young men, the shadowdancers whispering words we could not hear. They all stood for a time inhaling the smoke. Then they turned away, and the rest of us stood and left the fire. We followed our shadowdancers to where four runners stood waist-deep in water, holding four canoes steady. My Uncle Adibish, still holding his staff, got into the canoe where Godith's body lay. Beside Godith was a small bundle that I knew must be our dead baby.

I tugged at Hebbosheth's tunic. "Godith will keep my sister company on the Ghost Path," I told her. I hope she heard my words, hope she knew I understood why she thought Godith had to die and that I'd forgiven her—but she gave me no sign.

Three other canoes held bodies of the dead from Sabasut's meotick and he stepped into one of those. Since no one but shadowdancers can go to the secret cavern, the runners lashed the two unmanned canoes onto the two in which our shadow-dancers sat. Adibish and Sabasut laid down their staffs and picked up paddles. The great antlers they wore on their heads made the men seem huge in the small boats, big as Old Caribou. Knowing we were protected by such powerful beings was a comfort.

We watched until the canoes disappeared into the darkness. Someone said, "Eenodsha"—which is a blessing—and we all went to our sleeping places. My father had again made a three-sided shelter for me and Hebbosheth but the others had not yet set up their summer tents. They went back into the dunes where they would roll skins around themselves and sleep in scooped-out hollows.

When everyone had left the beach, the Old One and I sat together in our shelter's opening, just as we had on the night she told me the bear story. This time she said nothing. We did not speak but sat thinking about the day, looking back at the place where Godith had fallen, where the arrows still burned, green sparks rising into the dark, drifting up to join Godith's star pictures.

XIII

The next morning at dawn I felt Hebbosheth's bony finger jabbing my shoulder. I roused myself to find her still sitting in the opening, still looking down the beach.

"Someone is lying on the beach," she said. "I have been watching for some time and think it is a dead person—but perhaps not."

I knelt and peered over her shoulder. In the greyish dawn I could see a dark shape, something long and motionless far down the curve of sand. "Perhaps a big fish or a small whale has washed ashore," I said. Whatever it was it looked harmless.

"It is a man," the Old One said. She told me to creep outside, to keep down and run back into the dunes. "It might be a Dogman, there might be others. Tell your father and brothers. Tell them to be careful. Even dead Dogmen are dangerous."

I crawled out beneath the loose caribou hide, ran bent-over across the sand towards where my people slept. The dread Hebbosheth had spoken of in her story ran with me. My Old One had found her family, all the people in her meotick dead.

It was what I expected, to find my parents, my brothers, all my relatives killed. Then I remembered Nonosabasut—he and his people would be dead too! In my mind I was already moaning over their bleeding bodies—when I came upon them, still alive, all sleeping except for my father who had heard a fox bark in the hills.

"It is a warning," he said. "One of our watchers is telling us that someone is walking towards this place—coming along the travel line between us and the next bay."

I was so happy to find them all alive that neither the body in the sand nor the creature coming towards us from the hills seemed important.

"Go back to the Old One," Father ordered when I told him what she and I had seen.

Instead I walked along behind as he quietly woke my two older brothers and three other men. I watched him whisper something to each of them, saw them fan out and disappear. My father then went down to the beach. Walking past the black fire where we had gathered the night before, he crossed the wet sand to the water's edge—and I followed.

The dead man on the beach was Sabasut the shadowdancer. Where one of his eyes should have been there was a hole. The hole went right through his head but it was washed clean of blood. Only sea water bubbled out—one eye weeping while the other stared up with the same certainty it had always held.

This dead thing is Nonosabasut's father! When the thought came I must have made some sound, because my father turned and roared at me to be off—and I ran.

When I told Hebbosheth who the dead man was, her body jerked as if an arrow had entered her. "If Sabasut is dead then so also is my grandson Adibish," she said. She crawled back inside our shelter, lay down and closed her eyes. She told me to pull the bearskin over her, to cover her face. I began to settle down by her, but she growled, "Go away! Leave me alone!"

Because the Old One had ever taken my father's side against Adibish, I had thought she did not love her oldest grandson. Kneeling beside her in the three-sided tent, I remembered that she had once patted stories into Adibish's head, had told him all the secrets she now told me. And I knew that despite all the bitter words that had passed between them she still loved Adibish as she now loved me—perhaps more than she loved me. Now I feel glad that love can endure such disagreements, then I felt nothing but jealousy.

I told her that my father had sent men out to search for his brother, Adibish. But she didn't stir, so I left her and went back to the dunes. Nonosabasut and his brother were not there—I saw only women and girls, my little brother, Kakula, and other boys his age. Someone had carried Sabasut up to where the sand was dry and covered him with a caribou skin. Two old men were sitting, one on either side of the body; they were talking about Osagana, the great shadowdancer who had been Sabasut's grandfather. Above their talk I could hear Ashei's wails rising from a huddle of women and girls gathered near the body. I could not see Doodebewshet but knew that Sabasut's wife too must be enclosed within the circle, and I wondered at her silence.

Mother was alone at the fire. She had set a small stone pot of water to boil and was stirring something in a birch-rind vessel hung above the fire. It smelled like rabbit and dried juniper berries. I was about to ask for some when she asked after the Old One. Then, before I could answer, she quickly asked if I had seen Ianamish and Longnon leave camp. I told her about the fox bark, about my father sending my brothers and other men back into the hills.

"Your father must be gone there also." She scooped a few dried leaves from the leather pouch around her neck.

I watched her closely; she had deliberately turned her back on the cluster of women, was rubbing leaves between her fingers, crumbling herbs into the boiling water. Using her sealskin mitts, she carefully lifted the little pot and poured some of the hot tea into a birch cup.

"Take this to Hebbosheth, and bring me some moss—any moss you can find." She was thinking of something else, not really seeing me.

"The Old One wants to be alone." I held the tea, sniffing it, trying to remember when I had last eaten.

"Drink it yourself, then, and when you are finished, go and find the moss—but stay near the beach, your father has taken his spear."

Despite Sabasut lying dead within sight of us it seemed like any other morning—Mother not really hearing me, giving me orders, telling me to take food to the Old One, to take care of my brother, to bring moss back to our tent. She had been bleeding ever since the dead baby came, packing dry moss into a sling between her legs. The bleeding made her cross and I wished it would stop.

"You know there is no moss on beaches," I said. Then, because I had been rude, I bent towards her and murmured, "I am sorry, Mother."

"Your father did not speak to me before leaving. He left our sleeping place and went to Doodebewshet," she said. Her face crumpled, but I could not tell if she was angry or about to weep.

"I am sorry, Mother," I said again, although I did not truly understand why she was upset.

"Finish the tea—and here." She passed me a bowl of rabbit stew. "When you have eaten, go over there." She waved towards the marshland beyond the dunes. "Yesterday we walked through moss—bring me back some."

Mischievous spirits arrange the small events of our lives. This is something the Old One often spoke of, how small things ripple out into bigger things, become waves that can sweep life away. If Mother had not been bleeding . . . if I had not been sent to find moss . . . if I had gathered the moss quickly and taken it back to the beach instead of falling asleep . . .

In the marsh there was no moss of the kind my mother needed. I had known there would not be. The mossy place she remembered was in the forest, a shining green bowl surrounded by dry pine spills, then by tall trees. Yesterday, Demasduit, Kasathi and I, along with other children, had pulled off our moccasins and stepped into the moss, our feet sinking into green that was cool as water and soft as down. We lay in the moss and danced in it until our parents called out that Aich-mud-yim would get us if we did not follow more closely.

The marshland was nearby—Hebbosheth and I often gathered plants there. I knew the place well and made my way across without getting my feet wet, but the mossy circle where my friends and I had danced was half a day's walk in the forest. On this day of bad omens I was afraid to go that far into woods; instead I wandered along the edge of the marsh where the birch and balsam did not grow so close together.

Such a long time it seemed since we'd walked out from these trees, crossed the marshland and climbed up the sand dunes. Only yesterday, with Godith alive and waiting for us and

Sabasut walking beside his wife—everyone happy to be back on the holy beach.

Because sand dunes were now between me and the ocean, this boggy place was warmer than the beach. At its edge I sat down with my back against a tree and watched small birds cross and recross the marshland. The birds flew low over bright budding clumps of rose and meadowsweet, over alder and the small willow that has spring twigs of pale yellow and red and furry grey buds children love. I could see rosemary too and shining laurel, leatherleaf and teabush, and many ferns and rushes whose names Hebbosheth had not yet taught me.

I had slept little the night before, had been wakened at dawn and had eaten my mother's warm stew. I thought of going in search of a good piece of bark I could mark a picture on. But as the sun moved up the sky, the scent of buds and blossoms mixed with the pleasant pungent smell of warming marsh water and I fell asleep.

I must have slept for a long time. I woke quickly, knowing there had been some sound where now there was silence. I did not move but lay still, looking out at the marsh, and saw that the light had changed, the birds gone. Then the sound broke behind me, a rasping like ice moving downriver, but a smaller, more contained sound—one I had never before heard.

Then came my father's voice. "Stop it!" he said, then, less harshly, "Such grief is unseemly in a man—you must stop before we go to the beach."

The wrenching, half-strangled sound continued. After many heartbeats I knew it was a man crying—and I knew who the man was.

"Tell me what happened," my father said. They were so near I could smell his pipe. I heard him say, "Here," and knew he was passing the pipe to his brother. It was some time before the crying ended and then there was a long silence.

"Sabasut is dead," my uncle said.

"Yes, I know. I have told you—the sea brought his body in." I could tell from my father's voice that he had repeated this many times already.

"I loved him."

"Yes."

Though I could not see them, I knew my father would be standing, would be holding something in his hands—a twig or stone or the white bone he carried in his pouch along with the dried leaves he smoked. I had seen him stand like this many times, reasoning with my brothers, smoothing the bone between his fingers, trying to control his anger.

"You hated Sabasut," my uncle said.

"Men should not be so close to men."

"You considered us evil."

"Mistaken," my father said. "When you were still boys, you and Sabasut were deceived by that old wolf Osagana."

"Osagana was a great shaman—he will be waiting for Sabasut now . . ." Adibish made a gulping, guttural sound as if he was about to weep again.

My father cut him off. "Tell me what happened last night! Tell me now before you have to tell the others."

"It was the same as all other journeys we have made to the holy cave. The soft rumble of a calm sea, the smooth glide into darkness, the spray of light as our paddles lifted water, the wrapped silent bodies laid near our feet, our own silence—the feeling of contentment, the happiness of moving towards that holy place is like nothing you have ever known."

"Where is the holy place?"

"Beyond the headland that is like a whale—a place only shadowdancers can enter."

"Tell me."

"You must never speak of this," Adibish said, and waited.

My father said nothing, yet after a time Adibish continued. "At the whale headland we turn towards where the moon rises, to where waves slam against cliffs high as the moon, where canoes would be smashed to bits if we brought them near shore." From his voice I could tell Adibish was reliving the story, as Hebbosheth says a good storyteller must.

"But you do go near shore."

"There is a place where the air changes, sound changes, where the lift and glide of water below my canoe feels different. It is connected with the season, the moon, with the pull and push of tides. When all these things are right there is a path in the water. When the long stave of Ash-wa-meet is held out over its bow, when secret words are spoken, the canoe will find this path.

"That is the dangerous time. Although your canoe is pointed into the cliff's face, although no break in the rock can be seen, the shadowdancer must lay his paddle down, must trust the ocean, trust Ash-wa-meet and all good spirits to pull him and his dead along that narrow water-path and into the holy cave.

"This cave is not a round hollow worn into the cliff by water. It is a great gouge, as if some underwater spirit had pulled a spear from the ocean, gashing upward through rock as we would cut through rabbit hide. The cave is only one canoe wide at the waterline. There is no light. We move forward as if swallowed into the black gut of the mountain.

"Only when the canoe nudges against the cliff and can go no farther are shadowdancers permitted to spark flint and make rushlight. It is then we see how the mountain walls lean inward, slowly narrowing, rising so high that even holding the tapers above our heads we cannot see their meeting point.

"All the way up these cliffs are ridges of rock—shelves on which generations of our people lie. Only at this season, in this moon, in this tide-time can these ledges be reached. Even then it is difficult for they are high above our canoes. One shadow-dancer must climb the rock face, feeling with toe and fingers for familiar crevices. It takes all the strength of the one above and the one below to lift bodies from the canoe up and onto the stone shelves.

"Last night we had ten dead ones with us. To raise them and place them well back on the dry shelves took a long time. When it was done Sabasut and I said the words that encourage our dead to step quickly onto the Ghost Path. We called out each one's name, gave each a message to take to our Ancestors. Before leaving we asked their spirit guardians to guide our people safely to Perfect Time.

"I had never been so long in the holy cave. The tide was already turning when we finished. By the time we reach the opening it was running so fast that our canoes were spewed out into deep ocean. A misty grey dawn was coming on. Because they were now empty, the canoes tied to ours tipped and rolled. Tide and wave swept us straight out, past the whale headland, almost out to the bird islands. It took all the skill Sabasut and I possessed to keep from being thrown into the water. We had just managed to right ourselves when we heard Dogman muskets.

"Only then did we see their boat. It was at anchor beside the high cliffs of the largest island.

"These were the ones Dogmen call eggers, but it is birds they are after—boatloads of birds. Many Dogmen were standing along the topside of the big boat. They were shooting into the island, firing their muskets into the mass of nesting seabirds that cover the cliff face. Clouds of birds rose up, screeching, flying off. Dead and wounded auks fell onto the boat, into the sea. Swarms of gulls, gannets, puffins, turrs, a host of maddened birds, wheeled about trying to defend their nests, diving straight into Dogmen guns.

"The Dogman who saw us first shouted. Then they all turned and began shooting down at us. They were laughing.

"The fire must have hit Sabasut at once. He did not even cry out. My canoe was hit, water coming in. All four canoes were rocking and spinning. I could not see Sabasut and thought he could have gone into the water. I lay down and rolled my canoe, holding onto the bracing and treading water, but I could not see Sabasut anywhere. I managed to grab the hide strip that was tied to the canoe I thought was Sabasut's, and I pulled it along behind."

I tell you the story straight, Dogman, but Adibish did not tell it straight. Many times he stopped, once he began to whimper like a child and once he got up and walked a little distance from my father. I could hear him talking to Sabasut, as if he were still alive, promising his friend that he would take his body out to the holy cave.

When Adibish got this far in his story he began talking fast, urgently explaining to my father the difference between good Dogmen and evil Dogmen. He told about a good Dogman—the one he and Sabasut had met when they were boys, the one they had once guided in-country.

"Stop speaking!" my father snapped.

There was a long silence. Finally Adibish said, "That was all, that is all."

"How did you get where I found you?"

"I stayed in the water a long time, swimming under my upturned canoe. When the Dogmen stopped laughing and shooting they went back to slaughtering birds, and I swam away. My canoe sank but I kept pulling the other, hoping that Sabasut might still be in it, yet knowing it was riding too high to be carrying a body. When I thought it safe I surfaced and looked—and the canoe was empty. The paddle was gone but I managed to come ashore on a small pebbled beach not far from where you found me."

"I have something to tell you now, Adibish." My father's anger was still building and I wondered if Adibish knew that whenever my father used those words he always had an unpleasant thing to say.

"I do not need your telling, Washomish," Adibish said. My father's anger did not seem to frighten him as it did me.

"I think you do. I think you must." I could hear the gust of rage that had overtaken my father—and something deeper, a coldness that made me shiver and wrap my arms around my body.

"Sabasut is dead. Everyone on the beach thinks Adibish is dead also. Your wife and daughter weep. Our grandmother already lies with her head covered. No one would think it strange if you did not come back."

"You—you want me dead? You think to kill me!" Adibish sounded more astonished than afraid.

"I do not wish to kill you. But I will if you do not listen."

"Only listen?"

"You must agree to do what I say."

"And what is that, my brother?"

"From this day onward you will not speak of the great love between you and Sabasut, and there will be no more talk of the goodness of Dogmen. This very moon we will call the Circle together, make a plan to defend our hunting grounds, defend our salmon rivers, defend this beach, defend the living and defend the holy places where our dead lie. From this day onward the People must kill any Dogmen who come near our mamateeks."

"You talk like a savage—like one who has never heard the stories of Ash-wa-meet, who knows no great spirits."

"Great spirits have told us that the Euano are descendants of Nakhani the evil wolf spirit," my father said.

"Euano are like us, a mixture of evil and good. Let me tell you the story of a good Dogman—a Dogman who spared my life and the life of Sabasut when we were only boys . . ."

"I need no such story—will hear no such story!" Father interrupted him and loudly repeated the words he had already spoken. "From this day onward we will kill any Dogmen who come near us."

"That is called war," Adibish said.

"It may be."

"We are few, they are many. They have muskets, we have arrows."

"We have trackers and runners—young men who can live forever off the land, who know every hill and river, every cave, cove and beach on the Great Island. We have hunters who kill with every arrow. In one season we could kill every Dogman in Baetha. Even now we can do this. Soon it will be too late!"

"And then more will come—always more will come."

"This time we will not let them ashore."

"We cannot guard every bay, every beach . . ."

"We can try."

"Washomish, my brother, you know we have been told from Old Time never to kill creatures that walk upright like ourselves . . ."

"They kill us . . ."

Their voices became low, fading as daylight faded. I could not hear many words, but when Hebbosheth's name was spoken I cupped my ear and listened hard. Adibish was telling my father that he would agree to the Old One becoming our shadow-dancer again.

"Our grandmother is too old, she is not well. No, Adibish, you must continue as our shadowdancer."

"Why? Who will respect a shadowdancer without power?"

"You will have power in all that does not concern Dogmen."

"And if I refuse?"

"The dead have no power," my father said.

"You cannot believe that!"

"I do. I have seen the dead. This morning I looked into the face of your friend Sabasut, water washing through his skull, all his stories, all his mighty thoughts, all his power washed out through one little hole."

"I too have seen the dead. I have talked with the dead, I have talked even with Sabasut. His wound is healed, already his feet are on the Ghost Path. This day Sabasut will meet our ancestors in Perfect Time—he will ask them to protect us."

"I hope he learns wisdom in Perfect Time." Father sighed, and I could tell the worst of his fury had passed; now there was only sadness and grim resolve. "The old ways are gone, Adibish. If we hold back from killing others who walk upright, our own people are going to die—every one of us," my father said. Then he walked out of the woods.

He walked straight towards me, was almost on me before he stopped, staring down with such a look of astonishment that I might have laughed if I had not been so afraid.

Adibish came behind. He too stopped. For a heartbeat my

father and uncle looked very much alike, two bewildered faces peering down at me through the dim twilight.

"I was asleep," I said.

Father knew I was lying. He reached down and ungently pulled me to my feet.

"Shanawdithit means Listening One," I said, "my Old One told me so."

"Frighten the Listening One into silence," my father told his brother. He was almost smiling, studying me in a thoughtful way as if he had never seen me before.

Adibish bent forward and stared into my face. I had never been this close to my uncle, never in all my life spoken to him. This was not the great shadowdancer who had danced around our fire the night before; his tunic was dirty and torn, his face grey, a cut along his cheek was bleeding, the ochre paint was gone from his skin. His head was bare—his antlers must have been lost in the sea—and his long hair stank like rotting seaweed.

I stared back at him. This person could say nothing that would frighten me.

Adibish reached out and placed his hand on my head. "Do you love the Old One?" he asked quietly.

The hand on my head felt heavy, a weight pushing me into the earth, but I tried to hold my chin up, keep looking into his eyes. They were like Demasduit's eyes—dark and unknowable as bog water. My uncle repeated the question, saying the Old One's name as if I might not understand. "Do you love Hebbosheth?"

I nodded.

"Then you will never tell her what has been said here, never speak of this to anyone." Adibish straightened, his body unfolding against the rising moon. I could no longer see his eyes, only the black outline of him towering over me—his broad shoulders, his head, and above his head the great upward curving antlers of Old Caribou that had not been there before.

Now I was afraid. Adibish and my father turned away from me and walked silently across the marsh. I ran behind; twigs scraped my legs and the bog squished under my feet, unseen birds fluttered as I pushed through tangles of bush. The men stopped only when they came out on the dunes above the beach. I caught up then and stood quietly beside my father and uncle, looking down on our camp.

Tonight there was no fire and no noise. By the moon's light we could see a confusion of shadows moving this way and that. A straggly group of children were coming towards us, half running across the sand; behind them adults were hastily rolling and tying their belongings, women gathering up pots, food and babies. I could see Nonosabasut down by the water where men were pulling in our remaining canoes, hoisting them onto their shoulders. And there, rising from the moon-drenched sea, was the immense blackness of Aich-mud-yim—that monster I had dreaded through all my childhood.

"Euano!"

Adibish whispered, "Yes," and we stood, three of us staring at the huge thing crouching in the open bay, just beyond our holy beach.

Demasduit was the first to reach us. She did not notice me but ran to Adibish, sobbing, "Father!" I had never before seen her cry. I watched as she flung herself against him. "You're alive! You're alive! Father, the Dogmen are here!"

"You are safe now, safe." Adibish patted her head absently. "Go back to your mother." My cousin hesitated, then returned to Waunathoake.

Our shadowdancer's antlers had again vanished but he no longer looked exhausted. "Here they are, then," he said, speaking in an undertone only my father and I, standing so close, could hear. "Here, Washomish, are the Euano you wish to make war with."

"Is this the same boat the men shot at you from?" Father asked.

"The same—but the water is shallow here, that boat cannot get in to this beach."

"Why then are they here?"

"Perhaps they have just come into the bay for the night and will return to the bird islands at dawn, or perhaps they want to get fresh water, to catch fish, or to kill birds back in the marshlands . . ."

"Or to kill us. But how will they get ashore?" It was unlike Father to ask a question of his brother or to accept his words so humbly.

"They have small boats inside this big one, boats the size of our canoes but not as seaworthy. I have seen them—heavy, slow things made of thick wood."

All the people were now coming up into the dunes with their belongings, gathering around Adibish and my father, asking questions, telling how they had been waiting, hoping the shadowdancer was alive—knowing if he was, Washomish would find him and return with him to the beach. They were all glad, I think, to see my uncle safe, but so anxious to leave that they could think of nothing else.

Adibish neither answered the people nor made any move to calm them. He and my father continued to look out at the evil monster in our cove. After a time people stopped talking, the women dropped their bundles and settled like geese a little distance from the silent men.

Mother's face had brightened when she saw Father but she did not speak to him, only took my brother Kakula's hand and went to sit with the other women. Some women were carrying babies and toddlers; Doodebewshet was holding onto Ashei so tightly that I wondered how the girl's arm could stand the grip. Adibish's wife, Waunathoake, who had not gone near her husband to welcome him, sat between Demasduit and Gowet, the girl-woman who was to marry my brother Ianamish.

Nonosabasut and Tomasuth brought their father's body, now wrapped in caribou skin, up from the beach, and the old men I'd seen that morning sat down again on either side of the dead shadowdancer. His sons stood nearby, waiting to pick up the sling on which Sabasut's body lay. Other men and older boys all stood around Adibish and my father, waiting to be told what to do. I could see my father counting, checking on my older brothers and on the men he'd sent to search the hills. They were all there, together with Sabasut's people—all our watchers and runners had come to the beach when they saw the boat turn towards shore.

"Let us sit and think about this thing," Adibish said.

There was a ripple of sound, not quite a protest, then we all sat and were silent. No one told me to go over with the women and girls, so I sat near the men. When our shadowdancer finally spoke he repeated to everyone what he had already told my father about how the eggers had killed Sabasut. He did not speak of the love he felt for the other shadowdancer but he did say that we must leave the beach in case the Dogmen came ashore.

"But they will come . . ." my brother Ianamish said. It was not a question.

"Not until morning, I think. It would be dangerous to bring their little boats in at night," Adibish said.

"We have the night, then, to leave, to get away . . ." There was some muttering, then a man from Sabasut's meotick said softly, "Unless—unless there is another thing we can do?"

"There is another thing we can do." Father's answer was as quiet as the man's question had been. "We can destroy the Dogman boat."

He paused. No one spoke and he continued. "This is what we should do—what we must do. I am not alone in this, it is a plan told to our ancestors by Firewoman, a plan Hebbosheth spoke of to me long ago." He looked around for her support. "Where is she?"

"Nodurra! Where is she, where is the Old One?" my father called to Mother, but she too was looking, shaking her head. Everyone began looking about, standing, turning this way and that. But my Old One was not there, not safe in the dunes with the rest of us—even I had not missed her.

"She must still be asleep," I said. Far down on the opposite end of the crescent beach I could see the dark hump of our sleeping shelter. No one had gone to it, no one had wakened Hebbosheth to tell her of the danger.

"She wished to be alone," I said. It shamed me to know I had forgotten about her. She would not have forgotten me.

My older brothers were gone before I finished the words, racing along the circle of beach, keeping well back, flickering like striped birds through waist-high grass at the sand's edge. They disappeared into the shelter.

The dead weigh heavy. We saw, long before Ianamish and Longnon reached us, that the skin they carried contained nothing alive. A moan, soft as breath, swept the cluster of people when my brothers laid the Old One down in front of her grandsons.

My father leaned forward, carefully folded the bearskin back from her face. "We are here, Grandmother," he said, just as he had the day before.

He was weeping, as was I, as were many others.

Like the trees, like the hills or the caribou, Hebbosheth had been with us longer than anyone could remember. She had helped bring people into the world, helped others out of it. In her skull were the memories of many ancestors. I thought of the things she had promised to tell me, the dreams and stories, the names and memories, all that knowledge still inside her dead skull. Could so much truly be lost, be gone forever? I wanted to return to last night, to those wasted hours when we had not spoken. It did not seem a big thing, or even a strange one to turn back time—she had told me many stranger things.

Remembering the antlers that had appeared above his head, I screamed at Adibish, "Make her alive! Make my Old One alive again!"

He did not even look at me. He was speaking in a low voice to my father. "There are now two who must be taken to the holy cave."

"You are mad!"

"I am taking Sabasut there—this I have promised him. I will take our Old One also."

"Such a thing is now too dangerous. We will take the dead ones in-country with us," I heard Father say. And then Ianamish picked me up, carried me over and set me down among the women.

I began to ask Mother something, but she patted my arm, said, "Be still," put Kakula into my lap and went over to kneel opposite my father beside the Old One. "We must rub oil into her skin, paint her with ochre and wrap her." My mother spoke clearly, looking to both my father and Adibish, but the men did not look at her.

They were still talking to each other, quarrelling again, I thought, yet closer to each other than I had ever seen them. The quiet argument continued and little by little my people's whispering stopped, and even the babies became still. We were all watching Adibish and my father, straining to hear what they were saying.

The dark sea, the darker outline of the Dogman boat, the empty beach below, and us crouching in the dunes amid scattered belongings, the two men sitting beside the old woman, her dead face strangely peaceful and pale under the cold moon—all this seemed unreal, like a half-forgotten dream or a half-told story. Even my mother, the only one of us who could hear what the brothers were saying, my mother quietly kneeling beside the body—even she seemed a stranger.

The men stopped talking. Then I saw Father reach across the Old One's body and for just a moment take my mother's hand in his. I hold the gesture dear, a sign that there was love between those two.

Adibish stood and told us that we must leave the beach as soon as the Old One's body was made ready to walk the Ghost Path. He nodded at Auntie Santu and she came with many other women to help Mother. They carried the Old One farther back down into a hollow in the dunes. Our shadowdancer was still speaking, but I heard no more of what he said because I pushed Kakula off my lap and followed the women, keeping behind in case they might send me away.

The women lay Hebbosheth down and began digging into their pouches, unfolding eel-skin packets of herbs and ochre, mixing it with oil to make salves. I went and sat beside my Old

One. I took her leather pouch from around her neck and hung it around my own, pushing it inside my tunic beside the bag of coloured stones I already carried. Then I lowered my head to her breast and asked her forgiveness. I placed one of her knotted hands on my skull and held it there with my hand. I wished that something from her head would come into mine. But that did not happen. When Mother saw me she made a clicking noise with her tongue but did not tell me to go back with the children.

The women let me rub oil into the Old One's hands and feet, let me comb her hair, place her smallest scraper between her hands and arrange the bear claw that was her amulet so that it hung nicely around her neck. Then we folded a soft caribou skin around her, tied it and placed her on a carrying hide. All of us together lifted the hide, carried her body back and placed it down beside the body of Sabasut. Without a word, Adibish and Nonosabasut, together with two other men, picked up the bound bodies and moved away from the rest of us.

Father told the young boys and girls to gather together. We must leave the beach, he said, along with all the mothers of babies or children too small to go alone. My mother ignored this and put Kakula in my care. Doodebewshet and her daughter, Ashei, came with us, of course, and poor Godith's mother, Mishatut, and her husband, Ebanthoo, also because she would not release his hand. All the woman with babies inside them came, including Gowet who had Ianamish's baby inside her, these and a few old people—all the weak and helpless ones my father sent to a safer place.

"We will walk back across the marshland and into the forest as far as . . ." The old man who must have been told to pass along Father's instructions stopped—he did not seem to know how far we should go.

My friend Kasathi was the one who said, "As far as the place with green moss—we can sleep there."

The man nodded. "Take your sleeping skins and any small bundle you can carry and follow me. We will be very quiet and stay close together." He told us that our parents would catch up to us in the morning.

My brother Kakula and other small children were whimpering, afraid to cry out loud. Before we went down into the first hollow I looked back over my shoulder at the others. They stood as still as animals, men and older boys, our mothers and fathers, the women without babies—every one of them staring after us. I was overtaken with a terrible sadness and the wish to stay behind with my parents. But I took Kakula's hand and left with the weak and useless ones to cross the marshland and go into the woods.

XIV

How hard it is, Dogman, to tell a story straight. Whose story will I tell now? Not mine, for I was not there. Will I tell my brother's story? My mother's? My uncle the shadowdancer's story? Or the story Nonosabasut told his mother years later? Bits of each perhaps—although the stories of that night all follow different paths, they all lead to the same ending.

Our shadowdancer had only one thought that night: to take Hebbosheth and Sabasut to the holy cave. His plan was to carry their bodies over the hills to the little pebbled beach where he'd come ashore earlier that day, where he'd hidden the canoe. But he would need three other men to help carry the bodies back to that place.

"To do this you will take four able men from among us. Our Old One would think it foolish to put the living in danger to make ceremony for the dead," Father told him, naming other holy places where we could bury Hebbosheth and Sabasut.

But Adibish would hear of nothing else. He insisted that he was going to the sea cave even if no one went with him.

Nonosabasut spoke up then, said he wished to go with his father's body to the holy place. "Taking one canoe out to the cave should not be dangerous since the Dogmen's boat now rests just beyond our beach."

My brother Longnon told us later that our father only permitted Adibish to return to the cave because the boy Nonosabasut spoke so confidently and with such respect to his elders.

Of the four needed to carry Hebbosheth and Sabasut to the pebbled beach, only Adibish and Nonosabasut would go out to the sea cave. Many seasons passed before we saw the meaning in this—that even then Sabasut's son was being taken into the secrets of shadowdancers. The other two men would wait—if Adibish and Nonosabasut had not returned at dawn the waiting ones would leave. They would not come back to this beach. Instead, following old travel lines they would catch up with those already on their way in-country.

Before leaving Adibish promised his people that he would rejoin them before two sunsets. He called on Ash-wa-meet for protection. And then, according to my brother Longnon, our shadowdancer said that until his return both the people of his meotick and those of the meotick of Sabasut were under Father's direction.

The people still remaining in the sand dunes included my parents and my older brothers, Ianamish and Longnon, my mother's sister, Santu, with her son Manus, and the young woman Amet. Nonosabasut's brother, Tomasuth, was there and my friend Kasathi's brother, who was called Newin, as well as other men and big boys and some strong women. They had four canoes, two that were from our meotick and two from the meotick that had been led by Sabasut.

Only after Adibish and the others had picked up the slings on which the bodies lay and walked away did my father ask those remaining people to come into a tight circle. Then he told them what must be done. My father did not give reasons, did not ask permission. He quietly explained how they were to attack the ship, repeating the plan our Old One had presented to Osagana long before I was born.

Despite all Adibish was to say later, I always believed this was part of some agreement made between him and my father earlier that night.

Those on the beach did not argue. People were thankful to be given directions, thankful their children had been sent into the forest, even thankful that the moon had gone behind clouds, though it meant they had to find and make weapons in darkness.

The men all had bows and arrows and the boys had good sling-sticks hanging from their belts. These are used in games and could fling a heavy rock long distances. In addition to the sling-sticks, people took all the small baskets and nets they could find from their bundles. They filled these containers with dry grass soaked in seal oil, then pushed in a few stones for weight. They tied the bags of grass with thongs of caribou hide, leaving the ends long so the things could be whirled overhead and thrown. Following Father's instructions, they put arrows and spears into the four canoes and into each canoe they placed one small seal-oil lamp already burning.

My father explained that they must move silently, bring the canoes in tight alongside the Dogman ship, two canoes on each side, he said. They were to attack on signal, shoot arrows into any Dogmen who appeared, send burning catapults right into the big boat. Our fire would catch the folded canvas and ship's ropes. Even the small wooden boats Dogmen needed for coming ashore would be burnt. When our people saw fire on the Dogman boat they must quickly paddle away, return to the beach. Only then would they begin walking in-country. By dawn no trace of the People would remain on the white beach.

When all was ready, each person drew a piece of grass from my father's hand. This was to show who would go in the canoes and who would wait on the beach. My father let the men draw as well as the women and boys. Three men, three boys and two of the women stayed behind—my mother was one of these. She tried to change places with a woman in my father's canoe but he forbid it. "The grass has chosen," Father said, and so she was left.

"Helping the wounded ones was to be our job. We were to stop bleeding, and to carry them in-country, alive or dead. If none returned we would leave that place empty-handed, become witnesses to what had happened, charged with telling the story," Mother, the most unskilled teller of stories among our people, would tell us later.

At the edge of the water they all paused to ask for guidance from Ash-wa-meet and Crow, and especially from Firewoman whose plan this was. My father reminded these good spirits that for countless circles of time the People had not touched Dogmen's belongings or used Dogman tools, yet still we were being killed by Dogmen, going hungry because of Dogmen, having our holy places ransacked, our caribou fences destroyed. He told the good spirits how the Dogmen in this boat had spitefully killed the Great Shadowdancer Sabasut and tried to kill our own Shadowdancer Adibish.

Longnon, who lived through that night, later said our father spoke so powerfully that people would have followed him anywhere. My brother wondered that Hebbosheth had not chosen Father to be our shadowdancer instead of Adibish.

"We had four canoes, each with four people, some of them women and older boys," Longnon told me. "Father made sure there were two strong men in each canoe—Ianamish and I were together.

"We pushed off so quietly that not a gull took flight. The women began to whisper the names of every one of our people who had died because of Dogmen. The dead were with us that night, all around us. I could feel their spirits, the spirits of ancestors like salt on my lips."

Longnon remembered how his paddle folded into the liquid blackness, the soft murmur of names, remembered glancing back and grinning at Ianamish who had the job of holding the seal lamp steady, keeping the flame out of sight.

"Then the Dogman boat loomed above us, a great blackness lodged in the ocean," my brother said. "As we came near I thought of it burning into the water, thought of our arrows flying, of Dogmen drowning, the sea turning red. I had no fear—it did not matter if this killing was evil, did not matter if I died—I was glad that this time we were the ones bringing death."

Mother said that after the canoes slipped away there was a time of waiting. "A time as long as winter while we sat close to the water, squinting into darkness, seeing nothing."

Then fire appeared, blazing a line in the sky above the ship, racing along ropes, catching the oil-soaked sails—the dark sea brightening into a sudden burnished sunset.

"Come back," she was whispering. "Hurry, Washomish! Come back! Bring our sons back!" Those with Mother began jumping up and down, giving thanks to Firewoman. They could see the canoes that were landward of the big boat—both seemed to be drifting, floating like leaves above a shimmer of orange heat.

Even those on the beach could feel heat. They were shouting, "Turn away!" and "Come back!" Then there was a loud evil noise, a stink and bellowing black smoke that covered the canoes they'd been watching.

Of the eight people in these canoes, only my brother Longnon lived.

He told us what happened. "As Father instructed, we quickly threw our burning slings up into the ship. They were gone in moments—every one of them, right into the Dogman ship. We could see fire, sooty bits of canvas falling on us. Ianamish was standing, so were two men in the other canoe, shooting arrows up at Dogman who were trying to haul buckets of water out of the sea.

"Our canoes were close together; we were back-paddling, moving quickly away from the burning. Then a Dogman threw something down at us. I saw it coming—a thing big as a man's head with fire-hair streaming out behind. I shouted, 'Jump!' dropped my paddle and was underwater before the fireball hit our canoe. I came up in foul smoke, floundering and choking in the water, only guessing which way the beach was."

The two canoes that could not be seen from the beach had also used all their burning catapults. But Father and the people with him could see no fires on that side of the Dogman boat. And so they stayed and shot arrows up at Dogmen, who shot back, their long guns pointing straight down at the canoes.

Even when a shot killed the boy standing next to him and went into my father's head he stayed, his canoe bobbing just below the Dogmen muskets. Father did not give the order to pull back until the canoes began to sink. With the help of people on the beach, who splashed out and pulled them in, both boats managed to get to shore. By then a woman in my father's canoe was dead also—the woman Mother had tried to change places with—and a woman in the other canoe was badly wounded.

"My oldest son, Ianamish, and all the people who died with him were gone. One of these was Amet, the young woman who had married your cousin Manus just two seasons before," Mother told us. "People swam out and dived, searching for bodies even under the Dogmen's fire, but there was nothing. Seven bodies gone, blown away." She never spoke of this terrible thing without weeping, asking again and again, "How can flesh and bone disappear?" For her the loss of Ianamish's body was worse even than his death. Every sunrise for the rest of her life our mother would perform rituals to ease her son's way along the Ghost Path.

Everyone on the beach was close kin to someone who had been killed but there was no time for grief. Canoes were pulled in and filled with whatever belongings remained, the dead woman and boy were quickly wrapped and laid in slings, my father and the wounded woman were tended to. To stop the woman's bleeding they packed moss around her wound and tied it in place, but nothing could stop the bleeding from Father's head.

My father was still calm. He ordered Longnon and Kasathi's brother Newin to spend what was left of the night in the dunes above the beach. Told everyone else they must leave at once, go back through the marsh and into the forest, follow the travel lines of those who had gone ahead.

Mother was holding my father in a sitting position. She was drenched in his blood, but she said his voice was still strong. "You two will keep watch from the dunes until sunrise—be ready to shoot any Dogmen who try to come ashore in their little boats," he told Longnon and Newin. "At sunrise make sure there is no sight of us in this place. Only then can you turn away and begin the trek in-country."

Out in the bay the evil ship was still afloat. There was no fire now, just smoke and a terrible stench my mother thought was burning feathers. She told us that Father looked out towards the black hulk, and with great pride said, "I killed Dogmen tonight." She said he smiled.

These were the last sane words he ever spoke. Though, Mother thought even they were not sane and never forgave him the smile.

Of the ten and six people who went out in our canoes, nine were dead, one of them the brother I loved best, one the happy young woman who had married Manus when Firewoman danced. We never knew if any Dogmen died that night. I hope some did.

In the last winter of my life, a mad old Dogman stopped me on the steps of a church in St. John's—that cold grey place Cormack often took me into. The Dogman leaned close and pointed his finger in my face. "A ship I captained once were attacked by savages like her there. But we got even," he said. His eyes shone with pleasure to be telling his story to a savage. "Two days after, we backed a herd of 'em onto a point of land— we had nar cannon but we killed 'em with small shot—men, women and pups, we put a end to every one."

Ecshamut's meotick vanished after the boat burning, we never saw one of his people again. Standing outside that dismal church I remembered this and knew this Dogman had killed them—slaughtered a whole meotick of people who had no part in the attack on his boat. When I spat in the killer's face, Cormack thought me unmannerly.

When we children left the beach that night, walking across the fragrant marshland and into the deep forest, we did not know it was the last time any of us would see that holy place. I was hungry and tired but it was a dry, windless night and not unpleasant. I did not think about my parents and brothers left behind on the beach, did not think of Adibish and Nonosabasut walking along the coast path, did not even grieve for my dead Old One, even now on her journey to the holy cavern. I thought of nothing except myself—Shanawdithit moving quietly beneath tall trees, coolness brushing my face and arms, leaves and moss under my feet, my strong young body moving towards a safe sleeping place. I was alone inside myself, alone as the Great Traveller Miaoth when he sailed around Baetha.

After a time I saw that my brother Kakula was stumbling with tiredness, so I put him in my sleeping skin and Demasduit, Kasathi and I carried him between us. Everyone must have been tired but the only one to whine was Ashei. Doodebewshet stopped walking and ordered the old men to carry her daughter. The men ignored her but one of them scolded Ashei, told her that if she did not hush he would call Nakhani the evil wolf spirit.

We had almost reached the mossy place when four men stepped out of the shadows. Before anyone could make a sound, we saw they were of the People—watchers guarding Ecshamut's meotick. The men led us to where their families were sleeping, the very place we were walking towards. Ecshamut's meotick had thought to reach the beach the next morning. Hearing our story they knew they too must turn inland, away from summer food and the seal oil we would need so badly next winter. Seeing the Shadowdancer Ecshamut and his people I remembered that it was still springtime—other meoticks were still walking towards the sea.

Before sleeping I thought of all that had happened. It seemed impossible that we had spent just one night on the seal beach. But it was true and so was the Old One's death—and Godith's killing by his own people and Sabasut's killing by Dogmen.

I was barely ten summers old that night but I had seen evil. I lay down in my sleeping place and wept quietly until I slept. I did not know about the others, did not know the brother I loved was dead, my father destroyed, my childhood over—did not know that within two sunsets all of Ecshamut's people sleeping around me would be slaughtered by the Dogmen whose ship we had set afire.

XV

I come now to the desolate years when my people were blocked from our seal beach, when every good hunting ground was taken from us. Each season our meoticks moved farther and farther back into valleys, behind mountain ranges across which Dogmen seldom ventured. We used waterways that curve and double back, shallow rivers that loop through bog and marshland, rivers with falls, over which the awkward Dogmen boats could not go.

We were forced to move camp many times each season. We found small islands far up Eel Lake, left our caribou fences to rot, abandoned old travel lines, retreated into barren places where our ancestors had never made camp.

Our numbers became fewer, families combining until we knew of just two meoticks, ours and the meotick of the Shadowdancer Thebush. Thebush had decided that ours was an unlucky meotick and now kept his camping place some distance from us. Since we never saw the Shadowdancer Ecshamut or any of his people, we supposed that he was doing likewise.

Seasons would pass without us seeing other people. In our meotick Uncle Adibish was still our shadowdancer. I knew from Demasduit that he blamed much of what had befallen us on the recklessness of my father.

When my father looked at me it was as if he did not see me, as he did not see any of the world around him. Mother said his spirit had escaped through the wound in his head. She washed him and put food into his mouth. When we moved from place to place she led him by the hand like a child. Although his body still looked healthy, his lips were twisted into a scowl and the words he spoke were twisted too. Only Mother seemed to understand them.

I remember my father holding his head between his hands, silently rocking back and forth from sunrise to sunset. Sometimes bad spirits would get into his damaged skull, then he would scream, flailing his arms about as if he wanted to fight. The thing in my father that did not change was his distrust of his brother; it was always Adibish he tried to hurt when the evil thoughts entered his skull. When this happened it would take all my family, Longnon and me as well as Kakula and Mother and sometimes our cousin Manus, to catch Father and bind his arms until he became calm.

How strong life is. Even while we starved, froze, hid from Dogmen, moving continually, crossing and recrossing that vast barren in-country with our sick and feeble, with our mad and wounded, even after our gums began to bleed, after our bodies became dirty and our hair lice-infested—because we could never properly clean ourselves or our tents—even then people still loved and hated, were kind and unkind, played dice games; men and women still argued, lay in each other's arms; children were still born. Sometimes we even laughed.

Missing both the Old One and my brother Ianamish, the two people in the world who had thought me special, I grew lonely as I grew older. Strangely, for we had talked only a little, I also missed my father greatly. Everything had changed, not just my world but my place at its centre. Father was no longer listened to in our meotick and I was no longer the listener, the chosen one Hebbosheth told her secrets to. I still whispered to the Old One each night before I slept, asking her about Nonosabasut, asking what I should do to pull his eyes to me. She never answered.

After Sabasut was killed, Doodebewshet and her three children were among those who joined our meotick. This surprised me, for although our shadowdancer had been her husband's good friend, Doodebewshet never hid her dislike for Adibish and indeed for all of my kin. I thought it must be Nonosabasut, who greatly admired my uncle, who had convinced his mother to bring her mamateek into our meotick. However it had happened I was glad for it. I now saw Nonosabasut every day, circled him like a fox, watching from a distance, always wondering how to get him for my husband—but his name never passed my lips.

Amid all the moving, the constant search for food and safety, our mothers still tried to teach us how to clean skins, to preserve meat, to sew and make snowshoes, to cook, to care for babies and tend the sick—still hoping to make us into good wives for the young men. I still drew pictures, secretly listened to the conversations of others, still whispered with Demasduit and Kasathi whenever we could find a quiet place away from our mothers.

Much of the talk between us concerned the men we might marry. Our young men were full of anger, I saw it in my brothers Longnon and Kakula. Young men were taking chances that older, more cautious hunters would avoid—and they were being killed. Even in the families that made up Thebush's meotick, people who had not been on the beach when the Dogmen boat was attacked, four men were killed when they tried to get seals. There were now more women than men in our mamateeks. It was clear to us that some young women would not get husbands or have children. Demasduit, Kasathi and I often talked of how it would be to remain husbandless.

Kasathi, who had yearned after my brother Longnon since she was a child, said we must all find husbands. "We need men to hunt for us and children to take care of us when we get old," she said. She was sure there were young men in meoticks we did not know about. Kasathi was a sweet, agreeable girl but sensible and not shy; even before her moon bleeding began she asked Longnon to marry her. Now the man in our mamateek, he smiled foolishly whenever I spoke her name.

Demasduit had been moon bleeding for many seasons but did not seem interested in any of our young men. She said we might have children without having husbands. We knew this was possible because Gowet, the woman who was to have married my brother, gave birth the winter after Ianamish was killed. Gowet, being husbandless, still slept in her parents' mamateek but the little boy spent most of his time with my mother. Mother loved him dearly and called him Mish-mish, the pet name she'd once had for my dead brother.

"I do not wish to spend all my life in our gloomy mamateek," I told my friends. I was at once sorry I had spoken thoughtlessly. Kasathi would have to move into our mamateek if she and Longnon married.

"Who will you take, then?" Demasduit looked at me so sharply that I turned my eyes away before she could see inside my skull.

Sometimes they would tease me, asking who my secret lover was, wanting to know what happened to the moon-topped staff Hebbosheth had owned. They wondered if we might find it, wave it over the sleeping place of some young hunter—but who? One by one they named all the young men in our meotick and those they knew of in the meoticks of Ecshamut and Thebush, watching my eyes, pretending they could see which one we had to cast a spell on.

"None of them. Not one of them!" I said. My own moon blood had not come, but even if it had I would not for anything have spoken Nonosabasut's name to Demasduit or Kasathi.

To stop their questions I made up a story about a meotick of perfect men who lived apart from all others. These handsome spirit-men would one day walk out of the forest and claim the most beautiful among us, take us to live on that secret island in a remote lake—that happy place where the Old One had said Perfect Time still was and always would be. As I grew older I often imagined such a place before sleeping, dreaming of warmth and good food, of wide beaches, of teasing the sea, of lovemaking—not with a spirit-man but with Nonosabasut, who was alive and real.

If I did not let my friends see how their teasing worried me, they would grow tired and begin speaking of other things—which of us had the most beautiful eyes, how to find coloured shells to circle our tunics, the possibility of Kasathi's father asking Adibish to perform a wedding ceremony for her and Longnon when Firewoman next danced.

There was no longer as much ceremony and celebration in our lives as there had been. Cut off from our winter hunt, without the long spring trek to the beach, we did not meet people from other meoticks. Seasons blurred into one another.

In the depth of winter we froze, in spring we starved, but the most dangerous times were summer and fall when Dogmen with fire-sticks roamed the forest. We had not yet forgotten our special dances, but we could not always do them or tell the stories that are meant to celebrate each moon change. I blamed Adibish for this and thought that if Hebbosheth were alive she would have forced her grandson to observe all the rituals of our people.

I see now that Adibish did his best to keep the small ceremonies that marked our day-by-day lives. When any bird or animal was killed he asked its forgiveness and thanked the creature for giving us its life. He had inherited our Old One's bone stiffness, but when it was considered safe enough to have a fire he still storydanced. For my father's sake I disliked my uncle. Yet, remembering how he had risked himself to place the bodies of Sabasut and my Old One in the sea cave, I did not doubt his courage.

Even then, when it was difficult to find safe graves for our dead, Adibish faithfully carried out this task. Often he had to travel long distances carrying a body. As his own body stiffened he began asking Nonosabasut to help him, both with the preparation of the body and with finding a grave place. It became a common thing for these two to be away from our camp for days at a time searching out burial places Dogmen could not plunder. Seeing this we all knew that Adibish had chosen Nonosabasut to become our next shadowdancer.

The rare happy rituals—times when we could stop beside water and clean ourselves, the ceremonies of birth and marriage, of choosing a child's spirit guardian—those Adibish still performed himself. After a baby had lived three moons, our shadowdancer would draw a circle and look into the bone pieces to find the child's spirit guardian, and when Firewoman danced, Adibish still chanted the marrying songs of our people.

When Kasathi had passed four and ten winters, Adibish chanted a song for her and my brother Longnon below the swirling skirts of Firewoman. Although there was not enough food to have a true wedding feast everyone rejoiced, and Demasduit and I danced around Kasathi and Longnon, clicking our fingers and twisting our bodies so that the shells on our tunic fringes made a joyful sound.

I sewed a sleeveless tunic for Kasathi and drew a pattern of birds around the shoulders. My brother and my friend seemed happy together and I was pleased to have someone with her cheerful spirit in our mamateek.

Even after the People were blocked from the sea, our hunters secretly went to the coast for seals in early spring. Dogmen now occupied every bay, cove and seal beach. They had built shaky stick-platforms even on that beach where I had spent every summer of my life. Many Dogmen still went away during the winter, but now they left watchers behind to guard their storehouses and belongings. In previous springs four of our hunters were killed by these watcher Dogmen. Yet we were so desperate for seal meat and seal oil that our men were forced to go back, returning to these dangerous places again and again.

In the deep evergreen forest where the People had always felt safe, we could no longer camp beside the fenceways our ancestors had built. In fall and winter hunters had to track animals through deep snow, hiding from the muskets of Dogmen. They never saw the great caribou herds, only a lame or sick animal, one that had dropped behind or strayed from the travel routes taken by Old Caribou and his family.

Dogmen now followed our old hunting lines. They killed and skinned animals, caribou, bear and wolf, beaver, martin and lynx—any animal that had fur—leaving the flesh to rot in the forest, become food for crows and wolverine. These Dogmen hunters seemed to take pleasure in tormenting us—shooting at any of the People they saw, uprooting our food caches as heartlessly as they did our burial places.

Night and day runners guarded the forests around our tents, bringing news of approaching Dogmen. In one season we would be forced to move many times. Because of this we never had time to make our mamateeks warm and waterproof, the old and the sick never had time to rest, women pulled fish and meat from smoke racks before it had properly dried, men left precious unbutchered carcasses behind to rot.

Then, in the year my brother and Kasathi married, the last hiding place we knew became unsafe. Firewoman was still dancing in the northern sky—I remember frozen earth crunching under the feet of the runner who brought us word that Dogmen were coming towards our camping place. The runner was my brother Kakula. Excited and out of breath, he told us these Dogmen were dressed like none he'd ever seen, in blue tunics with shiny buttons. Listening to him, I thought how strange it was that I, who was three winters older than him, had never beheld a Dogman.

Adibish listened quietly. Then he told us that the blue tunics showed that these Dogmen were not the hunters or birders who had been tormenting us. "These blue jackets speak for a great leader. They will not harm us," he said, and I remembered my father once accusing him of guiding some Dogman across Baetha.

One of the young men—it may have been my brother Longnon—called out, "They are all the same—all Dogmen!"

Adibish did not even glance at Longnon but continued in the voice I'd heard him use when speaking to my father, the voice that made all things seem reasonable. "Not all Dogmen are monsters. To us they all look the same, but those wearing the blue jackets with shiny buttons are the ones who smoked with our ancestors, the ones who, in other times, spoke to the sky and left bright cloth behind on our beaches."

The short winter day was ending, twilight seeping to blackness. In the middle of our camping place a poor fire burned below a brace of geese. Flesh from the birds and a small roll of bibdid would have to make supper for all of us.

At the end of his speech our shadowdancer announced that he was going to meet these Dogmen. He would greet them as friends, invite them back to our tents for the night. "When they sit with us, they will see we are few and that we mean them no harm." He spoke calmly, as if this was a thing we had done many times.

"But the men coming towards us are many, many," Kakula said. He had counted two tens. "They are marching in two long lines, like beaters crowding caribou into a fenceway—and they all have muskets." My brother spoke out well but he looked frightened.

Adibish did not seem to hear. Waunathoake, his good silent wife, had already brought his robe and headdress. He continued pulling the bearskin around his shoulders, placing the great caribou antlers on his head. When he was ready he looked out at us. "People cannot run forever.

"If we are to live we must make peace with Dogmen. We must learn some of their ways and show them some of ours— how to treat animals, how to share travel lines, hunting grounds and the seal beaches we need so badly. This can only be done," Adibish said, "when we meet with Dogmen, talk to them, become friends."

These were the very words I had heard him say to my father the night they'd argued, but I think this was the first time our shadowdancer had spoken such thoughts to the People. My uncle then told the story Father had refused to hear that night.

It was a story about how he and Sabasut as boys had gone ice-fishing together and become caught in a blizzard. They had floundered in the cold and snow for most of a day before stumbling upon a wooden shelter.

"It was a kind of shack Dogmen hunters build in the forest—they are called tilts." Adibish's stories always held such scraps of knowledge, everything that had ever come to rest in his head had to be spoken—I remembered how impatient this always made my father.

The boys forced their way in and figured out how to make fire inside the potlike thing set down in the hut. The blizzard continued and they stayed inside for a long time—many days, Adibish thought—with nothing to eat but snow that drifted in around the door.

"I began coughing and could not breathe. Then I lost my senses. Thinking the smoky air was choking me, I tried again and again to go outside. In the end Sabasut had to tie me down to keep me from rushing out into the storm. On the third or fourth day the wind died but I was still very ill, still raving— and Sabasut would not leave without me."

When the Dogman came through the door, the boys knew they would be killed. "Sabasut was a brave friend. He stood over me, holding a piece of wood, ready to attack the Dogman who was himself holding a brace of rabbits and a long fire-stick." Our shadowdancer smiled at the memory.

"The man stood in the doorway looking at us, then he began to laugh. He put down the fire-stick and Sabasut put down the wooden stick. Dogmen carry many things. He had a heavy blanket, a pot for cooking, smoking material in a tin and containers that are named bottles. We had been using as little of the dry wood as possible; now the Dogmen pushed many logs into the burner he called a stove. Then he skinned the rabbit and cooked it along with a bit of the white powder he took from one of his bottles.

"In another bottle he had thick brown liquid, strong stuff that he forced me to swallow every little while. Sabasut and the Dogman moved me near to the fire and wrapped me in his blanket. His medicine was powerful; it made me sweat, made me feel better. In two nights and two days I was well enough to leave. That Dogman saved my life.

"Because of this I know Dogmen are not all evil. Because of this I believe they are people—people, just as we are people!"

When Adibish spoke these words a shocked hissing came from those circled around him. They, like Father, did not want to hear that Dogmen were human creatures like us.

One old man was brave enough to speak what many were thinking. "All of this was settled in past time. Remember, Adibish, that Old Caribou explained to our Ancestors how Dogmen were not truly people but the children of Nakhani. Good spirits have ever warned us not to trade or have any dealings with Nakhani's blood-soaked pups." As the old man spoke, others nodded and muttered their agreement.

I think Godith's mother was the first woman to raise her voice against Adibish. "Dogmen cannot do good, Dogmen have always brought death," she said quietly. Mishatut was alone by then, her husband having been killed by Dogmen while hunting seal.

How easy it is to say "killed," how quickly it falls from the tongue. But the killing of Ebanthoo was slow.

It had happened the spring before. Our hunters had already left the beach when they were attacked. Watcher Dogmen saw them and began to shoot at their backs. Ebanthoo was holding up a man who had already been shot, dragging him downhill towards the river where a canoe was hidden. One Dogman, having used all his fire, threw his axe at the backs of our hunters. The axe took Ebanthoo's arm off at the elbow. Yet they all managed to get into the canoe and push away before the Dogmen stuffed more fire into their long sticks.

A ways upriver our hunters pulled over; they made a fire and stopped the bleeding of Ebanthoo's arm by burning. When they brought Ebanthoo into our camp, blackened flesh hung in strips from the stump where his arm had been.

When Mishatut spoke, we all remembered the days and nights we had listened to her husband cry and moan—it had continued until he was too weak to make any sound. Then he began to stink, and the smell of rotting flesh was everywhere in our meotick. He lived for a full moon after he stopped moaning, Mishatut kneeling beside him, dripping water between his lips, until finally he died.

"Dogmen will kill us all . . ."

"Dogmen destroyed my child's grave place."

"Dogmen killed my grandson."

"They carry death—they hate us!"

Suddenly every woman in our meotick was calling out, naming fathers, husbands, brothers and sons killed by Dogmen, listing what Dogmen had done to us. They spoke of women who had miscarried when running from Dogmen, children who had starved because of Dogmen, mamateeks and canoes that had been set fire to, trapping lines and caribou fences that had been destroyed—every evil they could remember. Women opposing our shadowdancer!

"Will you now have us give them our food?" one woman asked, and this seemed the worst thing of all for I was very hungry. Everyone was hungry, saliva running down the chins of children as they watched the geese roast. If visitors came into our meotick, even Dogmen, they would be given our meal.

I wanted very much to speak out, would perhaps have spoken, but then Doodebewshet stepped forward. Even before her husband, Sabasut, was killed she had been strange, but I had not seen her often then. Since coming into our meotick she scowled at everyone, sometimes shouted orders at us, and never washed. A shadow of the beautiful girl she had been still lived below the dirt and meanness of her face but she had turned into what my mother called a bibin—a handmaiden of bad spirits.

Doodebewshet flung herself on the ground in front of my uncle and began to wail out her complaints one by one. "The Great Shaman Sabasut who was my husband would not have asked these things of us. Adibish has no reverence, does not address the spirits properly. It is because of him that this evil time has come, because of him that Great Sabasut is dead. Now my children are hungry, I myself am hungry. We have not received our fair share this season and now this madman will give the little we have to feed Dogmen!"

It seemed her lament would never end, but Ashei came and hushed her mother. The girl managed to get Doodebewshet up onto her feet but was not able to pull her away. The two women stood in front of Adibish swaying back and forth as if they might fall. I could see Ashei's eyes searching for her brother, whose job it was to carry their mother back to her mamateek whenever she began raving. But the swaying seemed to calm Doodebewshet; although she kept holding Ashei's arm, staring ahead like a ghost spirit, her keening stopped. Everything became quiet, so that when her next words came, everyone heard them.

"You, Adibish! You and my husband's grandfather caused my first daughter to starve—you will not starve this one!" As she shouted Doodebewshet jerked Ashei even closer to Adibish until both women's faces were just below our shadowdancer's, their bodies almost touching.

Except for the hunters and runners who were guarding a circle beyond our meotick and one small girl who was sick, all our people were now gathered around the Shadowdancer Adibish and the two women. Nonosabasut and his brother, Tomasuth, had returned. I could see them standing aside, watching. Their handsome faces held that closed, absent look of men who fear being made to look foolish.

For a long time Adibish did not answer. He stood looking down into Doodebewshet's eyes and I could see that he'd lost his certainty, become bewildered—just as he'd done years before when he discovered me listening beside the marsh.

Since the death of Sabasut, Adibish had seemed very alone. Without sons and with most men his age already on the Ghost Path, he may even have missed my father. I had long ago noticed that my uncle did not attend much to his wife and daughter, never talked or joked with them the way my father had with Mother and me. Maybe, as the Old One once said, women confused Adibish.

I believe it was that night, listening to the mad words of the woman he had once desired, that Adibish knew our people would never again rest—knew that our lives had become temporary, without permanence. He had lived five times ten winters, had become an old man without ever convincing anyone but Sabasut that the People had to live side by side with Dogmen.

After a time he interrupted Doodebewshet, saying that he would argue no longer. "We will leave this place, run from Dogmen, even those who come towards us in peace." His voice shook and when he reached up and took the antlers from his head his hands shook also. "I will show you the way to one last camping place. It is a place I saw when I was young, a place I travelled to with the Great Shaman Osagana. No Dogmen will find us there."

Adibish looked towards Nonosabasut, and as if it were a commonplace thing, said, "Nonosabasut, the son of Sabasut and the grandson of Osagana, will oversee the moving of our meotick."

At least two older men stood nearby, experienced hunters and runners, but no one spoke up to question our shadow-dancer's choice. Adibish went inside his tent, and Demasduit and her mother followed him, Demasduit looking back over her shoulder at me as if confused, suddenly unsure for the first time in her life.

See how it feels—see now how easy it is to have your place in the world torn from you! I thought. Then I looked away from her, across to where Nonosabasut was talking to Kakula, asking questions, listening carefully and nodding. His face looked stern but he touched my brother's shoulder with the tips of his fingers, the way I had often seen him do when talking to friends.

Then he turned to face the People. "A long time will pass before we will again make fire. We must eat now, finish quickly and then we will leave," he said. Lifting his face to the sky, he asked Ash-wa-meet for protection and gave thanks to the spirits of the grey geese we were about to eat.

When we had eaten, Nonosabasut told two young men to make the sick child comfortable in a sling they could carry. The rest of us were to divide ourselves so that each family had a strong person to help take the mamateeks down, to pull sleds and carry heavy belongings. He spoke as if he had been giving commands all his life.

While I helped Longnon and Kasathi take our tent apart, it came to me that perhaps Adibish and his family intended to stay behind. I was surprised at how unhappy this thought made me feel. Demasduit and I often had unpleasant words, yet I sometimes loved her and always considered her my sister. Also I would miss my uncle. Despite the long disagreement between our families there was something about my father's brother that I trusted. Perhaps, after all, I would not have been too unhappy standing beside him to greet the line of blue-dressed Dogmen. I knew that was what Nonosabasut would have wished, could see from the blackness of his face as he went from mamateek to mamateek that he was not pleased with this task Adibish had set him.

No one stayed behind. Nonosabasut went first, with Adibish and his family following. We walked into a night of freezing rain, walked all night and long into the next day before we stopped. Huddled in the shelter of a rock outcrop we made a weak fire and boiled spruce needles in enough water to give each person a few mouthfuls. Then we moved on through the next night. We walked in a line, the strong taking turns up ahead, beating a path through the ice-crusted snow, flattening brush and breaking the wind for those weaker. Nothing could protect us from rain or keep ice from forming on our clothing. We rattled as we walked, like the finger-bones of bears we'd once hung in trees to protect our dead.

We had never travelled such great distances in-country, had never travelled in such terrible weather. The ice weighed down the bundles I was carrying until the straps cut into my shoulders. Always some part of my body hurt; my arms and back, my hands and legs ached, my feet bled and my lips too, from ice slivers cutting into my face. In the end I walked bent over like an old woman, seeing only my feet, thinking of nothing except moving, going forward. Some walked with their eyes closed, stumbling out of line, having to be pulled back. My father was crying and falling to his knees every few steps. Longnon and I tried to help but he pushed us away, would let no one but my mother lead him. The sick child died.

Late on the fourth day we were far in-country, in a place only our shadowdancer knew, a brown exposed place beside a wide, hard-frozen river. As a young man Adibish had come here on a spirit quest with his teacher Osagana. Without the close encircling forest we were used to, this space seemed bleak and unprotected. But we were so cold and tired that no one questioned Adibish when he told us this was where we would make our camp.

We set up our mamateeks on the circle of brown grass. Beyond the grass a few birch and dogberry trees grew out of a waist-high tangle of spruce, balsam and juniper. Beyond this fringe of bush there was nothing—only barrens, vast and windy, between us and the distant hills, hills without trees, hunched down like beasts waiting to pounce. The place reminded me of that dismal camp Hebbosheth had spoken of, her first husband's meotick. But Adibish pointed to the spindly dogberry trees and said Dogmen considered them unlucky and would not come here. In our exhaustion this seemed enough.

In the confusion of arrival no one noticed that Mishatut was not with us. After her husband's death, Godith's mother had gone to live in the mamateek of Kasathi's family—distant kin who did not miss her until the next morning. Kasathi's father and her brother Newin went a day's journey back over our trail before they found her. When they returned with her frozen body the men told us she had wrapped herself in fur and curled down beside a rock. I was glad she'd had a more peaceful death than Godith and a less painful one than her husband. I thought of her often that winter, especially after I heard Mother tell Auntie Santu that Mishatut had been the wisest of us all.

There were only five mamateeks now in our meotick. Often there was only wood for one fire and we would crowd together in Adibish's mamateek, everyone quiet, barely staying alive, without the spirit to sing, to tell stories or shadowdance. The contentment I'd once felt within the tight circle of my people was gone. I hated the coughing and scratching, the old man who picked lice from his dying wife's hair, the crying children, the stink of unwashed bodies pressing around me.

I would rather be alone. Cold though it was, I often left the fire before it died, went back to our own mamateek, where I lay listening to the nearby snap of frost and far-off howl of wolves. Like us, wolves are hungry when the snow is deep, always on the move, always hunting, their night voices echoing through the low hills and desolate barrens.

"Maybe this is the home of Nakhani the evil wolf spirit," Kakula said one night when we were in our own mamateek, listening to the animals and waiting for sleep. "There are no other people here. Not once since coming to this place have we seen a sign of others—not even runners from the meoticks of Ecshamut or Thebush."

"I think people are vanishing from earth," Mother said. Her voice was dead, hard as the frost encasing our mamateek's walls.

No one spoke, although we were all there—Longnon and Kasathi and my younger brother, Kakula, along with me, the boy Mish-mish and my father, and Santu with her husband and son. Mother's sister, Santu, had always lived with us. Her daughters had both married into Ecshamut's meotick, but her son Manus, whose wife had been killed the night we attacked the Dogman boat, still slept in our family mamateek.

Usually Auntie Santu would say something to comfort my mother, but that night she was as silent as the rest. All of us were silent, too cold to sleep, already longing for daylight though night had barely begun.

"Few of the People are left, perhaps only us in this meotick. Only us in all of Baetha," Mother said after a time. She was sick herself, had become ill the day after we made camp. I thought she was dying but Kasathi said it was just tiredness and lack of food. When Mother spoke that night, I think she was secretly hoping Father would become alert and contradict her—as he'd so often done when he was well.

It was Longnon who played my father's part. "No, Mother, there are still many besides us," my brother said. "I myself have seen the shape of their canoes in clouds passing overhead, reflections from distant lakes and rivers along which our people move like leaves. There are islands within islands, endless forest through which Old Caribou leads his family." Longnon spoke from the sleeping place where he and Kasathi lay. His voice was dreamy, muffled, as if he were talking just to her.

"I tell you, my Mother," he said, and suddenly his voice was clear—he'd tossed aside his sleeping furs and was sitting up— "there are yet safe places in Baetha, forest where tens and tens of meoticks can be hidden, where the People will live whole lifetimes without seeing Dogmen. Someday I will take you there."

It surprised me to hear Longnon, who spoke seldom and only of fishing and hunting, say such things. His words reminded me of the things Hebbosheth had said; they comforted me, and I have repeated them to myself on many a black night. I repeated them then, curled my body around my brother's words and slept despite all the evil spirits that waited in the freezing darkness outside.

Inside every mamateek someone was sick that winter. In our tent there was Father, Mother, and Santu's son Manus, whose foot had become infected during the march in-country. To me it seemed that Manus, like Father, had some sickness inside his skull. He had ever been quiet, now he'd become sullen and silent. My brothers said that even when they were hunting together he hardly ever spoke.

There seemed nothing to rejoice about. Yet, secretly, I did rejoice—on days when the wind died and we saw blue sky, on nights when I lay down without the gnaw of hunger inside me. I thanked Firewoman that Nonosabasut was now part of our meotick, that during that mournful winter he had at last looked into my face and spoken my name.

It happened when Mish-mish and I were playing what he called the animal game. From the time he could speak my nephew had loved to watch me make pictures, was drawing himself before he was three winters on the earth. Now his drawing was as good as mine. I loved the boy, both for his own sake and for the sake of my dead brother, Ianamish. The animal game was a way to get Mish-mish outside, away from the sick stink of our mamateek. With a stick each of us would draw some creature in the snow, then see how quickly the other could guess what the animal was. Mish-mish had his father's happy nature, and that day we were kneeling in snow, laughing at the bird I'd drawn.

"If only it could lay eggs," I said—always I was thinking of food.

Then a voice from behind us said, "I can almost believe it might."

I knew it was Nonosabasut. Still, when I looked up and saw him my face flamed with heat. By then we had lived in the same meotick for many seasons. All that time I had watched him, listened for his voice, thought of him—yet my eyes still marvelled at his beauty. Perhaps I should not use the word *beauty* for a man, certainly not for the tall hunter standing above me. He was dressed in hides and fur, his skin the colour of warm earth, his eyes like the ice-blue sky behind him. Ah, but he was a beautiful man!

"I know you have a voice, Shanawdithit, I have heard it," he said.

I could not have spoken then, not to save myself from Aich-mud-yim, not to thank Good Ash-wa-meet. He smiled down from what seemed a great distance, then he turned and walked away from us.

In that place there were no encircling evergreens to protect us, and snow swept across the white lake making our mama-teeks shiver like large animals. Because we'd had no time to bring in deadwood before the snows came, women and children had to spend the short daylight gathering damp wood that gave little heat and made our fires smoke. The few berries, the small supply of bibdid and smoked meat we had was gone before the first moon of winter ended. We ate anything we could find: frozen birds, lichen, even dogberries—well named, for despite Adibish's belief in their protective power, these bitter berries made everyone who ate them sick.

Each morning, no matter what the weather, every healthy man was out hunting. But fur-bearing animals were all hiding, thick glitter enclosed beaver dams, fish slept below river mud and the great starving wolves were too savage to come upon. At dark, weary men would return with one or two small birds, a frozen rabbit, sometimes a fox or lynx.

People began to die. Three children perished first; several others, my cousin Demasduit among them, were too weak to stand. In the third moon of winter, when the nights were long and bitterly cold, when even the wisest old one was not sure the sun would ever return, one of the old men no one thought sick died. Then Father killed himself.

At the end I think my father's mind must have returned to him. One dark, rattling night he took his favourite spear and crept out of our mamateek. We should have seen him, should have heard him. But my mother being sick and the rest of us exhausted, we slept. He did not go far. Just beyond the dogberry and tamarack, my father held the whalebone tip against his heart and forced his body down onto it.

Early the next morning Longnon found him; a wolf was lapping up our father's blood. Even in his shock my brother was swift, and his arrow killed the big animal before it could turn and face him. Thus in his death my father brought us a little respite from hunger.

Father had been gone so long that our sorrow was not as large as it should have been, yet we did grieve. Inside our mamateek my brothers and I remembered our father before his mind went, how whenever he sat beside the fire he would be carving—toys for us children, a small canoe, dolls for me and my dead sister, combs for Mother and an arrow and set of bows for his youngest son, Kakula. My mother had not left her sleeping place for many days and we could not tell if she knew that her husband, the great hunter Washomish, was dead.

Those of us who remained upright rolled our dead in their sleeping skins, tied them with strips of hide and pushed them up into the forks of four spindly birch trees that grew a short distance from our mamateeks. For each of the dead Adibish made a song. He made a special song for Father, calling his brother an arguing spirit and cautioning Crow to watch his words when Washomish reached Perfect Time. After the songs were sung, we hung strings of bones in branches around the bodies to keep evil spirits away. Then we beseeched Ash-wa-meet to keep the rest of us alive until we could find burial places for our people.

One night after our father's death, Longnon whispered that he would tell Kasathi and me a secret thing if we promised not to tell others. We both made the promise, and he told us that there was talk among the men of calling some great animal from the Spirit World. Our Shadowdancer Adibish, and Nonosabasut, who was now his helper in all things, said that such a thing had been done in old times. Adibish, Longnon said, knew of a ritual that would bring the living body of a spirit animal back to save us from starvation—just as Old Caribou had saved Former People.

Inside our own mamateek, with our family sleeping around me, I dared to scoff at the idea. "Perhaps the confused spirit from our father's skull has now gone into Adibish."

And that night, for the very first time, I dreamt of Hebbosheth. *"It is a dangerous thing to draw creatures from the Spirit World,"* she told me, just as she'd done in life. The Old One was standing somewhere I had never been, at an entrance into a dark hill—a place very like this one, Dogman.

"Remember the scar on your hand, Shanawdithit," she said, and then she made her rude hissing sound and was gone.

A shapeless dread still shivered inside me when I woke. It lingered even when I went out into the wind and drifting snow, searching for buds of spruce I could boil into a tea for my mother.

When he came, I was on my knees, digging around some twisted spruce near our mamateek. Below the snow I hoped to find cones and lichen, and if I was lucky, the new buds that are good for breathing sickness.

Again Nonosabasut spoke from behind me. "A bear or caribou are the only animals with enough flesh to save us," he said, as if we were in the middle of a conversation, although he had not spoken a word to me since the day he saw Mish-mish and me drawing in snow.

No one was nearby, yet Nonosabasut kept his voice low. "A caribou, I think, since it is winter—and it would have to be large, larger than anyone alive has seen, a great stag big as Old Caribou."

Because my Old One's dream-warning was still in my skull, I knew at once what he was asking of me. To keep his attention and to postpone speaking myself, I shook my head.

"No? Then there are others I could ask." His voice was cool and I heard him move as if to leave.

"There are not!" The first words I ever spoke to him—words of defiance and denial. Unwise, Shanawdithit, unwise.

"I think my mother could do it . . ."

"Doodebewshet!" I was so astonished that I turned towards him and said the first thing that came into my head: "Your mother is mad! And she cannot make pictures!"

"She might with the help of Ash-wa-meet." He looked at me thoughtfully. "But my mother has slept with a man."

I looked up into his face, waited a heartbeat, then said, "So it seems." I was breathless at my boldness, laughing inside because now I knew he was teasing me.

"And?"

"And I have not." Forgoing the pleasure of watching his face I looked modestly downward.

"Here, I will help pull this up." He knelt beside me, digging around a wide snow-flattened spruce with his sealskin mittens.

While we cleared snow from the stunted tree, Nonosabasut told me the story our shadowdancer had told him. Hebbosheth had once told me the same story—and her telling had been better.

In Early Time there was once a winter that did not end. Ice did not melt from rivers, days stayed short, animals stayed asleep and the People starved. It was then that their shadowdancer, who was an ancestor of my Old One, received a vision. In this vision she was told to choose a young hunter and go with him in search for a special rock, one she alone would recognize.

When the rock was found the shadowdancer in the story drew on it, marking the image of an animal that had to be killed to feed her people. The shadowdancer returned then to her meotick, but the hunter had to wait beside the rock until the next sunrise. When the first ray of sun hit the drawing, the hunter was to be ready with his arrow. The sun would pull the young man's arrow along the beam of light and into the heart of the stone animal. The hunter would turn then, look away from the sun, towards darkness, and see there a living animal waiting for its death.

I let my voice slide over Nonosabasut's, finishing the story for him. "Only if the ceremony of the shadowdancer has been acceptable, only if the hunter is of good heart—only then will the spirit animal be drawn into our world. Only then will his arrow fly into the very place it did in the animal's image," I said. Then I asked why he was speaking to me of things no one but shadowdancers should know.

"Your uncle has said that the Old One chose you to keep her secrets. It is he who directed me to come to you."

"But Adibish is our shadowdancer—must not he kill the animal?"

Regret and pride, or perhaps anger, flickered across Nonosabasut's handsome face. "Do not pretend to me, Shanawdithit—you know what I am asking. It might be you have always known. Just as he has chosen you to draw the spirit animal into Present Time, so too will Adibish choose who is to kill the animal."

I think now that it was anger I saw in his face. I know now that Nonosabasut was unhappy with Adibish's choice of me as his helper. In my pride and excitement, such thoughts did not come to me then. It was only for modesty's sake that I asked, "Why me?"

"Because you watch and listen, because the Old One's secrets are inside your skull, because you draw creatures that seem alive—because in all our meotick only Shanawdithit dreams continually of the Spirit World . . ." He looked at me, turning his head so quickly that he must have caught the joy, and perhaps the triumph, in my face.

This was what I had been waiting for, what I had known since I first beheld Nonosabasut's face—that something connected me with him. That someday, if I had patience, he would need me.

Without asking, I knew he was the one Adibish had chosen to kill the spirit animal. I would gladly have left with him then to search for the creature, but he said we had to wait for a sunny, calm day. A day when we had some chance of finding the place Adibish had told him of.

The scar on my palm was nothing, last night's dream nothing, all the doubts I had ever had were nothing. Nonosabasut needed

me, and together we would find the rock through which the sun
shone down upon a valley at dawn.

Three days and four nights passed before a day without wind
came. I woke to the strange silence, to brightness glowing through
the skins of our mamateek. I stood up from my sleeping place,
wrapped a sleeping fur around my shoulders, and stepping carefully over my sleeping nephew, I went outside. Nonosabasut was
waiting, standing beside our mamateek; the rising sun shone on
his face, shone on his arm and hand, as he reached out, laid his
cool fingers lightly across my lips.

If some evil spirit had shot an arrow into him—into him and
into me—would we now be together in Perfect Time? I did not
think of such a thing then—only knew I would be happy to stay
forever in that heartbeat of joy and expectation, feeling his hand
on my face, his fingers on my lips, knowing exactly what I
wanted, yet not knowing, not truly knowing, what he was calling me to do.

Had I known would I have refused? When I returned to my
sleeping family, when I laced up moccasins, pulled on legskin
boots and fur mittens and crept out into that brittle, bright air,
had I known that I was walking towards darkness, towards lone-
liness, towards the hard, straight paths that Dogmen follow—
would I have turned back? I think not.

We tied racquets onto our feet and he turned without a word,
moved ahead swishing through the freshly drifted snow around
our tents, breaking a path down to the lake. He was wearing a
light skin jerkin but had a caribou hide looped around his shoulders along with his bow and arrows. Knowing I would return
before night, I wore only my tunic and hood above soft legskins.
I followed close behind, placing my snowshoes carefully down
upon his prints until we came to the icy lake, where even on this

calm day, small scuds of blowing snow quickly covered the prints we made.

We did not cross the lake but followed its edge until we turned in-country. We crossed a frozen marsh, circled the closest hills and began to move up the valley towards the third hill. It seemed a long way, but Nonosabasut said we were still on land where our men hunted. We moved quickly over crusted snow, but on the wooded side of the hill powdered snow reached up to our knees and slowed us down. In time we came to land Nonosabasut had never seen, a place he said none of our hunters had been to. We walked with the sun until it was almost overhead—until we saw the rock we were searching for.

"There it is," he said, and we stopped.

It was right above us, alone in that shadowless white world, a rock the shape of a giant black whale rising from a sea of snow.

We had walked hard since sunrise and were very warm. After we unlaced our racquets we washed our faces with handfuls of snow, then held snow in our mouths and swallowed half-melted (what children call) almostfood. Feeling refreshed, we squatted comfortably on our heels and stared up at the huge rock. The sun was climbing towards the centre sky but I could judge where it would touch the rock when it spilled into the valley at dawn.

Neither of us spoke. I do not know what Nonosabasut did—for a time I forgot him. I stared at the rock, holding my mind on the shape of the thing, the hardness of it, the cracks and fissures on its surface, searching for the great animal that waited inside. I waited too, only waited, neither impatient nor uncertain. Simply there. Knowing that what I needed would be given.

In time it was. As Firewoman appears in the sky so the shape of a bull caribou emerged from the rock, standing like some noble shaman surveying his valley. I looked until I was sure of him, until I knew every line of his body. Then I walked up to the rock and quickly began to outline the narrow flanks, the wide shoulders, the antlers rising like trees out of that fine head. I worked fast, using every coloured stone in my pouch, smudging in the white ruff above his heart, touching on brightness where light fingered the ripple of bone and muscle, smoothing a reddish sheen of ochre into his fur, drawing the long graceful legs, four sand-coloured hoofs, the white rolling eye.

When it was finished I fell backward exhausted. I lay in the snow looking up at the blue arch of sky and at the beautiful beast I had made. I knew I would never again draw anything as perfect. I was giddy with pride, with happiness, with hunger and cold. I would have liked to crawl into his skin, to sleep inside his gleaming sides, to share the warm breath I could see misting above his great raised head.

I remembered Nonosabasut only when I felt his arms slip around me. He lifted me until I was leaning back into his body, both of us standing, looking up at the caribou. Nonosabasut took my drawing hand in his and made a quick cut across the old scar Hebbosheth had put on my palm. We raised our hands, his above mine, and together we pressed my blood onto the place where the great animal's heart would be.

Nonosabasut turned me around so that my face was below his, where I could see nothing but the yellow and blue feathers his mother had woven into his leather jerkin. Keeping one arm around me he cupped his other hand under my chin and traced my lips with his thumb. I kissed his palm and tasted my own blood.

"There is still one thing we must do, Shanawdithit," he said, and undid the lacing on my tunic. His hand was on my back holding me as we fell together onto the caribou skin he had spread in the snow.

He drew me just as I had drawn the animal, his hands outlining my body, his fingers touching life into me. We became animals, animals inside animals, warm skin enfolding warm skin, became a world encircled by the breath of Old Caribou.

We slept a little then. When I woke he told me I must now go. We dressed and then he touched my lips again. "You will never speak of this, Shanawdithit," he said.

I did not answer, there was no need. He stepped to one side and I walked away. Not once did I look back at him or at the animal who had stood above us, watched our lovemaking, made us man and wife as surely as any shadowdancer could.

It was easy to follow the marks of our snowshoes, yet I took my time. I wanted to be alone, to keep what had happened to us separate from everything that had ever happened in our world. And so I dallied, holding happiness close, examining the patterns reeds make in snow, picking the frozen partridgeberries I'd seen beside the marsh on the way in.

I came out on the lake just as dusk turned into a cold clear night. Above my head stars glittered bright as ice chips, snow scrunched below my feet and below the ice a river ran black and cold.

When I knew our meotick was not far off I stopped. Soon other faces, other voices would break the perfection of this day. I stood still on the wide, white river and brought each part of the day, each heartbeat, to mind.

Nothing can change what has been; what has been must now always be. He and I will talk of this day all the seasons of our lives, I thought, and although my breath frosted on the fur of my hood I was warm.

Back in our mamateek I had not been missed. The hunters had not yet returned but Kasathi was making some kind of stew, using a large ugly root she'd dug up and a small fish Kakula had pulled through the ice. We decided the berries I'd picked could be boiled with a little water, mashed and given out to the sick.

When the hunters came back they had only two birds and a scrawny lynx. It was then it became known that Nonosabasut had not been seen all day. His mother and sister, being too weak to screech, began sobbing as if he were dead.

Nonosabasut's brother, Tomasuth, my brother Longnon and three others went out again, trekking back along the traplines, checking places where he might have slipped or fallen. I said nothing. Hours later they came back one by one. The hungry, half-frozen men assured Doodebewshet that they would have seen some sign if her son had been attacked by animals or taken away by Dogmen.

"Nonosabasut will take care of himself—by now he's built a shelter and is asleep," Tomasuth was telling his weeping mother when I went to their mamateek.

I was carrying a bowl of the hot partridgeberry drink into which I had stirred a little of the Old One's soothing herb. When I told Tomasuth that it would help Doodebewshet and Ashei sleep, he took the bowl gratefully.

At dawn the trackers spread out across the lake and frozen marshland. Halfway through the morning Tomasuth, Longnon and Newin were nearing the third hill when they saw Nonosabasut walking towards them.

"When he saw us he raised both arms, holding up a huge caribou head," Longnon told us later. The wonder of it made his voice boyish. "Nonosabasut was laughing, holding the animal's head above his own head, blood dripping down onto his face, running down his hands and arms. Behind him a trail of blood was melting into the snow."

It was Kasathi's brother Newin who raced back to tell us of the kill. When they heard his shouts every man in our meotick ran to grab spears, knives and containers. Following Newin, they came to the line of blood leading back to the remote place where Nonosabasut had killed the animal.

There, where Nonosabasut and I had lain, the men paunched and butchered the caribou. They drank his blood and divided his penis and liver among them, giving the first bite to Nonosabasut. All the while Adibish stood, looking out over the frozen valley, chanting songs of thanks to Old Caribou, apologizing for the indignities being performed on the animal's body and asking forgiveness of his spirit.

I stayed behind with the women, the children and the sick. Those of us who were well enough went to Adibish's mama-teek and built up the fire, put snow into leather containers and began melting it. Then we plaited three strips of wet hide into a tight twist, which we tied above the fire, attaching it to the centre pole below the smoke hole. When our men brought the body of the gutted caribou in, they cut off small bits for us to chew on while the meat was cooking. All of us sat in a circle, chewing and chewing, smiling at one another, the slippery warmth filling our mouths.

The great animal was hooked onto the braided line. As it unwound, the carcass twisted slowly, browning, fat feeding the flame until the flesh had cooked enough to eat. How wonderful it was to smell roasting meat! For the first time since coming to this dismal place there was talk, hope, and even laughter.

The old and sick sat nearest the fire, taking the most tender pieces of flesh, sipping hot marrow broth into which Doodebewshet had crumbled the last of her powdered egg. She was very proud of her son, smiling and nodding at the old ones as she passed the bowls around. It was the only time I ever saw her happy.

Some of the women began to hum Miaoth's song about when he sailed all around Baetha. The song told how the great traveller could call migrating birds down from the sky, lure bears from their caves and beaver from their lodges. Once Miaoth had tied his canoe onto an iceberg and been drawn into a deep fjord where he circled a whale, singing until the creature grew dizzy and rolled over, offering up its white underbelly to Miaoth's spear.

The old song went on and on. It made me think of Hebbosheth and wish she were beside me enjoying the flesh of an animal I had helped kill. Yet I was content, sitting by myself, eating and watching my people eat—listening to Nonosabasut's voice and remembering.

Again and again Nonosabasut was asked to repeat his story, tell how he had been shown in a dream what to do. How he had found the spirit rock Adibish had told him of and had slept beside it all night. He told how he waited while the sun rose, calling on Ash-wa-meet and all good spirits to send some animal that would save the People from starvation. When not speaking he sat quietly with the older men, beside my Uncle Adibish who had given over his place of honour to the young hunter.

When Nonosabasut spoke, his listeners leaned forward and watched him scratch in the dirt with a stick. "It was just sunrise. I was here and I saw the caribou there. He appeared, stood still against the sky as if waiting for my arrow—he gave himself to me. Not even a woman could have missed," he said, smiling around the circle of admiring faces.

The young man who had lain with me the day before seemed older, taller, his voice deeper.

We were warm, we had food and the Dogmen were far away. Nonosabasut talked and we ate, and when we were full we thanked all the good spirits who had given us a hunter with the skill of Miaoth. We praised Nonosabasut and made chants to him and to Old Caribou who had once again saved the People.

It did not trouble me that my part of the story was left untold. Some things must be done in secret and time unfolds all stories. I sat quietly, glad to be in the same world with him, loving him, imagining him years and years hence, an old man telling unborn generations—our children's children—the story of this day.

During the days that followed I waited, watching for some look or gesture, some sign that he and I were lovers, that when Firewoman next danced we would stand before all the People and be married. But he never spoke, never glanced my way. Telling myself to be patient, I waited as days turned into moons and moons into seasons.

XVI

So it was that Nonosabasut became our shadowdancer. Without any ceremony Sabasut's son moved into the role that Adibish had prepared for him. He began performing the old dances again. At night, when we gathered around the fire, I watched Nonosabasut's hands, overlapping, intertwining, his long fingers making shadow patterns on mamateek walls. I remembered those hands on my body and with all the spirit inside me I willed him to turn to me, to acknowledge me as his wife. If the Old One had been alive, I would have asked her, just as Adibish had once done, to hold her kuus staff up to the moon and say words that would make him mine. But Hebbosheth was gone and I did not know the words.

Unlike Adibish, our new shadowdancer did not keep his thoughts hidden. He spoke openly of making peace with Dogmen, of living side by side with them. Yet the old argument did not die completely. My brothers Longnon and Kakula, along with two or three others, disagreed with our new leader—though they seldom spoke such thoughts aloud.

The hungry winter ended and most of us survived. Nonosabasut was young and strong, he spoke to great spirits, he had brought us food—because of this people loved him, and opposition to his ideas seemed to melt as the snow melted.

We could not leave our bleak camping place, but even here the earth warmed, small animals returned, birds and wild geese flew in over the marshland and fish swam upriver. Soon there were green things to eat and all the sick, including our mother, began to feel better.

I was still young, just ten and four winters old. I did not know that half my life was over. When I saw that Kasathi was carrying Longnon's child some of the tightness inside me went away.

Always I hated to be in the forest or near fly-infested marsh after melt-time; always I longed for the smell of sea, for seafood cooked in seaweed, for icy water lapping around my feet, for silver fish rolling up onto white sand. But I was now doing woman's work and had little time to pine for those childhood summers on the holy beach.

My family still had three young hunters in our mamateek— my brothers Longnon and Kakula and my cousin Manus worked hard through every long summer day. After dark they would go fishing on the river. Mish-mish would go with his uncles, holding rushlight out over the water to attract fish to the men's spears. It was a lovely thing to watch—two moving flames for each canoe, one above and its reflection below, dancing on the black water.

Women's work was just as hard as the men's—sometimes harder because women had children to care for and meals to prepare while they were building smoke racks, keeping the fires going, and cleaning, stripping and drying whatever the men brought into camp. In our mamateek Mother and Auntie Santu were both feeble and could help only a little. It fell to Kasathi and me to render out fat, scrape skins, sharpen tools, gather wood, cook, make clothing, mend bedding furs and also to clean and thicken the walls of our mamateek against another winter.

I had no time now for making pictures or daydreaming, for hiding under trees, making up stories about young men, telling secrets, giggling. Kasathi and I spoke with Demasduit only when we met while gathering berries or firewood, or the plants we used for sickness and for cooking. My cousin seemed distant, quieter than she had been, thinner too. I thought her face more beautiful, with high cheekbones I'd not noticed when she was a child. Although he had bone stiffness, Adibish was still a skilled hunter, and Demasduit and her mother worked as hard as we did preserving food for winter.

In mid-summer when Kasathi gave birth to a healthy baby, we rejoiced but hardly stopped work. That night, the women in our mamateek marked the little girl's head with oil and ochre, and we whispered a welcome to the good spirits inside her skull. But we did not celebrate—celebration and the choosing of a spirit guardian for the child could wait until winter.

Winter was always there, gnawing at our backs like a wolf—the memory of last winter's cramped stomachs, the cold wind, the stink of sickness inside our mamateeks. We could not forget, not even with our hunters bringing in fox and marten, otter, hare, beaver and lynx. There were ptarmigan and inland birds too, and eel, trout and river salmon. None of these creatures had the rich fat of seals, the fat necessary for light and fire, the fat that would keep sickness away through a long dark winter.

We had seen no Dogmen since coming to this place Adibish said was secret, but whenever our men ventured near the seal beaches they found Dogmen on guard. In former years our hunters had sometimes been able to out-track these evil creatures, to go down to a beach at dawn and quickly take a seal or two. That year something changed—runners reported many more Dogmen in the hills above the beaches. Longnon said that all Dogmen now had muskets, were nervous and shot unthinkingly at everything that moved.

As the first summer of Nonosabasut's leadership ended, it became clear that we would be very hungry in the coming winter. Nonosabasut knew this. He left camp and went alone to one of our holy places.

My people have never piled stones into high, straight walls, do not build what you Dogmen call churches. Our holy places were shown to us by great spirits, by Crow and Firewoman, by Old Caribou and Ash-wa-meet. Even now, Dogman, even in this evil time when the great lonely headlands and the sea-washed caverns have been scooped out, hacked up and despoiled by your kin, even now there are secret caves whose entrances are hidden, small still clearings where no wind blows, no leaf rustles, where flowers bloom late and early. The Shadowdancer Nonosabasut went to such a place. He remained there all through the beautiful last moon of summer, fasting and asking guidance from the good spirits.

When our shadowdancer returned he stood before the People and told his vision. He had been shown a safe path our hunters could take to the sea, had seen a deep fjord—that same northern place where whales and white dolphin and harbour porpoise had once danced around the canoe of Miaoth the great traveller. I remembered the Old One's story and wondered if the spirit had told Nonosabasut that Miaoth was my ancestor, wondered if he had been directed to again ask for my help.

Nonosabasut was at the height of his manhood, aglow with the glory of his vision, more beautiful than even the Great Traveller could have been. Listening to my lover, I remembered how a young woman had swum out in the moonlight to meet Miaoth, how he had reached out and pulled her into his canoe. I wished that such a thing would happen to me.

I had not drawn in a long time—my hands were stiff from hard work—but that night I lit a small taper and while my family slept I drew whales and dolphins. Each night for three nights I practised. On the third night, Kasathi, waking to nurse her baby, found me drawing a chalky white whale on a flat blue stone that had markings like sea water.

She came and sat beside me. "You are doing this for Nonosabasut, I think."

I nodded and kept drawing, wondering how I had given myself away. After a long silence, sitting in the tiny flare of rush-light, I told my friend what had happened on the snowy hillside. I told her that Nonosabasut was my husband, said we were waiting for a time when he could speak of this to our mothers and to Adibish who was now my token father.

Kasathi did not give me that quick smile I had expected, did not even look up. She carefully unlatched the baby from one nipple and moved it to the other. Her breasts were filled with milk, round and softly brown, and I thought how good it was that her child had been born in summer when food was plentiful. When the baby fell asleep Kasathi stood and kissed me on the cheek.

"May good spirits watch over you, Shanawdithit, may Ash-wa-meet guide your hand." And still without smiling she went back to her sleeping place beside Longnon.

Nonosabasut never asked for my help. Four mornings after telling his vision, he raised the whalebone staff above the heads of our hunters. Without other ceremonies, without Adibish—without me—the chosen men walked away from our camp to search for Miaoth's fjord and the whales Nonosabasut had seen in his vision.

After he left I was desolate. Why had he not asked for my help, not taken me? I was deeply sorry that I'd told Kasathi my secret. I began avoiding her, shamed by the pity I saw in her face. I hoped she had not told Longnon my story of how Nonosabasut had called a caribou down from the Spirit World, began to wonder even if she might have told Demasduit. After a time I realized that Demasduit knew nothing. If she had known she would have teased me, laughed at the idea that Nonosabasut would choose me or that I could draw a living creature from rock.

Thinking over much about what Demasduit might say, I even wondered myself if our lovemaking at the spirit rock had really happened. Each night before sleep I made myself think carefully about that day, remembering each small thing as if it were a picture inside my skull. I imagined Hebbosheth's voice telling me that what I remembered was true—and since it was true, Nonosabasut and I were indeed promised to one another and he would speak of it when the time came. In this way I calmed myself.

Kasathi and I never spoke of Nonosabasut again. Our old, easy friendship slowly returned and we worked together happily, helping Mother and Auntie Santu build a steam house to use when the winter sickness came.

The hunters were gone almost a full moon, the camp strangely empty of young men, yet this did not disturb us. Three circles of seasons had now passed without Dogmen coming near us. We felt safe, were sure that our shadowdancer would return with the whale he had been promised.

It was deep fall, the most beautiful time in Baetha. Grey geese were still flying overhead, flocks so thick that even the rheumy-eyed old men Nonosabasut had left behind could bring down enough birds to feed us. When everything in our meotick had been cleaned and a new layer of hides covered our mama-teeks, when all the meat and fish we had was smoked and packed in a safe storehouse, then we began collecting wood, making a stack beside each mamateek.

After the steam house was finished, Kasathi and I, along with all the women and children, began spending our days berry picking in the marshland beyond our meotick. Berry picking is more pleasant than most women's work. Working and talking, eating together—even that short distance from our camping place—let us imagine we were on one of the spring treks we all remembered.

The thing I now tell happened when we were picking at the far side of the marsh. It was late in the day, light seeping away. The women who had been with us had returned to our meotick, but Kasathi and I stayed on, crouched down, picking our way around a grey boulder in the shelter of which her baby slept. The baby, who was almost three moons old, would soon wake and cry to be fed. When that was done we would follow the other women back to camp, eat whatever food Mother and Auntie Santu had prepared and then sleep. Perhaps I would dream of Nonosabasut. Already I was half asleep, thinking of him, dazed by the dusty blueness of fading day, by the movement of my cupped hands reaching under green leaves, filling with blue, blueness dropping into the skin pouch I'd tied around my neck.

The Listener forgot to listen. I knew this when it was too late, remembered the absence of bird sounds—although it was the time of day when small birds twitter and swoop (singing before night comes, I'd imagined as a child—singing to put off bedtime and darkness and evil dreams). The vast, empty marsh was completely still.

Even when I did hear something I thought it was the baby waking. I glanced over but she was still lying quietly, warmly rolled in rabbit skins, barely an arm's length from where I crouched.

Yet there was a sound. Not far away, not a bird or animal, and not Kasathi, whom I could see a little distance downwind, quietly picking. I bent forward and pressed a hand flat against the dark earth, forehead almost touching the moist bog. I held still and waited, watching brackish water pool around my hand. The sounds were not far off, coming from the dimness between us and the low hills. Kasathi must hear it. I pushed back my hair, raised my head a little and peered through low brush. She was half kneeling, letting a handful of berries fall into her birch bucket. I could tell from the way she carefully tipped her hand that her bucket must be full. I opened my lips to call out that we should go. Then I saw them.

Two Euano—Dogmen! Though I had never seen one I knew they were Dogmen, but *Euano*, our name for demon spirits, was the word in my head. They were big, not tall but big, and things hung from their bodies: knives and bags, furs and long sticks. There was a stink coming from them and darkness too, darkness in the air around them, heaviness, as if they should have four legs.

I was sure that they must hear my heart beating, expected them to turn and see me. But they saw only Kasathi. They came right up to where she was kneeling and then stopped. They towered over her, looking down. Then she looked up, only silence between them, silence and the blue misting evening that had seemed so beautiful. One Dogman said something, then reached down, grabbed her arm and jerked her up. The bucket tipped, blue spilling, Kasathi looking away from me, searching over her shoulder as if expecting someone. She was trying to save us, trying to keep the Dogmen from turning around, seeing me and her baby.

I reached out, hooked two fingers into the binding and quickly pulled the bundled infant through the bushes and into my arms. She was awake—two wide open, anxious eyes, an open mouth. I would have offered her my own empty breast but I had no time to untie my tunic. All I could do was stick a finger into her mouth and curl around her, folding us both into the soft spongy earth.

Kasathi made one sound, the beginning of a scream cut off before it could become a scream. I looked then and saw they had her on the ground between them, one Dogman under and one on top—her pinioned like a small bird being savaged by wolves. I did not look again but lay with my eyes shut, stomach cramping, my body curled so tightly around the baby that I might have been giving birth to the little creature. When my teeth started to clatter I bit on my arm until blood came.

I pressed my forehead against the ground and went inside my skull, listening to earth, calling silently to past time, begging help from that perfect place Hebbosheth had told me of. No help came. I silently cursed my Old One, prayed to any spirit, good or evil, to save us. In that hour I would gladly have traded all of Perfect Time for the power to bring Nakhani's fangs down on the necks of these Dogmen. Neither good nor evil answered me.

I pulled my mind back from the Spirit World and was suddenly, sharply, aware of everything—the chill of evening, the prick of broken twigs against my skin, the smell of rhodora, bog laurel and crushed berries, the salty bitter taste of marsh water mixed with my own blood. Finding myself alive, I was overtaken by such a great throb of relief that I almost cried out. It lasted only a heartbeat, but for a long time I lay still, feeling ashamed.

When I finally opened my eyes it was almost dark. My legs and arms hurt but I slowly pushed myself up on my knees and wiped mud from my mouth and eyes. All colour had drained out of the world. I knelt and looked out at the vast grey marshland, slowly, slowly turning until I had seen the full circle of earth around me. I could no longer smell Dogmen but still I waited, checking each rock, each shadow.

Only when I was sure they had gone, only then did I look down at the baby. Her eyes were still open, her mouth filled with berries, her small round face stained purple where I had pressed her against the berry-filled pouch and against my body. She was dead. I knew this, yet I cleaned the berries out of her mouth and tried to breathe life into her as I'd once seen Hebbosheth do with a choking child.

I closed her eyes and wiped her face as best I could. Then I reached inside the bindings to touch her tiny feet, whispering that she should hurry along the Ghost Path. These things I did quickly, without thinking, knowing they must be done from having watched Hebbosheth and Mother when my baby sister died.

When it was done I stood and took a few steps towards where I thought Kasathi should be. But it was so dark that I went back to the baby, undid one of her binding strings and tied it to a bush so that I would know where to find her body.

It took me longer than it should have to find Kasathi. She had moved—had been dragged or had crawled, farther away from us. She was on her side and had vomited. I eased myself down beside her, touched her face and lifted her head into my lap. She was breathing, short rasping breaths, her spirit fighting hard to live. I felt inside her mouth to make sure nothing was clogging her throat. I ran my hand down her neck and across her breasts—one nipple was torn, oozing blood and milk, and her tunic, the one I had made for her wedding, had been ripped apart or slashed and was tangled around her waist. Below, between her legs, there was blood, much blood and the slime of Dogmen.

I tried to wipe the vomit and blood from her face—crying and shaking, almost vomiting myself. I pulled the torn tunic down over her. I thought of going back to the baby, to take one of the skins she was wrapped in to cover Kasathi, but I was afraid to leave her. I raised her head and shoulders, resting her against me to ease her breathing. After that I knew there was nothing to do, no spirits to call to, no ancestors who would come to help us—nothing.

I sat in the dark marsh with my arms around my friend. I whispered her name and cried, my tears falling into her hair. By the time Mother and Auntie Santu found us, Kasathi had stopped breathing.

Mother and Auntie Santu and Doodebewshet washed Kasathi; along with the other women they anointed her body with oil and ochre. Demasduit combed her long hair and hung the strings of shell beads we had made as children around her neck, then the women wrapped her in her own bed skin.

I could only watch, telling them bit by bit what had happened in the marshland, repeating myself, crying, saying I was sorry again and again. Yet none of them seemed to blame me, not even Kasathi's mother. All the women of our meotick were there, together with two small children—the only babies left to us.

When he saw Kasathi's body, Adibish gathered the men and boys and led them into the night. They were only a few, three old men and some small boys the age of Mish-mish. My brother Kakula was older, the most able of the group and the only strong runner Nonosabasut had left behind. Kakula returned midway through the night to assure us that no Dogmen were nearby. Our old men and boys were patrolling the half-circle of marshland around our meotick, moving silently outward as if stalking game.

"We will find the demons who did this," Kakula told us. "Even Adibish has agreed we will kill them the instant we see them." He was watching our mother sew the body of her dead grandchild into a rabbit skin, the baby being no bigger than a rabbit.

"May I be the one to find them, may the spirits guide my arrow into their bellies, may I bring their heads back on sticks." My youngest brother's voice was as bitter as Father's had ever been when he spoke of Dogmen.

But the Dogmen were gone. While I'd crouched in fear, lain with my head touching earth, begging our ancestors for help, the hulking creatures who had savaged Kasathi had lumbered across the marsh and into the hills. Kakula did not bring back their heads, no one did. The men searched for three days and nights. They even followed Dogman spoor into the hills. Yet my people did not find the savages who killed Kasathi—I cannot say they killed her baby, my stupidity did that.

Adibish and his helpers came back into camp midway through the fourth day. He said that we must begin the ceremony for Kasathi and her baby at once, must take them to a grave place when darkness came. Only the boys were left to stand guard between our camp and the marsh. The rest of us stood in a circle—ten and six people holding rush-fire, each in turn speaking of Kasathi. I could not speak, but others remembered her kindness and recalled the happy, laughing girl she had been. Demasduit told of the games we had played, of the hours we three had spent under trees whispering secrets to one another.

Adibish spoke last. Holding the staff of Ash-wa-meet over the dead he asked all good spirits to guide Kasathi and her baby safely along the Ghost Path. Then we walked to the river and laid both bodies down in his canoe, all the women chanting a song Kasathi's mother had made for her daughter.

> For only a little while she was given life,
> this sweet earth to walk on,
> and for that time she walked lightly,
> joyfully and with love.
> Remember all you Spirits,
> this alone is required of us.
> Remember all you Spirits,
> and welcome my Kasathi into Perfect Time.

The sun was almost gone and the rushes we held had burnt to sparks, wisps of sweet-smelling smoke rising. I had not slept, not eaten, was still wearing the bloodstained tunic. I stood beside the water with my eyes closed, worn out with sorrow. I longed to empty my skull of thought, of memory, of everything that had happened since that moment when I knelt watching blueberries drop into my cupped hand—before I looked and saw evil.

One by one the singers stopped singing and the song dribbled into silence. I expected Kakula and the old men who had helped carry the bodies down to the water to go with Adibish to the burial place, but when I looked up, he was gesturing for them to stay ashore. Adibish was climbing into the canoe by himself.

"You who were her friends will take us to her grave place," he said. He moved Ash-wa-meet's staff until its eagle-feathered tip pointed first at me and then at Demasduit.

We both took a step back. I think Demasduit whispered, "No."

Adibish said nothing. He kept staring at us.

For all of our lives he had been the leader of our meotick, our great shadowdancer. He was still the elder of our family and Demasduit's father, and being my dead father's brother he was my token father. The pause before we obeyed him was not long.

Demasduit and I climbed into Adibish's half-moon-shaped boat. With our feet almost touching the wrapped bodies, we each took a paddle. The people on shore began a low moan that could have been mistaken for wind passing through trees. The sound followed us into the middle of the wide river and around the bend as we passed out of sight of our encampment.

Adibish remained standing, one foot balanced on either side of Kasathi's body, pointing his stave in the direction against which the river flowed. When he sat down, suddenly as if his legs had given away, he had to push the bodies to one side. Still he continued to direct us with his staff until we turned into a green reedy tributary that led back and back between rocky shores. The stream became narrow, so shallow that we had to move our weight sideways to keep from scraping bottom.

It was almost dark when Adibish spoke. "There," he said, pointing up to a place where rocks jutted like a ledge above the water, and we edged the canoe in to shore.

When we'd secured our hide-line to a crooked tree root, he asked if we could see anything in the cliff above us. "A red mark, like a blood-line pointing downward?"

Demasduit and I looked and after a time did see the mark—although we never would have if he had not shown us.

"Just behind the boulder to which the red line points there is a cave. When I was young, Osagana and I lived in it for a season. It is not a big cave but dry and safely hidden in the shadow of the broken ledge. Mishatut's body is there but there is room for others."

Either it was not possible for Adibish to climb the bank or he did not wish to do so. He told us what we must do, then sat in the canoe while Demasduit and I carried our friend up the steep hill. There were bushes and loose stones, and once I fell to my knees, but we reached the cave without dropping Kasathi. Demasduit sat with her while I went back down to get the baby. When I got down to the canoe I thought at first the old man had died, but he was only sleeping, chin on chest, snoring softly, his staff laid sideways across his lap.

I picked up the tiny bundle and carried it easily up the hill. But it was full dark by then and I was not able to find the cave under the ledge. I was frightened and closed my eyes. "Let me see, please, let me see," I whispered. And when I opened my eyes I could see a little—I have noticed that when spirits give it is either not *as much as* we ask or not *what* we ask.

I would not have found my way but for Demasduit. Hearing the rattle of loose rocks she called out, "Shanawdithit, is that you?"

"No, it's not me—it's Nakhani come to eat you." I was suddenly angry at us both for being weak and unskilled, for not being able to do this thing as well as our ancestors would have—as well as Nonosabasut would have.

Demasduit started to giggle, a thin silly sound that showed her fear. I followed the sound to the cave's mouth and by touching the rock face felt my way inside to even greater blackness.

When our senses returned we could barely make out Mishatut's grave—rocks piled over a hollow at the back of the cave, just as Adibish had told us. Together, Demasduit and I carried the bodies there and laid them down side by side.

"It is wrong to leave her here. A place so dark cannot be close to the Ghost Path."

Demasduit said just what I had been thinking. Always we have buried our dead where the spirit of light is strong, on headlands or in sea caverns that arch above shimmering green water. Godith's mother, who had given her life willingly, was here, yet it did not seem right that Kasathi and her baby should come to this place of shadows.

Demasduit suggested we make a song for the baby, although the poor little thing had not lived long enough for a naming ceremony or been given a spirit guardian. I touched the fur where I thought her feet would be and, our voices echoing off the rock walls, we sang the same small song our people had made for Godith. I wondered if his mother could hear us.

After that we did not know what to do. I would have drawn flowers or a rabbit or some small animal on the cave wall, but Adibish had forbidden us to mark the grave spot in any way. He said we must just put the bodies in the hollow and pile as many rocks as possible over them. Neither Demasduit nor I wanted to do this and we sat weeping beside the body of our friend until Demasduit said, "We will sing her song just once before we put rocks on her."

So we sat in the darkness and sang Kasathi's song, not once but many times, and for a short while it almost seemed we were children again, three of us singing under evergreen trees in the safe centre of Baetha. But in the end we had to put rocks on top of her and her baby—we had to leave.

Adibish heard us coming down the cliff and woke in a peevish mood, pretending he had not been asleep, needing assurance that we'd piled many rocks over the graves. I remembered the Old One lamenting for a baby sister whose doll and burial robe had been stolen by Dogmen—but Adibish did not speak of Dogmen, only said that wolves and bears would uncover bodies that were not properly buried. He made me and Demasduit promise that each season we would return to the cave, to make sure the grave place of Kasathi and her baby was intact.

"If their bodies are broken, dismembered or scattered, you must collect the bones and return them safely to earth," he told us. "If this is not done, the spirit of your friend will never find its way onto the Ghost Path that leads to Perfect Time."

When we had promised, he lay down in the canoe where the bodies had been and was asleep again before I untied the cord holding us to the tree root.

I kept even that promise, Grandmother. In the seasons that were left to me I went many times to Kasathi's grave place. Even when it was dangerous to do so, I returned. Even when Dogmen hacked down trees, cut trails up and down beside the river, I returned. Even in that last moon before leaving our camp to give myself up to Dogmen, I went alone to the cave. By then it had become the grave place of Demasduit also—and of her husband and child. That last time everything was as it should be. I placed one more stone on each body, six stones. Then I sat and wished for death, longing to stay forever in the enclosed stillness of a place that must now have been holy. But I had made another promise.

In the end I could go there only inside my skull, only by lying on the cold floor, the one place in that straight-walled room where I could see sky and clouds—see nothing that had been touched by Dogmen. I would lie on the floor and watch clouds move across the sky, clouds that had come over all the great forests and beaches of Baetha—places my eyes had once seen, my feet had walked on. In the time before they would come to scold and put me back between the white sheets, I would ask Firewoman to take me, not to the light-filled sea caverns, but to that small dark cave where my bones could be safely hidden beside the bones of people I had loved.

As we paddled down the shallow side stream on the night of Kasathi's burial a flurry of moths flew around us. Moth wings brushed our lips and eyelids like ghost spirits—the spirits of dead babies, Demasduit said. But I repeated what Hebbosheth had told me when my tiny sister died: "Babies have such pure spirits that they find the Ghost Path at once, without effort."

When Demasduit asked how I knew this, I said, "My Old One told me our baby was already in Perfect Time before she came out of my mother's body."

"She was not your Old One only. I also am a daughter of her grandson." Demasduit did not turn towards me but stared into the fluttering dark. Then she said, "I wished she had told me such things."

I knew this hurt was at the root of all the childish disagreements that lay between us. But I did not have Kasathi's kindness, did not say words that might have mended our friendship. So we slipped on through the silence, through moonless dark, leaving the moths behind, moving forward until the current told us we were in river water, until we saw the small fire our people had made to show where our camp was. Then we turned the canoe towards shore—and the love Demasduit and I had felt when we sat beside Kasathi's body was wasted.

As she pulled her paddle in, my cousin gave me a cold, appraising look. "I am older than you, Shanawdithit, I am more beautiful and I learn better. The Old One should have chosen me to be her listener." She said this before her father opened his eyes, but not, I think, before he woke.

Six sunrises later our hunters returned. They had killed many seals, and two blunt-nosed whales, the greatest prize of our people. They came walking towards us across the marsh, Nonosabasut and his brother and my brother—all our strong young men. They were singing, their voices coming ahead of them, giving thanks to Whale and to other good spirits. They strained under their heavy loads. Along with two canoes, they carried long thick strips of meat and sealskins. Bladderfuls of thick oil and good blubber hung from huge whalebones two men balanced across their shoulders.

The hunter's joy vanished when they saw our faces.

Adibish did not call them into his mamateek. Standing in the cool sunshine of early morning, he told the whole bitter story—or what he knew of it. Leaning heavily on his wife, for he was still exhausted, the old man spoke of his determination to find the Dogmen who had raped and murdered Kasathi. Then he told of the long search that had ended in failure.

Longnon, who was standing between me and our mother, had already asked where his wife and baby were. When Adibish said Kasathi's name, my brother made a choking noise. We wrapped our arms around him and held him upright.

"I am sure there were only two," Adibish said. "They were not with others and may have been lost or sent away because of some evil they had already done."

I wondered if he was moving towards his old song about there being two kinds of Dogmen, the few evil ones and the many good ones.

Nonosabasut may have had the same thought. He stepped

forward quickly and began a prayer to Ash-wa-meet, asking for the safe passing of Kasathi's spirit into Perfect Time. Then he gave thanks for all the food our hunters had returned with—food that would keep us from hunger through the winter season. He praised Old Caribou and Crow and the good spirits for giving him a vision of the sea fjord to which he had guided our hunters.

His voice was powerful, soothing, and he told of a place filled with whales, described the sight of whales blowing, plumes of water rising above their heads as they leapt and dove, trying to shake the harpoons embedded in their backs. The whales pulled against the long strips of hide, drawing canoes and men beyond the fjord and out towards open water, until at last life left the great bodies and they could be dragged back to shore.

At the end of Nonosabasut's story he spoke of each whale they had killed, giving thanks to each one's spirit guardian. He had not said such a thing but I began to feel that Kasathi had become a sacrifice to those spirits who had guided Nonosabasut and our hunters. Perhaps others had the same thought. Looking at the faces around me I sensed that people had lost their anger. A few were nodding, some even smiling as they listened to the words of our young leader. Only the faces of Kasathi's parents still showed their grief. The face of her brother Newin showed anger, just as Longnon's face did, just as all the faces of my kin did.

Because he was the husband of Kasathi, people did not hush Longnon when he broke the spell. "Are you going to tell them what we did?" His voice was loud as he pulled away from us. Suddenly he was standing directly in front of Nonosabasut, between him and the listening people.

"Tell them what you had us do!" My brother's hands were clenched at his sides, as if to keep them from hitting Nonosabasut.

With barely a pause Nonosabasut continued speaking. He was tall, almost a head taller than Longnon, and looked out over him as if he were not there. "It is fitting that we honour the dead and thank our spirit helpers before admitting our own human failings—I will tell them now," Nonosabasut said, and smiling, he placed his hands on Longnon's shoulders, obliging my brother to move aside.

Nonosabasut began to speak of two Dogmen he and our hunters had come upon in the far hills. It had happened just days before, on their way back from the fjord. The Dogmen were lost and starving; they had run out of shot and had crawled under bushes to the edge of a muddy pond. Lying on their stomachs lapping water as animals do, they had not seen our hunters.

Our men had wanted to walk past, leave the Dogmen to die—at least two would have killed them outright, I was sure one of these must have been my brother. When Nonosabasut reminded them that our ancestors had been told not to kill creatures who walked upright, someone laughed and said these Dogmen did not look very upright. The Dogmen heard and rolled onto their backs—it pleased me to think of the fear they must have felt when they looked up into the faces of six hunters.

At Nonosabasut's suggestion, our men sat on the ground and smoked while considering what to do with the Dogmen. After some talk our shadowdancer convinced the others that it would be pleasing to Ash-wa-meet if they gave the two Dogmen food and showed them the way to the coast.

While Nonosabasut told us about helping Dogmen he kept one hand on Longnon's shoulder, as if they were together in this thing.

Staring at Nonosabasut's hands I stopped hearing his words, remembered only how they had touched me. For a moment I forgot Kasathi who had been in the ground just six days, thought about nothing but Nonosabasut's hands moving over my body. What if that never happened again? A gulping sob came out of my mouth, a crow called, Mother's hand reached for mine. I was ashamed and began to rock back and forth, holding myself stiff, keeping my breath small and quiet so that Mother would not look at me and know my thoughts.

I had gone so far inside myself that I missed the movement of Longnon's fist until it slammed into Nonosabasut's jaw. I had never seen one of our people strike another. Even Adibish and my father, who for most of their lives had thrown bitterness at one another, even they had held back from violence such as this. Everything stopped. Many heartbeats after the blow no one moved. Nonosabasut stood perfectly still, his hand fallen from Longnon's shoulder, his face filled with shock.

Then Mother ran forward and pulled at Longnon's tunic. He did not seem to notice she was there, did not move until Nonosabasut's brother, Tomasuth, and another young hunter came. They wrapped their arms around Longnon and hauled him away, pulled him into Adibish's mamateek. Nonosabasut and all the other men followed, but when Doodebewshet tried to enter, shouting that she wanted to tend her son's injury, she was turned away. The bearskin was dropped down over the entryway.

Women and children stood around for a time, and then, not knowing what else to do, we began to work. Using piles of brush and small wood we had gathered while the men were away, the young ones built three fires. We women cut the huge slabs of meat into smaller strips and threaded it on sticks for roasting.

Neither Doodebewshet nor my mother took part in preparing the whale and seal meat. After she was turned away from Adibish's mamateek Doodebewshet simply sat herself down on the ground outside the entryway. She continued to call out, demanding to be let inside so that she could treat Nonosabasut's injured face. Then she began screeching that Longnon was as mad as his father, Washomish, that like his father he should be sent from our meotick before he killed someone.

Hearing this, Mother became even more angry. She took herself over to sit beside Doodebewshet, each mother calling out towards Adibish's entryway, demanding justice for her son. Together they made a terrible din, but no one reacted—not even me or Ashei, who as their daughters should surely have tried to still them. Everyone just kept on working until all the seal and whale flesh hung in neat rows over the fire, until each sealskin was stretched on a frame, until the whale blubber was rendered out, the fat and oil divided into birchbark containers so that every mamateek would have its own supply of the precious stuff.

While I worked a calmness came over me. I saw what I should do—if Longnon was sent away I would go with him. Kakula would come too, I knew, and our mother and Mish-mish if the boy wished. We would find another meotick, Ecshamut's perhaps. Ecshamut being the shadowdancer who had always camped nearest our meotick, we would know his people; indeed many had married into each other's families and so we had kin in his mamateeks. And if we could not find Ecshamut's people, my family would do well enough by ourselves with Longnon and Kakula to hunt for us.

I imagined us going to one of the secret places Hebbosheth had told me of, to the inland sea or to the canoe maker's island inside the lake. As Longnon had told Mother, in the immense land of Baetha there must be some safe place for us.

While making this plan I felt sure again, as if Hebbosheth were still whispering to me, telling me to take back my life just as she had done. The Old One's voice pulled my thoughts from Nonosabasut, peeling memory of him from my skin, shutting him out of my skull.

Then he came out of the tent and all my sureness was gone. He was alone, and would have tripped over his mother and mine had he been moving with his usual quickness. As it was he had time to stop. He bent down and, giving an arm to each, guided the two women from the entryway. When they were seated by one of the fires he smiled down at them and said, "I am sorry you have been unsettled." Both women seemed confused by his words but they stopped shouting and sat quietly.

When he turned towards us, all work stopped. With Doodebewshet and Nodurra silenced, our camp seemed eerily quiet. I could hear the river again, the crackling fires and spitting of fat. We waited. Nonosabasut looked at us, we at him. None of the other men came out from Adibish's mamateek.

I saw where Longnon's fist had made a dark bruise along one side of Nonosabasut's jaw, but the skin was not broken. Yet there was a difference in his face. His eyes had darkened; he seemed to be studying us, as if he had never truly looked at his people before, had never seen these tired sweating women, the half-starved children, all of us filthy with oil, blood and guts.

"I did wrong," he said. "I should have brought the Dogmen back to our meotick. Then I would have been guided by the wisdom of Adibish and of my elders." He held a thumb pressed into the hollow of his throat as if pushing the words out. "I am sorry," he repeated, though he did not look sorrowful.

After he spoke those words, all the men came out of Adibish's tent. Longnon came first and again stood in front of Nonosabasut, but this time my brother bowed his head. "I too am sorry," he muttered, then turned quickly away.

That seemed to be the end of it. People sat around the fires, lit pipes, began to eat and talk, children running about as if this were a meal like any other.

I saw our mother get up from beside Doodebewshet. She trailed Longnon into our mamateek and I followed her. Mother and I sat down beside Longnon. My brother was lying in the place where he and Kasathi had slept, enclosed in their sleeping furs, only the slow heaving of his shoulders betraying his grief. No one spoke. The day ended, I suppose we slept.

In the morning he was gone and Kasathi's brother Newin with him. They had taken bows and arrows, their spears and sleeping rolls, but none of the meat that hung everywhere about our camping place.

The bright, cold moon of late autumn shone, the river caught over and the marshland became a blaze of yellow, red and purple. In trees skirting the marsh, dogberries froze, glowing like small suns in the haze of morning frost. Longnon and Newin did not return.

Before the first snowfall, Mother became sick, as she often did in wintertime. I saw then that my thoughts of leaving our meotick were foolish—she would never survive another trek through cold and dampness.

Then Firewoman danced and Adibish told us that if she danced again that season we would have a marriage ceremony. I wondered which of the few young women in our meotick was to marry. Besides myself, my cousin Demasduit and foolish Ashei, I could think only of Gowet, who was Mish-mish's mother. Gowet had once been promised to my brother Ianamish and after his death had returned to her father's mamateek. I had often seen her talking with Newin and I wondered if he would now return and marry her.

The very next night Firewoman flung her rainbows of light out again, colours whirling and weaving above us as she danced. I had never seen her so beautiful. Everyone came outside to watch—even Mother, rolled in fur, wheezing but determined. I had been wrong about Newin—he had not come back. But Ashei was standing just outside the door of her family's mamateek. She was dressed in her ceremonial tunic and looked well pleased with herself.

Then I saw Demasduit on the other side of the fire. Leaving Mother with Auntie Santu, I went to stand beside my cousin. She and I had barely spoken since the trip to Kasathi's grave place. I touched her shoulder. "It is Ashei, isn't it?" I said. We had often spoken of how Doodebewshet spoiled her daughter, and I almost laughed, asking, "What man is going to marry that whiner?"

Demasduit did not turn her head to me, but her shoulder jerked impatiently. I dropped my hand and looked towards Ashei. She was folding the stiff bearskin back from the entryway to her mother's mamateek.

Her brother Nonosabasut came out. He stood tall and beautiful, looking straight at me. He began walking towards me—and I, stunned by happiness, stayed rooted to the ground. I cannot tell how long I was held in that moment, caught in the glory of Firewoman's dance, my lover coming towards me.

Beside me Demasduit moved, ran to meet him. Then she and Nonosabasut stood together before the People. All their near kin—his mother, Doodebewshet, along with Tomasuth and Ashei and then Demasduit's mother, Waunathoake—all came and stood beside the young couple.

Adibish came out of his mamateek and spoke words to Nonosabasut and Demasduit. He held the moon staff of Ash-wa-meet over them and told us they were now man and wife together. Then everyone danced.

And Shanawdithit walked down to the river. She wished for the courage to walk out on its thin glaze of ice, wished to die. But she did not—she kept on living and living. . . .

XVII

It was deep winter before we heard what had become of Longnon and Newin. When one of the little ones died of breathing sickness, Adibish, along with Tibeast who was the child's father, walked far upriver, taking the body to the same place where my father and also Tibeast's parents had been buried. Such places are not so hard to get to when the river is frozen.

When the two men returned, Adibish, who knew my mother was sick and worried, came at once to our mamateek. Mother and I were alone, as we often were that winter. My brother Kakula came in behind Adibish but he remained standing just inside our entryway as if guarding it.

Adibish had come to tell us of Longnon and Newin's whereabouts. Both men were well, he said. "They have made a rough shelter under a rock overhang beyond the first hill, half a day's journey from the grave place of my brother, Washomish."

It was the first time I had ever seen Adibish in our mamateek.

When I put a bowl of tea into his hands I saw that his fingers were curled and lumpy like Hebbosheth's.

"I thank you," he said, surprising me with what seemed to be a look of approval.

He sipped the hot drink, and Mother roused herself enough to ask if her son was coming back.

Adibish told us that the men had refused to return with him and Tibeast. "But they are not sick and have both food and furs. Before leaving I showed them a place farther up the hill, where the rock cut is deeper, where they will have more protection from snow and wind."

"Why do you come into our mamateek to tell us this?" Kakula spoke roughly, without moving from the entryway.

"Your brother asked us to tell only his close family where his camping place is." Our uncle's voice was mild, though he must have heard Kakula's rudeness. "He asked me to mark out the place for you and to say that if there is hunger in our meotick this winter, you, Kakula, must go to him to get meat."

Adibish took a stick and drew the way to Longnon and Newin's camp in the dirt beside our dying fire. Then he drank the rest of his tea and, without another word, stood and walked past Kakula and out of our mamateek.

Our mother lay back and closed her eyes. Kakula came near and hunkered down, me staring over his shoulder until we both memorized the marks showing the river, the hills and the line leading between the first and second hills, curling like smoke up to the cross Adibish had drawn deep into the dirt.

"I do not trust our uncle," Kakula said. "He will tell Nonosabasut." He scuffed out the map.

In the time since Firewoman danced, I had not looked into Nonosabasut's face or into the face of Demasduit. Even to say his name without flinching I had to steady myself. "Nonosabasut will not bring harm to our brother," I said.

"Longnon thinks he will. Why else would he want his camping place kept secret?"

I had no answer for him. In my heart I felt that Nonosabasut had more to fear from Longnon than Longnon did from him. But I would not have said such a thing to Kakula—or to anyone.

After Adibish's visit, our mother stopped eating and her illness grew worse. She had always suffered terribly from the cold but now she coughed up blood and painful sores broke out around her mouth and eyes. It hurt her to talk and I did not want to talk, so we spent the winter of her dying in silence. I used the last powder in one of Hebbosheth's eel-skin pouches to make a salve for her skin, then Santu and I took her to the steam house to help her breathing. It was not well built, and so small that only Mother and I could fit inside. Yet I spent whole days there in a strange, hazy peace, dribbling water over the hot rocks—hiding from the sight of Nonosabasut and my cousin, and from the gloom of our mamateek.

Every winter in that exposed place was bitter, but that season each mamateek had a little oil, so at least the cold and darkness was not constant. Santu's son Manus, Kakula and Mish-mish, like other men, caught a few small fish and sometimes a duck or partridge. This, together with the whale and seal meat Nonosabasut and his hunters had brought into camp, took us safely through the first four moons of winter.

It was near melt-time when Mother died. We were together in the steam house, curled on mats, asleep. I woke and knew I was alone even before I missed the rattle of her breath. I could not tell if it was the silence that woke me or if she had died long before. She looked peaceful enough, and was so small that I lifted her and carried her back to our mamateek.

Adibish's bones pained so much that he could not take our mother to her grave place. Kakula refused Nonosabasut's offer of help, but she was so light that all alone Kakula carried her body upriver to the place where our Father was buried.

Kakula was away a long time, longer than he should have been to put our mother in her grave place. When the river ice broke I knew he would have to come back the long way, crossing the wide exposed marshland. I began to worry, but Mish-mish was sure Kakula was with Newin and Longnon in their hidden camp. That would be good, I thought, imagining my brothers together at our parents' grave—together and safe. It was my only good thought.

My aunt Santu and her sick husband began using our steam house, Mish-mish and Manus were always out in search of food, and I spent most of my days alone inside our mamateek. I slept alone and ate alone, lived each day by keeping my mind from the day that would follow. Sometimes I forgot to eat—there was little food left anyway.

For a time I forgot even to wash and I let my hair grow into a wild tangle. I knew that if I did not stop grieving for my lost self I would turn into a bibin, just as Doodebewshet had done. I wished for someone to talk to, but Auntie Santu had her own troubles and Mish-mish was still so young that he thought I was grieving for my mother. Every night I pressed my ear to the earth, listening to the bones in my skull, straining to hear the voices of Former People, or even Hebbosheth's voice, telling me what I must do. No voices came.

As I became thin and ever more wraithlike, Demasduit grew more and more beautiful. She had moved into Nonosabasut's mamateek and seemed pleased enough with the company of his mad mother and foolish sister. Sometimes I would hear Demasduit's laughter. To me it was an unpleasant sound, out of place in the misery around us. I think I knew before she did that she was carrying his child inside her belly.

Always at melt-time I remembered our treks to the sea, always then I longed to leave the place where I was and walk towards the coast—something I would never again do. That spring I could not abide being around people—it is easier to be alone when you are lonely. I began leaving camp, walking great distances every day. This was unwise, but no one now noticed my comings and goings.

I did not cross the marshland but stayed close to the river, pushing through low brush and birch along its banks. Where the water was shallow I walked in the river, though it was still cold. One day, well upriver from our camp, I was walking along a sandbar, ankle deep in water, when I noticed a tall broken pine beside a grey rock I'd not seen before. I splashed ashore and found the rock was a canoe that had been abandoned and pushed under brush. Since the bark was dry with rot I knew it must have been there for more than one circle of seasons. When I saw Hebbosheth's new moon marked into the keel line, I claimed the little boat as mine.

After that I spent my days patching the canoe. The ribs were still strong and I took my time. Trying to remember everything Hebbosheth had told me, I cut out the rot and replaced it with fresh bark that I softened in the river, gumming patches outside and inside with a mixture of spruce resin, fat and my own hair.

I found Hebbosheth's moon-shaped drawknife in our mama-teek and made a rough sort of spruce paddle. The flint edge was still sharp and the upward-curved bone handle fitted as neatly in my hand as it must have in hers. I did not think of Nonosabasut all the while I was smoothing the paddle and shaping its rounded end. Remembering these things now, I know Hebbosheth sent her canoe to save me from madness.

I did not bring the canoe back to our meotick but kept it hidden where I found it. When the ice was all melted I began taking the little boat out whenever I could get away without being seen. I was so unimportant in our meotick that no one took notice of what I did.

I would leave our camp at dawn, walk to the sandbar, then paddle upriver until midday, trying each day to go a little farther. When the sun was high I drank river water, then lay down in the canoe, floating backward with the current. In the drift between sky and water I did not think and did not remember, feeling nothing but the pull of water below me, the movement of sky above. I imagined myself on the Ghost Path and was content.

But always I had to come back to the misery of our meotick. By then our oil was used and our whale and seal meat eaten and it was not yet full summer, still that time of year when only pale shoots of fern grow, when animals are thin and wary and even fish have little flesh on their bones.

When Kakula returned to camp with the haunches of a small bear slung on his back, everyone gave thanks and was glad—for a few days we would not be hungry. Only I, and perhaps Adibish, knew the meat came from Longnon. That night, inside our mamateek, Kakula told Mish-mish and me that he would not have come back except for the meat.

"Longnon and Newin live well. Their camp is in a more pleasant place than here," he told us. "They will never come back but they would be happy if others joined them."

Although I had seen Adibish's drawing and knew it was not so, I still imagined their camping place to be near the sea. Kakula said no, it was even farther from the sea than our meotick. "Their camp is on the far side of the third hill, near a waterfall. The hill is steep, almost a mountain, and stands like an island in a sea of marsh and barren land. Beyond the barrens on one side is the forest where they hunt. On the other side the marshland is circled by two small rivers."

Longnon and Newin's camp was much safer than ours, Kakula said. "Yet they are always on guard, always watching. I am a runner and thought I was well hidden when I crossed the barrens, but they knew I was coming long before I was at the foot of their hill."

Mish-mish only wanted to know what animals were in the woods around Longnon's camp. The boy had been born in this desolate place and had never seen the richness of life in an evergreen forest or the vast caribou herds that had thundered through my childhood. Our nephew knew Kakula did not have great hunting skills and teased him a little with questions about how he'd killed the bear. Yet, when he asked if Kakula would someday take him to Longnon's camp, my brother smiled and said that perhaps he would.

We talked for a long time. Before Mish-mish went to his sleeping place, Kakula warned him not to speak of Longnon and Newin's camp to anyone, not even to his friend Joisp, the only other boy his age in our meotick. After Mish-mish was asleep, my brother told me other things. He said Longnon and Newin talked constantly of making a meotick of people who wanted to fight Dogmen. They spoke of owning land, all the land they could see.

"But land is like water, like air—people cannot own land!" I said.

"They both know such a thing is against words passed down by many shadowdancers, but Longnon says we must now act like Dogmen and claim ownership of the earth." When Kakula said this he was leaning forward, watching my face, trying to judge my reaction.

"Hebbosheth also wanted to fight Dogmen, but she thought it evil to own the earth. People cannot own Baetha—to think such things is beyond evil. From Perfect Time we have known the earth owns us, as it owns all living things." When I said this I wondered if our brother also wanted to own fire-sticks—but I did not ask.

It was a soft night and we were almost outdoors, crouching in the shadow of our entryway, as far from our nephew's sleeping place as we could get. Santu and her husband were both unwell and were at the steam house, but Manus their son came while we were talking.

Manus did not ask to sit with us, but when Kakula glanced at me and we both nodded, our cousin lit his pipe and settled down beside us. Manus was a silent one and older than us, near the age of our oldest brother. Kakula and I did not know him well, but he and Ianamish had been friends and we trusted him.

Kakula looked from me to Manus. "You two must never speak of what I am going to tell you—not to anyone!" he said just as he had to Mish-mish. We both nodded, though it vexed me that my brother would think it necessary to say such a thing.

There was a crescent of moon, like Hebbosheth's mark, in the sky and by its pale light I could see excitement in both men's faces. Coldness touched the back of my neck.

"Longnon and Newin have the heads of two Dogmen set on poles outside their mamateek," Kakula whispered. "They have vowed to kill every Dogman they see. They say Dogmen are easy to track, and they are both good with arrows."

"Ah." Manus made a low, approving noise. He picked up a stick, scraped two marks in the dirt and made a line across them. "For Kasathi and her baby," he said. Then he began making other marks, one after the other. For each mark he whispered the name of someone killed by Dogmen, beginning with his wife, Amet, and my brother Ianamish, who had both died the night we threw fire at the Dogman boat.

Kakula and I watched. When there were many, many marks Manus put the stick down. "Soon my father and mother will walk on the Ghost Path. When they are gone, I will go to Longnon and Newin and help kill Dogmen," he said quietly.

"I will go there with you!" The words came from my mouth without thought. For the first time since Firewoman's dance I saw a life for myself, imagined what I could do with the seasons I had yet to live.

Both my brother and cousin looked troubled—even after the savage things we had spoken, this thing shocked them. Manus studied his hands for some time, then said it would be against the will of ancestors for an unmarried girl to live in the mama-teek of young hunters.

"It is also against the will of ancestors to kill Dogmen," I said. But they would not hear. "I will marry Manus, then," I told them. Manus was not beautiful and had a twisted foot from an old infection but he was tall and had a kind face.

When they reminded me that Manus was close kin, I persisted, saying I could marry Newin, the brother of my friend Kasathi.

"You cannot go, Shanawdithit," Kakula said.

"I will go, I will!" I was almost crying. "I will marry Newin and live with him and Longnon, I will clean hides and cook meat." I told Kakula that he was only my baby brother, not my father.

It embarrassed Kakula that I would say such things in front of Manus and he became cross. "You cannot marry Newin—he has asked me to take Gowet back to their camp if she will agree. Gowet is better at women's work than you are," he said. Then he smiled. "Ash-wa-meet may yet send you a husband, Shanawdithit. Young men from other meoticks will join Longnon's camp—I will keep a watch for you."

I hissed through my teeth and went and lay in my sleeping place. Turning my back on the men, I began to think over everything Kakula had said. I wondered if Longnon's camping place was near the place where Nonosabasut and I had killed the caribou, wondered how I might be useful to Longnon even without a husband. Perhaps I could become a canoe maker.

I fell asleep thinking of Hebbosheth's canoe and of the two rivers that ran along the marsh below Longnon and Newin's camp. And while I slept a voice inside my skull whispered, *Wait and listen, wait and listen.*

Days became warmer, fish came up the river and geese flew in over the barrens and there was enough food to keep us from starving. Kakula disappeared often from our meotick, staying away longer and longer each time, until whole moons would pass without his sleeping one night in our mamateek. I thought no one was taking heed of my brother's comings and goings, until I saw Adibish watching him the third time he came into our camp with meat.

Demasduit gave birth to her baby on the longest day of summer. It is considered lucky to be born on this day and indeed the child was strong and Demasduit herself was walking about soon after he was born. I stayed in our camping place that day, thinking Demasduit might have need of the herbs I'd gathered, but she did not call me to her tent, though I had once been her friend. Nonosabasut's mother, Doodebewshet, and his sister, Ashei, were the women who had helped with the birthing. It was they who brought the baby outdoors on the first morning of his life, rubbed oil and ochre across his forehead and whispered his name to the good spirits.

As is our custom, the baby's father came out behind them. Nonosabasut took the child from Doodebewshet and held him out for all of us to see. "When the season for my son's naming comes we will take him to the seal beach," he told us. "In that holy place we will choose his spirit guardian, and there we will give him the name Osagana after the great shaman who was my father Sabasut's grandfather."

By then many summers had passed since the People had walked to the seal beach, yet I did not doubt that Nonosabasut would take his son there. If only your son were mine! I thought, then we would go together. I imagined us coming out of the forest, looking down over that wide sweep of sand, sea and sky. I fought the need to weep, wanting to turn away, but was held by my love for the man and by the beauty of the child in his arms. Summer sun shone like a blessing on Nonosabasut's face and hands, on the body of his naked brown-skinned baby.

"The future will be better for my son," Nonosabasut was saying. He was very happy, smiling openly—as he had never smiled at me.

"As the Great Shadowdancer Osagana wished, so it will be," he said. "Soon we will make peace with Dogmen. They will join us in protecting the sacred places—our children will once again run and play on our holy beach—our shadow-dancers will again dance there. Our dead will again lie with their Ancestors in the great cavern of the sea." He continued to speak, but knowing the power his words had over me I left.

I went to the river, walked through brush up to the sand-bar and took my canoe out. I did not turn back at noon but paddled hard all through that long summer day. When dark came I was exhausted, and I tied up below the drooping branches of a poplar tree. All night I heard a sound like rain on a mamateek. Although it was the first night I had ever spent away from my people it did not come to me to be afraid.

When I woke I was very hungry. After drinking river water I left the canoe and went a little ways into the trees. I put my feet down quietly, searching the ground for fern, or the nest of some ground bird. Just where the small woods turn into marsh I found both fern and a nest from which I stole two of the hen partridge's ten eggs.

I was uneasy being so near the marsh and so I went back to sit beside my boat to eat. The fern was crisp, had a minty taste that went well with the richness of the brown spotted eggs. It was a lovely morning, the sky and water still pink with dawn, the still air smelling of summer and only a little cool on my skin. I thought I might take my tunic off and swim when I finished eating. The pleasure I was feeling in these things—the morning, the taste of food, the thought of washing myself in the river—shocked me. I marvelled that my body could play traitor to my mind's grief.

I had sucked the last juice from the second egg and was about to stand, when a hand closed over my mouth.

"It's me! Longnon." My brother took his hand away. "I thought you might scream," he said. Instead of sitting, he straightened up and stood, leaning a little away from me as if listening for some sound from upriver. "What are you doing alone and so far from our—your—meotick?"

"I have a canoe—it was made by our Old One. I come on the river often."

"I looked over your canoe while you were away robbing nests. I could have taken it, anyone could have—if that happens you will have to walk back across that open marshland." He sounded angry, looked stern and much older than he had just summers ago when he and Kasathi had danced with Firewoman.

"Nothing will happen," I said. "I will drift down to the sand-bar and walk downriver to our camp." I had not gone on the marsh since Kasathi was killed there, had never considered how I might get to our meotick if something happened to the canoe. "Nothing will happen—I come on the river often," I said again, feeling he was not really listening.

"And I have seen you often, but this time you came much farther. Why?" He folded his arms and looked at me the way our father used to, as if he were trying to see inside my skull.

"You have become very like Father," I told him.

"Were you looking for me?"

"No," I said. Then I wondered if I had been, wondered if I had come to tell him the words Nonosabasut spoke when he held his newborn out to us.

"The meat you and Newin send keeps us from hunger," I said, hoping to turn his mind away from me.

He nodded. "What has Nonosabasut done?"

"Would I come upriver because of him?"

"With you all things are because of him."

No one but my Old One had ever guessed my feelings. My surprise must have shown.

I saw the breath he took before saying her name. "Kasathi told me," he said. "She always knew, even before you told her." Then he asked again, "What has Nonosabasut done?"

"He and Demasduit have had a baby—a son," I said. Then I repeated what Nonosabasut had said the day before, about making peace, about going back to the seal beach and living together with Dogmen.

"Euano!" Longnon spit on the ground, turned and walked a few steps into the woods.

Sorry, and afraid for what I had just done, I sat and waited. My brother's burden of hate was big enough. Why should I add to it?

After a long silence I asked about his camp, asked how Gowet was doing. But he would speak of nothing but Dogmen, told me how he and the others had stolen into a Dogman cove, hidden under the wharf and cut loose a Dogman ship. "We let her drift across the bay, took her rope and sails, and smashed all the muskets she was carrying."

"So, you did not take the Dogman weapons?"

He gave me a hard look. "No," he said, "but I might next time. It was not difficult to take a Dogman ship—next time we will go to a different bay, then another, then another. I have learned that Dogmen are easily confused—to trick Dogmen we only have to do nothing in order, nothing straight."

"How long before it will end?"

"It can never end until we or they are all dead. Dogmen hate us even more now that they know we will fight back. Perhaps you should warn Nonosabasut of this. If he tries to have dealings with them it will be the death of you all."

"The way it was for Hebbosheth's family," I said, remembering her terrible story of the meotick filled with dead people.

"Perhaps that way, perhaps some other way. Dogmen carry death in their breath, on their backs—between their legs."

When he spoke again it was to tell me about a message tree near the place where I hid my canoe. He described the lightning-struck tree I had noticed earlier, told me to put a piece of marked bark in that tree if Nonosabasut ever made plans to contact Dogmen or to bring Dogmen into our meotick. He again told me to warn Nonosabasut that Dogmen had become even more savage.

"If you hear of their coming, listen and let me know how many and if they are blue-coat Dogmen or the other, untidy ones." He picked up a piece of bark and showed me the marks I would need. "Kakula is a good runner but does not hear things you might hear. You are the listener."

When my brother said this he smiled, and for a heartbeat I saw the younger, light-hearted Longnon and remembered the wintery day he and Ianamish had taken me to their traplines. "Do you remember walking across the ice towards our meotick?" I asked. "You carried spears and two brace of hare and Ianamish carried me on his shoulders. We saw wolves—it was sunset, pink and purple turning blue, and there were only us three, walking through blueness, towards the smell of meat, towards the smoke rising from our campfire. Do you remember?"

He shook his head, but later when he pushed my canoe out into the current, he reached in and brushed his palm along the moon mark Hebbosheth had cut into the keel. "Baetha," he whispered, and I knew he remembered.

Around this time Mish-mish and his friend Joisp, along with two younger boys, began fishing on the river during the day. Because of this I often could not go to my canoe. Since I would not walk across the marsh I was forced to spend time around our camp. Working with other women, I saw Demasduit often. She was so pleased and proud of herself that I could have slapped her sweet smiling face.

Nonosabasut, as always, hunted with his brother and other men, but one day he and she and the baby went together out across the barrens. They managed to kill a half-starved caribou that must have wandered from the herd's travel lines. The meat was tough, but like the others I ate it and smiled. Our shadow-dancer did not speak again of Dogmen or going to the seal beach, but even if he had, I could not have gotten to Longnon's message tree without being seen.

Late that summer my cousin Manus, along with Nonosabasut's brother, Tomasuth, and the hunter Tibeast, ventured back towards our old camping places. They hoped to find caribou and if they did not, vowed to continue on towards the coast in search of seal.

The men carried a canoe and walked back the way we had come many winters before. Then they took the canoe down Eel Lake and portaged inland to a place not far from our old abandoned winter camp, the place where our caribou fences once stood. Our fences had fallen and were rotting into the ground. Near Great Spruce Lake they came upon a mamateek that had been burnt seasons before. Nowhere in all that vast country did they see any sign of the People.

It was after they left the burnt mamateek that Tibeast was killed. He was walking ahead, and the shot went into his heart. He died at once. Manus and Tomasuth dropped to the ground and stayed under the canoe until nightfall. For days after they were followed—hunted, Manus said. "Always we could hear Dogmen. Once we were shot at but they were far off."

They managed to get back to Eel Lake carrying Tibeast's body. The Dogmen did not have canoes, so Manus and Tomasuth were able to find a grave place for Tibeast in a rock covered pit beside the river.

This was the story Manus and Tomasuth told us. Tibeast's wife and his father were comforted, knowing he died quickly and was buried in a safe place. I listened and watched the faces of Tomasuth and my cousin while they talked, and I knew they were not saying all that had happened.

If my brother had been in our meotick I know Manus would have told him the true story, but Kakula was again in Longnon's camp. Manus and Kakula had grown closer—I often heard the low murmur of their voices late into the night. One was my brother, the other my cousin, and it angered me that I was not included in these talks. Perhaps because of this, I determined I would find out what, in truth, had happened to Tibeast.

Manus's father had died in late winter. After that, Auntie Santu began to leave the steam house when darkness fell, was again sleeping in our mamateek. Days passed before the night came when Mish-mish went to sleep early and Santu stayed a little later in the steam house. Even when we were alone it took time before I could persuade my cousin to tell me what had really happened on the hunt.

"Although we saw no large animals, everything went well until we came upon the burnt mamateek," he began at last.

I sat beside him, discovering that Manus was a better story-teller than I would have expected.

"From the state of the hides we could tell that the fire must have happened more than one winter ago. Yet there were still evil spirits about the half-burnt mamateek—as if someone was watching us. We left the small clearing quickly, not even taking time to look for bones or people.

"Dogmen are not great trackers and very soon we knew we were being followed. After that, one of us would keep behind and to the side of the two carrying the canoe. We were still far from the coast, not even out to Spruce Lake, and I was the one scouting behind when they first shot, but the muskets were too far away to hit me. We did not turn back but veered inland a little before crossing again over our own footprints. By then we knew there were two groups of Dogmen—five or six in all and they seemed to be hunting together. That is what it was, hunting!

"At sunset we hid the canoe and searched until we found tall, strong trees to sleep in. Although we had chosen trees a good distance from each other, I expected to wake up encircled by Dogmen. I stayed awake a long time. Then I promised my spirit guardian that if I lived until morning I would become a hunter of Dogmen. After that I squirmed down into a place where three thick branches met and slept until dawn.

"When I woke it was fine and dry and there were no signs of Dogmen. Tomasuth thought they had passed us in the night, but I did not think so. Dogmen dislike moving about at night more than we do—and there would be signs if they'd come our way.

"Being the oldest it was I who told Tomasuth and Tibeast that we should spread out a little, lie in wait, and kill one pack of Dogmen as soon as they came by. We three had hunted together before and knew how to draw our prey into a trap. Dogmen are easier to kill than bear or caribou, and arrows, unlike muskets, would not give our position away. I explained how we could kill the first pack, then track the other and do the same."

Manus must have forgotten that Tomasuth was the brother of Nonosabasut. He was surprised by the man's outrage at the idea of killing Dogmen.

"I could not understand him. Dogmen had been tracking us for a full day, they had shot at me, were trying to kill us—and now Tomasuth talked as if sending an arrow into them would make all good spirits turn away from us forever," he said.

Tomasuth and Manus argued so bitterly that Tibeast had to put himself between the two men to keep them from hitting each other.

"Our anger disgraces us both," Manus told me. "Tibeast was the wise one. He remained calm, telling us that we must be mad to fight with one another when there were Dogmen to fight. He made us sit down and talk, made peace between us, said if the Dogmen continued to track us that day, the next morning we could talk again about hunting them. In the end we agreed with his words and kept walking towards Great Spruce Lake.

"We did not hear or see any Dogmen in the morning. It was late afternoon—Tomasuth and I were carrying the canoe—when we heard shots."

Manus stopped here in his telling. "I should not tell a woman this," he said.

I sat quietly, quietly, and then, because some things must be told, he continued.

"Tibeast was not dead when we found him—not dead at all. The shot had knocked him back and he was half lying, fallen against a rock. He was staring at us and his hands were pressed to his chest. He was trying to catch his own blood, to lift it to his mouth to drink. But the blood ran out of his body too fast, it ran between his fingers and down his face. When he saw us his hands dropped. He looked at me and said, 'Do it.'

"'Kill Dogmen?' I asked.

"He moved his head and made his lips smile. 'Me first,' he said.

"I understood and did what he wanted.

"Afterwards, Tomasuth and I wrapped Tibeast in his sleeping roll and put him in the canoe. It was a slow, awkward portage but we managed to carry him all the way to Eel Lake in the canoe. No Dogman would portage their heavy boats that far in-country, and even if they had, none could make it down that whitewater. Because of this we knew we would be safe if we could get to the lake. I don't know why they gave up tracking us—perhaps having never seen all three of us they thought Tibeast was travelling alone. We never went near the coast, yet they had hunted us as if we were wild animals!"

Even crouching in our mamateek telling me this, Manus was in a rage of despair, his usually quiet voice becoming loud. "Do you think Dogmen eat us or wear our skins?" he asked. "Or is it for pleasure that they make such misery of our lives?"

The next day he left our meotick and did not come back. I knew he had gone to join Longnon and Newin. Everyone knew. Just as people knew that the moon before that, Gowet had gone to become Newin's wife, just as they knew the meat Kakula brought into our camp was killed by Longnon or Newin. Yet, outside the mamateek of my family no one spoke of the names of these people who had gone from us.

Seeing that we faced another winter without seal oil, Nonosabasut began to talk again of a whale hunt. It did not matter that this time he had no vision. Adibish advised him to go away to a place where he could fast and speak to his spirit guardian. But Nonosabasut said that having once shown him the way, these good spirits would surely expect him to keep going to the whale fjord to which they had directed him.

Of the six strong hunters who had gone to find whale the year before, only Nonosabasut and his brother, Tomasuth, now remained in our meotick. After much arguing, Adibish convinced our young shadowdancer that he and Tomasuth with a few unskilled boys or old men could not harpoon blunt-nosed whales and herd them to shore, neither could they carry meat and canoes all the way back from the fjord.

Half-frozen rain, foretelling an early winter, was falling the day Nonosabasut came to our mamateek. He was asking for help. In past times Adibish would have called Kakula to his mamateek, but Nonosabasut was too near to my brother in age and too far from him in inclination to hold such power.

And so he came to us, and Adibish with him. They stepped into our mamateek and stood by the entryway, their tunics stiff with rain from crossing our camping place. I was surprised. But they, I thought, were more surprised—as if they had not expected to see me and Mish-mish there as well as Kakula and Auntie Santu.

We were squatting near a weak fire with Mother's gaming discs scattered on a hide in front of us. We were humouring Auntie Santu, letting her teach us the dice-and-bowl game our parents used to play night after night. Some of the bone discs were very old and may have been carved by Hebbosheth or even by a more distant ancestor. I had carved five of the pieces myself. Most discs are square but I have always made mine canoe-shaped.

When Nonosabasut and Adibish came into our tent I was holding two of the canoe discs in my hand, staring down at traces of the ochre I'd rubbed into the patterns. It had taken me a full winter to make five discs. How safe I had felt then, how warm and well-fed, how I had daydreamed about Nonosabasut as I incised patterns into the bits of bone.

Remembering this, I looked up and saw him, and loving him, I smiled. He saw my smile, hesitated and looked bewildered, as if he had never seen me before and was wondering who the women in Kakula's tent could be.

I thought that when he married my cousin I had stopped hoping, but hope is stubborn. All of us—even you, Dogman—hope without reason. That dreary day when Nonosabasut did not know my face was the day Aich-mud-yim reached inside me and took away hope.

XVIII

Because my kin—Kakula and Auntie Santu and Mish-mish—and I asked, Longnon, Newin, Manus and Kakula all went to hunt with Nonosabasut and Tomasuth. But they did not find whale. It was too late, ice had come early and the fjord was frozen solid. The snows came early also; there was hunger again and much sickness. Before the second moon of winter passed, word came that Dogmen were coming towards our meotick.

As before it was Kakula who brought us the news. My brother was no longer an excited young runner. He had just come from Longnon's camp, his face was grey with exhaustion and he carried only a string of weasels and one hare. He told us he had seen four Dogmen, all well-outfitted, all but one wearing jackets with shiny buttons. He said they were coming, but still on the other side of our frozen river.

Everything seemed like that long-ago time when Adibish had failed to persuade us to invite Dogmen into our tents, when we had left our old winter place and walked through sleet and snow until we came to this bleak place. The words Nonosabasut now said were shadows of the words Adibish had spoken: that we must invite these Dogmen to eat with us, no longer consider every Dogmen our enemy, that Dogmen with shiny buttons must be trusted.

Like Adibish, he repeated the plea his great-grandfather Osagana had made: "Dogmen have found the seapath to Baetha—they will never leave. We must accept them and greet them as we would civilized people. We must talk to them, learn to live with them. If we do not, we will all die."

Nonosabasut reminded us that, as boys, his own father and Adibish had been saved from death by a good Dogman. In time, he told us, Dogmen would discover that all creatures belonged to the earth, not the earth to Dogmen. We would exchange knowledge, exchange goods, and then Dogmen would let us return to the seal coast and to our holy places.

It was a sweet dream our shadowdancer showed us. We listened in silence. Doodebewshet did not call out against her son as she had against Adibish. No one called out—poor and hungry people want to believe. But Aich-mud-yim had taken hope away from me. I knew the earth Nonosabasut spoke of could never be, not this side of the Ghost Path.

Nonosabasut waited a moment. When no one spoke he told us to build a fire, to begin roasting the meat while Kakula led him and Adibish downriver to meet the Dogmen.

"I would put on dry footwear and leggings first," Kakula said. He went towards our mamateek and I followed.

"Every morning Longnon goes to the message tree beside the sandbar," my brother told me. He had grabbed up a burnt stick and was scratching marks on a piece of birchbark: four lines, three circles, and another mark that meant our meotick.

I knew what he was asking. Already I was pulling on leggings, finding mitts, unhooking snowshoes from the antler on which they hung.

"Wait until Nonosabasut and I have gone to meet the Dogmen before you start. It will be hard going, but keep to the bush until you're well upriver. I'll lead Nonosabasut a ways downriver before crossing over—that would be best anyway, better for us not to walk across the ice straight into Dogman muskets."

He rolled the birchbark up and pushed a bone ring around it. When he passed it to me, we both smiled. If I could get the message to Longnon, he and the others in his camp would come and kill the Dogmen.

And so Nonosabasut brought the Dogmen into our camp and Dogmen sat around the People's fire. Dogmen smoked our pipes and ate the little food we had, while Nonosabasut spoke, telling them reasons why we must all live peacefully together.

Even Kakula admitted that Nonosabasut was magnificent that night. Standing tall above the circle of seated people, the horns of Old Caribou on his head, the moon staff in his hand, the skin of Keathut the bear around his shoulders, her claws hanging from his neck, the splendour of our shadowdancer made Dogmen seem poor and pitiful creatures.

After welcoming them to our meotick, Nonosabasut spoke of how the People had lived in Baetha for uncounted circles of seasons. He told them how, since past times, we had roamed her forests, crossed and recrossed her lakes and rivers, gathering food, gathering wisdom. These things Dogmen must also learn, he said, if they are to live in this cold place—how to share belongings, how to give and receive gifts, how to read signs and make cures, how to build canoes and mamateeks, how to respect Baetha and all things that live in it, on it and around it.

Nonosabasut was magical. "Even I almost believed him," Kakula told me later. "He talked right through the night, talked on and on, told them the story of First People, of Ash-wa-meet and Crow and Firewoman.

"All four Dogmen fell asleep where they sat. Then we could look at them as much as we wished. One rolled onto his side and Ashei touched his hair, which was a strange ochre colour. Then she ran her fingers around the buttons on his blue jacket—until Nonosabasut spoke sharply to her, ordered her to return to her place beside their mother."

I alone did not sit around the fire with Dogmen. For the first part of that night I plowed waist-deep in snow, keeping to the banks of the river for as far as possible before moving out on the frozen lake. On the ice I was not much faster because the wind was against me, cold as knives on my face. I knew I would find the place—in winter the water froze in ridges around the sandbar where I swam in summertime. I kept moving, warming myself with the thought of Manus saying Tibeast's name, his arrow making a line into the body of a Dogman. I found the message tree and slipped the rolled bark into the place Longnon had shown me.

Kakula left our meotick at dawn. We must have crossed paths but I did not see him.

I was back in camp early enough to see the Dogmen, to smell the sharp stink they give off, to watch them drink the last of our tea. Before they walked away, Nonosabasut placed a caribou hide on the shoulders of each Dogman. They each pushed one hand towards him, holding it out until he took it for a heartbeat and then, looking foolish, dropped it.

We all nodded and watched until they crossed the river and marched out of sight. Everyone seemed pleased with the meeting. Nonosabasut told us the Dogmen had promised to return with food and oil. How he understood this I cannot say, but he seemed sure.

Everyone settled down to wait. I was the only one not waiting for food, I the only one who got what I waited for.

The day Kakula returned he passed a string of frozen turrs to women beside the fire, then came into our mamateek and dropped something into my hand. "Look when you are alone," he whispered, then stumbled to his sleeping place and lay down, asleep almost before his body touched the furs.

I did not open my hand, although I was alone, or as good as. Auntie Santu was quietly dying in the shadows and never opened her eyes unless I tried to give her water or clean the filth out from under her. I sat in the half dark holding the three round discs in my hand—buttons from the jackets of three dead Dogmen. The satisfaction I felt was near to happiness.

"One got away," Kakula told me when he woke. "He was better on snowshoes than the blue-jackets and ran when the other three fell. Still, he shouldn't have escaped . . ." My brother sipped the hot broth I'd gotten from the women who'd cooked the birds.

"It was my fault. Longnon, Newin and Manus killed the others quickly. My arrow pointed at the fourth but I had never killed a Dogman before. I held back and he got away." The birch cup in Kakula's hands shook, and I thought he would weep. "Thinking of Ianamish, even thinking of Kasathi and her baby, I still could not kill a creature standing on two legs," my brother said, then he went back to his sleeping place.

Nonosabasut, Tomasuth and Kakula hunted every day; everyone who was not ill hunted and foraged. But winter had come down so suddenly and the snow was so deep that we never found enough to eat. For each winter moon one of us died. The baby that Tibeast's wife gave birth to died because she had no milk, then the poor woman herself walked into a blizzard and did not come back. Doodebewshet and Ashei and the boy called Joisp were sick—we were all weak and a little sick. All of us would have died except for the meat Kakula continued to bring to us from Longnon's camp.

I am getting near the end, Dogman. Do you want to hear how we all died? Even Demasduit—and Nonosabasut, even him! All banished from our beloved place by your savage ancestors.

The river was still frozen when it happened. Mish-mish and I were on our knees trying to hack a hole in the ice near shore. Nonosabasut was farther out, he and Tomasuth together with Demasduit, who had the baby tied to her back.

By sticking an evergreen tree down in the ice when it was soft they had managed to keep a small hole in the river open all winter. Each morning they would rotate the tree, knocking away new ice until the hole was large enough to fish through. Sometimes they caught a small fish or two but that morning there were none. They had pulled up their lines, were turning towards shore— towards where Mish-mish and I knelt.

I looked up and saw many Dogmen, nine or ten walking fast, coming out onto the ice behind Nonosabasut and his family. One Dogman pulled a sled and all carried muskets; they had long knives and hatchets, ropes hung from their belts.

I think I cried out. Nonosabasut and the others looked back and saw the Dogmen. Demasduit and Tomasuth began running towards us, but Nonosabasut did not run. He broke a bough from the tree they'd been using, turned and faced the Dogmen. He stood very still, holding out the green bough of friendship and talking. I could not hear but well knew that he was welcoming them, telling them the foolish dream of his father and grandfather.

For a small time they let him speak. Then three Dogmen came forward—the old one jerked the bough from Nonosabasut's hand and two others began to tie his arms with rope. He shook them off as easily as a wolf shakes a rabbit.

Nonosabasut turned and saw that other Dogmen had caught Demasduit. They were holding her roughly so that her tunic fell open showing her breasts. The baby on her back was screeching. Nonosabasut leapt at these Dogmen, grabbed their jackets, to pull them away from Demasduit, implored them not to harm his wife and child. They paid him no heed; one was laughing while he tied a rope around Demasduit's arms. Nonosabasut put his hands around that Dogman's neck and jerked him backward.

A Dogman pressed his long musket into Nonosabasut's back and shot him. Still he kept his hands wrapped around the throat of the biggest Dogman, holding on until one of the others brought a hatchet down into his head. Seeing Nonosabasut fall, his blood spreading across the ice, Tomasuth ran towards his brother. In an instant he too was dead.

Through all this Mish-mish and I had not moved nor made a sound. I forced my eyes to look away from Nonosabasut and saw that his son had been pulled from Demasduit's back—had fallen, or been placed, on the ice. Demasduit was wailing, struggling to reach her baby, but they pulled her back and tied her to the sled. The Dogmen must have seen us. Yet they turned away and left, satisfied, I suppose, with the killing they had done, satisfied to take the woman, Demasduit.

I did not move, though I could hear Mish-mish calling my name, could see that the Dogmen had vanished into the trees on the far side of the river. I knelt as if frozen, my hands splayed out. Then someone stumbled over me and I fell forward, banging my face into ice.

Everyone who could walk was coming down to the river: two women and one small girl, the boy Joisp and the old men, and my brother Kakula, who pulled me upright. Ashei and her mother came, and then Adibish. He was last, lurching along on his crippled feet, calling his daughter's name as if he already knew she would never answer. His was the only voice. All the rest were silenced when they saw what had happened.

I only watched, staring at the beaten, thin-faced people who shuffled out onto the ice. One by one they passed me, went to stand between me and the bodies until I could no longer see the two spreading circles of red.

I did not go near, but after a time, without looking at the bodies, I walked forward a little and took the mewing baby from Adibish, who had picked him up off the ice. I tucked the poor thing inside my tunic and turned my back on the slaughter. Behind me a moaning began, a soft sound like snow swishing across a frozen lake. I went up to our mamateek, where I found Kakula already tying on his snowshoes.

I longed to ask if this had happened because we killed the Dogmen with shiny buttons. But seeing the rage he was in, I knew I could not look to him for a comforting lie. His breath was coming fast, his hands shaking so he could not do up the rawhide laces.

Without speaking I knelt down, pulled the thongs tightly around his moccasins and knotted them. I stood and looked into my brother's eyes and saw they were filled with cold hatred, like the eyes of the starving wolf that had once followed us.

"Do not go alone—get Longnon and the others and then kill as many as you can," I told him. I would have gone with him but for the baby squirming against me, trying to find a breast to suck on.

I could not even keep his child alive. No woman had milk, and three sunrises later Nonosabasut and Demasduit's child died.

Kakula did not come back.

Mish-mish and I were the strongest people in our meotick. We were the ones who, with Adibish and two old men, had to drag Nonosabasut and his brother down the long frozen river, haul the bodies up the steep bank and into the cave where we had placed Kasathi and her baby. I remember no ceremony, no songs—only hands that bled from the pulling thongs and knees that burned from slipping on ice-crusted rocks below the grave place. I remember cold and pain and bitter determination.

I do not know why I lived. All around me there was hunger, hopelessness, sickness and death. Demasduit's mother, Waunathoake, who had been ill for many seasons, finally died. Joisp's parents died, both of them on the same night, and neither of the old men lasted through the winter. Doodebewshet and Ashei rolled in their sleeping skins and moaned, puking and shitting, until Adibish roused himself from grief long enough to come asking if I would clean the two women. In the end I went to sleep in their mamateek, and Mish-mish went to live with Adibish.

In Doodebewshet's mamateek I was sleeping in the very hollow where Nonosabasut and Demasduit had slept. Terrible dreams I had—dreams of him and me lying inside a caribou skin, Demasduit watching us, me watching them, dreams of her calling her baby, of me calling her. I dreamt constantly, crying myself awake, weeping to find myself still alive.

One morning in melt-time Mish-mish came running, shouting that he'd found Kakula asleep in our family mamateek.

My brother was much changed, Mish-mish said—and indeed he was. Kakula had always been paler than the rest of our family; now his skin was ash colour, his head was pulled askew, rawhide strapped around one of his shoulders seemed to be keeping his arm in place.

He had not gone to Longnon's camp for help the day Nonosabasut and Tomasuth were murdered. "It would have taken too long," he told us. "I wanted to catch up with the Dogmen who had taken Demasduit, thinking if I came upon them in the night I would get her back, kill some Dogmen—two at least. It began to snow a little but I could still see the tracks of their sled. Through the afternoon I pushed on, promising myself that even if I did not free Demasduit, I would kill as many Dogmen as I could before they killed me.

"By dark the snow turned into a blizzard, whiteness every- where, covering the Dogmen's trail, covering earth and sky, rocks and trees—nothing left to guide me."

Yet Kakula was not afraid, he had a good sleeping skin with him and had spent more than one night alone in the forest. He began to build a wind break, using his racquets to dig a hollow in the soft snow, then twisting boughs off evergreen trees.

"I was in a hurry, sweating, angry with myself for losing track of the Dogmen—Longnon would not have lost them! My legs slipped from under me, I fell forward into the snow. When my senses came back I was lying face down, pinned to the ground by the point of a rotten tree stump.

"I must have fallen hard—the tree stick had gone through my shoulder like a spear. My arm on that side had no feeling. I pivoted my body slowly upward, trying to pull loose, and again lost my senses. When I woke the next time I was weaker, and so cold I knew I would soon die. With my good hand I somehow managed to get hold of one of my arrowheads. Holding it flat I slid my hand between my body and the ground. I touched the still-rooted tree where it went into my body; it was only the thickness of a finger—a small thing to kill a man.

"I began to rub the sharp edge of flint back and forth against the wood, warm blood trickling down on my hand. Twice more my senses left me, but each time I came back, each time I was weaker, each time I kicked earth with my legs to know I was still alive. Then I felt the arrowhead and continued cutting through the thing that pinioned me to the ground."

When my brother finally cut himself free he crawled to the hollow and found it had filled in again with snow. Too weak to do more, he dragged his sleeping skin around his body and lay face down on the wet bushes with the stick still pointing up out of his shoulder.

It was Newin who found him. "The night was not as far along as I had imagined—if it had been I would have died. Newin was returning to camp from a day's watch on that edge of the forest. When he saw the arrowlike stick rising out of a strange snowdrift he thought he'd come upon a dead Dogman. Newin is not a big man but he hoisted me up against his back and half dragged, half carried me to their camping place. I owe him and Gowet my life—it was she who fed and washed me and cleaned the hole in my shoulder until it closed over."

Kakula told us he would have returned to our meotick sooner, but Gowet insisted that he was too weak to walk all the way. To get his strength back he began walking each day with Longnon or one of the other men.

"Every day they all hunt and fish, and as they go each one is guarding part of the circle of land and water that Longnon says is theirs. Even the women guard-walk—there are two women now.

A man and woman came into their camp last fall—they'd been walking all summer, coming down from some northern place from which they had been driven by Dogmen furriers. Each day I was feeling stronger. When I saw the ice breaking up, Longnon and I walked down to the sandbar. We uncovered your canoe and with that I managed to get downriver without any trouble."

Nothing could ever again make me glad, yet it was a good thing to know that Newin and Gowet, our cousin Manus and our brother Longnon, were still alive. I thanked Ash-wa-meet for saving my youngest brother. Although he could not yet hunt and would have to live in Adibish's mamateek with Mish-mish and the boy Joisp, it was good to have him back with us.

We were still keeping fires in three mamateeks—Adibish's, and the one I lived in with mad Doodebewshet and her daughter, and the mamateek where an old man and woman lived with a little girl and her mother. To save the wet wood we had to gather each day Adibish said we should all be in one mamateek, but neither the old couple nor Doodebewshet would hear of it.

The cold had knotted Adibish's hands and feet so that he could hardly stand. Mish-mish, Joisp and I had become the hunters for our meotick. When Kakula returned, we had been living for three days on the water in which we had boiled spruce boughs. I was so hungry that when I saw the haunch of caribou and two brace of geese sent from Longnon's camp I began to weep.

Two moons later Dogmen came for the last time.

Mish-mish and Joisp brought the warning. The boys had watched the Dogmen's boat come partway upriver, saw it go aground in a shallow place less than a half-day's journey below our meotick. The Dogmen left their boat and were now ashore, walking towards us. They were many, the boys said. Although the snow had now melted the Dogmen were pulling two loaded sleds, one covered in blood-red cloth. Mish-mish and Joisp were sure the other sled carried fire-sticks.

Adibish told us to go out on the barrens and hide; he himself would wait for the Dogmen in his mamateek. Hearing this the old couple said they would do the same. "Surely it is better to perish beside your own fire than freeze to death on the open barrens," the woman said.

It was Kakula who said we must either all go or all stay. There was no argument. All of us—thin and weak, crippled and sick—managed to drag ourselves out of our mamateeks and through the few trees that separated our camping place from the barrens. Those who could grabbed sleeping furs and bits of meat. Adibish was able to lurch along by keeping himself upright with two sticks. Doodebewshet and the old couple were too weak to walk without help, and both the little girl and her mother, a feckless creature, had run out without moccasins.

We did not get far into the barrens. Those who were strong enough flattened a circle of brush and spread out the furs so that we could all lie down, out of sight of the Dogmen. Kakula and the two boys had bows and arrows. They would be able to kill some Dogmen, but the fire-sticks of others would surely shoot the rest of us as soon as we lifted our heads above the brush.

Lying on our stomachs we were without dignity, but not uncomfortable because we had coverings and it was a sunny, mild day. Although we'd hurried, this had taken some time and we had just settled when Adibish announced he was going to crawl back.

"I crawl better than I walk," the old man said. Remembering when he was young and could make his shadow dance along the walls of our mamateeks, I felt sorry for him. But then I thought, Adibish has lived to grow old, which is something Nonosabasut did not do, something I am unlikely to do.

Kakula would have gone with him but Adibish forbade it. "If I am taken or killed, you and these boys must get our people to Longnon's meotick. Only you, Kakula, will know the way to that place."

My uncle looked towards me and I knew what he was going to say. "Shanawdithit is strong, she will come with me," he said. "If I falter, you will help me, get me to the Dogmen, for I must speak to them—must explain."

It took a long time to crawl back. The ground was wet and uneven, covered in thorny bushes that caught my hair and scratched my face and hands. I was stronger than Adibish and often got a little ahead, stopping to rest whenever his breathing became loud. At the edge of the barrens we hesitated. This forlorn place had never been circled by forest and over time we had burnt the lower branches of the few trees that did grow between our camp and the open land.

Adibish whispered that we should make for the largest dogberry tree, but I shook my head and pointed to a patch of stunted balsam and spruce. I had spent much of my childhood under such trees and knew well that we could hide ourselves better below low green boughs than behind the bare trunk of a dogberry—no matter that Adibish thought that tree had magical power.

Peering out from our tangle of trees I could see the whole of our meotick, see what a poor place our camp had become— sad strings of meat hanging beside entryways, two broken canoes tipped on their sides, green, untidy wood scattered around our dying fire, badly chinked mamateeks from which bits of birchbark and hide fluttered. As I waited, lying shoulder to shoulder with the old shadowdancer, I felt the soft air, sniffed the sweet spring greenness and thought this a better place to die than inside one of our stinking mamateeks.

They came soon enough. As Mish-mish had warned us there were many—twice ten and more—pulling two loaded sleds, carrying muskets, with ropes and long-handled axes slung about their shoulders. Six of them were dressed in the blue jackets with shiny buttons. Two of the Dogmen I had seen before—the one who had brought the hatchet down on Nonosabasut's head and the laughing big one who had helped tie Demasduit to the sled. I wanted to run at them, kill them, feeling in that moment that rage and bare hands would be enough. Instead I pressed myself into the damp earth and waited.

They seemed unsure of what to do—went into each mamateek and came quickly out. One Dogman was holding the huge caribou head that Adibish and Nonosabasut wore when they became shadowdancers. Adibish's shoulders stiffened and I thought he might call out, even stand and try to take back the headpiece. When one of the blue-jackets shouted at the Dogman, he turned and carelessly tossed the great caribou head back into Adibish's mamateek.

The Dogmen gazed around; two or three called out something and one shot his musket into the sky, sending a family of crows aloft, cawing out warnings above our heads. Since our fires were still warm, the Dogmen must have known we were nearby, yet they did not search the bushes or go beyond our camping place.

Instead they built a kind of mamateek with stuff like the sails on Dogmen's ships. I did not think it would be warm in winter but I was filled with amazement to see how quickly the great billowing thing was made. Outside on its centre pole, they hung a red, blue and white cloth, like the one Hebbosheth used to keep under her rabbit bedskin.

Three of the blue-jackets pulled the sled that held the red-covered box across the bare ground and into the white tent.

Other Dogmen unloaded some things from the other sled and carried them into the tent also. They stood outside just looking around for a time, as if waiting for a sign from the good spirits—but Dogmen do not have good spirits. And so, pulling the remaining sled, all of them turned and walked down the way they had come, towards the river.

Before they disappeared into the underbrush that bordered the river, one Dogman turned, looked back, raised his musket and shot into the sky again. The sound echoed off the three hills. Our people lying behind us in the barrens must have thought Adibish and I were both dead, but neither they nor we moved until the sun began to set.

It was dark before we all came back to our meotick. We were cramped and hungry, and Adibish could not have stood up if I'd not been there. We were curious to know what was in the Dogman tent, yet no one wanted to go inside.

Lying on the ground half the day seemed to have brought some sense into Doodebewshet's head. In her usual gruff way she told us we should light a fire, cook food and eat together while we considered what to do with the ghostly white tent.

I knew what we should do. I, who had not spoken around our fires since the night of Godith's death, spoke. I reminded them of my Old One's story on that long-ago night, about how Dogman gifts had brought sickness and death to everyone in her family. As we ate, I boldly told my people that we must set the thing alight, give it and everything inside it into Firewoman's keeping.

Not even Kakula agreed with me. After we had talked some time, Adibish went into his mamateek and came out wearing the head of Old Caribou and carrying the staff of Ash-wa-meet. He told us he would sit before the tent's entryway all night so that the good spirits would keep any evil from escaping into our meotick. Perhaps Adibish was brave, perhaps he just understood Dogmen better than the rest of us did—or perhaps his magic had shown him what was in the cloth-covered box.

Next morning we all stood outside, watching as he entered the tent, as he slowly eased open the lid of the box with the shining handles.

Demasduit's body was not rolled in skin but dressed in fine white stuff, sewn with tiny beads; her eyes were closed, her face almost as pale as the shiny cloth she lay on. All around the box were piled gifts—beads and tea and pots of white powder and the tobacco Dogmen use in their pipes.

Much moaning and many songs we made for Demasduit, who had been good and beautiful and wise. It seemed that Doodebewshet had truly loved her son's wife. Ashei too loved her, and of course Adibish dearly loved the daughter he had hardly spoken a word to for all her life. Kakula and Mish-mish told happy stories about our cousin's childhood. I did not speak, did not make a song for her. I pushed my thoughts back and tried to think tenderly about the round-faced laughing girl who had once told me and Kasathi her father's secret stories.

Although his feet were a little better, as they always were when spring came, Adibish did not go to the grave place with Demasduit's body. With the coffin there was room for only two people in a canoe. So in the end, Kakula, Mish-mish, Joisp and I had to make two trips to the grave place. Demasduit's coffin was well-made. Heavy. Even using the ropes Dogmen had left, it took four of us to get the box up the hill and into the cave.

When we returned to our meotick, Ashei was standing beside the river. She told me that Adibish wished to speak privately to me, that he was waiting in his mamateek. I went there and found him dressed as if for a ceremony—his face and hands painted with ochre, the skin of Keathut the bear over his shoulders, the finger-bones of Keathut around his neck, and on his head the antlers of Old Caribou. He had become the shadow-dancer I remembered.

We were alone. He nodded for me to sit opposite him and, without a word of greeting, put his plan before me.

"Clearly all Dogmen now know of this meotick. Evil Dogmen killed Nonosabasut and Tomasuth, and they took Demasduit away. But good Dogmen returned my daughter's body. They treated her with respect and left behind gifts of friendship. I once travelled with one of those who brought Demasduit's body back. He is known to me . . ."

And two are known to me, I thought, recalling the men I'd watched while they put the white tent up and carried the coffin into it. *Your good Dogmen and evil Dogmen are the same*, I could have told him. But I remembered my father speaking those very words and knew it would be useless to fight against this old man's lifelong belief.

His plan was the one he'd spoken of when we were hiding on the barrens. Kakula would lead everyone in our meotick upriver to join with Longnon and Newin's people. Their camp was still unknown to Dogmen, and they had runners and good hunters. When Kakula was not in our meotick we had only Mish-mish and Joisp strong enough to hunt, and they were just boys and not properly taught. We would not survive another winter in this place.

"We must leave now," Adibish said, "when the woman and little girl, even the old couple, are beginning to recover from their winter weakness."

As he talked it became clear I was not to go with those travelling to Longnon's camp. I sat and waited, knowing that Adibish would not ask, but would, as he always had, assign me whatever role he thought proper.

"Nonosabasut's mother is old—she and his sister, Ashei, both have the coughing sickness that always ends in death. Once Doodebewshet's sons and her daughter-by-marriage would have protected and cared for her through her last seasons."

He looked into my eyes. "But my daughter and her husband, and Tomasuth also, have already placed their feet on the Ghost Path. Now there is no one but you and me to care for Doodebewshet and Ashei."

When the shadowdancer said this, I knew he had seen my guilt, seen that I'd had some part in killing the Dogmen he'd told us were good. There was no need for him to speak of this. In my pouch I still had three shiny buttons belonging to those blue-jackets Nonosabasut had welcomed into our camp. I, too, since I had not given them Longnon's warning, should be held responsible for the deaths of Nonosabasut and Tomasuth, and for Demasduit's capture. I wondered if he knew that.

"Doodebewshet has always been very unhappy, now she is also very ill. I believe Dogmen have medicine that will make her more comfortable, perhaps even make her well," he said, and began once again telling how Dogman's medicine had saved him.

I watched my uncle speaking and saw that the guilt in his heart was as heavy as the guilt in mine. Had he and Sabasut not placed a bear cub at Doodebewshet's breast? Had they not stolen the life of her baby? Stolen her spirit too, according to my Old One.

"Perhaps she can become well." I said this although I had seen blood coming out of Doodebewshet's mouth and knew that no matter what medicine Adibish's Dogmen had, she and Ashei would both soon die.

He told me then how he and I would take the sick women towards the coast. We would take my small canoe to a place where good Dogmen had attached wooden mamateeks to the earth. Together we would take Doodebewshet and Ashei there.

I would have to stay in that place and care for the sick women. Adibish would not stay but would come back, try to return to Longnon's camp where our remaining People would have need of a shadowdancer.

It did not matter what I did, where I went—nothing mattered. "I will take care of Doodebewshet and her daughter as long as they live," I said, and saw a flicker of relief in his eyes.

The next morning I went alone to the cave where Kasathi and Nonosabasut and Demasduit—so many people I loved—were buried. I stayed there all day, sitting first beside one body then moving to another. Godith's mother was there also, and the babies. I put stones on their graves and I talked to them all. I told them we were leaving this place and promised them that Kakula and Longnon would surely come to the cave.

I talked to Hebbosheth also, though her body was not there but out beyond the white beach, in the sea cavern Adibish had taken her to. I told my Old One that I still held all her stories inside my skull, promised I would bring them when we met beyond the Ghost Path. Almost I could feel her hand patting my head—almost.

Adibish danced one last time on the night before we left. He was old now and his feet crippled, but his hands could still make animals slide and leap around the mamateek walls. When the dance ended he told us the story of Miaoth, the beautiful young man who had paddled all around the Great Island in his canoe. He reminded us how Miaoth's people had almost forgotten him, how, after he had been gone for many winters and many summers, they thought he would never return. Adibish wanted us to believe that like Miaoth we would all return to our families. I do not think any of us believed him.

I still carried ochre in Hebbosheth's pouch and I placed my ochre fingerprint on the throat of Kakula and Mish-mish before they left. I promised them that we would meet again in Perfect Time.

It was high summer when we left. Such a season that even in that poor place one forgets winter, thinks earth will provide everything.

It was hard for Adibish to portage even my small canoe, hard also for me and Ashei to hold Doodebewshet upright and moving forward through the forest. Because of this we kept to the water as much as possible, paddling downriver between long ranges of mountains, through vast marshlands, worlds of green forest and water meadows shining in the sun. When Adibish praised the canoe, I told him who had built it, showed him the mark his grandmother Hebbosheth had made.

He touched the Old One's half-moon with his fingers. "I remember," he said, and placed his fingers on my forehead. It was as near to a blessing as I ever got from that stubborn old man.

Although we saw many animals, Adibish did not hunt. We lived on fish and on minty plants that grew beside the river. When Doodebewshet and Ashei slept, when I did not have to hear their coughing and moaning, sometimes then I could pretend it was a long-ago spring and I was moving towards that summer beach where caplin rolled endlessly in—still roll, I suppose, if Dogmen have not destroyed them too.

Adibish seemed to know where we were going. When we found what he called a fishing station it was just three grey buildings leaning against one another over the water, and in the cove, two Dogman ships. The ships seemed empty, but three or four Dogmen came out of the buildings to stand on the rickety wharf and watch us.

The river coming down was shallow. We had to pull the canoe up on the far side of the beach and walk across towards the Dogmen. We did not want to do this but Adibish said we must, so Ashei and I, clutching our sleeping skins in one arm and holding Doodebewshet up with the other, shuffled awkwardly over the loose round rocks.

Adibish walked with us as he'd said he would. Then he looked and saw our canoe had slipped away and was drifting out, so he started back. We women stopped to watch. Doodebewshet began her mad cursing, which turned into a coughing fit, and Adibish splashed on into the water after the canoe.

I heard the musket, watched him fall forward into the sea, watched him float face down, his sleeping skins tangled around him like seaweed. Ashei screeched, two Dogmen came towards us, shouted something, Adibish's body sank, and there was only Hebbosheth's canoe rocking in the sunshine.

The London Times
SEPTEMBER 14, 1829

Died—At St. John's Newfoundland on the 6th of June last in the 29th year of her age, Shanawdithit, supposed to be the last of the Red Indians or Beothicks. This interesting female lived six years a captive amongst the English, and when taken notice of latterly exhibited extraordinary mental talents. Hers has been a primitive nation, once claiming rank as a portion of the human race, who have lived, flourished, and become extinct in their own orbit. They have been dislodged, and disappeared from the earth in their native independence in 1829, in as primitive a condition as they were before the discovery of the New World, and that too on the nearest point of America to England, in one of our oldest and most important Colonies.

BOOK THREE

THE SCAVENGER

XIX

In Cambridge it was raining, that relentless drizzle Judith always forgets when she is away from England. Ian just nodded when she suggested they take a taxi straight to the garage where the station wagon was stored. Passing buildings that would normally evoke lively conversation between them, he was silent, staring down at his hands. They were beautiful hands. Judith reached out and he took her hand, holding it between his—but still he didn't speak. They were cheerful people, optimistic by nature, but right now they were tired, both of them, tired and sick of talk.

Throughout the trip they had talked constantly, considering what they might do, what their options were. Could they go back to Koobi Fora on their own? Might some private foundation finance the project? They'd have to begin again, once more work their way through the practical and political obstacles that protect such ancient places, the aggravation of prolonged paperwork, the haggling, the bribes.

These circular conversations always ended with one of them assuring the other that Clive would not do anything to damage their reputations, that surely he intended them to complete their work in Koobi Fora. In the end they fell silent, knowing, despite all, that they were being manoeuvred into a position of disadvantage.

The man in the garage simply entered their names in his computer and passed over a key. The key was tied to a block of wood on which *Number 7* had been scrawled with black paint. The man led them in a hard rain around back to his junkyard. He nodded towards the row of battered steel sheds he rented out as lock-ups and raced back into the garage.

As they walked towards Number 7 shed, their wet sandals making soft sucking sounds in the oily mud, Judith began to weep. In all their years together Ian had never seen her cry, had never heard her cry; unpleasant gulping sounds pushed up out of her lungs. He dropped his haversack and put his arms around her, clumsily, for she too had a haversack on her shoulder.

"There now, there now . . ." he kept saying, fumbling with the lock, finally leaning her against the wall as if she were an old woman and might fall over. And indeed she did, sliding down so that she was sitting in mud, still weeping, when, at last, he managed to open the awkward door.

Ian pulled her up and inside. He rolled down the door, all the while holding her against him, patting her damp back. And Judith, taking slow deep breaths, gazed beyond his shoulder at a yellowing Plexiglas skylight. Opaque it was, spattered with leaves and bird droppings, yet it transformed the grey-blue outdoor light into warm amber. The air in the shed was warm too, as still as the air inside tents or in tombs that have been sealed for a thousand years.

"Luv, luv—what is it? What's wrong?" Bewildered, he kept asking, holding her, patting her.

And finally the sounds became less harsh, stopped and she could speak, could explain that she couldn't bear to see him so unhappy, could tell him that all day she'd been thinking about that Australian archaeologist who threw himself off a cliff when he was forced to retire.

"God, Judith! You don't think Clive is going to make me jump off a cliff!"

Ian had started to chuckle—she could feel the smothered laughter in his chest.

"I will hate Clive Aldridge forever and ever if he doesn't let us go back to Koobi Fora," she said. As the words were spoken she began to laugh, for who would not laugh at such childishness in a grown woman?

Suddenly they were both laughing, laughing together as Ian eased her along the side of the station wagon, falling with her onto the folded-down back seat, falling atop heaps of sleeping bags, car blankets, pocket books, sweaters and old raincoats. Amid the belongings they so carelessly discarded whenever they left England, they made careless love, and afterwards they lay listening to rain hitting the steel shed, watching rain shimmer across the stained skylight.

"We're foolish to fret so much over nothing," Ian said. "No one at the Institute can make us do anything we don't want to do." He kissed her. "It'll all work out, luv—haven't we always been lucky?" And with great solemnity he quoted from a newspaper clipping someone had sent them months before: "'Even among anthropologists, a branch of academia noted for eccentrics, the Muirs are considered odd—reclusive and clever and exceedingly lucky . . .'"

They had laughed when they first read the article, and they laughed now. They untangled themselves from the untidy pile and sat smiling at one another, enchanted by the splashes of golden light playing across their mud-smeared faces, their aging mud-smeared bodies.

Ian thought they should go see Clive just as they were, naked as jays except for one sandal that had stuck firmly to Judith's foot. It would show him, Ian said, what they thought of his regal tone, his commanding correspondence.

They'd hardly believed the first letter, a brusque, four-line request (order?) above the signature of their old friend and colleague, newly appointed director of the Institute of Human Origins. They were to return to England within the month, no reason given. Subsequent letters became yet more urgent. Then, in a final phone call, Clive reminded them, albeit gently, that Ian's retirement was, in any event, due well before the expected completion date of the Koobi Fora project. He said he expected to see them both within the fortnight, and hung up.

After leaving the lock-up, they checked into a hotel. Bathed and dressed in clean but wrinkled clothing, they presented themselves at the administrative offices of the Institute, which had recently moved to a glass and steel complex on the outskirts of Cambridge.

It was still raining and after the usual platitudes regarding the weather, Clive apologized for the terseness of his correspondence, the absence of any reason for this summons to England. He told them they were being seconded to a subgroup working under a newly formed United Nations Commission.

Head tilted, chin resting on the back of one hand, Clive stared intently at them across his desk. "It was impressed upon me that

I not mention the UN or any details of this undertaking until you were in my office."

He explained that the broad mandate of the still-unnamed commission would be to investigate the root cause, or causes, of twentieth-century genocide. "You two will direct one of six international working groups asked to examine bodies at specific sites, to record as much as possible about the day-by-day lives of the victims," he said.

"The world has run out of forensic pathologists, then?" Ian's tone reflected his irritation, at both their unceremonious removal from Koobi Fora and at the assumption that they were obliged to agree to this proposal.

Clive ignored the question. "Our co-operation on this could have very positive ramifications for the future of the Institute," he said, and when neither Judith nor Ian replied, he proceeded to explain the project at some length.

This phase of the study would concentrate on the bodies of non-combatants in the former republic of Yugoslavia and in Rwanda. The Muirs would serve as co-heads of a select team that would include academics from a dozen member nations. "I am bound to say this is a prestigious invitation. The Institute is flattered—you should be flattered," he told them.

Though Clive's office was large and bright, more pleasant really than most of the cramped offices within the colleges, there was no view of grass or river from its oversized windows. Nevertheless he pushed back his chair and went to look out at the surrounding tower blocks. For some time no one spoke. Judith and Ian stared at Clive's back and he stared out the rain-steamed window.

"Over 800,000 people were slaughtered in Rwanda alone," he said. "There have been other massacres since, but that was the worst—800,000 men, women and children murdered in a hundred days." Before turning to face the Muirs he traced the number on the window glass, repeated, "800,000."

Clive Aldridge was black and somehow that made a difference. Judith wasn't sure why, but it did. When Ian spoke of the impossibility of dealing with such numbers his voice had changed, and she knew they would accept the appointment.

Clive knew too. He returned to his chair, smiled at them warmly and reached forward, placing his hands protectively atop the large globe that stood on a pedestal beside his desk. Judith leaned towards the globe, expecting him to point out the country to which they would be sent. Instead he touched a thin brass ornament that ran along the equator and lifted the northern hemisphere, revealing a landscape of decanters and tumblers nesting in plush green valleys.

So here we are, Judith thinks, six weeks later, speculating on how many thousand pounds have already been spent to transport their group to this quiet field, wondering exactly what they will do next.

It is clear that the bodies have been lying in this ditch for some time. Spring runoff is now drying up, mud has caked cocoalike around skulls, around arm and leg bones that protrude, slimed with weed, clotted with hair and scraps of filthy cloth.

"*Bodies deteriorate differently under different conditions.*" Barely twenty Judith had been the first time she heard Ian say that. Timid, convinced the lecturer was encouraging her to drop his oversubscribed course, she'd gritted her teeth and stayed.

She does the same now—holding herself still, controlling her revulsion at this tangle of bones—legs overlaying pelvises, arms flung wide, fingers clawing at ribcages. Faced with such disorder Judith cannot even estimate how many bodies lie here. She thinks fondly of the bones she is accustomed to— white bones, bones cleaned by time, sculpted by wind and sand, bodies long removed from whatever slaughter caused their death.

For more than thirty years—a period Judith will shortly come to think of as a long, extended innocence—she and Ian have worked in the field, shovelling their way down old trade routes from southern Turkey, through Syria into Eritrea and Ethiopia along that crescent of earth where *Homo erectus* evolved into *Homo sapiens*.

Judith has been told there are places in the Arctic where the soil is so thin that when a body falls, one can see its shape outlined in greenness for a hundred years. Not so in the dry drifting soil of the Great Rift Valley. To find bones there, the Muirs must watch for a slight rise of earth, the shadow of a buttress built to keep out advancing hordes—built to no avail, as a few weeks of careful digging always revealed.

Despite small wars, those limited engagements and local uprisings one reads about, the Muirs have only once found themselves in the path of an approaching army, forced to abandon their invisible city—the one they will forever imagine as perfect. But there are always other cities, more bones, bones upon bones, layers of bones piled against a thousand crumbled fortresses.

Staring down at this fresh slaughter Judith reflects upon humankind's long commitment to violence, the many manifestations of violence on which her and Ian's reputations—their lucky lives—have been built.

"I suppose we'll have to consider it our penance for being born in this savage century," Ian had remarked the day they agreed to come to this place—after it was all settled and they were eating with Clive at a smart restaurant near his office. Even then Judith had not been convinced. Why should she and Ian, who had contributed nothing to the century's bloodshed, do penance?

Ian is standing on her left, arms folded across his chest, gazing thoughtfully down over his glasses. A British photojournalist named Thornton is in front of Ian, closer to the ditch than any-one else, his leather hiking boots inches deep in green scum. Other UN observers stand on either side, representatives of a variety of non-governmental organizations, shoulder to shoul-der with the young academics Clive had promised—forensic entomologists, forensic anthropologists, sociologists and others. Behind them are reporters and liaison people, fieldworkers holding colour-coded tags and clipboards. Shovels and scoops, stretchers and body bags have yet to be unloaded from their convoy of white UN vans.

On this side of the ditch there are twenty-three UN people— Judith counts them. A multicoloured, multilingual group, they have arranged themselves neatly and now seem reluctant to move. Like tourists who visit archaeological sites they wait for someone to tell them the significance of what they are looking at.

They have been carefully briefed: bodies are not to be touched until locals are consulted, there may be ceremonies, religious leaders must be invited to chant words, sprinkle holy water— whatever custom dictates. Judith supposes the bearded priest, standing on the other side of the ditch with a group of silent vil-lagers, has been chosen for this purpose.

She knows this may take some time, tells herself to relax, to focus on the bones. Counting slowly, matching skulls to spines, she calculates that the remains of six people lie in the ditch. There is no sign of weapons—of course weapons could have been stolen. But she doubts these people had weapons; they were probably workers, or the family who owned this field. She imagines a harvest interrupted, people collected at gunpoint, men from the fields, women and children from the gutted buildings they passed a kilometre or so down the lane. She had noticed a stone barn, and the shell of a house, its clay roof-tiles fallen in, partly hidden now by weeds. These could be the bones of the farm family—three half-grown children, two parents and a grandmother, or grandfather. It is difficult to tell but she suspects the third adult is female—something about the shape of the skull suggests this.

She is only guessing, filling in time. It will take weeks, months—maybe even years—to establish who these people were, what their relationship was to one another, and to their murderers.

Judith Muir has brushed soil from skull bowls used to collect human blood, has dipped her fingers into the ashes of sacrificed children, cupped the broken skulls of murdered kings in her hands—but time had purified those bones. Not here. Evil still surrounds this place, hovers above the bodies, vibrates through her own body urging her to leave. She wants to shout *Run!*, to herd everyone back into the vans, to take off down the lane—a quiet lane, as beautiful as any English lane this time of year. It would be the decent thing to do, to go and let time do its work. Let some future scholar determine who was sacrificed here and why.

But leaving is not possible. Behind her the Scandinavian sociologist is already whispering words into a tiny microphone. Atop one of the UN vehicles, the cameraman from Global hoists a TV camera onto his shoulder, aims his long lens at the villagers across the way. The process has begun, words are being fed into university computers, into newsrooms, pictures are being bounced off satellites. Before an hour has passed, words and pictures will merge into story, will be relayed to a thousand television stations. Images, of these filthy scraps of cloth, that worn shoe, the mud-filled cranium to which hanks of hair still cling, will be flashed around the globe. Millions will watch while eating their evening meal.

Apart from the whispering sociologist, everything is silent. The people across the way, twenty or so adults and children, wait quietly for some sign that the ceremony is to begin. The mayor, who had greeted them the night before, stands in front, between the dark-robed priest and a one-armed woman. Judith recognizes the woman from a file picture: she is the village teacher. The teacher and the mayor, whom Judith understands were on opposite sides during the killings, now stand side by side. None of the villagers, not even the children, look at the bodies. They stare across the ditch at the outsiders.

Judith imagines accusation on every face. Even the schoolteacher, the one who reported this site to the committee, looks reproachful. Judith resents their resentment, thinks, *We are here to help, to discover why this happened, to prevent it from happening again.* She would like to tell them this—will tell them, given the opportunity—although she hardly believes it herself.

She moves closer to Ian.

Knowing her thoughts, he pulls a hand from under his armpit, lays two fingers along her bare arm and, without turning his head, whispers, "Close your eyes and think of England."

She does, but not in the way he means. Her mind skims over their lovemaking, recalls instead her aunt's cottage near Gillsford. A ditch very like this one runs beside the cottage;

334

the water is thick and shiny, more reddish in colour, smelling of wetness, of a million primitive life forms that have bred and died beneath its sluggish surface.

"They drained the fens to get rid of the fenpeople," Aunt Min once said when Judith asked about the water's colour. "Them old kings wanted shut of fenpeople but our blood seeps up betimes." (Our blood! the child had thought. Why our blood? She hadn't dared ask.) She wonders if Aunt Min could have held some residual memory of an ancient slaughter.

The journalist in front of Ian hunkers down and his feet slide farther into the muck. Judith fears for his expensive boots. But then he steadies himself, rests his camera on one knee and points it down, almost into the rib cage of the skeleton she believes to be the grandmother. Looking closely, she sees what Thornton is photographing. The sternum has broken and inside the crushed chest cavity lies the head of a child. The woman's skeletal fingers still cradle the small skull.

She hears a sharp *crack*. Ian's fingers loosen, slide down her arm. He drops to his knees, then pitches forward. Dead in a second, dead before his body sprawls atop other bodies, dead before mud and blood can mix, splash up onto his wife's feet, spatter poppylike across her fawn trousers.

Ian is dead. In that instant Judith Muir knows that every thought she has ever had is wrong. All the answers, those grand possibilities, the carefully constructed theories delineating the upward curve of civilization—all false, all a disguise for what we humans are, what she is.

What she is makes guttural sounds, kneels in muck pawing at Ian's back, trying to roll him onto his side, trying to lift him, pull him out of the slime, separate him from this miserable, rotting family, a family whose deaths she would gladly condone—as she would the death of every soul in this wretched village—in exchange for Ian's life.

But Judith is powerless. She can make no exchange, can change nothing, cannot even move his body. She curves her body around his, crouches over him with her face pressed into his still-warm back. The animal-like sounds gradually stop; time passes and there is a terrible quiet.

The village people have vanished. On this side of the ditch the UN people have leapt behind vans or flattened themselves to the ground. One by one they stand up. Horrified and embarrassed they reach out, extend their hands. Judith ignores them. She stays in the ditch, kneeling in mud, in blood and bones. Her eyes are closed. Below her cheek she can feel the rough weave of Ian's shirt; it is an old shirt, much washed. This morning in their hotel room she had passed it to him, commented on the thinness of the cloth: Time to buy a new one, she'd said. This morning . . .

Eventually she is dragged up out of the ditch. With someone holding her on either side she is moved, stumbling towards the nearest van. Ahead of her someone opens a door and she falls in, falls on her side across the cold back seat, eyes closed, ears closed, hands covering her face, the reddish ditch water caking on her clothing, her skin, on the black leather beneath her.

X X

Two months later, edging the wagon down a narrow English lane, Judith can still smell that ditch water. Surrounded by a network of highways and superhighways, by the Midlands, by Cambridgeshire, Suffolk and Norfolk, separated from that place by oceans and continents, the rank smell of the ditch is still in her nostrils, its mud still encrusted in the pores of her skin.

She had hoped to reach the cottage by noon, has wasted hours in a tangle of flyovers, underpasses and byroads—one leading into a vast shopping centre the like of which she'd never seen, huge jail-like buildings surrounded by a labyrinth of parking lots that took ages to escape from. Even when she found the right access road, she'd driven past twice before spotting the car-wide break in the thicket. Trees and brush had narrowed the path to a tunnel. Yet she knows this place, knows now where she is. Hands that have been gripping the wheel for hours relax.

Judith has no confidence that the cottage will be there. Not until she comes upon it, crouched in its circle of tall grass and taller weeds, can she believe it has survived. She stops the car and gets out, stands for long minutes looking at the only property she has ever owned. Very different it is from the thatch-roofed, rose-draped cottages one sees on teapots and biscuit tins. Judith cannot remember there ever being roses, and the roof is of tarred felt over which a yellowish fungus has grown. The grey stone walls would be attractive except for the large area beside the door that has been patched with mismatched bricks—" . . . before my time," Aunt Min used to say, implying she would have made them do a better job of it. Yet her aunt never had the bricks replaced, never made any changes to the cottage, as far as Judith can recall—and surely she could have after the war, when her dependant's money was coming in?

The spring rain has stopped but it is cool, the sky overcast, the knee-high grass still wet. As she hoists her haversack onto her shoulder and pulls two grocery bags from the wagon, Judith is aware of her bare legs and wet sandalled feet. Pray God the old stove is still in the cottage and working.

She has always felt artfully pretentious when referring to the place as a cottage—not that she's had many occasions to refer to it. She and Ian had only visited once. Even then, a year after Aunt Min's death, the solicitor in Gillsford seemed to have forgotten its existence. He'd taken half an hour to find the large key, now tucked in an outside pocket of her haversack.

The key is unnecessary. The plank door is held shut by a slab of stone. She pulls it backward, then tips it end over end away from the step. The frame is warped and she must force the door open, lifting as she pulls. Inside, the place is dim and damp and it smells of mice. No matter, she is alone. Faint with relief she pushes the rusting bolt in place and leans back against the door.

It has taken all this time. Weeks and weeks to get here, to get to a place where there are no questions to answer, no forms to fill out, no decisions to make. A place where she no longer has to watch herself, guard against the sympathy and sorrow, the embarrassment others feel when they meet her—as if she were responsible for their feelings as well as her own. All this time Judith has been afraid she might splinter, give way to the awful public hysteria one sees on television. She knows, now, how such scenes are obtained—people are paid to lurk in airports and outside hospitals, waiting to harvest grief, and blood too. Death and violence made visible.

It happened to her only once. Only that day—the one question, "How do you feel?" called out from behind one camera, a camera held inches from her face, moving slowly downward over her bloody clothing.

After that, things had been arranged. They had hospitalized her, protected her from the media and perhaps from much worse. Some official had assigned two silent women to sit beside her, to wash her, keep her safe and comfortably drugged. Judith cannot remember that time, cannot help wondering how many went without care because of the attention given to her, the bed she occupied, the medicine she so willingly took.

Even after she got back to England, that urge to howl, to lie on the floor moaning, would overtake her—in waiting rooms and in the offices of solicitors and accountants. Even in their own small office at the museum, to which Clive Aldridge had kindly come to offer his condolences—to urge her to take as long as she wished to recover, to assure her there would always be work for her at the Institute—even there, Judith had to concentrate on containing herself, holding her skin in place, keeping those sounds inside her chest.

No one, of course, had thought to protect Ian's father—certainly not Judith. As she floated between starched sheets, no thought of eighty-nine-year-old Jonathan Muir had entered her drug-addled mind.

At suppertime, in the nursing home outside Churston Ferrers, the old man had seen his son die on the seven o'clock news.

"Hard to tell how much he'd took in," the attendant said. A cherubic boy with white hair, he had been feeding Jonathan at the time. They had been watching the news, and when the man on TV pitched forward, Mr. Muir's body jerked as if he too had been shot. It made his tray fall over, the boy told her.

Two days later, with Judith still becalmed in a far-off hospital bed, Ian's father died of a massive stroke. She had loved the old man. He'd been very like his son, a collector of odd facts, artifacts. A cheerful, practical kind of man who'd given up travel writing to teach junior school, keep house and raise Ian when his wife died in her early forties.

Judith closes her eyes and sniffs the cottage's damp. She would like to lie down right now, lie down in a corner and sleep. She feels tired, heavy. How strange that she can feel heavier, less elastic, more encumbered, when so much has fallen away. Somewhere in the room there is movement, the dry rustle of paper or leaves. Aware suddenly of how uncomfortably the haversack pulls at her shoulder, how the plastic bags cut into her fingers, Judith opens her eyes and, with what feels like a huge effort, pushes her back away from the cold door. She crosses the room and deposits her load on the dirty table.

The air in the cottage is icy, much colder than that outside. She rummages through the grocery bags, finds matches and goes to the ancient stove some ancestor fitted into the space that had once been a fireplace. Gingerly lifting the damper she finds nothing more unpleasant than a crumpled mass of paper—left by squatters, she supposes, or by people who simply think of the abandoned cottage as a public shelter. There has been no caretaker—the solicitor who handled Aunt Min's estate will have died years ago.

Ian saw the cottage only once. Aunt Min died suddenly, unexpectedly, in Judith's second year of graduate studies. Later, the solicitor, whose name she now remembers was Witherstone, wrote asking her to come and sign a transfer of deed or some such document. She and Ian came down by train, checked in at the hotel in Gillsford and hiked across the flat fields to the cottage. It had smelled bad even then. They had simply propped the door open and gone around back to drink their Thermos tea and eat cheese-and-pickle sandwiches under the blossoming apple trees.

Afterwards they walked along the towpath. Pushing aside rushes and brambles, they listened to frogs and speculated on what might lie buried below the rust-coloured mud of the canal—flint axes and iron spears, the bones of lock-keepers, perhaps the bones of those murdered fenpeople Aunt Min claimed as ancestors. Recalling human remains that had been preserved for thousands of years by the acidity of bog water, she and Ian mused on the possibility that not just bones but intact bodies might lie encased in silt below the canal.

It was late afternoon before they got around to examining the cottage. The single downstairs room had looked pleasant enough. Judith remembers the gold-pink light of sunset filtering through dusty windows, spilling across the stone floor, onto handmade chairs and a worn deal table.

The two upstairs rooms, with low ceilings and narrow windows that went almost to the floor, were dark and less inviting. The only furniture was two washstands and two bare beds with rusting springs. Pushed far in under the dusty eaves were the outlines of other things—the old tin bath, barrels and many boxes into which someone must have packed Aunt Min's belongings.

It was dark when she and Ian locked the door and left. They'd walked back to Gillsford, taking shortcuts across reclaimed fields of grass and oats, past sleeping cattle, heat rising from the shadowy bulk of their bodies. There were still cottages along the canal then, only a few and not one showing a light. They talked about how they might make the cottage habitable—as if it had not been inhabited by generations of Kirkmans, by the lock-keepers, her father's parents, grandparents and great-grandparents, by the recently dead Aunt Min for all of her eighty-six years. They would install new floors and plumbing, Ian said, add a bathroom out back, repair the roof and repoint the stone walls. Judith imagined a sunroom, pots of flowers, shelves for books and pottery, walls the colour of country butter.

On that sweet, spring evening anything seemed possible. Their future was already assured—Ian had just published his paper on the Tollund Man and a colleague had invited them both to join his expedition in West Turkestan when Judith finished her thesis. Before long they would have their own research team, would unearth lost cities, become as well known as the Leakeys. And when they grew tired of travelling they would return to England, come to live here, uncover communities of ancient fenpeople, become even more famous. Clearing the orchard and garden they would grow fruit again and vegetables. In old age they would sell things to passersby, sit outside the cottage surrounded by piles of knitted scarves and tea cozies, by sacks of potatoes, baskets of apples, jars holding sprays of flowering currant, lilac and sweet-smelling mint.

How confident they had been, holding hands, laughing at the impossible idea of themselves old, reliving Aunt Min's life. Ian had tucked her hand under his arm, had said, "I'll learn to plumb and you'll learn to knit."

"I know how to knit, sir! Have talents you know not of." She had pulled him towards her, falling with him onto the spring grass—sky falling with them, the moon suddenly near, outlining his head, the curve of his neck and jaw, her hand reaching up.

Judith finds herself weeping, standing with the lifter in her hand, tears streaming down her face, dropping onto the cold stove. Weeping changes to wailing, howling, then she is banging the iron lifter against the stove, filling the world with such a racket that birds roosting in the chimney whirl noisily upward. She begins to tremble, mouth, hands and knees shaking so violently that she has to hold onto the stove to keep upright. Slowly she gets control of herself, makes herself stop, tells herself she can weep later, remember later—later when the fire is going, when she is warm. She thinks about heat and food, rubs a hand across her eyes, strikes another match, concentrates on the mundane task of lighting a fire.

How long everything is taking, as if time slowed when she crossed the doorstep, and how cold the room is, like winter. Stone walls must hold cold as well as heat. Still, it is a marvel, after years of neglect, that the walls are standing, that they have not been hauled to some nearby suburb where such stones are prized. No thanks to her that the place has not been vandalized.

During that brief visit she and Ian had arranged through Mr. Witherstone to have taxes deducted from their bank account. That was all they had done. They had never come back, had barely mentioned the cottage. It was a place for their future, for that distant, still unthought-of time when their nomadic life would be over, when they would become old and settled.

"Damn!" The fire is not catching. Darkness is drawing in, filling the corners of the room. The cottage has electricity. In the thirties, when wire was strung pole to pole out to the old boot factory, Aunt Min's brother, Judith's grandfather, had electrified the cottage. He'd done the work himself, installed two dangling bulbs, one in the hall upstairs and one downstairs above the table. Along the back wall, just left of the stone sink and its rusty pump, there is a switch, an ugly iron lever protruding from a steel box. It takes two strong hands to push the lever up. Before going to bed Aunt Min used to do what she called "throwing the switch," so that neither she nor the child would thoughtlessly turn on a light if they got up during the night.

It took only one light to guide German bombers, Aunt Min said. One light and the Huns would be dropping bombs smack down on their cottage, on her friend Rosemary's house in Gillsford, on her school or the church—or even worse, on the nearby airbase from which squadrons of silver planes took off each sunset, lifting like birds into the distant sky, flying in formation towards the North Sea, towards Berlin.

Watching the tiny glow each match makes before sputtering out, Judith remembers that feeling of responsibility, the whole weight of the war depending on a child not showing a light, on thousands of English children—and German children too, for surely there must be German children waiting in the dark as she was—remembering not to show a light as they fumbled across dark floors to pee-pots. The idea had frightened her then, it still frightens her. It would be useless now, after all these years, to try to throw the switch. Wires will have corroded, the electricity long since disconnected.

The thought of lying down returns. She is very, very tired. She could fall asleep, die of hypothermia and not a soul would know. How long before the bank would notice that nothing was being withdrawn from her account? Would they then report the dormant account to the Institute? Clive Aldridge might send out a research team. They would discover her beside the stove, dead and dry as leather, preserved like the Lindow Man. She, like him, would be found by accident, for no one would think to look here, her forwarding address being a post office box in Gillsford.

Judith shakes herself and slams down the damper. She will have to find something dry to burn. She blows her nose and wipes her still-moist eyes with the sleeve of her sweater. There used to be a woodbox. She turns, holds another match aloft, and there it is looming in the corner behind the door. Before lifting the top, still covered with peeling oilcloth, she has to remove a hammer, a box of nails, three rusty soup tins, an attractive but filthy lamp and a tin jug containing a hardened brown substance that could be molasses or paraffin, or something more unpleasant. It is a sturdy jug, with a wide mouth and a good flat bottom, and looks very like the one Aunt Min used to measure out potatoes for her customers—only Aunt Min called it something else.

She remembers squatting in the yard, watching a tinkerman hold a jug like this one on his lap. The man had made a fire in which he heated his soldering iron until it was red hot. The glowing tip would magically turn solid lead into a bubbling silver liquid. It might have been this jug he was mending—and sure enough, when she turns it over there is a lead patch where the handle is soldered to the round belly of the jug. She likes the jug. Before setting it aside she sniffs its putrid contents. Maybe she can clean it.

Keeping the woodbox filled had been one of her childhood duties, the job Aunt Min assigned to her on the first morning after she arrived—a kind of cure for grief, she supposes. Too short to see into the box she'd had to reach up and drop wood in piece by piece over the edge. She was only four and terrified of the woodbox, of its deep unknown interior, a place where anything from Germans to goblins might hide—and of the very real possibility that the heavy lid, propped open by Aunt Min with a junk, would crash down on her arm.

The top of the box is waist high now. She lights another match and leans in, sniffing the clean, remembered smell of wood shavings and chips and junks. Windfall and sawed-up branches trimmed from their own apple trees had kept the old stove going. The almost-empty box still holds a pile of twigs and six or seven good junks. As a teenager she'd taken over the cutting and splitting herself. Is it possible that she might have cut the very wood she is now piling onto her arm? She is thinking this when there is a movement among the shavings; she flings the junks she's holding to the floor, grabs a handful of twigs and slams down the lid.

"Pray God the chimney is safe," mutters Judith the atheist, who never truly prays to God but upon whose mind Aunt Min (a non-believer herself, now that Judith comes to think on it) has inscribed a hundred prayers. Watching flame lick into the shavings and catch the newspaper, she thinks she should have fished one out—then she would know when the last fire was lit here.

She would like to make tea but knows the water pump, a cranky, creaky affair at the best of times, has not been oiled or primed in years. No matter, the supermarket bags contain wine and cheese and bread—candles too, she belatedly recalls. And there is milk and fruit for breakfast. She must go out to the station wagon while there is still a little light, must get the torch and the sleeping bags.

Only when she is sure the fire will keep burning does she go outside. The tree-encircled garden is already dark. In the cooling air the familiar smell of fen water mixes with the smell of mint gone wild, crushed by her feet. Looking back at the cottage Judith can see a faint glow from her fire reflected through the grimy downstairs windows, see smoke wisping up, grey against the black sky. These signs of habitation induce a small rush of satisfaction—followed instantly by guilt that such feelings are still possible for her.

Back inside she drops the iron bolt across the plank door and spreads both sleeping bags, one atop the other, near the stove. Tomorrow she will root out mice, she will find pots, scour the rainbarrel, scrub the table and stone floor. Tomorrow she will wash the windows, examine the attic rooms, weed the garden, chop wood, oil the lamp and prime the pump. Tonight, with fire and food, in the blessed absence of people, wrapped in the familiar-smelling sleeping bag, Judith hopes to sleep.

XXI

On her fourth day in the cottage, having used what little rainwater she's managed to collect in the newly clean tin jug and having run out of both bread and wine, Judith decides she must go in to Gillsford. The rain has finally stopped. As she backs the wagon down the narrow path and eases carefully out onto the access road, the sun breaks through.

In her childhood there had been no access road, no paved highway, just a gravel cart-track following first the canal and then the river into Gillsford. Aunt Min did not have a car of course, or a horse either. The Kirkmans had never kept animals. They owned no barns or fields, just the cottage lot, which was part vegetable patch, part herb and flower garden, and around back, the small apple orchard. Aunt Min said her ancestors had been bog-watchers not farmers, bog-watchers and eel-catchers who became lock-keepers.

Early in the century lock-keepers like Aunt Min's father, who lived in rent-free cottages beside the canal, were replaced by steam and electric pumps. The lock-keepers and most of their dwellings are now long gone. Aunt Min had somehow managed to hold on to the cottage, making her modest living from the orchard and garden.

On market days a farmer named Hemmings would pick Aunt Min up, along with her baskets and boxes. Judith usually refused the ride. Walking was more pleasant than jolting along in the wagon, having to pull over and be smothered in dust every time a car or lorry passed. Walking was faster too. Crossing through fields and over narrow plank bridges it was easy to get into Gillsford before Mr. Hemmings.

From the six-lane highway Judith catches glimpses of places where old gardens and cottages once stood, transformed now into neat neighbourhoods, twenty or so identical houses built around artificial duck ponds. Near the outskirts of Gillsford, where the deepened canal meets the Thorpe, the master lock-keeper's house has become a smart restaurant.

Gillsford too has changed, is bigger, surrounded by suburbs. The high street is unrecognizable; it has been widened, the huge old trees Judith remembers are gone, every one. The houses and small shops are gone too, given way to glass and steel banks and insurance companies. Three or four large shops built since her childhood are already in various states of decay, their windows boarded, plastic fronts sprayed with graffiti. She is wondering where people shop, when, at the end of the high street—right where the market used to be—she sees a big Tesco store. Small businesses branch out on either side from the supermarket; several take-aways, a hairdresser, a video rental shop, a sweet shop, a combined chemist and post office, two clothing stores and a flower shop. These, together with the supermarket, make a three-sided enclosure for the huge parking lot.

After she finds a spot for the wagon Judith walks slowly around the half-circle of shops. Is it possible that someone in Gillsford might recognize her? Some of the people she went to school with must have stayed—but many left, including her best friends Jean and Rosemary. She sometimes gets a card from Rosemary, who works for a pharmaceutical company in Switzerland. Jean's family moved to Canada two years after the war ended. It had seemed a wildly adventurous thing to do at the time. Aunt Min said they would all be eaten by polar bears— and perhaps they had been, for despite her solemn promises Jean had never written.

Judith feels dazzled by brightness, by noise and colour and the multitude of things. After the dim silence of the cottage everything startles her, especially the smells—chip fat and rotting fruit, car exhaust and curry, and that peculiar scent that wafts from gift shops. Judith, who has spent very little time shopping, is astonished to see such shops in Gillsford, one that sells nothing but herbs and spices, one filled with trinkets, plastic earrings and jewelled hair clips, another with just candles, one with flimsy underwear, one with party supplies.

In the corner once occupied by Aunt Min's rickety stall there is a laundromat called Wishwash. A large white cat sleeps in the window. The spire of St. Matthew's sweeps up behind Wishwash but the laundromat blocks any view of the church itself or of the churchyard. As a schoolgirl Judith spent many a Saturday mooning among the graves. Daydreaming beneath the trees, feeling out the words on weather-worn headstones when she should have been helping sell herbs and apples, marrows, lettuce and potatoes, garish tams—and tea cozies, the knitting of which constituted her aunt's only domestic talent.

Next time she will bring her laundry into town. While her

wash is being done she can go around behind and find the old side gate into the churchyard. She will buy clippers and tidy Aunt Min's grave, which must be overgrown. Judith has not seen the grave since the day of her great-aunt's funeral. She vaguely remembers ordering a marker—or did she only plan to order one?

What a self-centred creature I am, Judith thinks, but only briefly, reminding herself of how little time she and Ian spent in England, how busy they always were—recruiting people, arranging transportation, begging for permits and funding—tedious work that had to be done before one arrived at a site. Still, she should have visited her aunt's grave. She hopes it is marked, hopes it is on the far side of the churchyard. It would be unfair that one who set so little store by cleanliness should be eternally surrounded by the smell of bleach and fabric softener.

Inside Tesco she is surprised at the many things besides food one can buy here—flowers and clothing, tools, even furniture—surprised too at how much she needs, and very glad for the cart. After picking up food and wine, she sees a fleecy dressing gown, a shovel, a broom, an axe, cleaning supplies, skin cream—Judith has begun to worry about the invisible mud caking her skin, wonders if she's contracted the disease that afflicted the rulers of thirteenth-century Cairo, a hardening and roughening that makes skin unpliable. She buys dishes, pans, two large plastic buckets and then, on impulse, a huge container of drinking water.

Leaning on her overloaded cart outside Barks and Bits, which seems to be a toy store for dogs, Judith looks out over the glittering sea of cars and sees there is an enclosed playground in one corner of the parking lot. After depositing her purchases in the wagon she walks idly over to the chain-link fence. Inside, screaming children race about, swinging from and clambering over tubular affairs painted in red, yellow and blue. It is almost noon and a row of potted saplings along the fence casts brief shade on plastic benches where parents, mostly fathers, sit. The men read and chat, smoke and eat take-away food, keeping a sharp eye on their offspring.

Amazing how English children are guarded. In most of the world small children still play in the streets, only going home to eat and sleep. Probably as I did at that age, she thinks.

Although Judith remembers little of her childhood, there are times when she is swept with a pervasive sense of loss she knows is connected with those first four years of her life. Most of the memories that remain are sharply clear but disconnected—the scent of a certain lip gloss, wartime songs, damp steps leading downward into darkness, and morning sun outlining the slanted shadows of iron railings on a pavement. Encounters with such sights and smells and sounds leaves a residue of sadness that may linger for days.

When she got older Judith asked about her parents. Aunt Min, a sister of Judith's grandfather, said both her brother and his wife died in their fifties. She remembered little about their only child, Judith's father. Mark Kirkman had left Gillsford right out of school. Aunt Min had never laid eyes on Judith's mother, but knew her nephew had married a girl named Ethel. She remembered getting a note from the couple saying they'd had a baby girl and were living in a flat near Holborn Post Office where Mark was a sorter.

Judith can almost remember the flat—three rooms on the ground floor where the toilet was, the dark hallway smelling of pee and Jeyes Fluid. When her father was called up, her mother let Judith's closet-size room out to a friend called Mildred Elsy.

After that, Judith slept in her parents' bed, alone five nights a week because her mother had taken a night job in a factory down near the railway yards. Judith's mother was always home when she went to sleep, but Mrs. Elsy would wake her every morning, give her breakfast and see that she got off to infant school. Mrs. Elsy did not work in a factory but in the Express Dairy, which Judith thought was a farm with cows but which Mrs. Elsy said was just a soda bar. There did not seem to be a Mr. Elsy. Years later Judith came to realize that Mildred Elsy did not like children and wondered if the woman took care of her in exchange for the room or out of friendship.

"Out through the door with ya," Mrs. Elsy would say after breakfast, her being always in a hurry to get to work. This meant Judith had to leave the house early, had to walk to school on her own. She didn't mind. Most mornings she would meet her mother coming home from the night shift—it was the happiest time of her day, the one happy memory she has held on to.

They would come together at the corner, beside the iron fence of a little park across from the school. If her mother wasn't there, Judith would wait, holding her gas-mask box and her satchel, looking at the dry fountain where a beggar girl balanced a broken water jug on her shoulder. She has a clear memory of the girl's stone face, but cannot recall her mother's. She remembers her mother's hand, though, soft fingers with painted nails touching her shoulder, a sweet-smelling kiss, remembers watching her mother's legs, pale and childlike beneath a print smock, vanish around the corner.

Even on days when she waited a long time for her mother, there was still an hour to while away before the doors were unlocked and the school bell rang. Other infants would already be there, three- and four-year-olds whose mothers had wartime jobs. They would sit quietly on the school steps watching big children swarm over mounds of bomb rubble that was cleared from streets and dumped in open spaces every night: hunks of concrete, twisted pipes, sections of brick walls, jagged strips of steel and glass, smashed cars and furniture. The wreckage of London spilling across what Judith supposes had been a playground.

The smell of meat frying pulls her into the present, to Hamburger Hannah's, a box-size take-away beside the playground. Holding coffee, onion rings and a large Hannahburger, Judith returns, pushing open the narrow gate into the fenced enclosure. She ignores the young man occupying the other end of the bench, sits on the warm plastic and bites into the first cooked food she's eaten in days.

The playground is a surprisingly pleasant place despite its chain-link fence and dismal surroundings. Its colourful tubular constructions remind Judith of modern art—indeed, the total effect is more pleasing than most modern art, softened by the sunny blur of moving children. She wonders if Ian will think so. Then she remembers. A low sound, something between a howl and a moan begins deep in her chest. Her mouth is filled with half-chewed food. Trying to control the sound, she sputters and, much to the alarm of the young man sharing the bench, begins to choke. Without raising his eyes from his book, the man stands and moves quickly away. Judith swallows, takes a gulp of coffee, and after a minute or two the sound stops. Using several of Hannah's paper napkins she blows her nose and mops her face.

In Cambridge someone pressed a book entitled *Five Rooms in the House of Grief* into her hands. The sepia-toned cover showed a hallway with five doors, a gauzy figure moving towards one of them. Judith left the book on a chair in the airport. She wonders if these embarrassing bouts of despair will continue for the rest of her life, wonders if the book might have helped. Probably not—grief is not a house but a country.

She closes her eyes, leans back, raises her face to the April sun and listens. Children laugh and squeal, call out to one another. Their voices seem thin, farther away now that her eyes are closed. Somewhere girls are singing a kind of chant that sounds vaguely familiar. *"Blast off! Blast off! Don't go there!"* the song ends. Despite the ominous words these children sound happy, happy and safe—but then so had the ruffians she recalls scrabbling over the sharp-edged mélange of war.

So much danger. Yet Judith doesn't recall anyone getting hurt. *"Blast off! Blast off! Don't go there!"* There had been warning signs of course, and sometimes an old man wearing a tin hat would come by, shouting at the children to get the hell down. As soon as the Air Raid Precautions man was out of sight they would return to the heaps of rubble—untangling twisted bikes, bird cages and baby buggies, pushing aside filthy sinks and toilets, uncovering cups and window frames, doors and door knobs, bolts of half-burnt cloth, scraps of clothing, books and fancy bits of plaster.

Each child made a pile of stuff they considered useful or saleable. Most worked in teams, one guarding and one gathering. Sometimes a teacher would look out from a schoolroom window, but since the park was not part of the school property they never came outside. Not even when terrible fights broke out over the ownership of valuable items. The boys were especially rough, they could make even big girls cry. Even a frightened four-year-old shivering on the steps knew enough not to raise her eyes to watch these fights—often the boy who lost would turn on some girl or smaller boy.

Except for the moment when her mother takes her hand and bends forward to kiss her, Judith is always alone in these snatches of memory, a small forlorn child sitting on cold steps or standing on an empty sidewalk.

Have such memories held her back from having children? This thought has never occurred to Judith before. For a student of the past she sets surprisingly little store by her own. Too late, she considers the question, considers also her mother's neglect— and decides to forgive her. Had Ethel Kirkman been unusually careless? Probably not. Preoccupied with the war, with the fatigue of factory jobs, absent husbands, with air raids and inter-rupted sleep—it's a wonder they didn't all go mad.

Sitting in the sun listening to the sounds of children at play, Judith wonders how many women did go mad, how many chil-dren were molested, murdered, or simply disappeared during those war years. It would make an interesting research subject— but why would anyone bother? There are fresher, ever more bloody wars. All over the world women and children huddle in wastelands, creeping out at night to find food and water, thou-sands are raped, tortured and slaughtered daily—generations of the newly disappeared to study, research, write books about.

She reflects on these things, thinks how fortunate she was in the location of her war. No guerrilla armies had prowled the streets of London, no uniformed assassins had interrupted the orderly flow of refugees leaving the bombed city. All alone four-year-old Judith Kirkman had reached the safety of Gillsford, the offhanded kindness of Aunt Min.

Resolving again that someday soon she will tend Aunt Min's grave, she stands, and after stuffing her leftovers into a conveniently placed garbage container, smooths down her hair and walks briskly out of the playground. From the corner of her eye she sees the man return to his bench. Judith cannot blame him. Who could enjoy sunshine and a good book while seated beside a crazy woman who moans and spits food about?

She is immensely relieved to find the cottage as empty as

she left it. No official waits to inform her that she cannot occupy a dwelling without plumbing or electricity. Having already cleaned out a cubbyhole under the stairs, she stacks her groceries there, then hoists the heavy water container up into the dry sink. The shovel, scrub pail, cloths, a brush and a huge plastic jar of an unpleasant-looking blue substance called DirtAway she puts down near the woodbox.

On the plank shelf behind the table she arranges the old tin jug, the pots and a cheap set of cream-coloured dishes she bought in the supermarket. Later she will clean the windows and scrub the floor. Now she goes outside and picks some of the tiny spring flowers that grow near the trunks of trees—flowers Aunt Min called wood anemone. Judith puts the pale blossoms in a cup of water, sets it at the centre of the table and stands for several minutes admiring the niche of domesticity she's created.

XXII

By mid-May Judith has hacked back most of the weeds around the cottage and planted a small vegetable and herb garden beside the door. Hoping to keep animals out, she encloses her garden with a fence of twigs woven together with Aunt Min's coloured yarn. Although she doesn't want them eating her seedlings, she is glad for the rabbits and badgers, as she is for the many birds that nest in low bushes beside the ditch and for the owl who calls at night from her ruined orchard. They add movement to the landscape without disturbing her solitude, the remoteness she feels from the vast network of highways, the pods of brick houses, which in fact encircle her just beyond the fields.

She has set mousetraps. Some wildlife she will not tolerate— she has killed and buried thirty-seven mice. She has scoured the woodbox and filled it with windfall. She has scrubbed every surface in the downstairs room and started clearing out the two attic rooms. Eventually she will cut paths through the orchard, perhaps find the old well.

She works slowly. Days follow no pattern—sometimes she rises before dawn, sometimes sleeps till noon, when hunger and a full bladder wake her. During this period Judith often feels that she is on the edge of wisdom, that some significant truth is within reach. Then time skips and she finds herself in the garden, knowing the sun has moved, knowing by the ache in her bones that she's been kneeling for hours.

She prowls at night, walking by moonlight along the canal path, pacing inside around the table if there is rain. On other nights she takes the lamp upstairs. Her ancestors lived simply but they never threw anything away. For uncounted years Kirkmans have stored every unneeded item under the eaves—every tool and dish, every threadbare bit of clothing, moth-eaten sweaters and stiff, hardened footwear, scrub boards, walking sticks and broken umbrellas. The tin half-bath she remembers using is filled with Aunt Min's knitting wool; a barrel is stuffed full of feather pillows and worn mats. Iron bake pots hold twisted nails, small boxes contain never-used, lace-edged handkerchiefs, letters, two pocket watches, balls of twine, pencil stubs and many buttons and keys. There is a wooden packing crate addressed to W. Wilks & Son, Grantham, Great Britain, the word FRAGILE stamped below in still-red letters.

At first Judith thinks that the box holds only straw and mouse droppings. But no, nestled among these are twenty-four identical teacups. No saucers and no plates. Judith lifts the cups out one by one—perfect, smoke blue, transparent things; pale pink flowers circle each rim and on the bottom is a tiny Chinese letter she cannot read. Salvage dredged up from the canal or looted from a barge? She will never know. Judith packs twenty-three cups back in the straw, takes one downstairs.

There are other boxes but these contain no surprises—corsets and purses, chipped dishes, stained pictures, perished rubber hot-water bottles, and a hundred green and brown glass bottles, many of which once contained Dr. Anderson's Tonic Wine. Larger bottles and jars are lined along one side. The cheap little case she brought with her from London when she was a child is there too, strangely alone with nothing stacked around or over it, pushed far under the eaves in the room where she used to sleep.

With centuries of belongings to be sorted, the upstairs will take months to straighten out. Judith finds the job soothing, she wants it to last. Very like her other life it is, sitting in a circle of lamplight examining each broken and discarded thing her ancestors ever owned, speculating on the lives of relatives as distant from her as the people of Koobi Fora.

She makes little mounds of their treasures, discarding the ugly and unusable into a pile that is burnable and a pile that will be bagged as rubbish. She saves anything she finds useful, interesting or beautiful—a few books and letters, a good tin bucket, a barrel that she drags outside to catch rainwater, the mouse-proof stone jars in which her aunt had stored a winter's supply of potatoes, apples and flour. Her own suitcase she ignores. She knows down to the last hair ribbon every item inside. She will leave that for last—wait until new grief has made space for old.

Every week or so Judith drives into Gillsford. She has no curiosity about the place or its people, never reads the community notices she sees tacked up in Tesco, never looks at magazines or newspapers. She and Ian had not taken much interest in affairs that did not impinge upon their work and she now feels completely indifferent to world events. She lives in ignorance of each day's body count, what atrocities have been committed, which countries face famine—tells herself that she's paid her dues and is better off not knowing which Cain is slaughtering which Abel.

Nor has she gone to visit her aunt's grave, searched out the law office where the deed to her cottage is stored, or even checked to see if her mail is being forwarded to the post office box her bank pays rent for. Her bank card still works; someone is making sure her cheques are deposited. At shops and restaurants she speaks only when necessary, to order a meal, to purchase seeds, nails, lamp oil, tools, food and drinking water. She saves the rain-barrel water for washing dishes and for taking baths in the tin tub she has brought downstairs. For scrubbing walls and floors and watering her garden she uses bog water dipped out of the canal with Aunt Min's bucket.

The cottage's roughly plastered walls are the colour of strong tea. When she has time she will whitewash the walls—is white-wash made anymore? There used to be someone called the Lime Man. He wore a white canvas coat over his regular clothes and came each summer to do the walls. He had a horse and cart, and buckets of cream-like lime that he spread with a wide brush—and not just on the inside walls. Judith remembers that he limed fences too, and the well and the privy and halfway up the trunks of all their fruit trees. At night the orchard glowed. From her bedroom window she could see lines of white truncated ghosts standing guard behind the house.

The whitewash has long since washed away. The rows of fruit trees now blur into a tangle of underbrush, entwined with mallow, bramble, thistle and some large-leafed plant that might be rhubarb. It is impossible to walk through the orchard. Owls, badgers and rabbits own the place, together with a fox who sometimes sits on the edge of his kingdom to watch Judith work.

Always she is aware of Ian's absence, but it is worst at night. She lies awake missing their shared thoughts, the talk, the sex, the laughter. Most of all she misses the living physical presence of him; his loss is like an amputation. Sometimes she can distract herself by listening to circles of sound that surround the cottage. Animals move through the garden, grunting and coughing, disturbing the congregation of crows who roost in nearby trees. Then small birds nesting under the eaves begin to flutter and chirp in their sleep, nearby a fox barks, the owl calls from the orchard. The sounds thread around and under one another, weaving a net as she drifts towards sleep.

On other nights the silence is so complete that it wakens her—no furnace, no refrigerator, no throb of electric generator, a sound common to every excavation they ever worked at. On such nights the cottage and garden seem wrapped in black flannel and Judith lies awake straining to hear something beyond her muffled world. If she listens long and hard she can imagine a low hum, is never sure if the sound is inside her head or an echo of distant traffic on the new highway beyond Gillsford.

Several of her favourite books are in the wagon and during her first wakeful nights she got up and tried to read. The light in the cottage is bad, but it wasn't just the light. She kept drifting away, losing the thread of words, even in novels she'd read before. Neither poetry nor biography, not even a picture book filled with images of the Maya underworld hold her attention.

The only way Judith has found to distract herself on such nights is to make lists of the things she must do before winter: she will rebuild the collapsed privy, prune the trees, dig a larger garden; have wiring installed, the chimney checked, the roof made tight. Rain comes in around the door. Also the well must be located, cleaned and reconnected to the kitchen pump, from which only a dribble of blood-coloured water can now be forced.

Sadly, all these jobs involve workmen—men, and perhaps women, who must be bargained with, told what to do, told how to find the cottage. They will drive trucks and backhoes down the path, will want to talk, ask questions, want to know who she is, why she is here. They will notice things, these kindly workers. They will go home to ask aged parents if they remember Old Min Kirkman, tell them her niece, the one who came to live with Min during the war, is living out in the cottage. Squatting they will probably call it. They will describe how she looks, her unmade-up face, her uncombed hair, her wool socks and heavy work boots, the man's shirt hanging out of a skirt she picked from a sale bin in Gillsford. They will see that she has no bed, no running water, no electric lights, no radio or television. For all Judith knows it may be illegal to live this way—workmen might report her to some authority or other.

With daylight she forgets these petty fears, forgets her lists. The future exists only on silent, moonless nights when she cannot walk and cannot hear the sounds of other creatures.

During the day, as if of their own accord, her hands find work, leaving her mind to float thoughtlessly in some netherworld of its own making. In that place she and Ian are together, enfolded in warm air, walking on soft earth below which unimagined cities wait to be discovered. Often Judith emerges from this other time to discover that she has completed some small task—finds herself staring into a newly cleaned pot, holding freshly chopped kindling or a plate she has eaten from. She is neither bored nor lonely. Hours slide into days, days become weeks, spring shimmers into summer—without words, without decisions, without thought.

Her hands. Kneeling in the garden one day, holding the threadlike roots of some plant she must just have pulled up, Judith realizes that her hands no longer feel stiff. She touches her cheek; the mud there is damp, from her own garden, not the dry alien mud that has covered her skin for so long. She tries smiling, grimacing, opening and closing her eyes. Her skin is pliant.

Something has happened, what she is not sure. She stands and her newly supple body unfolds effortlessly. She circles the cottage, taking long exaggerated steps, swinging her arms, rotating her hips, delighting in the fluid movement of limbs, breathing in warm air, seeing how deeply green the garden is— it must be midsummer. To celebrate she will bathe outside. The slipper-shaped tub, which she has been using for weeks, is easy to move. She has no trouble pulling it out to the garden, setting it down in the bed of wild mint she's been weeding.

Judith fills the tub with water from the rain barrel, collects her bathrobe, towels, soap and a bottle of wine. She strips and sinks into sun-warmed rainwater, lies there looking down at her body—a strong useful body, it has given her much pleasure. She and Ian had enjoyed their bodies, enjoyed lovemaking. They were both unusually healthy—"robust," Aunt Min would have called them—could endure long uncomfortable journeys with pleasure, could eat strange food with no ill effects, did not succumb to fevers and insect bites that sickened many who came out from England. Ian, especially, never had an ache or pain— healthy until the moment he died.

Can comfort be taken from such a thing? From Ian's missing that torturous closing-down of movement and speech and memory, the long decline his father endured—missing too the happy, foolish old age they might have spent in this garden.

> Drip, drop, dropping in the sea,
> Who pulls the rope with me?
> Come, come, coming to the fair,
> No, no, the fair's not there!

Words from a song girls skipped to in her childhood come unbidden to mind. Judith lies in the tepid water reflecting on the songs children sing so cheerfully. Many foretell death, another of the devices we humans use to live with the terrible knowledge that we all must die. She is weeping again. Quietly this time, not howling or moaning or banging her head, just weeping silently as she opens the wine and pours a little into the stolen cup.

If Aunt Min had known about the hidden crate surely she would have sold the cups at Gillsford market. Judith is thankful they were left for her to find—are still there for someone else to find. After draining the wine she holds the empty cup up to the sun. A nimbus of light shines through the thin china; when she moves the cup a silvery blue shadow glides along her pale body.

Now would be the moment for once-upon-a-time to happen. That moment she had imagined as a young girl, the moment when her rescuer would appear, come slashing through the underbrush and carry her off to a wider world. She searches the circle of trees for a glint of sword, the shining banner, the sudden rushing breath of a horse, white and dappled green beneath the leaves. Once upon a time. Once upon a time such fancies may have held her, but that was long ago, before Ian, to whom it would never have occurred that she needed rescuing.

And neither do I, Judith thinks. Even now, even in this terrible time, she knows she will survive. *Survive* is a good word, *endure* might be more accurate—both are words she's not considered before, never had to measure herself against. She closes her eyes, lies quietly, mellow with sunshine and wine and the smell of crushed mint. For the first time since coming to this place she is aware of time passing, can feel the summer's day slip away, life happening while she lies listening to the sounds of birds and insects, to frogs along the ditch and a dog barking in the field beyond the orchard—the field where she and Ian once made love.

When she has finished crying, when most of the wine is gone, she gets out of the tub. She dries herself, then quickly rinses her dirty clothes, hanging the wet garments in trees around the clearing. After tipping the bathwater onto the garden she wraps herself in the newly purchased bathrobe and goes barefoot into the cottage and upstairs. In the low-ceilinged bedroom where she once slept, she crawls out under the eave and retrieves her suitcase.

She sees then that it is not really a suitcase, just her old school satchel. Had everything she owned fit into this small case? Probably not—how much could a four-year-old child be expected to carry? Things must have been left behind, probably with Mildred Elsy in the flat. For the first time Judith wonders what became of her parents' belongings, what became of Mildred.

The satchel is made of heavy brown cardboard meant to resemble leather; it has two rusting clasps, and a cracked handle onto which her gas-mask box is still tied. When Judith picks the satchel up, her hand remembers the handle, remembers holding it tight, standing in a vast station surrounded by wailing children, by smoke and the noise of trains. Some of the children had proper suitcases but most carried their belongings in school bags like this one; a few had flour bags or pillowcases. They all had name tags and cardboard gas-mask boxes strung around their necks.

Other children were being hugged, kissed and wept over by mothers and grans. Mildred Elsy stood beside Judith, the woman's gloved hands folded around a purse she held against her stomach. Mrs. Elsy had been kind those last terrible nights, letting her keep the light on beside her bed and making her cocoa in the mornings. Yet there was no warmth between them; even a four-year-old could see how stiff and uneasy they were together.

Judith had kept looking at a group of children who'd been placed way up at the front of the queue—several were on crutches, had arm or leg casts or huge bandages, two were in wheelchairs. One, the one Judith's eyes kept returning to, had a cloth-covered face like a rag doll with no eyes, just black dots for nostrils and an empty slot for a mouth.

"What's wrong with them?" She must have whispered the question aloud, because Mrs. Elsy said, "They're wounded dear. They're being moved to rest homes out in the country."

The wounded children didn't seem to have mothers either; they were guarded by four nursing sisters in black capes and starched white caps.

They're worse off than me, the child had told herself, but probably not out loud, because Mrs. Elsy didn't say anything else and they just stood there for a long time, silent and apart from the great rush of emotion swirling around them. Judith had tried to keep the wounded children in view but the crowd ebbed this way and that between them and the wounded children did not move.

"Miss Kirkman's your Dad's auntie, luv—she'll be good to you 'til he gets back," Mrs. Elsy said at last. She patted Judith's tam and tucked the gas-mask cord under her collar.

Judith cannot recall replying. She had never heard of Amelia Kirkman until Mrs. Elsy found the old woman's address among her mother's things and got after the childcare people. Then the whistle blew and a man with a clipboard came to look at her name tag. He wrote it down before gently prodding her into the long line of fearful, tearful children.

Two railway men in dirty overalls hoisted the smallest children up the high step onto the train. Judith followed the boy in front until a conductor pointed her to a seat and told her to sit there and not to budge. The seat was not high enough for her to see out the window and was made of wooden slats that hurt her bum. A big girl beside her was told to watch out for the four-year-old, but when the girl asked her name, Judith curled into a corner, pulled her school coat over her head and cried into the woolly dark.

She doesn't remember much about the journey. She must have slept. Later a smiling woman in a uniform came around with milk and sticky buns for everyone.

Judith carries the satchel downstairs thinking she will light a fire and make tea. But the cottage is still warm, and bright too, late-evening sun spilling in through the open door. She makes herself a cheese sandwich, pours the remaining wine into the grey-blue cup and settles down on a kind of couch she's made by piling sleeping bags and cushions against the wall facing the door. She has gotten into the habit of eating her evening meal here, leaving the door ajar so she can see the garden and the edge of trees from which the fox sometimes emerges at sunset.

She eats and waits but the fox does not appear. When the room cools she closes the door, decides to light the fire and make tea. While the kettle boils she goes through the contents of her old satchel. Nothing she doesn't remember—red plush slippers with bunny ears and a threadbare flannel nightdress, a pencil case with a hidden drawer containing two sticks of chewing gum, a cigar box filled with crumpled hair ribbons, her school tam and the picture book *Bertha Badger and Her Friends*. Judith's name and the address 5 *Nag's Lane* is written inside the book in a hand she cannot recognize. There are no documents, no photos of her parents, no letters from her father. Had Mildred Elsy not considered such things important, or had she stowed a trunk somewhere for safekeeping? A trunk no one has ever claimed.

The thought that she will never know doesn't bother Judith greatly. She sits with her feet on the fender and leafs contentedly through the Bertha Badger book. The pages have a smell that she remembers. She lifts the book to her face; a smell that is like vanilla but not vanilla seeps from the shiny cream-coloured paper.

She drinks tea and slowly turns the pages. It was the vanilla-y scent and the pictures, not the words, that captivated her as a child. Bertha Badger's underground world, shown as if you were looking down into a box, is mysteriously filled with sunshine, a sweet little town of winding streets, a school, a tiny church, a market where clothed badgers stand behind flower and vegetable stalls much nicer than Aunt Min's. Bertha's garden has an arch of vines over the gate and perfect lines of roses edge the path to a thatch-roofed house. There are tiny chairs inside the house, a table upon which teacups and teapots, cake and cookies are arranged. There is a couch with a fringed throw, woolly mats, windows with flowerpots and checked curtains.

She studies each picture for a long time, every detail is familiar, the colours softer than colours one sees in books nowadays— warm faded browns and oranges, pale pinks, transparent greens and blues. Colours that must have existed in a time before plastic.

Judith loves the book and is delighted to have found it. The satchel and the rest of its contents she slings onto the junk pile accumulating beside the woodbox. This collection of unburnable rubbish is growing daily; it contains dozens of bottles and tins piled into two dented buckets, a rusted kettle, rake and scythe, several mouldy pillows and blankets and three feathered and beaded hats. She promises herself that tomorrow she will bag everything and take it all in to Gillsford, where she hopes to sneak it into the tip behind Hamburger Hannah's.

She puts the book on the table and is about to pour herself another cup of tea when she notices the gas-mask box still lying on the sleeping bag. She picks it up. The cord that had attached it to her school case has broken but the box itself is still tied shut.

Children at infant school had to practise putting the gas masks on and taking them off. Judith hated the stiff rubber pressing against her face, the tight strap and the nasty smell, but especially the feel of having to hold her breath. She cannot recall seeing the gas-mask box after she arrived at Aunt Min's. The knots will not come untied. She is about to toss the box in with the other junk when the cord suddenly loosens. The old cardboard has come unglued—it falls apart and a skull rolls out onto the sleeping bag.

Judith Muir is not alarmed; she has, after all, seen many skulls, has often dreamt of them—odd, rather pleasant dreams of white skulls inside white temples, light-filled places where she and Ian walked hand in hand. Ian had maintained these dreams were signs of good fortune—since his death she's had no such tokens. She stares down at the object lying on the red polyester sleeping bag. It has landed face up. It is not white and for a minute she thinks it might be made of wood, one of those beautiful carvings you sometimes still see in parts of Africa.

She crouches down, picks the skull up, runs a finger along the junction of the coronal and sagittal sutures, finds the line where they fuse and knows instantly she is touching bone not wood—is holding a human head. She stares into the empty eye sockets. Who are you? What are you doing here?

As long as she can remember Judith has been intrigued by skulls, has considered them beautiful, elegant things, the most evocative part of the human skeleton. This one is particularly fine, with high cheekbones, widely spaced eye sockets and a strong, gracefully curved jawline. Unfortunately it seems to have been dyed or varnished. Can this be the work of some ancestor, anxious perhaps to preserve the skull of a loved one, or a despised enemy? Thoughts of bloody war trophies, of murders inside the Kirkman clan, fratricide by poison or knife, death creeping across this very floor—all these thoughts and others pass through Judith's mind.

"Not a word outside the house," Aunt Min would say after telling of some mad, disgraced or dishonest relative—though never a murderer, nor anyone who stole crates of teacups.

How could a skull have gotten into her gas-mask case? Aunt Min surely would not have put it there. Squatters perhaps, high on drugs, making a joke? But the story doesn't ring true. The upstairs rooms seem not to have been disturbed and the box was tied with its own cord, the satchel neatly tucked in below the eaves.

How nicely the skull fits her hand. Certain things do fit neatly into the human hand—skulls and shells, the worn handles of tools and walking sticks and guns. Judith has never killed anyone, never even shot a gun, but she has held Ian's small pistol more than once, always struck by how the smooth metal cradled against her palm, how her fingers naturally curved into position to accommodate the deadly extension. Ian had been a peaceful man, but it is not unknown for excavation sites to be plundered and therefore it was sometimes necessary to show that you had a gun. Her mind veers to that last moment, someone crouched down, a finger tightening on a trigger.

She is pulled from her dark vision by the rattle of rain hitting the windows, the thought of her underwear, skirt and shirt hung in trees outside. Placing the skull on the nearest flat surface, she rushes barefoot into the wind and rain. In the purple darkness she can see her shirt dangling from a branch like some white ghost; other garments have scattered but in a few minutes she finds her skirt and underpants. She gives up on her bra and darts back into the house.

Drenched and breathless, she pulls the door shut against the wind, stands gasping—staring straight into the face of the empty skull. It rests on her school satchel, atop the pile of junk, and it stares back at her just as it did the first time she saw it.

Saw it. Put down her school satchel, reached into the rubble, touched the smooth round thing, lifted it up with both hands, peered into the eyeless sockets, felt fear, delight, kinship—mixed with desire to own this strange object.

The memory is like a film clip—a little girl dawdling, no other children about, not a soul. She carries the skull over to the school steps and sits down. Using her limp cotton skirt she carefully wipes away a coating of chalky dust. The skull is interesting; she would like to talk to it as she talks to her doll, has a feeling it might talk back, which her doll never does.

They sit in the quiet sunshine for some time, but after a while she hears far-off voices, a kind of singing she thinks might be older children practising inside the school. She is afraid they might come out and find her sitting here on the steps—big boys would take the skull away from her. She decides to put her find in her gas-mask box. It fits neatly, just as it had in her hands. It is safe now, and hers. Later, when she is alone, she will hold it, look at it more carefully, ask it questions.

The child tosses the despised gas mask onto the pile of debris and walks out of the little park. She looks just as she had before, carrying her satchel in one hand and the retied gas-mask box, with the skull inside, hung over her shoulder. Then, just past the stone girl, she sees Mrs. Elsy coming towards her, almost running, and the child stops still, waiting . . .

Judith remembers each detail: the uneven paving stones underfoot, the cracked satchel handle nipping her fingers, Mrs. Elsy in her navy smock coming closer and closer. The smock has *Express Dairy* written across its front and when her small, resisting body is pulled into Mrs. Elsy's wide bosom, the child's nose and lips are pressed against the rubbery letters.

Standing with her back against the door, Judith stares through gathering gloom at the skull, but she can summon nothing more. Only Mrs. Elsy with her rolled-down stockings, the flower-print turban tied over her pincurls, the peeling letters on her smock. Judith sighs. All her trying will not conjure up another image from that day. Her feet are icy; the wet laundry she holds scrunched against her chest has soaked through her bathrobe.

She changes into dry clothing, woolly socks, and fills the hot-water bottle from the still-warm kettle. Before crawling into her sleeping bag she picks up the skull, turning it in her hands, thinking to find some markings along the back—but it is too dark. She sets it down on a nearby chair, sleeps and does not dream.

XXIII

J udith wakes early, the warmth of sun on her face. Unlike on other mornings, today she immediately opens her eyes, sits up and stares at the skull. It is dry and clean, no tissue remains. She reaches out and lifts it from the chair. Settling back, easing herself into the swath of sunlight that falls diagonally from the window across her sleeping place, she cradles the skull in her lap and drifts back to sleep.

When she wakes again, sun is shining straight into the empty sockets. She peers into the skull and sees that not only are the cranial portion of the head and the mandible intact, amazingly, so is the fragile internal network of facial bone. Turning the skull carefully, Judith gently runs her hands over its smooth surface, wishing, as she had when a child, that it could talk, answer her questions.

She puts the skull back on the chair, gets up and makes tea. Cup in hand, she goes outside into the bright morning, where every leaf, each blade of grass is a point of light. She walks slowly around the small clearing, sips her tea, thinking about what she will do, already leaning into the future, knowing she will miss this present, the timeless silence, the birds, the fox.

To stuff the rubbish, together with leftover food, into garbage bags, to roll up the sleeping bags, sweep the floor and push her clothing back into the haversack takes less than an hour. When her things are in the wagon Judith wraps a towel around the skull and tucks it in a plastic bag. She places it in the passenger seat and carefully arranges her jacket over it.

She goes back into the cottage to take a long look around—maybe a last look, she thinks, then tells herself not to be morbid. She closes the heavy door, lifting and pulling to get it fitted into its warped frame. Apart from the carelessly trimmed weeds and the shiny windows, all is as it was when she came. Resisting the urge to peer into the empty room, she gets in her wagon and backs down the path.

After depositing her junk in Hannah's tip and storing the car in a lockdown space near the station, Judith catches the train and is in Paddington by eight. Twenty minutes later she is checked into a small shabby hotel near Lancaster Gate. On their infrequent trips to London she and Ian always stayed in this area—what Ian called a "walkable distance" from the museums and art galleries they visited whenever they had time.

Her room is pleasant, with pale green walls, a desk with a lamp and a tiny bathroom where there is water that she turns on for the pleasure of feeling it splash into her hands. Her third-floor window looks down on the street, on small shops and restaurants, a fish-and-chips shop, a tandoori take-away, a newsagent and flower shop. People come and go. It looks very like Bertha Badger's world. The small Gothic church opposite has been stripped of stained glass and subdivided; floor braces cross the huge arched window that faces her window. A cheery yellow and red sign announces the church is now St. Andrew's Primary School. Through the top section of the window Judith can see directly into a brightly lit classroom where two women are at work. One cleans the blackboard, the other mops the floor. Both wear saris.

Mesmerized by the graceful swirl of arms, by how the green and orange cloth is never spattered by dirty water, never touches a mop or a sponge, Judith pulls a chair to the window and watches until the women finish their work, leaving the room suddenly dark as if a play has ended.

She stands, stretches and, with barely a glance, walks past the skull, which is still resting on the bed in its blue Tesco bag. In the bathroom she turns dials and watches steaming water fill the porcelain tub. Should she examine this urge to find where the skull came from, to what living body it was attached? It will probably be a fruitless task and not a simple one. There must be millions of skulls on earth—one cannot imagine the uncounted billions buried beneath the earth. There are thousands of skulls in London alone, not only in graveyards but inside churches and museums, in laboratories and universities. Why should she feel this sense of ownership, of obligation, for this particular skull?

Settled into the bath she considers the related questions of why she dislikes the idea of telling anyone about the skull, why she resists asking colleagues for help. The Institute she is employed by has databases, methods for the technical analysis of archaeological finds, the ability to date remains by the carbon-14 method. Were she to ask, these resources would be put at her disposal. Judith knows she will not ask.

Replenishing the endless supply of hot water, cleansing her skin with rose-scented soap, foaming shampoo into her hair, Judith reflects on the seductive nature of creature comforts.

This is what we all want, she thinks, running water, food, a comfortable bed, a sheltered room inside a walled city. Did the owner of her skull die fighting for such things—on the winning or losing side? Finding the answer will involve patient research through old records, work she has never done alone, work that will likely seem dull without Ian, who could make trawling through dusty papers seem almost as interesting as field-walking buried settlements.

Bathed, dressed and exceedingly hungry, she finds herself hesitating at the door, uneasy about leaving the skull in her hotel room. Chiding herself for this irrational protectiveness, she nonetheless slides the skull into her haversack—then finds herself sauntering along Queensway, wondering if it would like Greek food. She's been thinking of the skull as English, but it could be Greek, could be anything. Her countrymen have plundered the world, killing and conquering and collecting.

Upon returning to the hotel, Judith focuses the brightest lamp in the room on the desk and settles down to a more thorough examination of the skull. The forward-projecting cheekbones, the suture line where the cheek and upper jaw meet and the absence of a ridge above the eye sockets all indicate it is the skull of a woman. The skull has been varnished to a deep brown. The varnish unfortunately smooths out cranial sutures that may have provided information related to disease and aging. The most obvious clue, the code R29-H624 written along the back of the cranium, indicates that the skull has been part of a catalogued collection and almost assures eventual identification. The marking is quite clear, inscribed on top of the varnish in black ink with a wide-nibbed pen.

To Judith the dark varnish suggests the skull might be a relic from the Victorian Age—a time when the passion for collecting extended not only to such things as wax fruit, fossils, stuffed birds and macabre jewellery made from the hair of dead relatives but also to human heads, especially heads of people from what the English identified as exotic cultures. She has come across papers written on a subject these Victorians called the "science" of phrenology, which asserted that the power and range of people's mental abilities can be gauged from the size and shape of their heads—a variation of many offensive pseudosciences that have emerged throughout history, all aiming to sort and cull the human race. She runs her hands over the skull. It is quite beautiful—there are no signs of blows to the head, no bullet holes, no trephination. Of course there are a thousand other ways of dying, or being killed.

That night, despite the unaccustomed comfort of a mattress, Judith sleeps poorly and dreams of skulls. Not her usual pleasant dreams—these are nightmares in which she is alone, on her knees, digging beneath the floor of the cottage, uncovering hundreds of skulls. They are arranged neatly like eggs, and each has a small white square with names that fade as she bends to read. Somewhere there is ditch water; she smells it just before the cottage dissolves into darkness and she is creeping through a wet field, grass or stubble beneath her bare feet. In the air around her something brushes past—a cloud of bone. She is cold with fear, but a light appears, becomes a window, round and shining like a sun. Beyond the glittering glass there are skulls, stacked in a pyramid like those she's seen in atrocity pictures—except that the top skull wears a hat and spouts blood that ripples down like red silk over the other skulls, a dark river flowing around her feet, filling the world beyond her dream, and then she hears horses, many horses trotting steadily towards her.

She pulls herself out of the dream, wakes, opens her eyes—the horse sounds are still there. Real, the unmistakable sound of hoofs on pavement. She gets up, goes to the window. It is morning, the street below is bright and quiet, quite empty until a boy in a white apron comes out of the take-away to slosh a pail of water across the sidewalk. Then a woman holding a briefcase gets out of a car, unlocks the door of the school in the church and goes inside. In a minute Judith sees her enter the classroom opposite; the woman places a sheet of paper on each desk, then leaves the room. Everything Judith looks at has the quality of a dream, a languid, altogether more pleasant dream than the one she just escaped. She can still hear the horses, the sound growing ever more faint until it dissolves into silence. Nightmares, Judith thinks, almost smiling—nightmares receding into a different time.

Taking her haversack, to which she's returned the towel-wrapped skull, she goes to breakfast at the sandwich shop next door. She has slept poorly; the strange, liquid feeling of swimming through dreams stays with her. She resolves to walk herself alert, strolling south to Bayswater, then on up to Oxford Street. She takes her time, lingering before windows that are filled with glitter of a different class altogether from the stuff that awed her in the Gillsford shops. Tubercular mannequins flaunt garments designed in Madrid and London, in Paris and New York—Madras cotton skirts lined with Chinese silk, Mexican jackets embroidered like tapestries, tights patterned in plaids and checks, flower-splashed coats, hemp trousers from Brazil, sweaters knitted in Peru, Tibetan felt hats covered with tiny crimson bows. There are boots and shoes of Bolivian leather stained the same orange-brown as the skull. Some windows are filled with jewellery—bangles carved in Zaire, glass beads from

India and clay beads from Thailand. There are beautifully glazed tiles from Iran, mahogany furniture made in Honduras, carpets woven in Iraq, Egyptian linen and Chinese lamps.

The sidewalks around her are crowded with tourists who have come from these very countries to shop in London—only the rich, of course. Judith has seen the poor—the lucky herd cows and goats, grow food, knit sweaters, make carvings and weave rugs. The unlucky, whole tribes of men, women and children, smash rocks, dig through garbage, harvest vast single-crop fields; they dig in open-pit mines, melt down bits of wrecked bicycles and cars, break apart the hulks of huge ships with hammers; they pry open discarded computers and television sets with their bare hands.

The window displays depress her. They represent a world she and Ian had thought to escape from—had escaped from. Yet, she reflects, contemplating an evening gown that seems to be made of ostrich feathers, weren't we also pillagers? Much of what she and Ian had dug from beneath the warm earth of Syria, Eritrea and Ethiopia now rests in Cambridge—on temporary loan for research purposes, but in England nevertheless, as safe as those teacups in Aunt Min's attic.

Hungry and dispirited, having walked almost to the British Museum without finding the kind of shop she's looking for, she comes upon Copperfield Glassware and Ceramics. In the window, draped about with some shimmering silvery cloth Judith cannot identify, stands one tall white vase. Beside the vase is a card—"Thor," the card informs in a flourish of black ink—and, in the lower right-hand corner in discreet Gothic type, WE ACCEPT VISA / WILL INSURE AND PACKAGE FOR TRANSPORT.

She steps inside, into a world of water-green carpets, water-green music and indirect lighting that plays on slowly rotating, glass display cases. Beside a counter that seems to float like a slab of ice, a man stands. He has a round blank face, a dark suit, a shirt and tie, and he will not meet Judith's eye, not even when she nods and says "Good day" pleasantly.

She questions him about the window sign. Under pressure he admits that Copperfield sometimes packages items not purchased in their establishment. "However, it is expensive," he says. "Quite expensive, and we do not, of course, insure such items." He names prices and waits, clearly expecting Judith to remove her worn haversack from the sheen of his countertop and leave.

Coolly and firmly Judith suggests that the man show her a selection of Copperfield boxes. "I need something rigid, not cardboard but not heavy, something the size of those old gasmask boxes we carried during the war." She is pleased to see that the man is annoyed at her tone, at the inclusive "we," at the accuracy with which she's judged his age.

The box she chooses is made of balsawood, has a fitted cover, is padded in white linen and is indeed expensive. She refers to the skull as "a family heirloom," keeps it swathed in its cheap towel as she places it reverentially inside the little coffin, watches the clerk bed it down in popcornlike Styrofoam. By the time the package is wrapped, tied and sealed with red wax that has been imprinted with the Copperfield lion, the man has warmed a little. After she's paid, he presents her with his card, which reveals him to be Harold Holes Esq., Curator and Appraiser for Copperfield International. Having apparently decided that Judith is some wealthy eccentric up from the country for the day, he asks if she would like a cup of tea before returning.

She declines, bids Mr. Holes a regal farewell and repairs to the nearest pub. In celebration of what she considers to be her first truly successful encounter with the outside world since Ian's death, she devours a steak-and-kidney pie and downs a rather too-large glass of dark beer. She takes a taxi to her hotel, goes directly to the desk clerk and tells him she would like to see the person in charge.

"That's me," the boy says. He lifts part of the counter and nods her into the small office.

He is handsome, young—too young, Judith thinks, and asks for the manager.

"I assure you, madam, I am the manager." He has a Swiss accent. "My father owns this hotel—also two others in the Terrace around the corner. They have even younger managers—my brothers." He smiles broadly; apparently this happens often.

She takes the beautiful package from her haversack, explains that it contains a valuable heirloom and that she would like it placed in the hotel safe.

"The safe is not up here—it is a huge thing, built into the basement wall," the boy tells her, holding out his hand, expecting her to pass over the box.

But Judith says no. She will go to the basement with him. And so she does, walking cautiously behind, down steep steps to a shadowy, low-ceilinged cellar. She follows the fellow across the room to a great grey safe and watches him kneel on the dusty floor, turn the clocklike dial several times this way and that. The careless, knowing way he spins the dial impresses Judith, who had once, briefly, been keeper of the combination to just such a safe, had never opened it without referring to numbers taped to a drawer of her office desk. The young man pulls down the iron handle and opens the heavy door.

He looks up at her. "Do you want to put it in yourself?" he asks politely. He thinks she is mad, wonders if he should call the police—he could be helping to plant a bomb in his own basement. He is clearly relieved when she passes him the package, stands watching as he pushes it well back, behind old company ledgers he tells her his father insists upon keeping, although everything is now computerized.

As she watches him lean into the darkness of the vault Judith tries to account for the immense burden of guilt she suddenly feels. "Why?" she asks herself. The young man, dusting his well-pressed trousers, turns a startled face to her and she realizes she spoke aloud. "Would you mind giving me a receipt?" she says.

Judith is exhausted. Back in her room she falls onto the bed, lies wondering if she should go down and retrieve the skull. She could just carry it with her wherever she goes. She considers this, imagining how the young fellow downstairs would react. Both he and the man at Copperfield had been uneasy about her, had thought her eccentric, unbalanced. Judith has always heard that one is noticed more in small towns, but no one had noticed her in Gillsford—whereas here in London two men can now describe her in great detail. Something is wrong—in her voice, her attitude, about the way she looks perhaps.

She pushes herself to her feet, goes into the bathroom and stares into the mirror. She has aged; her hair has greyed and she is thinner than she was, the worn shirt hangs awkwardly from her bony shoulders. Judith can hardly bear to look at her face; it has the shocked, slightly mad look of someone caught between two realities. *God! I'm an old woman!*

She'd never considered herself old while Ian was alive. Never considered him old either, and they hadn't been—anthropologists, like orchestra conductors, are noted for working well past sixty-five. She and Ian had never given a thought to age or to retirement, not until Clive Aldridge mentioned it in one of his prescriptive letters. Judith leans on the sink, looking into the mirror, studying the crone; she sees the dazed face surrounded by a mass of long wiry hair streaked with grey, a wild woman with rough sunburned skin, tears running down the deep creases around her nose and mouth.

She wets a cloth and wipes her face. She must make herself more presentable, more like the customer Mr. Holes would wish to see walking into Copperfield. Finding notepaper and a pen in the desk drawer, she pulls the room's one chair over to the window and settles down. It is still light outside, the classroom across the way is empty; people are returning from work, coming out of little shops with newspapers and fruit, containers of milk and wine, going home . . .

Clothing, she writes firmly at the top of the paper. Judith has never given much thought to clothing, never owned more than two washable Marks & Spencer skirts, a jacket, a pair of trousers and a few blouses. All gone now, scattered, burnt or buried. She'd returned to England wearing new sandals and a bright rayon dress she had never seen before. Only her haversack, containing underwear and her worn work boots, remained. She's been wearing things she and Ian had left in the station wagon—old sweaters and trousers, wool socks, a raincoat she's had since university, with the cheap floral skirt she bought from a bin in Gillsford.

Before dark she has a page-long list. That night there are no dreams, although she is again woken by horses. She takes the next day to transform herself—gets her hair cut, her nails done, buys cream and lip gloss and clothing that will go unnoticed, plain blouses, a jacket, two tailored skirts, black trousers, a smart black raincoat and a black, white and red scarf the clerk says will go with everything. She buys neat walking shoes, tights and underwear; she replaces the haversack with a large leather bag in which she can carry money and maps, a note-book, pens, lunch—and when the time comes, a skull.

Judith makes all her purchases along Queensway, trying not to notice where things are made, consoling herself with the thought that she is avoiding the excesses of Oxford Street and giving business to small-shop owners—a notion she is disabused of when, paying for her leather bag in a shop called Pampas, she sees that the receipt is from Selfridges.

Having rendered herself inconspicuous, Judith spends the next week going from archive to archive. Sometimes travelling by bus and tube but more often walking, she visits the British Museum, the British Archives, the London Metropolitan Archives, the Natural History Museum, the Museum of London, the University of London Institute of Archaeology and six libraries. She spends little time in any of these places—all she is looking for is a file or a computer on which the numbers R29-H624 are recorded.

The work is not as enjoyable as it would have been with Ian, but it keeps her busy. It comes to her that she has done research alone before—once, over thirty years ago, when she was working on her thesis.

She and Ian had known each other for six months and were teetering on the edge of a commitment she knew would be huge, would be forever. He was twelve years older, the first man she'd dated—the first man she'd ever known really. That spring Judith took fright, went off to Hertfordshire where construction work-ers had discovered a large Iron Age grave. She told Ian not to phone and not to visit her.

At the end of the second day she knew she had made a ter-rible mistake, knew that if she dated a hundred men she would never find another Ian. She'd managed to hold on for three more days before phoning to tell him so. She stayed on at the site for five weeks, studying layers of earth, researching centuries of land use in the city block where the men—gas workers, in fact, laying down pipe—had made the accidental find.

Ian came down from the college on weekends and they were married at the end of the term. Judith now considers her dissertation unremarkable and is mildly ashamed of some of her conclusions. But the Hertfordshire research had impressed upon her how one can follow a paper trail of words for centuries, long after the cathedrals and fortresses themselves have been buried in silt and rubble.

Somewhere in London there's a record of my skull, Judith thinks—noting the possessive *my*.

She returns to the British Museum. On this visit she is more persistent and is eventually directed to a basement room with an imposing plaque proclaiming it to be "The Sir Gabriel Lumney Antiquities Indexing Centre." Beyond the door is a small windowless office, walls of grey folders, a desk, a computer, and Ms. Menzies, perky and fighting her drab surroundings in a bright pink suit.

Without elaborating, Judith asks to have the number R29-H624 traced and watches Ms. Menzies tap it into her computer. The woman nods brightly, tells Judith she will do a search and that she should come back the following day.

"Your numbering system is not part of our database," Ms. Menzies informs her when she returns. Is she sure? Ms. Menzies smiles pleasantly—today she is wearing lime green—and points a well-manicured finger at her computer. "Quite sure."

They discuss the possibility of some small museums having a system that has not been programmed into Ms. Menzies's computer. "Maybe some private collection dating back to the Victorian period when people were collecting everything—even human skulls. I think they believed that one's intelligence and moral fibre were determined by the size and shape of one's skull," says Judith, who is finding it useful to pretend less knowledge than she has.

"Phrenologists . . ." Ms. Menzies murmurs thoughtfully, and agrees that an individual collection might still exist in some private home, even in one of the community museums in various boroughs. She thinks this unlikely, however. "Between 1975 and 1985 a huge effort was made to consolidate a database of all the bits and pieces of bodies held by various institutions around London. Even church relics were given numbers—a job not without complications." Ms. Menzies grins, apparently relishing the memory of enumerating the bones of saints and martyrs. She asks Judith if the object carrying the number is, in fact, a skull.

There is a chair. Judith longs to drop into it, to unburden herself to this smart, cheerful woman. She resists the chair, remains standing while she considers her answer. "I am not sure precisely what the object is," she says finally. "A human relic of some kind, I imagine. My young nephew has an interest in such things. His parents do not approve, but when he heard I was coming up to London he asked me to check on the number." She has never been a good liar and is aware of how lame her explanation sounds.

"Ah." Ms. Menzies gives Judith an appraising look, the first she's received since acquiring her new wardrobe. The woman behind the desk is no fool; there is an infinitesimal silence before she picks up a form and holds it out. "Perhaps you can get more details from your nephew. Meanwhile, if you complete this Information Request, I will try a cross-check with other data banks."

"I am at a hotel, you may have to leave a message." Judith fills in just her name and phone number—then, as an after-thought, the number on the skull. She passes back the form, says her thank-yous and turns towards the door—then turns back. "If I don't hear from you I will check again in a week or so." She hesitates. "Is that all right?"

"Quite," Ms. Menzies says, and rewards her with a smile.

She is at an impasse, can think of nothing more to do. Judith spends five days wandering through parks, through Kensington Gardens to Hyde Park Corner and across to Green Park. Wearing herself out, walking for hours beneath the shadow of old trees, watching gardeners replace pale summer flowers with masses of orange and yellow, watching carefully supervised children feed ducks and swans and waterhens, she is growing fond of London's parks. There are benches everywhere. In the morning, before starting out, she often sits beside the four fountains just inside Lancaster Gate. On the way back to her hotel she may have a glass of wine in the restaurant beside The Serpentine or take a long sit-down on a bench across from Peter Pan.

She begins to recognize characters who walk the same paths, sit on the same benches at the same time each day. These people do not venture far into the parks but linger in places where they can hear the roar of traffic, watch the crowded pavements to which they return at night. A sad, lonely way to live, Judith thinks, sitting at midday on her bench beside the Lancaster Gate fountains, musing on her own friendless state, on the dull ache of sadness that seems to have replaced the coating of mud.

Yet, when one looks closely, the park people seem more preoccupied than sad. A young woman with blue hair smokes and hums, a pale bearded man becomes suddenly robust, stands and waves his fist whenever a pigeon pitches near his bench. The flute player and the bottle collector are not about today, but between the hedge and the park fence she can see the feet of the cardboard-box sleeper, he who will soon wake, crawl out of his coffin and ask her for money. These people go on from day to day; they sleep and wake, eat, beg, use public toilets—they stay alive. Their perseverance amazes Judith.

How pleasant it would be to go to a warm café (the sun is not so strong as it was) with someone like Ms. Menzies, to drink tea and chat about inconsequential things—the changing season, the price of shoes, their common interests in bones. All her friends have been temporary—except for Ian, of course. The rest have been colleagues one loses track of at the end of each expedition.

Ah well! Judith stands. Shucking off her self-pity, though not her sadness, she walks across to the fountains and down three stone steps to the nearest statue. The figure is cracked, its surface mottled with some kind of black fungus, the bowl on the woman's shoulder broken so that water dribbles off to one side instead of splashing neatly into the little pool at her feet. Thinking how strange it is that this statue is left damaged, when everything else in the park is so well-kept, she stumbles against a pushcart and the very real woman squatting beside it.

Judith pulls back, stops, transfixed by the sullen face, the rootlike hands that sprout from a voluminous brown overcoat. The woman glares but continues eating, one hand moving between the ground and her mouth as she scoops up seeds and bits of cake and bread that people have tossed down for the birds. Her other hand grips the wheel of a child's pushchair that is filled with stacks of folded cardboard, a neatly rolled blanket and many stuffed plastic bags.

She's probably my age, Judith thinks, averting her eyes, stepping carefully around the crumbs to get onto the narrow stone walkway connecting the four small pools that together make a large square with a stone sculpture at each corner.

The stone women are all young; drapery falls softly over rounded arms, breasts and thighs. Only on her second time around does Judith see that each woman must represent a season and that each has deteriorated in a different way—a nose is missing from one face, another has lost part of her garland of flowers, the fourth has no hands, nothing to hold the sheaf of grain balanced on her knee.

The weathered state of the sculptures is deliberate—the women have been maimed for effect, made to look as if they are antiquities. While she is pondering this, a parallel idea flits into her mind. She can go in search of the stone girl, the wrought-iron fence, the corner where she and her mother used to meet.

Pray God some of it is still there, she thinks, rejecting the impulse to return for her raincoat, though her hotel is not ten minutes away and the sky looks threatening. She is suddenly, terribly impatient. She will find the post office where her father worked, find Nag's Lane, find the park where the skull had been tossed in with bomb rubble.

The street woman observes Judith with detached malice, forgets to watch what she is eating, finds something unpleasant in her mouth and begins to choke. Judith doesn't notice, is already hurrying towards the tube station where she will get the Central Line to the edge of Camden.

XXIV

Nag's Lane must be somewhere nearby, Judith thinks. She continues circling streets around the post office depot, where, if Aunt Min was correct, her father sorted mail before becoming a soldier. She wonders what kind of man her father was, what kind of boy? Aunt Min had been unforthcoming about her nephew. "A quiet one—sallow" was all the information Judith ever got from her usually talkative aunt.

Perhaps her father had disgraced himself in some way before leaving Gillsford? Yet Aunt Min had spoken with relish of other family scoundrels: fenmen, and women too, who had lived on the edge of the law; the eel-catcher who sold the same eels two or three times, stealing them and reselling them; the woman who came back from waiting on table at some rich man's house, with a damask tablecloth wrapped around her under her coat.

On long nights, lying in the darkened cottage, the old woman had told of wayward fathers who took off for Spain or Portugal, mothers who crept out to steal coal and grain from barges being ferried pass their doors. So numerous had these stories been that, as a child, Judith imagined she and Aunt Min to be strangely honest mutations in a family of rogues.

Now she thinks it more likely that with years of retelling her great-aunt embroidered the past with colourful characters. Perhaps she hadn't had time to concoct similar exploits for the quiet, sallow boy who left Gillsford right out of school.

The whole area around the postal depot is now given over to businesses, shops and restaurants, a small paint factory, loan offices and banks, the Thames Water Authority Offices and various institutions. Turning in the other direction she finds a few residential streets behind Grey's Inn and Theobalds Road, but nothing that wakens any memory.

Still she walks on, north towards the viaduct, where she imagines her mother's factory may have been. But the road is cut off—above the hoarding Judith can see the top sections of giant platforms that will support a flyway slicing across the city. She goes back to Theobalds Road where she buys a *London A–Z* and a cheap plastic raincoat—for it is now raining steadily, the filth-encrusted pavement oozing black slime that soaks through her expensive shoes.

Wet and tired, she turns in to a restaurant, discovering too late that it is a self-serve deli where she must load her own tray from a hundred glass cubicles. However, she is pleasantly surprised with the hot soup and with her table, which is pushed up against an old-fashioned iron radiator. Judith removes her shoes, shoves them in under the radiator and sits warming her feet while she eats. Searching through the *A–Z* she discovers there is no longer any such place as Nag's Lane in London. Maybe there never was.

When her shoes have dried somewhat she leaves the restaurant and crosses to the other side, walking towards an insurance billboard on Holborn Road and the grass she can glimpse between the buildings on Theobalds Road. The green place turns out to be a tiny park, smaller than the one she remembers, without a fountain and without iron fencing. Concrete slabs act as fence and seats. On one slab stands a life-size, black cast-iron dog. Judith likes the dog. Ian had often commented how representations of animals—terracotta bullocks from the Indus Valley, sculpted deer from the tombs at Pazyryk, those jade elephants found in the mausoleums of Ming royalty—all seem more human than the aggrandizing statues of their owners. She circles the dog slowly, watching how its eyes follow her—a good sculpture. A plaque informs her that the monument was erected by the Humane Society of London to honour a Labrador retriever who, "on the night of September 9, 1940, in the middle of a blitz, pulled two children from a burning house near this spot."

She had been sent down to the country in 1941, in mid-May she thinks. "You came with the primroses and swallows," Aunt Min once told her, making her arrival sound like a story, a fairy tale. Therefore the air attack that killed her mother and the date on which she found the skull was probably in the second week of May 1941. A different blitz, yet Judith is heartened by the dog monument, the first acknowledgment she's seen in any London street that the Second World War happened. It is something she hadn't noticed before, how all signs of war have been erased in fifty years.

"'The struggle of man against power is the struggle of memory against forgetting.'" Ian had read that out to her once. They'd been in an airport somewhere, she holding a plastic cup of lukewarm tea, he a pocket book. He'd sensed her boredom, and marking his place with a boarding pass, he closed the book—a novel by Milan Kundera—and asked what she thought of the quotation.

Judith recalls the vastness of the almost empty airport, the luxury of time—night and a missed plane having disconnected them from the world of obligations. How long ago that now seems, how strangely innocent the man and woman who sat meditating on memory and power.

Was Kundera right? they wondered. Should wars be remembered, slaughters remembered? How—in triumph or in sorrow? And by whom—the slaughterer or the slaughtered? But the slaughtered cannot remember. Their surviving countrymen, then? Are war trials enough? Names cut into granite enough? What of those huge World War One guns one sees painted and affixed to concrete? Judith asked; she has long hated those display guns. Surely Kundera was not suggesting that high streets be decorated with outdated weapons?

"Being a writer he is probably thinking of words," Ian said, "memory pressed between the covers of books."

They'd spent an enjoyable hour arguing, unable to agree on what books may have moderated the view of tyrants, changed history, prevented a war. If Ian were here they could talk about that again—discuss the dog monument, her walks around London. The mystery of the skull would have given Ian immense pleasure, just as the mysteries of lost cities and lost tombs had.

But Ian is not here to share her enjoyment. Ian has become ash, ash scattered over his parents' graves—no marker, no memorial. All that remains are the fragile memories stored inside her skull. Judith tells herself to stop; she is tired and must find a tube station.

But there seems to be no station on this side of Theobalds

Road. After ten minutes she gives up searching and catches a bus going towards Lancaster Gate. From the bus window she sees that the Holborn Public Library is directly opposite and considers getting off, but it is already late and she is damp and exhausted. She'll come back in the morning.

The sound of horse hoofs wakes Judith at seven-thirty the next morning, as they do every morning. She eats breakfast as usual, in the nearby sandwich shop, and is at Holborn Public Library by ten.

Inside the front door she faces a stairway that is blocked with a chain from which a handmade sign dangles. TO PLAY CENTRE AND COMMUNITY INFORMATION, the sign reads, and an arrow points to a door beside the stairs. Following the arrow Judith finds herself in a crowded room that was clearly never intended to accommodate a play centre.

A few feet from the door three young women lounge on plastic chairs while three toddlers pull toys from bins. The women, girls really, are dressed in a careless, mismatched way Judith believes to be accidental. One woman is black and has a long neck, the profile of Nefertiti. The other two have deathly white skin and black lips; all have elaborately curled hair. They do not talk, do not read the neatly stacked brochures—and who can blame them, Judith thinks, glancing at the titles: "How to Get Rid of Vermin," "Identify AIDS," "Attend Rate Hearings," "Report Abuse!," "Safe Storage of Household Poisons." But neither do they notice the dog-eared fashion magazines littering every surface, or see the children playing at their feet. Their eyes flick quickly over Judith, dismiss her and return to listless contemplation of the mud-coloured carpet.

I know more about the long-dead inhabitants of Koobi Fora than about these women, Judith thinks, and is startled by a voice from her right, asking, "Can I be of service?" The speaker smiles pleasantly from her glass cubicle.

When Judith explains that she is looking for the library, would like to see maps and newspapers related to this immediate area, the office woman tells her the public library is one floor up. "The main entrance way's been closed for months, they're repairing the steps—but you probably need the reference library. Just sign here and take the elevator to the top floor." She slides a ledger under the slot and nods towards the corner. Judith signs her name, squeezes around behind the young women and enters an elevator so old it has a folding lattice door.

The third floor is bright and surprisingly comfortable. It has high windows, several large tables with heavy wooden chairs, a librarian with a card-index file behind her. Three old men and one middle-aged woman sit, each at a different table. On a worn leather sofa below one of the windows another man, older even than the others, is sound asleep, snoring softly, an open newspaper spread across his knees like a blanket.

Judith asks the librarian if she can see histories of this area during the Second World War, "Maps too and newspaper clippings if you have them," she whispers, not expecting much but impressed by the attitude of people seated round about, so intent on taking notes that they do not lift their eyes to look at the newcomer.

Telling Judith to make herself comfortable, the librarian goes to the shelves. She does not consult her cards but simply walks around choosing material at random—a blue file box, a thick hard-covered book titled *The Boroughs of Hampstead, Holborn and St. Pancreas 1930–1949 — The Question of Incorporation*, along with a set of black loose-leaf notebooks. The notebooks are numbered one to five. "Personal Accounts of the War Years," compiled in 1986 by the Holborn Historic Committee, is written in ink on the first page of each binder. All other pages are typed.

Judith places her hand on the notebooks and knows she will find something here. Such moments are the drug that has fuelled her career—hers and Ian's both. The finding is wonderful, the published papers, the accolades are satisfying—but this moment before the find, when success is sure but mystery remains, is pure exhilaration. For this she and Ian had faced danger and discomfort, had forgone home, family and friends. With her hand on the rough surface of the binders Judith holds herself suspended in this wondrous moment and thinks, Yes! Yes! And I would do it all again!

The first binder—its typewritten letters already fading to brown, pages beginning to yellow—is filled with reminiscences of life in the area at the outbreak of war. A woman named Mary Kent wrote, "Our house was at the top of Postpool Lane. People lived above one another, only the rich and middle class had kitchens. My parents had their bed and a table and a chest of drawers in one room. Us children slept in a kind of closet where only the bed could fit. No bathroom—water came from a sink on the landing and we had to go down four flights to the toilet. We were lucky, some had to go up the street to the public toilet. All the houses had bugs, sometimes you couldn't see the walls for them. We went to the baths in Merlin Street—I think it cost 5p—you got a towel and a bit of carbolic soap but the hot water always went cold before you finished."

Marvelling, Judith rereads these lines. These are working people living in the middle of the twentieth century, in London, a wealthy city, the capital of the richest empire the world had ever seen. Aunt Min, with her snug cottage, her fruit trees and vegetable garden, had been rich by comparison. Had Mark and Ethel Kirkman been as poor as Mary Kent's family? Not quite—if you counted her closet bedroom she and her parents had three rooms. But they had shared a toilet with other flats— Judith remembers the dark landing, the stink. She cannot remember bugs or public baths.

Binder number two is filled with government publications— brochures urging children to collect metal, to plant vegetable gardens, to avoid suspicious objects. Others told parents how to protect their family during air raids, how to kill vermin, how to cook without sugar, meat, eggs and butter, how to identify spies. Here too were the conditions of enrolment into the Civil Defence Service, requirements for men and women joining the ARP, the duties of air raid wardens, rescue crews, ambulance drivers and attendants, first-aid post attendants, searchlight wardens, instructions on how to report incidents, to give first aid, to put out a fire.

Judith is content to go slowly, is drawn to the human voices that break through the jargon. "I was on ambulance duty and went without sleep three nights once. The rescue people would patch up those they could, cover the dead with ARP blankets and lay the serious cases out on stretchers for us to take to hospital. Children were worse, sometimes you had to take badly wounded children away from their parents. Sometimes it would take hours to get to a hospital. More than once we ended up carrying the wounded on stretchers to the hospital." A war nurse wrote this in pencil at the bottom of a list of materials that should be carried in ambulances.

"We would come up beside what had been a row of houses, half levelled to the ground, others partly caved in, roofs sagging above empty air," one member of a rescue team wrote. "There'd be a choking pall of plaster dust over everything, mixed with the sickly sweet smell of escaping gas. Both light and heavy reserve men would clamber over the rubble, forming teams, passing down the debris of doors, windows and joists as we began our search for trapped casualties. Sometimes someone would crawl out of one of the adjacent houses with cuts, gashes and shock—some quite unhurt with blackened lips and dust-grey hair, their eyes shining bright with relief at finding themselves alive . . ."

Judith cannot remember air raids, cannot remember sirens or the terrible bombing noises these people write of. She cannot recall taking shelter in the underground, where, according to one writer, "There were rats and an appalling stink that built up overnight."

Could she have forgotten such things? The memory she has of the war is of the shiny planes she and Aunt Min used to watch lift off, watching them turn smoothly in formation before they vanished into the evening sky—a peaceful image compared to what she is reading.

She covertly studies the people around her. The well-coiffed woman is about her age, the three old men attending so quietly to their books must have been teenagers when the war was on and the ancient man asleep on the sofa surely lived through the war, probably fought in it. Just such ordinary people had done these things. One would expect them to never stop talking about their experiences. But they had stopped, had gone back to their jobs, rebuilt houses and parks and streets, they'd replanted trees, kept having children. Extraordinary acts become ordinary, are forgotten, buried below the silt of everyday life. No bragging or complaining, no horrifying stories passed on to children and grandchildren, no standing on street corners holding out pictures of a world on fire. Nothing. Not a word spoken about those years, not until the Holborn Historic Committee took up the struggle against forgetting—and thank God they had!

Judith stands and stretches. She's had a good morning, is enjoying herself. When she asks the librarian if it is permissible to leave the reference material on her table while she goes for lunch, the woman nods brightly. Downstairs in the reception and childcare area, the young mothers have been replaced by two grannies. They look much more content, are deep in conversation about someone named Tanya who's going to get herself in trouble if she doesn't watch out. As they talk, one knits and the other shares out a packet of sweets among three small children. She calls out to the woman behind the glass, "Like a sticky-chew, missus?"

Judith doesn't catch the answer. It is a nice day and she walks briskly around the block before going into a café. She eats quickly and almost runs back to the library, passing through the reception area with barely a nod. She cannot wait to get back to the third binder.

Halfway down the first page her eyes light on the sentence "Coram's Fields was not far from the post office depot." This account is by a man named Henry Rubinstein: "I was on sentry duty at the gates in Coram's Fields. In the middle there was an open-fronted summer house with a pretty green copper roof—a gift of Viscount Rothermere to commemorate the death of two sons killed in World War I. We wardens would doze on benches inside at night—someone would always come around with a billycan of hot tea, so strong and sweet it might have been cocoa."

Judith gets out her *London A–Z*—Coram's Fields seems too large to be the playground she remembers. She keeps reading. A little farther along the same man says, "Later we got moved out of Coram's Fields to a children's playground. They made part of it a searchlight station. We had a dugout and sandbags; from up top you could look across to a tiny roundabout where there was a drinking fountain under a worn stone statue of a girl with a water jug—it stood up over the public lavatories."

Her girl with a jug! Judith's impulse is to rush out of the library and find the statue. Instead, she carries the binder over to the librarian. Pointing to Mr. Rubinstein's description of the girl atop the public lavatories she asks if the statue is still there.

The woman reads the page, turns and reads several more pages. She pulls a street plan of Camden from a file and studies it. "No," she says finally, "those old public lavs were mostly done away with. There's a tube entrance on that spot now—no statue. It was probably blown to bits in the war."

"Oh!" Judith cannot hide her disappointment. "Were you here during the war?" she asks. Then, realizing her mistake from the woman's shocked face, she adds, "Oh, I am sorry—of course you're much too young."

"A little," the librarian says, but she doesn't seem put out. She tells Judith to keep the road map, suggests that she look in the blue box. "It's full of newspaper clippings, quite a few old news photos too. If you're wondering what the statue looked like you might find a picture there—and we do have a photocopier you can use."

Judith returns to her table, reads for another hour before finding anything else she recognizes. Near the end of binder number four, a woman named Doris Brannan tells her interviewer, "I was working at the Express Dairy in Chancery Lane and one day when I went in for the evening shift the firemen were all around the street. The shop was gone, bombed—my mum and me were evacuated after that. We went to her brother's in Salisbury in Wiltshire for the rest of the war."

That is all. She goes through the blue box but finds no photos of anything she can recognize. Mildred Elsy had the morning shift—was she killed when the Express Dairy was bombed? Judith thinks it likely; she stares for a long time at one picture, a wasteland of grey rubble that seems to stretch for miles. There are no streets, no light poles, no houses. One smokestack and three chimneys in the foreground are the only things standing, the only things identifiable—black smoke still rises. There are no people. The caption reads, "Early morning of May 11, 1941—huge amount of damage in raids during past two nights, estimate 957 killed, 1,443 injured and taken to hospital. Raid exceptionally severe last night; reports already in indicate that 52 high explosives, 1 parachute mine, 9 unexploded bombs and hundreds of incendiary bombs landed in the borough."

A clear plastic envelope taped inside the cover of the clipping box shows a 1940 map. From the smudged copy she can make out that there were at least ten churches in the area. There were three small hospitals in addition to the Foundling Hospital and the Royal College of Surgeons—both of these, Judith knows, house small museums, but they are on the far side of Grays Inn Road and therefore unlikely to have been the source of her skull.

The day is almost over. Her fellow researchers are stirring, returning books, pulling on coats, but Judith sits squinting at the map, thinking of the many vaults, graveyards and hospital labs from which her skull might have been propelled by one of those explosives. And of course, as Ms. Menzies said, there was always the possibility of a private collection—one of the bombed houses could have contained the glass-fronted cases of some eccentric phrenologist.

The librarian wakes the old man in the corner. She gently herds him to the elevator before coming over to Judith. "Will you need this material again?" she inquires, gathering up the box, the book and the four binders.

Judith considers asking to have the map and the photo of the May 11th bombing copied—but why? She simply thanks the woman, says, "I think I've found everything I need."

This is not true. The material that had seemed so promising in the morning has revealed almost nothing—only that her memory of the statue was right and that the Express Dairy did once exist, but nothing about places where rubble was dumped, nothing about the skull. She feels only mild regret; she has enjoyed the day and finds herself wondering what she will do when the mystery of the skull is solved.

Outside the air is cool, night unrolling across London's skyline. She crosses the street to the bus stop. Summer is over, she thinks. I have lived through a season without you.

There will be others—other summers, other winters, other springs—season after season stretching out to the end of her life. The thought of all that time fills Judith with bitterness she can taste.

Feeling ill, she steps back from the curb, closes her eyes and takes several slow, deep breaths. She will walk a ways, will not think about a future without Ian, will not think about any future. Except tomorrow—she will concentrate on what she must do tomorrow. Where will she continue her search? Perhaps it's time to concede failure, to turn to Cambridge and her colleagues at the Institute for answers.

She opens her eyes, feels slightly better and sees she is standing beside the window of a fish-and-chip shop, sees that a man on the other side of the glass is staring at her with grave concern. It takes a second longer to recognize that he is the old man who was sleeping in the library. Their eyes meet, they both nod; he returns to his supper and Judith walks away.

Half a block down the street she stops, does an about-turn, hurries back, and, without giving herself time to reconsider, goes quickly into the restaurant.

He is still there. The only customer, back to the door, still staring out the greasy window, enjoying his pot of tea, his plate of fish and chips. Judith goes to the pass-through and orders the same.

"Here's your tea—I'll bring your fish and chips." The grim-faced woman passes out a tray containing a large yellow teapot and a thick mug. "Milk and sugar on the tables," she says.

Walking past three empty booths, Judith pauses beside the man, and he turns, startled, to face her. "May I join you?" she asks, then boldly sits without waiting for his answer.

She takes her time, setting down the tray, pulling her coat off, bunching it down behind her, stirring the tea before pouring out a mugful. "I saw you in the library," she says unnecessarily, knowing he has already recognized her.

The man seems neither interested nor annoyed; he carefully places the chip he's picked up back on his plate. He is wearing a not-quite-white shirt, a maroon tie and cardigan; his jacket is hung on the booth's hook. He watches her, waiting.

"My name is Judith Muir," she says, holding her hand out just as the waitress puts a huge plate of fish and chips down on the orange Formica.

"More tea, then, Ben?" The woman's tone is completely different from the one she has used with Judith.

"Not right now, ducks." He smiles, and Judith sees that he is not as old as she'd imagined.

"Ben—Mr. ... ?" Judith says, taking care not to look directly at him, dousing her chips with salt and vinegar.

"Ben Aldford," he says.

The woman goes back to her kitchen and Ben Aldford goes back to eating. There is a long silence. The chips are good, home-made, the tea is strong and hot.

"I lived nearby when I was a child. I've been doing research about this area during the war," she says after a few minutes. There is no response, so she eats and drinks, lets her body sag against the comfortably padded booth for a while, then remarks how grateful she is that the Holborn Historic Committee compiled personal accounts of the war years.

They are each into a second pot of tea before Mr. Aldford relaxes enough to tell her that he grew up not two blocks east of the Holborn Library, in the Bourn Estate. "Was nothin left of it when I came home from the Navy—me and Nita moved in back of her mum's. I'm still there—on me own these five year."

"Did you see much of London during the war?" she asks, wondering how many such questions he will allow.

"I was stationed in Scotland, up in Scapa Flow—didn't see much of London while the Blitz was on. Got back once on compassion leave when Mam and Pap were killed—sittin at their own table, neither of 'em fifty!" The man shakes his head and picks up his cup.

Judith fears the conversation has ended. But after a few sips of tea he begins talking again.

"That was May of '41. We buried Mam and Pap in the churchyard behind St. Etheldreda's—the church'd been bombed, a big heap of rubbish pushed up against one wall, crows everywhere, great black things swooping about, makin that terrible din all through prayers. The whole neighbourhood where we lived was gone, blown away—crows and rats everywhere. Families got resettled in sheds and basements and attics—you never saw people livin so close, worse than on shipboard."

Judith asks if he remembers other piles of rubble.

"Course I do! I got a good memory—remembers every minute of them few days. Wasn't just around here had bomb damage—craters all over London, mountains of rubbish. I minds a place across from Hyde Park Corner where they dumped everything—bits of houses and stores and churches, streetcars and lorries. Everything in London smashed and tossed all together—you wondered how they'd ever get it put to rights. I kept thinkin there could be people under there, bits of people. More than once I got a start, seein a rat scurry off or a scrap of muddy rag flutterin from under smashed concrete. They had to clear the streets, you see, had to get ambulances and lorries through. There's things underneath London streets that don't bear thinkin about." He turns his face to the window and falls silent.

Judith lets him be and they sit, staring silently out at the street, both imagining the terrible detritus of war that must lie in the yellow earth beneath these paving stones.

She has read that below London there is thirty feet of stratified archaeology, wars piled upon wars, covered over and pressed down. Maybe that shouldn't happen; perhaps parts of cities should be left in their bombed-out state—piles of rubble, wall-less houses, even bodies—as testimony to what we are capable of. Judith knows they have done that somewhere—in Rwanda, she thinks—left the bodies of wives and mothers, fathers and children rotting inside the school where they took refuge, where they were massacred by militants who used guns, grenades and machetes to kill fifty thousand in one day. Such sites might be more powerful than words.

Judith's morbid reflections are interrupted by the woman who comes from the kitchen with hot tea and a serving of lemon tart for each of them. "You a relative of Mr. Aldford's, then?"

"No," Judith says. "No, I'm just a friend." But she is not his friend, she is picking his brain. Ashamed of the lie, she glances at the old man, but he doesn't appear to have heard, is still gazing into the street. What an offensive term that is, Judith thinks— *picking his brain*—as though she were a vulture feeding on the dead. Scavenging . . .

He speaks suddenly, loudly, as if to the window glass. "Them out there got no idea what went on right along this street. Folk around here had it worse than we did at sea. Rescue workers'd be on the go night and day. My last night home I relieved Tom Drover—took his shift on an ambulance. They were just white wooden boxes mounted on Ford chassis, closed in back with a canvas curtain—no springs. Sewer and water lines got busted, some streets awash with mud that hadn't seen light since Roman times, some blocked with rubble that was still hot. Ambulance tires would go. Twice that one night we got to hospital with dead people in back."

A few minutes later he turns—surprised, Judith thinks, to find her still seated across from him. "I'll be getting along now, missus," he says. He puts a note on the table, pulls himself up and, before she has a chance to speak, takes his coat from the hook.

"Wait!" she says—she is in a panic. "I want to ask you some-thing else. Do you remember a stone beggar girl with a jug on her shoulder?"

He pauses with one arm in the sleeve of his jacket. "No," he says. "No, never." He steps back; her urgency seems to have made him nervous. "Maybe I'll see you again in the library." He makes a polite dipping gesture with his cap before pulling it firmly down about his ears. "See you, missus," he says, and starts for the door.

"Wait!" She pulls money from her bag, drops it on the table, jerks on her coat and starts after him. She is vaguely aware that the kitchen woman has come out and is watching the scene with interest.

He is on the sidewalk either buttoning his coat or waiting for her, impossible to tell from his sad, impassive face.

"Mr. Aldford, just one more question. Was there a place called Nag's Lane somewhere near the postal sorting office?"

"Nay, not up there!" He looks at her and blinks. "Didn't you say you was from round here?"

"I was. That is, I was born around here—up by the postal building in Nag's Lane—but I was sent down to the country during the bombing and never came back."

"Nag's Lane weren't nowhere near the postal building, missus—was a mile or more away! A good ways down, near Little Turnstile. I minds it well, had a field and a big barn at the end. Back to grandfather's time coalmen lodged their horses in Nag's Lane barn overnight. Only six or seven houses on the whole lane, along with a pub where the coalmen used to go after leavin the barn."

Suddenly his sad old face is alight with pleasure. "We boys loved them horses but we was deadly afraid of the coalmen—thought they was bogeymen. I minds us standing outside the pub door, darin one another to peep into the dark smoky place, see what the noisy crowd of men was doin. Black-faced from the coal they'd be, some of 'em still wearin them heavy leather caps that covered up their necks and shoulders. Pure petrified of 'em we boys were—and them only poor working men havin a pint before goin home to supper."

"There's no Nag's Lane on the map now—what happened to it?"

"Got built over in the fifties. No need for horses any more—coalmen either, comes to that. Was just a dead end anyway, more of a path than a lane. There's a big office building there now—that one with a little shopping place down underneath."

How stupid she's been! Judith thanks Mr. Aldford effusively, wishes him all the best, then thanks him again. She would like to kiss him, to whirl him around the dirty sidewalk. She restrains herself and, smiling like a fool, simply shakes his hand.

She watches him walk away, waves to the fish-and-chip woman in the window and then takes the first bus that comes by. Judith knows now exactly where her skull came from—would have known all along if she'd correctly located Nag's Lane, which was, as Ben Aldford has pointed out, a mile or more from where she's been looking, separated by a small park from the Royal College of Surgeons.

XXV

Next morning she is up and dressed before the hollow echo of hoofs wakens her.

She has found out where the sounds come from. Returning to her hotel the night before, thinking of Ben Aldford and the barn in Nag's Lane, Judith asked the boyish hotel manager if there was a barn nearby. A stable, he told her, explaining that the horses she hears each morning are kept in a refurbished garage. Well catered-to these horses are; they do not haul coal but take keen young executives on early morning rides through the park. In the afternoons they are curried and groomed by schoolchildren learning equestrian skills.

Judith is thinking about the horses as she leaves the underground, wondering if they miss green fields and open countryside—or is a park enough? She comes up at Kingsway and Holborn, within sight of Little Turnstile, which is a lane so narrow she can touch either side. She finds the office tower Ben Aldford spoke of and eats breakfast in a café beneath the building—a not unpleasant place. Artificial sun shines down from a pretend skylight; there are potted palms and water splashes down over a slab of pink marble.

One cannot imagine that on this spot grimy coalmen once gathered to smoke their pipes and drink, that somewhere nearby stood a barn filled with the smells of hay and horse shit, with the rumblings of large, exhausted animals. No sign remains of horses or beer or coalmen, or of the terrible leavings of war that must, together with wires and cables and sewers, lie buried in the earth around these very walls.

Looking at the amount of marble and concrete and steel that surrounds her, Judith reflects on how it once took centuries for walls such as these to collapse, for frost and erosion to accelerate decay, for sand and silt to bury buildings and battlefields. Today bulldozers can make the past vanish in hours. She nibbles toast, sips her cold tea and delays her visit to the Royal College of Surgeons, holding on to the pleasure of anticipation, and suppressing a faint, irrational awareness that she might be doing an imprudent thing.

It is a short walk across Lincoln's Inn Fields, a grassy square through which people in business suits and court robes take shortcuts, where two women play ball with a circle of toddlers, where a young man lies stripped to the waist soaking up the morning sun. This, she thinks, must be the park where she picked up the skull. Yet she feels no vibrations, no ripples of memory; she can see no fountain, no school. The morning sun falling through the wrought-iron fencing is not as she remembers.

Crossing the street towards the Royal College of Surgeons, Judith realizes that she's been here before, at least once, for a lecture given by some famous American on the pathology of teeth. She climbs two wide marble steps and pauses beneath the Greek-columned portico to read a plaque informing her that this building is home to an ancient organization once called the Company of Barbers. Established in the twelfth century, it evolved in the 1500s into the Company of Barber Surgeons. Judith wonders when the word *Barber* was dropped from the college's august name.

Inside, she ignores the uniformed attendant at the reception desk and wanders leisurely around the great foyer. She takes her time, scrutinizing portraits of the college's founders, lingering beside glass cases that display specimens associated with significant figures: the inoculation lancets—like small pocket knives they are—used in 1768 on Empress Catherine of Russia; the bladder stone of King George IV; a necklace of human teeth brought from the Congo by Stanley; samples of Joseph Lister's catgut ligatures; a denture belonging to Sir Winston Churchill; the skeleton of the Irish giant Charles Byrne; teeth retrieved from soldiers on the battlefield of Waterloo; the lymph nodes of a Zulu chief. All this and more Judith sees without even entering the rooms that house the vast Hunterian Collection of human and animal skeletal remains, of teeth, floating fetuses, microscope slides and thousands of surgical instruments.

Her search for this place has given her much pleasure, whole hours when she did not think of anything else. Knowing the search is almost over depresses her.

Eventually she approaches the desk and asks to speak to the curator, who will surely only confirm what she now knows— that her skull is part of the Hunterian Collection.

"I'm sorry, madam, but both Mr. Grenville and his assistant are out of the country at present. Perhaps some other of our staff could help you?" The man smiles politely and asks her to sign her name in the guest register.

After listening to Judith's deliberately vague explanation he directs her up two flights to the office of Dr. Jane Berryman, the college's chief archivist.

Dr. Berryman comes around from behind her desk smiling. "It's a pleasure to meet you, Dr. Muir—I recall you and your husband visiting my college."

Having been anonymous for months, Judith is deeply shocked to hear her name fall so casually from the lips of this fair-haired young woman. She shakes the extended hand and sinks into a cushioned chair.

Jane Berryman has returned to her seat; she is still talking but Judith has gone deaf. "Yes," she says, "yes," with what she hopes is appropriate emphasis. Trying to collect herself she counts the decorative items arranged on the archivist's desk: a glass paperweight bearing the crest of some university, a blue coffee cup, a four-inch half-circle of wood with a knob on the flat side. Judith wonders what it can be—it is painted in that lovely oil-on-water pattern once used on the fly-leafs of old books. There is a matching pen holder, two red file folders and a flecked crystalline lump of something that might once have been someone's heart or kidney.

" . . . I was especially interested in your conclusions regarding things that may become accidently incorporated within grave fill," Jane Berryman is saying. Apparently she is referring to the last paper Ian and Judith published, is talking at such length that Judith knows her own dismay has been noted.

She cannot think what she will say to the elegant, chattering woman. So she sits quietly, avoiding Dr. Berryman's direct gaze, focusing on a framed document on the wall behind her shoulder—a diploma probably. Judith squints to read the words written on parchment in an expansive flourishing hand:

"Lincoln's Inn Fields is the topographical centre of
London; London, as will be seen by a glance at any
map of the world, is the centre of the terrestrial half
of the globe (to which fact is due its being the com-
mercial emporium of the world); hence, Lincoln's Inn
Fields is the very centre of all the land of this earth."

It is the kind of imperial declaration Ian would have enjoyed.
Judith cannot keep from smiling at the pompous anglicism.

The quotation obviously amuses Jane Berryman as well; she
swivels her chair around and reads the curlicue signature:
"'Charles William Heckethorn, 1896'—his manuscript is in our
library. Wonderful quote, isn't it? Like something out of Gilbert
and Sullivan. The parchment is my own doing—a calligrapher
friend copied it out and I had it framed. I fancy it matches the
mad, godlike passion that animated many of our original collec-
tors—don't you think so?"

Judith feels calmer. She nods, takes the slip of paper from
her bag and passes it across the desk. "Does this artifact number
seem familiar to you?"

The archivist barely glances at the paper. "The number
appears to be ours—not the system we use now, of course, one
that went back to the 1800s, and continued until 1950 for sections of the collection."

"Could you tell me anything about the object this number
was assigned to?"

"Probably. The R indicates that it came to us as part of
the Odontological Society's collection, which the college acquired
in 1909. If that is so, the item is a human or animal skull, teeth
or bone. I can narrow it down by going through old cata-
logues. Fortunately, they have been transferred to computer."

Dr. Berryman touches a button on her phone, dictates the number and asks someone to bring the information to her office. She returns her attention to Judith. "May I ask where this number came from?"

No! Judith thinks. But of course the question is reasonable, and inevitable, one she should be prepared for—but is not.

The silence is uncomfortably long, but Dr. Berryman waits, head tilted, hands folded on her desk until the office door opens. A young man comes in, passes a sheet of paper to Jane Berryman and, after one quick, questioning glance, retreats.

Judith watches the archivist skim what seems to be just one paragraph; she rereads the page twice before lifting her eyes. Judith would like to snatch the paper and run—might have done had Dr. Berryman not known her name.

"'R29-H624—the skull of a Beothuk woman named Shanawdithit who died of consumption in St. John's in the British Colony of Newfoundland in June of 1829. This female primitive was believed to be the last of her race. The item is on permanent loan from the Odontological Society of Great Britain who acquired it in 1840 from William Carson, a graduate of the University of Edinburgh, medical doctor and member of the Boeothick Institute of Newfoundland.'" Dr. Berryman reads in a flat monotone and then, without looking up, adds, "An attached notation indicates that the skull was one of several thousand items destroyed in May of 1941 when the College was bombed."

"Shanawdithit," Judith whispers.

The name seems familiar but cannot be. There is a noise in her ears, a tightness in her chest—Pray God I'm not having a heart attack, she thinks. "Is it possible for us to meet for lunch?" she asks, responding to a sudden, overwhelming need to be outside, well away from the vast, silent collection of body parts assembled within these walls.

Jane Berryman agrees, they arrange a meeting place and Judith quickly leaves the beautiful building. She spends a pleasant hour walking in a circle around Holborn before meeting the archivist at noon in a tiny restaurant off Chancery Lane. When they have ordered, Judith tells Dr. Berryman what she remembers about finding the skull—Shanawdithit's skull. She tells the story quickly, thinking she need not do this, suspecting she should not.

Jane is satisfyingly astonished. She, or perhaps her assistant, has spent the past hour looking up the Beothuk. She passes over a copy of Shanawdithit's obituary from *The London Times*, and Judith reads it aloud, repeating the last line.

"'They have been dislodged, and disappeared from the earth in their native independence in 1829, in as primitive a condition as they were before the discovery of the New World.' According to this she was buried in Newfoundland, 'Interred in the C.E. Cemetery South Side of St. John's,' it says. How did her head get to London?"

"Apparently the doctor who attended her—a Dr. Carson—performed a post-mortem and decided that her skull exhibited certain peculiarities. He sent it to the Royal College of Physicians where it became part of the Odontological Society's collection, which was later acquired by us. More details regarding the skull's irregularities are contained in notes made at a lecture given by Dr. Carson some years later," Jane tells her.

Judith is indignant. "I assure you there is nothing peculiar about Shanawdithit's skull—it is quite a beautiful skull!" Realizing that she sounds like a proud parent, she smiles, shrugs, changes the subject, and they drift into discussion of the mythology that surrounds human heads.

The women have much in common, are soon using first names, chuckling together at people's attitude concerning human remains, from prehistory up to the Victorian Age and indeed into our own time, when they have transmogrified from holy relics into grotesque art objects entombed in plastic. They talk of travel, of archaeological sites they have visited—the stone walls of Zimbabwe, Mayan temples and Etruscan tombs—then return to the Beothuk, wondering how such a people could have lived in a place for thousands of years and left almost no material records of their existence.

"Even our Early Bronze Age people left barrows and stone towers," says Judith.

"The Beothuk's most permanent structures were caribou fences. They were hunters and gatherers—still in the age of flint. They hadn't gotten around to metal weapons, ramparts and stone walls. They were not as warlike as our ancestors." Jane chews thoughtfully on a carrot stick. "Could that be why we are here and they are not?"

"So the most barbaric of us survive to populate the earth . . ." Judith's voice trails away, and they finish the meal in silence.

As they are about to leave, Jane brings the conversation back to the skull, to Shanawdithit, to ownership. "Tonight I will be phoning Max Grenville. He will be very interested and . . ." She pauses. "I assure you that he will expect me to have the skull back in our collection when he returns."

"The skull is not in my possession right now," Judith says, and seeing the flicker of disbelief cross Jane's face, reinforces one lie with another, a story about having sent the skull to an independent lab for analysis.

"I won't ask you to name the lab." Jane Berryman seems uncomfortably aware that she has been unprofessional, much too soft on Dr. Judith Muir. Belatedly she tries to regain some ground. "However, if this is Shanawdithit's skull, it is an item of great significance and my superiors will need to know exactly when you expect to return it to our collection."

"It may take a month, perhaps a bit longer," Judith tells her. "The lab people are very apologetic but they seem to have a backlog."

"Ah . . . Should I require a signed statement verifying that you will return item R29-H624 to the college as soon as it is again in your possession?"

"IOU one skull." Knowing she's won permission to keep the skull a little longer, Judith can relax. However she has not missed the point—Jane Berryman has done her research, has committed the skull's reference number to memory, is more interested than she seems in having it returned. "I'll sign anything you wish, of course—but with or without my signature you can be assured I will return the skull. And if I fail to, you know you can always find me through Clive Aldridge at the Institute."

The women shake hands. The archivist murmurs something about this being a matter of trust, and very unorthodox. It is after one—bells ring from a nearby church as Jane Berryman walks briskly towards Lincoln's Inn Fields. Judith watches her turn the corner before strolling off in the other direction.

She turns in to Great Turnstile, then Little Turnstile, where she settles down to think in the same café where she ate breakfast. Sipping coffee, she reflects on the lies and half-lies she's told Jane Berryman, wonders if she has damaged her own reputation, finds she is not overly concerned.

Judith spends the next morning in the holy quiet of the British Library. Among the material she is given are several publications that contain articles on the Beothuk written by a woman named Ingeborg Marshall. Marshall's source material is impressive. From artifacts and archaeological data, as well as from journals and correspondence, church records, maps and government decrees, she traces a history of bungled government policy and ruthless brutality. Many Beothuk were murdered outright, others "accidentally," as was a chief named Nonosabasut. He was, Judith gathers, killed trying to prevent the abduction of his wife. Mistreatment, starvation and illness led ultimately to the extinction of the Beothuk race.

Checking a biographical note at the end of one article, Judith finds that Ingeborg Marshall is a research associate at Memorial University of Newfoundland and the author of a forthcoming book on the Beothuk.

Faced with evidence of another's long-standing interest in the Beothuk, the energy Judith's been carried along on collapses like a bubble. Suddenly exhausted, she returns most of the material unread, pulls on her coat and leaves the library.

Trudging through a fine mist towards her hotel, she examines the last few weeks, sees that this search has become a way for her to postpone life. Coldly analyzing her actions, Judith concludes she's been using Shanawdithit's skull just as these Victorian phrenologists, the ones she and Jane Berryman laughed at, had used the skulls they collected.

She imagines them more kindly now—old men returned from their travels, removed from the excitement of discovery, the sun, the attention, sitting in their dim, cluttered rooms, facing oblivion. No wonder so many of them resorted to writing papers on the significance of their collections. She chides herself for being like them, for being jealous because someone better qualified is writing a book on the Beothuk. *Come, come, coming to the fair / No, no, the fair's not there.*

Shamed, Judith resolves that tomorrow she will return the skull to the Royal College of Surgeons. Jane Berryman, who now knows its importance, will be pleased to have it back where it belongs in the Hunterian Collection.

After that, Judith thinks, I will go back to the cottage. She remembers the birds fluttering, the cup filled with flowers, the fox at the edge of the orchard. These things still exist, are all still there. She will learn to live quietly, ignore the world. If not happy, she will at least be content—as she was before she found the skull.

By the following morning she feels more cheerful. Perhaps she has judged herself harshly. It seems unlikely that she would ever let the skull become an all-consuming obsession. Nevertheless, she will this very day return it to the Hunterian Collection.

Having thus reassured herself, Judith decides to go first to the British Museum, to see the interesting birchbark dish mentioned in one of Marshall's papers. She is pleased to note that her curiosity has not vanished—mere curiosity seems a benign motivation.

Judith finds the small container in the North American collection of the museum's Ethnographic Department. Beside it in the glass case is a card that reads, "Birchbark vessel once owned by a Beothuk Indian (Nfld.)." After identifying herself she is given white gloves and permitted to hold the dish.

It is made of two pieces of birchbark folded into the shape and size of the tin pans Aunt Min used to bake bread, and is the same colour—a burnt brown. The seams are sewn with spruce root and a spruce-root chevron design is stitched along the upper rim. The dish is quite a beautiful thing, a work of art, Judith thinks. She wonders if Shanawdithit could possibly have held the object she is holding. Turning it over she finds that it, like the skull, is marked with black ink: "Red Indian Meat Dish for Deer's Flesh—found near Red Indian Lake by W.E.C."

She passes the dish back to the hovering attendant and asks to see the museum file on the artifact. From it she learns that W.E.C. stands for William Epps Cormack, explorer and president of "The Boeothick Institute"—she notes the change in spelling. A photocopy of a page from Cormack's journal records that he took the birchbark dish, along with other burial goods, from the grave of a Beothuk chief named Nonosabasut. The body of this Beothuk was one of several discovered by Cormack at a gravesite near Red Indian Lake, deep in Newfoundland's interior. An additional note explains that Nonosabasut's skull and the skull of his wife Demasduit were also taken by Cormack. In 1827, two years before Shanawdithit's death, he donated both skulls to the Royal Museum in Edinburgh.

Judith is suddenly angry. Cormack's words swim on the white paper. The people who drove the Beothuk to extinction— even others, those like Cormack who claimed to be their friends and protectors—these same men returned later to pillage Beothuk graves, hack off heads and ship them back to England!

Afraid she is going to vomit, she pushes her chair away from the desk, bends forward, holds her head over a wastepaper basket. Staring down into the black plastic she contemplates the morality of her life's work—are she and Ian fellow plunderers? And yet, and yet—what would we know of the Turkana Boy, dead these 1.53 million years, were it not for Leakey and Walker? she wonders. What of Ur were it not for Woolley, of Koobi Fora without the Muirs? Or, if it comes to that, what would I know of Shanawdithit's vanished world were it not for Cormack and his like?

A finger touches her shoulder, a glass of water is word-lessly offered. Even as she drinks the water, thanks the kind attendant, as she leaves the museum, passing rooms filled with tools and weapons, with hats and shoes and musical instru-ments, with dishes and hinges and locks and funeral cards and tennis racquets—everyday possessions of the long dead—Judith knows the certainties that supported her career have dis-solved. Never again will she look at such things without doubt, without sadness.

Once out of the museum and into the bright day she feels refreshed, begins to think clearly, knows just what she is going to do. She walks all the way over to Leather Lane, sits for awhile in the grassy square admiring the iron Labrador dog. Except for a magazine article she once read on L'Anse aux Meadows, where the Ingstads found the oldest European settlement in the New World, Judith knows nothing of Newfoundland or of Labrador. Before leaving she pats the dog's head—it may be a long time before she returns to this part of London.

At lunchtime she goes back to the hotel and retrieves the skull from the safe, noting with amusement the manager's relief to be rid of the mysterious package. Back in her room Judith sits with the sealed ossuary in her lap, thinking of the woman to whom this skull belonged.

The small, unreasonable act of contrition she is about to perform will make not the slightest difference to anyone, cer-tainly not to Shanawdithit. Judith has forgotten Jane Berryman, and when she remembers it will be far too late.

XXVI

Judith has rarely travelled alone and unencumbered. She and Ian were accustomed to filling out bills of lading, certificates of inoculation; applying for permits to dig, permits to billet foreigners, permits to transport artifacts across borders. She is pleasantly surprised at the ease with which a trip to Canada can be arranged.

The skull is not mentioned. Not even at Heathrow, where she watches with horror as two young men are pulled from the boarding line and marched off between security guards. Judith is not questioned. She murmurs, "Careful—a gift for my sister," as the balsawood case glides through the X-ray machine. What condescending smiles people beam at fussy old ladies, she thinks as the box is returned to her, along with her expensive carry-on bag and a lined raincoat she has purchased as protection against the fog and snow of which the Russell Square travel agent warned.

In an attempt to break a lifetime inclination towards thrift she has booked executive class. The music is soft, the magazines glossy; she is given the choice of six air-conditioning settings, three London newspapers, a menu from which she can choose steak or salmon for dinner. She rolls her coat around the balsawood box, slides it into the large overhead compartment and settles into her seat. The jet lifts into a dawn sky—outside its thin aluminum skin there is only blueness, below the Atlantic heaves and churns. Inside lights are dimmed, cushions are brought, wine is served, salmon arrives with salad and hot rolls and linen napkins.

After eating Judith wipes her hands on the warm damp towel, accepts a blanket and settles down to sleep. She recalls the many small, uncomfortable planes she and Ian travelled in over the years. Usually dirty these planes were, smelling of fuel oil, noisy too and often cold, freezing cold, even in the desert. Ian never slept on these flights but she did, slept deeply with her legs flung across his lap. She longs for Ian, for his bulky presence in the seat beside her, his hand holding hers. A strange thing, longing, a dull all-consuming ache for what is impossible. So thinking, she falls into a half-sleep where dreams and longing jumble with memory and imaginings.

She is awakened by a loud, disembodied voice telling passengers that they will be landing in St. John's in ten minutes, that they should turn their watches back by three and a half hours. She shrugs off the gloomy residue of her dream—something about birds, bad luck birds, crows or ravens—sets her watch and gathers her belongings. She follows other passengers into the airport, which, like half the world's airports, seems to be in the process of expansion.

Judith tells herself that everything will be fine, assures herself that even if the skull is discovered she will stay calm, will simply insist that as an anthropologist, she has every right to be travelling with human bones. She knows this is not true—one cannot move from country to country with unidentified, undocumented body parts. Awkwardly holding the skull box, her shoulder bag and coat, she joins the queue that is moving slowly between sheets of unpainted plywood, inching towards a counter behind which three Canadian Customs officers stand.

There is an air of relaxed friendliness in the room; Customs people and passengers chat while passports and hand luggage are checked. Beyond a glass wall whole families wait to greet the travellers. Each person who passes through the doors is surrounded, hugged and kissed, then led off in a flurry of talk as if they have been away for lifetimes.

Judith reaches the Customs desk, has her passport checked and—just as she had hoped—exits into the baggage area clutching the Copperfield box with its red wax seal still intact. After retrieving her suitcase she goes out into the November afternoon. Cool it is and sunny, without a sign of the fog or snow she has heard about. She finds, or more precisely is found by, a cheerful taxi driver, and before dark is comfortably settled in the hotel her travel agent booked.

For the first time Judith Muir has arrived at a place without a well thought-out plan—or so she tells herself the next morning as she gazes out at the sun-dazzled sea, at cliffs that rise steeply on each side, black cliffs that are saved from appearing ominous by brilliantly painted houses. Judith cannot imagine how people get to these dwellings, which seem to be tucked haphazardly, like bits of coloured paper, into crannies of rock.

After a late breakfast she leaves the hotel and walks down to the street nearest the harbour. Towns built on hillsides cannot be ugly and St. John's is almost beautiful—would be beautiful but for the architectural barbarism of its recent past. As in

Gillsford, plastic-fronted shops and offices have been abandoned, left to crack and sag like rotting teeth between the dignified older buildings.

When she comes to an ugly flyover, Judith turns back, walking behind shops and offices along the almost-empty Harbour Drive. Half a dozen fishing boats and a Russian trawler are tied up on this side of the harbour, and on the other side she can see a line of docks where two more ships and an orange container-barge piled high with blue boxcars are moored. The hills behind the docks are wooded and seem uninhabited except for five huge tanks that carry the familiar logos of multinational oil companies.

Back at the hotel Judith buys a guidebook, and instead of returning to her room, goes into a tearoom-cum-bar. Wicker furniture is grouped under potted palms; the place is comfortable and empty and has a magnificent view of the harbour. She settles down near a window, orders a drink and leafs through the guide to St. John's.

According to her book, the Battle of the North Atlantic was fought just beyond St. John's Harbour. Here merchant ships had rendezvoused with the Allied warships assigned to lead them through minefields and wolf packs. The water she is looking out on has been fought over many times, the book informs her. For centuries cannons and fortifications have surrounded the harbour, and hundreds of Frenchmen and Englishmen, and not a few Spaniards and Portuguese, slaughtered one another in order to hold those cliffs, which were seen as an entrance to the New World. That wave of killing ended in 1762 when the final battle of the Seven Years War was fought in the hills around the harbour.

Her book does not mention the Beothuk. She wonders if they ever inhabited this part of the island. She finds an appendix listing "Statues, Monuments and Plaques in and around the City." Studying several pages of black and white photos, she eventually sees the name she is looking for in a caption below one of the smallest pictures: "This monument marks the site of the Parish Church of St. Mary the Virgin during the period 1859 to 1963. Fishermen and sailors from many ports found a spiritual haven within its hallowed walls. Near this spot is the burying place of Nancy Shanawdithit, very probably the last of the Beothuks, who died on June 6th, 1829."

Apparently there is no monument, not even a statue—just a stone cairn with words engraved on a brass plaque. Shanawdithit's name, prefixed by the name her captors gave her, and not honouring the Beothuk woman but her burial place. The burial place of Shanawdithit's body, that is—her head rests in a chest of drawers, safely tucked between pillows in Judith's room on the fourth floor.

Judith puts the guide down and sits glowering at her reflection in the window—she is beginning to look like a witch again. She adjusts her mouth, sits upright, reknots her scarf and picks up the guidebook. Tomorrow she will find the cairn.

As always, resolution makes her hungry. She orders fish chowder, which she devours absent-mindedly as she works out the exact location of the monument, described vaguely as "near the base of the Southside Hills, below the railway bridge."

Contrary to much of her life's work (for do not heads from Koobi Fora, from Eritrea, from Ethiopia, rest on shelves in Cambridge because of her?), Judith Muir has decided that Shanawdithit's skull must remain in Newfoundland. The obvious thing would be to contact the Newfoundland Museum, a picture of which is on the cover of her guidebook. She asks the waitress where the attractive brick building is located.

"Just down Duckworth Street—but it's useless goin down there—been barred up these twelve-month." The woman gathers the silverware and empty soup bowl. "Like a cup of tea, love?"

"Nothing else, thank you." The waitress, Judith thinks, is about her age. She sounds like Aunt Min. With her pulled-back hair and large white apron she even looks a bit like Aunt Min. Judith would like to ask the woman to sit down, would like to listen to her for awhile. Instead she asks why the museum is closed.

"The government's building a new one up back of the Paramount. A dirty big thing they're callin The Rooms, for all it looks like no rooms I ever saw. If you go out front you'll see the top of it, all pointy glass like ski hills." The waitress smiles, says, "I suppose we'll get used to it."

When she shrugs and leaves, Judith feels momentarily bereft. Ah well, there is a university—the university with which Ingeborg Marshall is associated. Doubtless it has a department of archaeology or anthropology that can become custodian of the skull until the museum is finished.

The Hunterian should be asked to leave the skull here on permanent loan; it could be the cornerpiece of a major exhibition, perhaps for the new museum's opening. The possibilities of such an exhibit excite Judith. She would have Shanawdithit's skull surrounded by her drawings, by Beothuk artifacts, the birchbark container from the British Museum, Cormack's original journals, and bring in Native people from all over North America, artists and writers and musicians, have lectures and discussions.

Dr. Jane Berryman would be delighted to come—as would dozens of others. Judith finds a pen, begins scribbling down names of people who would make interesting speakers.

Suddenly she stops, reins herself in, reminds herself that she has vowed not to make an obsession of the skull.

Yet someone should do it, someone should build an event around the skull. Shanawdithit would get her moment in the sun, and afterwards the skull would stay in St. John's. Lawmakers have ways of making what is illegal legal, what is stolen theirs. Judith seems to recall that the British government passed a statute prohibiting the British Museum from returning the Elgin Marbles—surely the Newfoundland government could do the same.

On her second morning in St. John's, Judith phones the university. But when given Ingeborg Marshall's extension, she hangs up and calls a taxi instead. Before parting with the skull she will visit the place where Shanawdithit was buried.

The taxi man has never heard of the plaque, never heard of Shanawdithit, but he knows where St. Mary's Church was. "Mom's father and mother were married over there—Mom says Nan was some put out when they hauled it down."

Along Water Street she sees a flower shop and on impulse tells the driver to pull over. When she returns, with sunflowers and some kind of wild, wheatlike grass (everything else in the store had looked too forced, too arranged), the driver tells her there is no graveyard up where she's going. "Vanished along with the church—according to Mom, people tried to save it but the mucky-mucks paid no mind. Never do, do they?"

Judith doesn't answer and they drive on in silence. A little way beyond the flyover she had walked to the day before, they cross a small bridge.

"We're on the Southside now, missus—used to be a lot more people livin over here years ago," her driver says, then, as they get beyond the line of houses, "St. Mary's used to be along here on the hill. Not much to see now."

There isn't much to see—one lane of broken asphalt, the other lane dug up and cordoned off with detour signs, no sidewalks. When Judith sees a place to turn she tells the driver to pull over. She will get out. She's worn flat shoes and wants to find the marker on her own. She pays the man, takes his card and says she will phone him in an hour.

"Where from?" he asks, nodding at a boarded-up red-brick building on one side and a chain-link fence on the other.

"I'll call from that little restaurant we passed just before we crossed the bridge," Judith says, and when he looks alarmed, she has to assure him that she is perfectly capable of walking that distance.

The man shakes his head but drives off, and she is left standing beside the abandoned building, which, she now sees, has NFLD. LIGHT AND POWER CO.—1927 chiselled into its facing. Seagulls and pigeons roost along a brick ledge below the sign.

It is a grey day—not misty, but the air holds dampness and the faint stink of harbour sewage. There is no traffic, no people; not even the birds move.

Judith crosses the street and stands staring through a chain-link fence into a vast hollow where the entire face of the hill has been blasted away, a scene of such desolation that she is reminded of the hillside at Abu Simbel that last day before the valley was flooded.

Academics from all over the world had gone to Abu Simbel begging for more time. Judith wonders if anyone tried to save this hill. The temples of Ramesses and Nefertari had been saved, moved block by block, to higher ground, yet they all knew there was more—priceless Nubian antiquities and almost certainly bodies—still inside the hill, all soon to be drowned by the

Aswan High Dam. A sad day—it was hopeless of course to try to stop progress, or what people think of as progress.

Ian told her to cheer up, said water and electricity and flush toilets were more important than clay tablets, painted tombs and mummified bodies. They'd been young and she had indeed cheered up. That night, in a huge construction shed, the protesters and a group of Russian engineers toasted Lake Nasser, drank and danced until dawn came, and the water. Judith wonders what the lake is called now.

Before her on the chain-link gates a large sign proclaims, CONSTRUCTION AREA—AUTHORIZED PERSONNEL ONLY, but there is no construction, no personnel. Just a great circle of flattened rock, large enough to hold four or five pantheons. The rock-strewn plain is encircled by level after level of blasted cliff, a monstrous stairway leading into the sky. No blade of grass, no tree, not one grain of soil—not even an earthworm could survive here.

The only opening into the dismal amphitheatre seems to be here at the gates. A hundred or so yards beyond the fence is a small, windowless building, probably a watchman's shed. She wonders if anyone is inside and what there is to watch over. Though secured with a heavy chain and padlock, the two gates can be eased apart about a foot.

She has her hand on the chain, is positioning herself to slip between the gates, holding the flowers out so that they will not be crushed, when she sees two people coming towards her. They are far away, look like toy figures walking on the moon. She pulls away from the gates and steps back a little.

She doesn't take her eyes from the men—they are men, Judith can eventually see that. The one wearing a white construction hat and dark coveralls is holding the other's arm, propelling him forward, shouting at him, occasionally jerking him so that the second man lurches about, would fall were he not being held up.

Later, much later, Judith will convince herself she knew, felt something at that moment—not recognition, something else, something like the frisson that ripples along exposed skin in that instant before rain falls on a desert, before the sky rips and water splashes on sand for the first time in years.

Certainly she is relieved that she hadn't stepped inside the gates, and she is a little angry at the hard-hat man, thinks he is using too much force against the trespasser. When they come up to the gates, however, Judith can see how the other, the man wearing the brown cords and the waterproof jacket, is resisting, pulling back with all his might against the one pushing him forward.

"Why the hell didn't you come sooner?" The watchman scowls at Judith. "I phoned you crowd almost an hour ago, soon as I spotted him. What's wrong with ye? Think the numbers of people ye got working in there ye could keep Skipper stowed away safe!"

As he talks the watchman is easing the silent man through the space between the gates, pushing and pulling, threading him through sideways. The old man has stopped resisting; he lets himself be manipulated, be set upright against the outside of the fence like a straw figure.

The watchman goes back to the other side of the fence, takes off his hard hat, fishes a square of blue cloth out of his coveralls and mops his head. "This can't go on, missus." He looks pleadingly at Judith. "I can't be scravellin over them rocks, draggin Skipper 'round day after day. S'posen he goes arse over kettle and breaks a leg! S'posen he gets a heart attack! Who'll be to blame then? I ask you that—who'll be to blame?"

After this plea the man plunks his hat back on, announces, "Next time I'm callin in the police." Then he turns away, disappearing into the shed before Judith has absorbed the meaning of his impassioned speech.

The straw man just leans against the fence. He is very thin, has a narrow weather-beaten face, receding grey hair and grey eyes—intelligent eyes, Judith thinks. He stares at her and waits.

She wonders what to do. The man is sweating a little. She can see dampness on his forehead—being pushed about, struggling too, must be tiring. She looks for somewhere they can sit while she works on the problem.

"Do you live nearby?" she asks, speaking slowly, carefully, thinking he might be deaf as well as mad.

He doesn't answer but continues to stare at her. His face shows nothing, not anger or hope, not amusement or fear. And when he finally speaks his voice is low, mild, without emphasis. "Who are the flowers for?" he asks.

Judith has forgotten the flowers. She is holding them under her chin with both hands, like a nervous bride. She looks down from all that greyness, and the glory of yellow and orange catches her as if she's never seen colour before. She has the illusion of being enfolded in sunshine. Tension leaves her shoulders and with it the sensation that's been with her for a long time, the nagging feeling that she is doing something wrong.

"The flowers are for Shanawdithit," she says, the name falling from her lips lightly, as if she's been using it all her life.

The man's face changes completely—pleasure is followed by puzzlement which is followed by sorrow. It happens in an instant, then his face is blank again.

"You're too late—they've hidden her," he says. And he crumples, slides down against the fence until he is sitting on the asphalt, covering his face with his hands, weeping, though he makes no sound.

She drops the flowers and bends forward, half kneeling in front of him, but she is afraid to touch him, afraid even to speak. When the van comes, they are still there, squatting awkwardly beside the chain-link fence, surrounded by all that desolation, by sunflowers scattered on the grey asphalt.

The van is white, and on its side are the words HEALTH CARE CORPORATION OF EASTERN NEWFOUNDLAND wrapped around a meaningless blue and green logo. Two young men get out; they wear white trousers and white shirts that have the same logo on the pockets. They are polite with the man, easing him to his feet, chiding him gently as they lead him over to the van.

Judith follows, stands irresolutely beside the vehicle as they help him inside. One of the young men thanks her in a way that lets her know she is dismissed.

But before the door can be closed the old man leans towards her and says, "You'll never find her. Never." He shakes his head.

"How do you know—what do you know about her?" Judith asks.

He is holding one of the flowers. "I knew her," he says, "but that was before they took her away."

And then the attendant shuts the door. "Thank you for waiting with him," he says, and gets into the driver's seat.

"How can I get in touch with you?" Judith taps on the window glass, but the man in the back seat doesn't answer. He is looking down, pulling petals one by one from the sunflower.

The driver rolls down his window. "Call the Waterford Hospital, ask for Dr. Reddy," he tells her, "Dr. Hartman Reddy." Then he eases the van around and drives down the road towards the bridge.

She turns back to the fence, to the ruined hill upon which St. Mary's Church once stood, where there had been a grave-yard, where a grave had once held Shanawdithit's body, where later a marker had been erected. Nothing remains.

It seems wrong to leave sunflowers in the dirt, so she picks them up and weaves them one by one into the chain-link fence. Her feeling of doubt has returned. She walks slowly back across the bridge towards the little café where she finds her taxi waiting.

"Is the Waterford Hospital far from here?" she asks the driver.

"A few minutes west, in by Bowring Park." He pulls out a map and shows her, informing her that most people around town call it the Mental.

"Ah!" Judith says, and asks to be taken back to the hotel, where she is surprised to realize it is only noon.

She eats a large lunch and thinks about the man who says he knew Shanawdithit—a woman who died a hundred and seventy years ago. He is mad, of course. Nevertheless, after a shower and a short rest, she finds the number of the Waterford Hospital and makes contact with Dr. Reddy.

He knows at once who she is speaking of, assures Judith that the man has been safely returned, has eaten and is napping in his room. "His name is Kyle Holloway. He is one of my patients— more I cannot tell you," he says, "not without Mr. Holloway's permission." However, he does agree to see Judith the following afternoon at two.

The next day, delivered to the main entrance of the Waterford by her faithful taxi driver, she stands for a minute admiring the building, which still retains traces of its Victorian origins. Less forbidding, in Judith's view, than the steel and glass monstrosity where Ian's father spent his last years.

Dr. Reddy is young but he looks tired; behind his glasses dark smudges circle his eyes. "Mr. Holloway has told me to give you whatever information you require," he says. Gesturing to the chair beside his desk, he asks if she is a relative.

She tells him that she is neither a relative nor a friend of Kyle Holloway, knows nothing of the man, had never seen him before yesterday's encounter. "It is just that I have a special interest in an historic figure, a Beothuk woman named Shanawdithit—and Mr. Holloway said he knew her. Impossible, of course, but the way he spoke almost convinced me." Embarrassed by the vagueness of her claim to the doctor's time, Judith repeats the few words Kyle Holloway had spoken.

The doctor nods. "He has a long-held obsession with Shanawdithit. He reads constantly and of course knows what is going on in the town, knows they've recently blasted away the hill where she was buried—although as I understand it, her actual burying place was destroyed years ago."

Dr. Reddy's office has no door; staff people come and go, taking files from one pile on his desk or dropping files on another pile, scrawling names and times on a whiteboard that covers one wall. Nevertheless he manages to give Judith a summary of Kyle Holloway's history, tells her the man was born in Newfoundland, served in the Royal Navy during the war, but did not return to the island until 1985 when he was in his late sixties.

"He went around in search of a church and graveyard that no longer existed, became a vagrant—what the police call a public nuisance. From what I've heard he was a frightening sight, wild-eyed with long dirty hair, wandering around the downtown streets, accosting people with his story about this Beothuk women he'd once talked to. He practically lived in the museum on Duckworth Street. Once he interrupted a council meeting and on several occasions walked in on classes at the university."

"And how did he end up in here?" Judith asks. She has interrupted his day, can see his staff is impatient and is afraid Dr. Reddy might be pulled away any minute.

"As I understand it—this was before my time here—when anyone tried to tell Kyle what had really happened to that church he was looking for—it and much of the graveyard was blasted away and dumped as fill to make what is now called the Harbour Drive—he would go into a terrible rage, not with them but with himself. Kyle would shout and weep, bang his head against whatever was nearby and take off up towards the Southside Hills. Still, he was considered harmless until the day he smashed a glass case down at the museum. Apparently he was trying to rescue the bones of an aboriginal child—really only a plaster cast of bones, but the museum people were naturally upset. The police arrested him and in the fullness of time he was sent here for psychological assessment.

"This was some years ago. I've only known Kyle as a mild-mannered, intelligent man. We talk sometimes; he has a great interest in Newfoundland history and geology. We have his record of service with the Royal Navy—it shows that he made the rank of Leading Seaman and was honourably discharged at the end of the war. There's one notation recording that he was once absent without leave for ten days and another stating that he volunteered for an extremely dangerous mine-laying operation off Narvik Harbour in Norway—no indication that he suffered from paranoia of any kind during the war. It seems possible that his condition was triggered by some trauma just before he returned to St. John's." At this point Dr. Reddy is interrupted again—a form requires his signature.

Judith knows she should go, but does not. Afraid he will end the conversation she asks a question as soon as the office worker leaves. "Mr. Holloway seems very frail—must he be confined to an institution at this point?"

"On the three occasions when we released him into the community he was returned by the police. He has grown increasingly frail but is generally in good health—one of those thin, wiry men. Really, he shouldn't be here, but he has no next of kin on file and there is no other place for him. He is free to come and go, and in recent years has seemed content—at least until this destruction began again on the Southside. He tried to stop the blasting, almost got himself killed, so we had to put restrictions on his movements."

The doctor takes off his glasses and rubs his eyes. "What they're building will be a sewage treatment plant, if they ever get it finished. A month or so ago they stopped blasting, so we let Kyle go out again—but it's not working too well."

The doctor sighs, replaces his glasses and says cheerfully, "For all that, I'm hopeful that in time Kyle will calm down, get back to his old routine. He used to help with the flower garden in summer and spend bad weather reading in our small library. He's always happy in the library—he's there now, waiting for you. I hope you don't mind—the librarian will be at her desk and, as I say, Kyle is harmless, has never laid a finger on anyone." And Dr. Reddy, a kind man who has gone well beyond his professional duty, stands and waits for Judith's nod before leading her to the library.

Midway through the afternoon, Lillian Dawe, the librarian, brought them both coffee. At six o'clock, she apologized when she had to turn them out. She held the library door open, and they both nodded pleasantly to her as they passed through. Kyle looked happier than she'd ever seen him. He was excited, still talking, describing something to the woman, " . . . a green valley, everything covered in moss," he was saying.

Lillian Dawe told the inquiry that she'd watched them walk down the corridor towards the main door. Kyle was wearing a tan shirt and trousers, no outside jacket, she said. They stopped at the door and the woman pointed outside and laughed. The librarian supposed the Englishwoman must have been surprised to see snow—it was not a blizzardy kind of snow, just those November flakes that float down so silently you're amazed how fast they cover everything.

The Englishwoman patted Kyle's arm before she left. He watched her go through the door, then walked back towards the elevator by himself. Lillian was sure of all this.

She herself had locked the library and gone out minutes later, had waited a long time for her bus, which was late because of the snow.

There was no sign of the Englishwoman—she must have gotten a taxi.

———

He had told her to come to the park across from the Waterford. There is a bench just beyond the street light that shines down on the gates. He gets there before the light comes on. A purple-pink afterglow of sun catches at the edge of snowflakes, flickers on Peter Pan's snow-covered head and on the wing tips of his fairies. Kyle doesn't feel anxious; he knows the Englishwoman will come. He sits in the shadows and waits.

It is quite dark when she arrives. Her taxi stops at the park gate. She begins to cross the street towards the hospital, but when the car pulls away she turns and comes into the park. He stands and she comes towards him with the box, holding it out to him. When he tells her he doesn't want the box, she takes Shanawdithit's skull out and passes it to him carelessly, he thinks, as if it were some ordinary thing—a football or a cabbage. He takes the skull but then has to sit down for a spell.

He is amazed at how this can be. How he can be holding her head between his hands after all those years with only her voice. "It's you!" he says. "It's really you!" Lifted on a wave of hilarity, he begins to laugh.

When Kyle finishes laughing he feels better. He stands up, tucks the head inside his jacket and pulls up the zipper.

Having forgotten the Englishwoman, he turns away. He walks farther into the shadows, follows the old railway track through the park and on down the Waterford Valley. Her head fits nicely between his sweater and jacket, but he has to cross his hands over in front to hold her in place. He moves at a good pace, glad he took time to find his heavy boots, his padded jacket and the wool mitts that are cupped around the bulge of her head. Snowflakes cling to the wool until the mitts begin to look like small white animals. His mother used to call these shotgun mitts. Kyle thinks about his mother, about her stories of a garden and angels and birds that looked like no birds he has ever seen.

He gets down to the railway station more quickly than he would have thought possible—no railway now, of course. Art Norman's house is gone, the street's gone, even the church Art dragged him out of is gone, half the Southside Hills blasted away.

Soon there'll be nothing. Grass will grow over the railway station, over Water Street. Kyle wonders if they will just let the harbour silt up once the town is gone. The government will want to maintain what they call a presence, a toehold for the mining and oil companies. Something out at Cape Spear perhaps. One Coast Guard station should do the trick, five people in all of Newfoundland—not Newfoundlanders, of course.

Soon he is climbing up towards the Brow, keeping back from the paved road, keeping to a side path that is steep and narrow, a white line wavering between bushes. Everything is white, his hands and feet, his jacket, the very air around him is white. But Kyle knows where he is, knows he will soon smell the sea, find the tall rock that marks the turnoff to Freshwater Bay. When he comes to the place, he is breathing heavily. He sits awhile with his back against the rock, waiting for his heart to slow down.

The path beyond the rock is more twisted, disappearing around cliffs as it drops steeply towards the ocean. He hasn't seen the ocean for a long time, not the real ocean. Then he slips, falls, face down—Jesus, I've smashed her! he thinks. He rolls carefully onto his back and lies still for some time, staring up as a million wings whirl and swirl above them. When the wings stop moving, he sits up, unzippers his jacket and takes her out. She is all right—all in one piece!

"You're not going to finish me off now, Dogman, not when we're so close . . ."

So delighted is Kyle to hear her voice that he stands, pushing himself up without thinking. A sharp pain shoots along his right leg. He waits, gauging the pain, losing track of the voice, although he has the impression it is still there, still telling him something. He takes a step, finds he can walk, but it will be slow going.

Instead of putting her back inside his jacket he holds her close with his face against her smooth skull. They continue on for an hour, maybe two hours. The pain has gone, his leg is stiff, but he is warm and not a bit tired. He would like to keep on like this forever, walk for days and nights with the familiar path underfoot, the sharp cold smell of ocean in his nostrils, her husky mutter filling his head. He remembers that terrible place in Norway, or was it Russia? That grey, cold cove where old women loaded boats, hundreds of shuffling, grey crones hauling and pushing and humming—a desolate keening sound you could hear for miles out to sea.

Kyle begins to tell her how that sound reminded him of her, of her and of the old hag his mother used to talk about. But Shanawdithit is not interested. She is telling him a story about her Old One, a story he's heard before, but never mind. They move forward, snow still falling, her voice and the snow all around, enclosing them in a white cave that is filled with nothing but story.

Then they are pitching and falling, tumbling together, spinning downward into the ravine. The snow has stopped. Here is the green valley, the little stream, the moss that long ago covered the army truck and its driver, covered the broken beer bottles and knives, the rifles and rusting torpedoes, covered the spears and arrows, the shards of bone, the broken skulls of men and women and small children. Moss, given time, will cover everything.

ACKNOWLEDGEMENTS

I am deeply grateful to my uncles Jack and Clyde Vincent, who served in the Canadian Navy and the Royal Navy during World War II—their memories provided crucial background material on conditions at sea during the Battle of the North Atlantic.

I am indebted to members of the Newfoundland Writers' Guild and to many friends and relatives who have helped and encouraged me during the writing of this book. In particular I want to acknowledge my gratitude to Joan Clark for keeping me on track, to my sister Francis Vardy Reddy for her lifelong support, to Anne Hart for sound editorial judgment, to physical anthropologist Sony Jerkic of Memorial University for kindly introducing me to skulls, to Don and Sue Morgan for that early, essential fact check of my manuscript and to Georgina Queller for her final check. I am grateful to my daughter Jennifer Morgan for many things, including assistance with the practical logistics and for her help with the naming of Beothuk characters.

I thank Pedlar Press and poet JonArno Lawson for kindly giving me permission to use the phrase "cloud of bone" from his book *Black Stars in a White Night Sky*. Foremost among the books that have been important to me in writing this novel was Ingeborg Marshall's definitive *A History and Ethnography of the Beothuk*. I hope she will not disapprove of the use to which I have put her work.

Sincere thanks go to my agent Leona Trainer and to staff members at Knopf Canada for their enthusiasm for my work. I want especially to thank Stacey Cameron for her cheerful and invaluable help as editor.

Foremost among the books that were important to me in writing this novel was Ingeborg Marshall's definitive *History and Ethnography of the Beothuk*. I hope she will not disapprove of the use to which I have put her work.

Other books that have provided background for this story include *The Beothucks or Red Indians* by James P. Howley, *The Raven and The Totem* by John E. Smelcer, *William Epps Cormack* by Bernard D. Fardy, *Mythology and Folktales of North American Indians* by E.J. Brill, *Closing the Ring* by Winston Churchill, *The Fiercest Battle* by Ronald Seth, *A History of St. Mary's Church* edited by Donald Kelland, *Under the White Ensign* by Herb Wells, *Corvettes Canada* by Mac Johnson, *Tales of the North Atlantic* by Hal Lawrence, *In Great Waters* by Spencer Danmore, *The War at Our Doorstep* by Tony Murphy and Paul Kenney, and *A Safe Haven* edited by Shannon M. Lewis. Files of *The St. John's Evening Telegram* and of *The Daily News* have also been of great assistance. I must apologize to my sources for taking liberties with the dates on which certain events took place—for example *The Hood* was sunk in May of 1941, not, as I indicate, much later.

I want to thank the Newfoundland Museum, the Centre for Newfoundland Studies at Memorial University, the British

Museum, the British Library and the Royal College of Surgeons of England and the college's museum—the staffs of which left me to follow real and imagined lines of research without hindrance. Special thanks go to Holborn Public Library on Theobald's Road for allowing me to read archival material related to everyday life in London during World War II. I have quoted several passages from sections of the collection that was compiled by the Holborn Historic Committee in 1986.

Finally, I want to thank the Provincial Government and the Newfoundland and Labrador Arts Council for awarding me a Senior Artist Research and Development Grant, thus enabling me to travel and do research in the places where my story is set.